RETURN TO MATEGUAS ISLAND

"The real power in *Return To Mateguas Island* lies not so much in its inclusion of supernatural rituals as in its exploration of simmering emotions that lay just under the surface...Thus, its power and strength are most evident in its explorations of interpersonal relationships...the supernatural force described serves as a catalyst for events; not the end-all of these explorations. And it's the centrifuge of a whirlwind of emotional forces that swirl around all involved in the backdrop that is Mategaus Island and its mystical heritage ... the compelling draw of the island and its mysteries create suitable devices for a novel that excels in emotional interconnections with a dash of supernatural suspense added in for good measure."

D. Donovan, eBook Reviewer, *MIDWEST BOOK REVIEW*

"This is a quick-paced story portraying a wide range of human emotions, deadly supernatural forces and ancient Native American beliefs ... It explores the depths of love and loss, dedication and defiance, innocence and desire - all in spite of the threat of losing everything. This is supernatural fiction at its best with a hint of coming-of-age enlightenment to appeal to younger readers as well as readers of all ages."

Melinda Hills, *READERS' FAVORITE*

"Return to Mateguas Island by Linda Watkins was a gripping read ... Excellent storyline, excellent characters in an all-round thrilling read. Linda's attention to detail is second to none and the book is very professionally written. Loved it!"

Anne-Marie Reynolds, *READERS' FAVORITE*

"Linda Watkins' contemporary dark fantasy, Return to Mateguas Island: A Tale of Supernatural Suspense, is well-written and fast-paced. While this is the second book in Watkins' Mateguas Trilogy, the author gives enough background to enable it to stand on its own, but the first book, Mateguas Island, is as marvelous, dark and brooding as this one is, and I'd recommend starting from there ...The Indian folklore that serves as the basis for this trilogy is so compelling, and Terri's interactions with Charlie, the elder Indian at the museum were powerful and intriguing ... Return to Mateguas Island: A Tale of Supernatural Suspense is absorbing dark fantasy, and it's most highly recommended."

Jack Magnus for *READERS' FAVORITE*

"Great page turner! It didn't take long to get into this suspenseful paranormal read!"

Erth, Amazon Customer

"...the characters are well developed and delight you. There is intrigue in almost every page and the suspense is apt to kill you. And, as usual, the author has left us in suspense, because you know there's more to come. Waiting for the next book will be frustrating, so maybe I'll just go back and read the first two again. Brilliant job, Linda Watkins. Thank you for an amazing read!"

Jan Raymond, Author of *The Pha-yul Trilogy*

"In all good books there have to be believable, connectable, and emotional characters that make you feel. The author has succeeded in creating a great cast of protagonists, who live and breathe the mystery and fear, and they took me along for the ride. A great story and a very satisfying read. Highly recommended and worthy of 5*"

Bookcollector, Amazon Customer

"Soon after arriving we find ourselves back on the thrilling roller-coaster ride we experienced in the previous book. This time around there are more characters, twists, and clues that take us even deeper into this mystical realm that plagues the swamp, surrounding property and those that live there. With each page you will find yourself drawn in so deep that you find your heart pounding as you experience these terrifying supernatural events that haunt both Karen and her daughter Terri."

J. Wallace, Amazon Customer

"This book was so good that I can't wait for the next book!"

Kindle Customer

"The author weaves an unpredictable tale that has the reader around her little finger. This page turner is spooky and mysterious, couldn't help but read with a vengeance."

Brenda, Amazon Customer

"I held my breath at each turn. The flow of the story is great, the characters realistic, and the setting for me close to home. I can not wait for the 3rd."

A. Nixon, Amazon Customer

Return to Mateguas Island

A Tale of Supernatural Suspense

LINDA WATKINS

RETURN TO MATEGUAS ISLAND.
Copyright © 2014 by Linda Watkins.

Editing by Kristina Circelli (www.circelli.info) and
Diane Donovan (www.donovansliteraryservices.com)
Cover design: H. William Ruback (www.incolordigitaldesign.com)
Background photo, front cover:
Linda Watkins (www.mateguasisland.com)
Background photo, back cover: Wink Houghton
Interior formatting: Mallory Rock (www.malloryrock.com)

Published in the United States of America by Argon Press
Library of Congress Control Number 2014920666
ISBN 978-0-9908831-0-4 (PB)
ISBN 978-0-9910554-8-7 (EB)

ARGON PRESS

www.ArgonPress.com

ACKNOWLEDGEMENTS

Again, I must acknowledge my faithful "betas" who took time out of their busy schedules to read and critique the first draft of this work. My heartfelt thanks to Marge, Ruthie, Scott and Pat - you are the pillars this final edition is built on.

I also want to thank my editors, Kristina Circelli and Diane Donovan for their insight and help in sculpting RETURN TO MATEGUAS. I hope I have done you proud.

This book is dedicated to all those people who freely give of their time and money to save the lives of dogs that have been abandoned and abused. You are truly special angels.

As with its predecessor, MATEGUAS ISLAND, all net proceeds from the sale of this book will be donated to the Raison d'Etre Fund for Dogs, Dedicated to Rescue and Research.

"There is no death. Only a change of worlds."

Chief Seattle

PROLOGUE: JULY — MATEGUAS ISLAND

SHE STOOD IN THE middle of the lawn, arms outstretched, her face turned toward the sea. Her flimsy cotton skirt, drenched by the relentless rain, clung to her body, making her seem almost naked in the moonlight. The wind whipped her hair around her head.

Behind her, standing at the second-story window of the old house on the hill, a man strained to see her more clearly through the violent storm that raged all around them.

What the hell is she doing?

The wind howled and gusts threw the rain against the glass pane like so many pebbles tossed carelessly at a lover's window, obscuring his view. For a moment, dizziness almost overtook him. He glanced down at the floor. The pool of blood was larger now. He pressed a towel to his side, trying to stem its flow. Then, unable to help himself, he looked out the window again.

Her arms were now raised to the sky and, in the moonlight, he could see she held something in her hand. Thunder roared,

1

shaking the house. Black spots appeared before his eyes and he feared he would lose consciousness.

Is this how it's all going to end? After everything that's happened? Right here, in this house?

His attention was abruptly diverted by the sound of a car pulling in the driveway, its headlights rapidly approaching.

What now? he thought as thunder shook the room again and he was blinded by the flash of lightning that followed.

Then all was silent.

TWO MONTHS EARLIER –
MONTEREY, CALIFORNIA

"SET THE TABLE, GIRLS. Dinner's almost ready."

Sophie Andersen put down the book she was reading and moved to do her mother's bidding. Terri remained seated, her laptop in hand, typing away.

"You, too, Terri-bug. Get the good wine glasses from the china cupboard. We're celebrating tonight."

"Celebrating? What's happened, Mom?" asked Sophie as she laid out the silverware on the dining table.

"You'll find out soon enough and, Terri, I mean now. Get the glasses!"

Terri glanced over at her mother, sighed and put down her computer. "So, what's the big deal, Mother? Good glasses or jelly jars, it's all the same to me."

"Well, it isn't to me. And it's my surprise so we do as I say. Now hop to it."

Sophie gave her twin a meaningful look. Terri responded with a slight shake of her head as if to say 'not now.'

At eighteen, the twins had grown into striking young ladies. Both tall and slender, they had inherited their parents' athletic good looks. But there were differences now between the two. Sophie was softer, her hair long and flowing, and, contrary to current style, chose to wear skirts and dresses that sometimes looked like a throwback to a different generation. Terri, on the other hand, embraced everything the modern world threw at her. She sported multiple piercings and tattoos and was rarely seen in anything other than faded jeans and baggy sweatshirts. But their twin bond was still strongly in place and each knew she would move heaven and earth for the other.

The girls quickly set the table then excused themselves to wash up for dinner. Once out of their mother's sight, Sophie pulled Terri into the bedroom.

"Are we still going to do this tonight?" she asked. "Mom's got some big surprise and if we bring this up now, we'll ruin it."

Terri gave her sister a withering look. "It *has* to be tonight. We can't crap out now. If we want to leave next week, well, it just has to be now. We've put it off long enough. We'll let Mom have her big whatever, then we'll tell her. Are you still with me?"

Reluctantly, Sophie nodded her head. "I'm with you. He was my dad, too, you know."

Terri smiled at her sister. "Yeah, I know. And he was the best dad ever. Dex is good, but not like our real dad. He was special."

Sophie nodded again. "Remember how he used to read us all those stories or make ones up himself? He was always there for us. He wouldn't have left us alone in that storm - not him."

Terri put her arm around her sister. "We need to find out what really happened and this is our only chance. So, tonight's the night. Okay?"

"You still think Dex will side with us?"

Terri smiled. "Yeah. I hacked into his computer. He's been keeping in regular touch with all his old friends. I think he really wants to go back and see the place again. It's his home after all."

"I can't believe you did that! What if he'd caught you?"

4

Terri laughed. "I'm too good, you know that. I got Dad's computer smarts. Believe me, Dex doesn't have a clue."

"What doesn't Dex have a clue about, sugar?"

The twins were startled by the deep masculine voice coming from behind them and turned to see their stepfather standing in the doorway. Dex Pierce, at forty-six, was still a very attractive man even though his blond hair was now speckled with gray. He ran a commercial fishing operation out of Monterey Bay and was quite successful. Folks in the industry said he just seemed to have an internal radar for finding fish. He'd traveled with them to California after their father's death on Mateguas and married their mother two years later.

"Come on now, Terri, fess up. What are you hiding from your old man?"

Sophie blushed and stared at the floor. Her twin, however, didn't flinch "We're going back to Mateguas, Dex," she said. "We're leaving next week."

Dex stared at his stepdaughter, unable to believe the words she'd just spoken. "Mateguas? Why? Does your mother know about this?"

"No," replied Sophie. "We're going to tell her tonight."

"Oh boy. She's not going to like this. But why go back? What's there that you're looking for?"

"We want to find out what really happened to our dad," replied Terri. "Mom isn't telling us the whole truth, you know that. And, what with college coming this fall and all, this may be our last chance."

"Where'd you get the money for the trip? And where will you be staying?"

Terri smiled. "We've been planning this for a couple of years. We've saved up - mostly money from Grandma. And we've rented a house. I believe it used to be yours."

Dex stared at her. *My house! They're staying in the house I built. Oh God, I'd like to see that place again!*

"My home's a rental now? How'd you find out about it?"

5

"Through Louise McKinney," answered Terri, a smug smile playing on her lips. "She arranged it. I got her address from Mom's Christmas card list."

Dex looked at his stepdaughter with new respect. *She's really covered all the bases. I'd love to go with them. But what about Karen? She'll never agree to go.*

Shaking his head, he looked at Terri. "Okay, I gotta admit you've done a good job getting things together. But what about your mother? You know how she feels about Mateguas. How are you going to convince her?"

The girls looked at each other, then Sophie spoke up. "We're hoping you'll help."

Dex laughed. "That's an awful big assumption, honey. Why would I want to upset your mother by bringing up all that stuff again? Bill's been dead for ten years now. That chapter of her life is over and done with. I won't let her be hurt by all that old garbage again."

Sophie glanced at her sister, seemingly deflated by Dex's words, but Terri maintained her confidence. "Dex, we know you want to go back. I can see it in your eyes whenever you see anything on TV or anywhere that relates to Maine. It's your home, where you were born. Don't you want to step onto that island again just one more time? If you would help us convince Mom, well, then we could all go and maybe, just maybe, it won't be as bad as she thinks. Maybe, we'll all just have a little fun."

Dex sat on the bed thinking, knowing in his heart that she was right. He *did* want to go back - had wanted to for years. And he would've if it hadn't been for Karen.

Maybe now is the time, he thought. *Time to see that rock again and fish those waters. Yeah, this may be my only chance, too.*

Smiling, he turned to Terri. "Okay, you're right. I want to go back and I'll do what I can to talk your mom into it. But I won't let her be hurt, understand? She went through a very rough time ten years ago and I won't let her go through that again. Okay?"

Terri nodded. "You've got a deal, Dex."

He stood up, reached in his back pocket and pulled out his wallet. "Now assuming we can get your mother to agree, why don't you see if you can book two more seats on that flight. Use my credit card." He tossed the card at Terri who already had her laptop open to the airline's webpage.

"You got it," she said grinning happily.

"Okay, that's settled. Now I have to get in touch with Brad about taking over my charters."

He turned to leave the room, but stopped in the doorway and looked back over his shoulder. "One more thing. Your mother has something she wants to surprise us with tonight. Let's let her have her moment before you bring this up. Okay?"

"Sure. No problem," agreed Sophie. "Got any idea what she's all excited about? Something to do with her jewelry business?"

Karen had begun making jewelry from sea glass soon after they'd moved back to California. She'd started playing around with it as a hobby, but found she had a knack for design and soon was selling some of her work to local jewelry and curio shops.

"I haven't got a clue," replied Dex. "But let her have her moment, girls. Don't take that away from her."

"Okay, Dex. We get it. Now I think we'd better get back out there. Mom's going to wonder what's happened to us."

STATE HOSPITAL, BANGOR, MAINE

THE MAN THEY CALLED 'John Doe' shuffled down the corridor, eyes vacant and mouth turned down in what appeared to be a permanent scowl. He was tall, but very thin, elbows and hipbones jutting out at irregular angles as he walked. His hair was long, pulled back into a ponytail; strands of silver interspersed amongst what once had been sandy brown. An unkempt beard covered the lower part of his face, making him look older than he actually was. He had on institutional pajamas, an old tattered robe and LL Bean flip-flops that slapped annoyingly on the linoleum as he shuffled along. Sliding down his nose were a pair of gold wire-rimmed glasses. Overall, to those old enough to remember, he looked like some forgotten remnant from the Haight Ashbury District of the sixties.

"Hey, John," an orderly called out as he passed by. "We could use some help in here with the medical records software."

The man stopped, turned, and nodded. Then he walked quietly into the office and sat down at the computer. He used sign language to ask the orderly what the problem was. The orderly explained and the man nodded again then settled down to work. As his hands flew over the keys, the tension in his face relaxed and the beginnings of a knowing smile played at the corners of his lips. And, at least for this moment, he was content.

DINNER REVELATIONS

KAREN SET THE SERVING dishes out on the table then went to the liquor cabinet and got out a bottle of cabernet sauvignon she'd purchased from a boutique winery in Paso Robles. She handed the bottle to Dex along with an opener as he entered the room.

"You got out the good stuff tonight, princess," he said as he studied the label. "What's the celebration all about?"

Karen smiled, moving to the head of the table. "You'll see. Okay, everyone sit down, I have an announcement to make."

She waited as they took their seats and, when she had their undivided attention, smiled. "Okay, here it is. I received a phone call today from the Museum of Modern Art in San Francisco. They've asked me to submit several pieces of my jewelry to a juried exhibition they're planning for early fall. Isn't that exciting!"

Dex got up and gave her a hug and a kiss. "That's fabulous, Karen. Isn't it, girls?"

Terri and Sophie broke into applause and then each got up and hugged their mother. "Which pieces are your considering?" asked Sophie, returning to her seat.

"Oh, I'm not sure yet, but some of the blue for sure. It's harder to find. And the red, that's even rarer. Dex, pour the wine, please. I want to make a toast."

Dex complied with her request as Karen raised her glass.

"To my family. I couldn't have done it without all of you!"

Sophie and Terri exchanged glances, knowing that soon they would be putting quite a damper on their mother's ebullient mood, then raised their glasses, too.

Conversation during dinner was lively and centered around the upcoming art exhibition. After the meal was over, Karen stood up to clear the table, but Terri reached out and put a hand on her arm to stop her.

"Mom, you know how proud we all are of you, but Sophie and I have something we need to talk to you about and I'm afraid it may be upsetting."

Karen looked at her, puzzled, then sat back down. "Go on. What's on your mind?"

Terri took a deep breath. "Mom, Sophie and I want to go back to Mateguas."

Karen stared wordlessly at her daughter. After several moments, she turned toward Sophie. "Is this true, Soph? Or is this just some kind of cruel joke?"

Sophie looked down at her hands, silently trying to summon the courage to answer her mother. After a few moments, she looked back up.

"Yes, Mom, it's true. We've been planning it all year. We want to find out what really happened to Dad."

"Find out what happened to your father?" repeated Karen, incredulous. "You know what happened to him. He drowned in that blasted swamp behind the house. What more do you need to know? I don't understand this at all. Dex, help me out here."

She turned to her husband for support, but could tell immediately by the expression on his face that very little would be forthcoming.

"Oh, don't tell me you're in on this, too? Sure, it makes sense. You want to go back and see all your old friends. Immerse yourself in that wonderful Maine culture again. Am I wrong?"

"Now, princess, don't get your panties in a bunch. Yes, I'd like to go back. See my home again. What's so God-awful wrong in that?"

Karen clenched her hands together and frowned. "Okay, girls. You want to know more about your father's death and I guess I can understand that. I've tried to shield you from a lot of things, but now that you're almost grown, I guess it's time to tell you."

Terri and Sophie exchanged looks then leaned forward, waiting to hear what their mother had to say. Dex frowned wondering what Karen was going to reveal that wasn't already common knowledge.

"The first thing you have to understand is that Mateguas was not a good place for Bill. No, things went very wrong for him there."

She paused and looked down at her wine glass. "Pour me another," she said handing it to Dex. When the glass was again full, she continued.

"Your father and I were not getting along and hadn't been good together for quite some time. I'm sure you have memories of some of the fights we had, don't you?"

"Yeah," said Terri, nodding. "I remember one in particular. Your wrists were bruised. Dad hurt you."

Karen bit her bottom lip, remembering. "That's right. That was one of the worst of them, but there were others, too. In fact, I was contemplating divorce when he died."

The girls looked surprised by this and Dex leaned back in his chair, a puzzled look on his face.

Karen saw his look of disbelief and frowned. She took another sip of her drink then continued.

"And that's not all that was going on. There was trouble at work, too. He was in danger of losing his job again - mostly because of his drinking."

She paused to let her words sink in. Sophie's mouth was open in surprise, but Terri seemed strangely calm, a smirk on her face.

"So, how did you find out about this, Mom?" she asked. "And when? Last I remember, Dad said we would be moving to the mainland when he was promoted to an R&D position."

"That's what he wanted you to think, Terri. But it was all unraveling for him. He was despondent, depressed, and I'm afraid his drowning may not have been accidental."

"Are you saying he committed suicide?" asked Sophie.

Karen nodded. "I think that's a distinct possibility, dear. So, you see, there's really nothing to be gained by going back. It will just mean more heartache for you both."

They were all silent for a few minutes until Karen, thinking she had made her point, began to get up to leave the table.

"Not so fast, Mom," said Terri.

Karen hesitated. "What?"

"I don't buy it."

"I don't understand - what is it that you don't *buy*, Terri?"

"Well, as Sophie said, we've been planning this trip for awhile and last year when you and Dex were in San Francisco, I went rummaging around in the attic and found Dad's old laptop."

She hesitated for a moment, watching her mother carefully.

"That old thing? I'd be surprised if you could get it started."

"Well, I did. You know you've always said I have Dad's computer genes."

Karen sighed. "Okay, so what did you find?"

Terri smiled. "Most of it was corrupted, like you'd expect, but I did get some of the more recent stuff off. You remember how Dad was always making lists, always organizing things?"

Karen nodded. "Sure, he was a stickler for details."

"Well, right before he died he was busy planning for the future, making lists of things to do when he moved into R&D

and stuff like that. Names of realtors on the mainland, too. It sure didn't sound like a man contemplating suicide, Mom. That's why I don't buy it. That's one of the reasons we have to go back."

Karen had the decency to blush when she realized she'd been caught in a lie, but she quickly recovered. "Okay, you found some lists. That doesn't mean he wasn't depressed. He had ups and downs - especially when he was drinking."

"Nice try, Mom, but I still don't buy it. Dad was in good spirits in the days before the storm. And he wouldn't leave Sophie and me, not willingly. No, I don't think he killed himself, Mom."

Dex, who had been silent during this exchange, now leaned forward toward his wife. "I don't buy it either, princess. If a man wants to end it all, he uses a gun or goes out to sea and jumps overboard - makes it quick. He doesn't wander out into a storm, leaving his family behind in a potentially perilous situation, hoping that he'll drown in a swamp. No, I'm with Terri on this one. Bill wouldn't have willingly left his family."

Karen gave him a hard look. "You just want to go back to that God-forsaken place, too. That's why you're siding with them."

Dex leaned back in his chair. "Sure, I want to go back. I never pretended otherwise, you know that. I've brought it up before, but you always shot me down. It's where I was born - where my parents are buried. I'd like to place a bouquet on my mom's grave just one more time. And where's the harm? The girls want to know more about their father's last days. It's natural. If there's nothing to be found, well, then, where's the harm in it?"

Karen bowed her head, staring at the table, deep in thought. Then she sighed again, looked up, and forced a smile. "Okay, you win. I can't fight you all. We'll go back, but as a family. However, don't expect me to engage in any of your detective work, girls. You're on your own there. I'll just spend my days wandering the beaches looking for sea glass.

"And you'd better be prepared to find out some things about your dad that won't be pleasant. But if that's what you have to do to end this, then so be it. And, Dex, I'll expect you to bring us the bounties of the sea for dinner every night while we're there. That'll be your penance."

Dex laughed. "No problem! Lobster, clams, tuna - you name it, princess, and it'll be yours."

He got up from the table, walked over, and kissed her. She smiled again, this time more genuinely. "Well, now that that's decided, when do we go? Maybe next month. The weather should be very good by then."

The girls looked at each other. "We're going next week, Mom. Terri and I already have our plane reservations and we've rented a house."

Again, Karen frowned. "Next week? There's no way Dex and I can leave that soon, is there, Dex?"

Dex looked at her contritely. "Actually, there is. We've already checked the airlines and Terri's got us on the same flight. And they've rented my old place. You remember it?"

Karen couldn't help but blush. It had been at his house on Mateguas where they'd first made love and just thinking about it brought back to her vivid memories of the passion they had shared.

"Princess?"

"Yes, Dex, I remember. It's a beautiful place. The girls chose well. But what about your fishing commitments? Can they be cleared with such short notice?"

"I've taken care of that, too. Brad will handle them. Don't worry, I won't lose any business that can't be regained."

"Brad? Isn't he awfully young to handle the boat by himself?"

Dex smiled. "He's twenty-six, Karen. At that age, I'd already been running my own operation for two years. And he's been with me for three years - I trust him. He'll do fine."

Karen frowned. "Well, it looks like you all have just about thought of everything. Nice work, going behind my back. So, I guess it'll be next week. Think I'll straighten out the kitchen then check the weather. It's early in the season there and things may still be on the chilly side."

She picked up her glass and some plates and walked to the kitchen, deep in thought.

Oh Christ, back to that nasty little island. Yes, and once there, the girls will ferret out all our dirty little secrets. Bill and Maggie, and me and Dex. They'll find out some things, things they won't like, but they're adults now - I think they can handle it. But one thing's for sure - they won't find out the truth. No, only I know the truth and I'm not about to reveal it to them or anyone else.

Her hands shaking slightly, she carefully put the dishes in the dishwasher and wiped down the counters.

I have the knife with me here. That's all I needed to complete the ritual. The box with the blood powder and other stuff, I returned to its original hiding place, at our old house, before we left Mateguas. If I need it, I can somehow cajole the new owners to let me inside. But, maybe, that won't be necessary. I've kept my promise and made sacrifice every month. That should protect us. And the girls are adults now. Yes, maybe I'm worrying for nothing and it will end up being just another summer vacation in Maine.

But she looked down at her trembling hands and knew she was just kidding herself. No, it wouldn't be just an ordinary summer vacation. They were going back to Mateguas and every fiber of her being told her that they would be lucky if they survived.

ON MATEGUAS ISLAND

THE OLD HOUSE ON the hill stood silent, its occupant staring out at the waves crashing against the shoreline. She looked up at the blue sky and smiled, thinking about the phone call she'd received from her mother.

Dex is coming home. That thought gladdened her, but it was soured by the knowledge that he would not be alone. *That haughty bitch! Coming back so she can look down her nose at all of us again. Well, there will be some surprises for her, you bet!*

Maggie Maguire glanced toward the stairs. *My son is up there doing his homework. Bill's son. Yeah, I'll bet any money, Dex hasn't had the balls to tell her. She'd never come back here if she knew about Bill's child.*

Smiling, she walked to the kitchen to warm up some tea. Waiting for the microwave, she let her mind drift back to when she first met her boy's father, Karen's first husband.

It was right out there on the beach. Gosh, he was so good-looking. I think I knew right then that we belonged together. And he knew it, too.

What was that I yelled at him? Oh, yeah, 'there's no secrets on this island, Bill.' Well, there were none for me back then and, hopefully, this time there will be none for her. We'll see how she likes having all her dirty laundry aired. Everyone thought how noble she was after Bill died. What bullshit. He'd still be alive if it wasn't for her. She had something to do with his death, I'm sure of it.

The chiming of the microwave startled her out of her reverie. Taking her cup of tea, she walked back to the living room and stood for a moment by the rocker, watching the sea churn below. Suddenly feeling tired, she sank down into the chair, placed her cup on the side table, and began, slowly, to rock, back and forth, back and forth. The movement mesmerized her and her thoughts became dull and heavy as she closed her eyes.

When she woke up it was dark. Her son was sitting on the couch, watching her. She smiled at him as she got up and stretched and tousled his red hair with her hand.

"Sorry, Billy. Guess your mom is getting to be an old lady - taking naps in the afternoon just like Grandma. Bet you're hungry?"

The boy nodded vigorously.

Laughing, Maggie put her arm around him. "Okay, then, let's us heat up some of that venison stew that your grandma brought over and maybe mix up some mashed potatoes to go with? Will that work for you?"

Again, the boy nodded, smiling, as they walked to the kitchen to begin their meal.

Later, after the boy had gone to bed, Maggie poured herself a glass of wine and returned to the rocker. Sitting down heavily, she sipped her drink.

School will be out soon and Billy will be sterning with his grandfather on the lobster boat. I know he's looking forward to that. The sun just rises and sets on my dad according to Billy. Guess he thinks of him more like a father than a granddad. Wish Bill had lived to be a real father to him. I know he would have been proud of his boy.

She sighed, remembering her lost love. *We never really got a chance. If only I'd called him when I found out I was pregnant. If he'd a-*

known, maybe, just maybe, he'd have left that bitch and would still be alive. But I couldn't call him. He'd warned me not to. But still, I should have.

Beginning to feel depressed, she stared out at the sea searching for solace. *There's no good to be gotten dwelling on it*, she thought. *Hindsight's great but you can't let it ruin your life. I have the boy and that's all I need. And that bitch, she'll get her comeuppance. It'll happen, I'm sure. I just have to be patient. This island won't be good for her. No way!*

With a smile, she leaned back in her chair and began to rock. *Yes, something will happen when that women sets foot on this rock and I'll be right here laughing when it does!*

ONE WEEK LATER:
THE FERRY

AFTER LANDING AT THE airport in Portland, Karen and her family took a cab into town. With time to kill, they walked around the waterfront, stopping to pick up groceries, then made their way to the ferry terminal. There was no bridge to this island; access was only by ferry or private boat.

Arriving in time to catch the four o'clock, Karen was feeling tired and a bit out of sorts. As she approached the terminal she hesitated, a look of distaste on her face.

"You know," she said, "we could stay in town and just go out to the island during the day. That might be more fun."

"And lose our deposit on the house?" Dex exclaimed. "No chance, princess. 'In for a penny, in for a pound' as the old timers say. You just hop aboard the ferry - there's no turning back now. It's not going to be that bad!"

Karen scowled. She was about to say more, but decided against it, shrugged and stepped aboard the boat.

Once inside, she glanced around the cabin then sat down on

20

one of the hard wooden benches. *Jesus, it's like stepping back in time. This boat hasn't changed in the least since Bill and I got on it ten years ago. Still claustrophic as hell.*

Dex leaned down to her. "I'm going outside. Want to feel the salt air on my skin again. Care to join me?"

Karen shook her head. "I'll get enough of that damned air when we're on the island, thank you. And don't fall overboard while you're out there. I'm not inclined to lose another husband to this place."

Dex laughed, kissed her on the cheek, and headed to the stern of the boat. Sophie stayed inside with her mother, but Terri went out front and stood silently at the bow of the boat letting memories wash over her.

This is right where Dad and I stood that first trip over, she thought, smiling as she remembered how he'd kept his hand on her shoulder all the way. *He was so happy then - so full of hope for the future. And, I was so excited. If only that feeling could have lasted.* A tear slipped down her cheek.

She leaned over the rail, watching as the bow cut fiercely through the still-frigid water on the way to her former island home. There was a cool sea breeze but she didn't mind it - somehow it felt and smelled just right.

When they finally pulled into the dock on Mateguas, Dex was the first off, helping the deckhand secure the boat to the pier. He grabbed their suitcases and jogged to the parking lot to find the car that came with the rental house. His old friend, Pete McKinney, had assured him that it would be gassed up and waiting for them when they arrived. Sophie and Karen emerged from the cabin shortly after and, carrying the supplies they had bought in town, made their way up the gangplank. Terri, however, lingered at the bow for a few minutes, smiling as she took in all the sights and sounds of the busy wharf.

Dex found the car easily, an old Subaru Outback, rust-covered and well suited to island life. The key was in the ignition and on the dash sat a note from Pete.

"Louise and I would love it if you and Karen and the girls could come for supper Sunday night. Give me a holler and let me know. Welcome home, old buddy. Maybe we can get in some fishing while you're here? Pete."

Dex smiled. *Yes, it's good to be home.*

He brought the car around and started loading it while Karen surveyed the activity on the wharf.

"Hey, princess, remember the first time you stepped onto this rock? Remember that handsome young man who made goo-goo eyes at you?"

Karen couldn't help but laugh, remembering. "You were outrageous. I blushed so hard I think I turned into a beet!"

Smiling at the memory, she turned back to watch the men working on the wharf. On a lobster boat at the far end, a young boy was helping an older man load traps onto the back.

Pointing toward the boat, she turned to get her husband's attention. "Hey, Dex, isn't that boy a bit young to be working on a boat?"

The boy, seeming to sense he was being watched, turned and stared back at her. When she saw him full face, her mouth dropped open in surprise.

Oh my god, that kid's the spitting image of Bill - except for the red hair. As that thought flashed through her mind another image from the past reared up. *That girl, always that girl!*

Dex noticed the change in Karen's posture as she stared at the boat. "What's up, princess?" he asked putting his hand on her shoulder. "Everything all right?"

Karen whirled around to face him, pointing at the boy. "Did you know? I know you've stayed in touch with people here. Did you know about him?"

Return to Mateguas Island

Confused, Dex looked over at the lobster boat and recognized it immediately - it belonged to Rusty Maguire, Maggie's father. The boy was standing in the stern and, suddenly, it dawned on Dex just why Karen was so upset. Girding himself, he hesitated for a moment before answering. "Yes, I knew. He's Maggie's son and she says that your late husband is his father."

Karen's blue eyes flashed angrily. "And what else haven't you told me? Any more surprises?"

"Calm down. I'm sorry. I would have told you long ago but the subject of Maggie and Mateguas has always been a closed one for you. Any time I brought it up you shut me off. I was going to talk to you about this tonight. I'm sorry it was sprung on you so abruptly."

Karen glared at him then turned to watch as the lobster boat motored out to sea.

"People say he's a real nice kid, princess. Shy, but smart. Spends a lot of his time with his grandfolks. I know for you he's a living reminder of bad times, but he's the girls' half-brother and I think they might want to get acquainted with him."

Karen took a deep breath trying to keep her anger in check. Then she turned back to face him. "Okay - so now I know. Anything else? You tell me right now if there's any other big secret you've been hiding."

"Well, there is one more little thing," he said slowly.

"Go on. Don't stop now."

"The house - the one you all inherited. It belongs to Maggie now. She's the one who bought it from you."

"She bought my house?" Karen asked, her voice rising. "How could that be? I never would have sold it to that little slut."

Dex tried to remain calm. "Listen - enough with the name calling, okay? Like it or not, she's a friend of mine. I don't condone her affair with your husband - that was a foolish mistake on both their parts. But it was a long time ago. And so what if she has that house and all the bad memories that go with it? You didn't want it, did you? She lives there alone with the boy. She never married or had any serious boyfriends since Bill died. And she's still headmistress of the island school."

23

Karen pursed her lips. "Well, aren't you just the little town gossip. Got any other juicy tidbits of information to pass on?"

"Come on now, Karen. Sounds like all she has is the house and the boy. Maybe you should feel sorry for her."

Karen laughed. "Sorry for her? Not on your life."

They stood quietly staring at each other, and then, with a shake of her head, Karen turned and walked down the wharf trying to get her emotions under control.

Maggie had a child. Bill's child. A boy. A boy who should have been mine. Conflicting feelings of anger and despair dug deep into her core as she remembered another child - one whose life she had ended before it had even begun.

Oh God, why did we come back here? I don't know if I can stand it. A tear slipped down her cheek. *No good will come of it. Just bad memories and heartache.*

 ## DR. TODD'S PARTY

DR. HORACE TODD (HOD to his friends), Chief of Medicine at the Bangor State Hospital, was pouring himself an after-dinner drink when he felt his cell phone vibrate. Having promised his wife that tonight, for once, he would not let hospital matters interfere with their plans, he ignored it. But, as he joined his dinner guests in the living room, curiosity got the better of him and he pulled it out of his pocket to see who had called.

"Hod, not tonight, please," his wife pleaded when she saw him with the cell in his hand. "You promised."

Dr. Todd smiled. "I know, dear. I'm just looking to see who it was. Not to worry. I have the service fully covered for tonight."

He glanced down at the phone and a perplexed look came over his face. "Funny, it was Hemingway. Now why would he be calling me at home?"

"Hemingway? Not the dead author, Hod?" chimed in one of his guests with a laugh.

"Oh, no. Not him, Charles. Our Hemingway's an orderly. Been at the hospital longer than I have. Knows more than most of the nurses and I dare say some of the doctors, too. He's aware I'm off duty tonight and it's not like him to interrupt me for something trivial."

He stared at the phone then looked up at his wife. "Sorry, dear, but I'll have to return this call. I'm sure it'll be something I can handle over the phone. Don't worry."

Dr. Todd got up and walked over to his study dialing as he went. A few minutes later, he returned to his guests.

"Sorry all, but the strangest thing has happened and I fear I must go in to the hospital."

"What's up, Hod?" asked Charles. "One of your patients escape?"

"Oh, no. Nothing like that. It's John - John Doe. He's beginning to talk."

"John Doe?" his wife asked. "Is that his real name?"

"No, dear. We don't know his real name. But you should remember him. I brought him home when the computer went on the fritz. He fixed it up in nothing flat. Hasn't spoken a word that I know of since he was found seven or eight years ago."

His wife was silent for a minute, thinking. Then she nodded. "Oh, yes, I remember him. He's the one who looks like John Lennon, right?"

Dr. Todd laughed. "He wears his hair long and has wire-rims, if that's what you mean, yes. Hemingway says he's very agitated and Dr. Specks wants to sedate him. Hemingway's afraid if they knock him out, he'll shut down again and stop trying to speak."

"Can't you handle this from home, dear?"

"No, Esme, I can't." He looked regretfully down at his cordial then turned back to his wife. "Why don't you get me a cup of java so I don't fall asleep on the way to the hospital?"

His wife dutifully got up and, shaking her head, went to prepare him a cup of coffee. As he waited, he sat back down.

"Well, what's this guy's story, anyway?" asked Charles. "You say he's been mute for seven or eight years?"

"Yes," replied the doctor. "Think back, about seven and a half years ago - you remember that man who was found on Puffin Island by a group of teenagers who were going there to party? His photo was all over the news back then."

One of the guests nodded. "I remember something about that. They found him half-starved and hypothermic. Looked like a wild man in the newspapers. Is that your 'John Doe'?"

The doctor nodded as he took the cup of coffee from his wife. "Thanks, dear. Yes, no one claimed him so he was brought to us. He was amnesiac then and still is today. And he couldn't or wouldn't speak. So, we don't how he ended up on Puffin. I daresay, though, that he probably didn't go there voluntarily. There's nothing to entice a man to that island but an old abandoned house and a few rocks."

"How long was he there? Does anyone know?"

"No, no one knows, but I bet it was some time. It's a wonder that he survived."

"What makes you think he was there a long time, Hod?"

"The man has an old lesion on the back of his head that looks like an untreated wound, right at the base of his skull. The margins didn't heal properly, leaving a very prominent scar. If he'd been anywhere on the mainland with a wound like that, he would have been taken to the hospital and had stitches. And looking at the scar, I could tell it was old."

"Think he slipped and fell? Maybe he was on a boat and went overboard. Washed ashore on Puffin?"

"Well, maybe, but I have my own theory as to what happened to him."

His guests waited patiently as he sipped his coffee, eager to hear his hypothesis about the man called John Doe.

Finally he spoke. "I think he was a crime victim."

"Why do you think that, dear?" asked his wife.

"It's all pretty elementary, to coin a phrase," he chuckled. "Given the location and size of the wound, I think someone hit him with a blunt object, possibly a shovel, then his assailant took him to Puffin and dumped him, thinking he was dead or would

27

die soon. His inability to speak may be due more to this psychological trauma than actual physical limitations."

"Do you think he was a drug dealer or someone involved in organized crime?" asked one of the guests.

"I don't think so. A fingerprint check turned up nothing, so it's not like he was a wanted criminal or anything."

There were murmurs among the guests as they digested the doctor's theory. Pleased with the intrigue he had proffered, Dr. Todd finished his coffee and handed the cup back to his wife. Then he got up and went to the hall closet to put on his topcoat. Before he left, he walked back to the living room to again apologize to his guests.

"Sorry I have to leave, but I don't want John clamming up again. He's a gentle soul, likes to work in the garden, and is a whiz with computers - he takes care of all ours at the hospital. I won't be late, Esme. You all have a good time."

With those last words, Dr. Todd left the house, his heart beating rapidly in anticipation of what, if anything, his patient, John Doe, had to say

 **MAGGIE**

THE PHONE RANG. MAGGIE put down her dishcloth, wiped her hands and walked to the living room to answer.

Before speaking, she checked the caller ID. "Hi, Mom. What's up?"

"They're back, honey. Came on the four o'clock ferry."

Maggie grimaced. She knew who her mother was referring to.

"How you know for sure, Mom? You camped out down at the wharf?"

Emma laughed. "No, honey, but your dad and Billy were down there loading traps and they saw them. Dad called me right up on the short wave. Think that woman saw young Bill, too. Sure would like to be a fly on the wall at her house tonight! Bet old Dex is going to get an earful!"

Maggie laughed. "Well, maybe he'll finally wake up and begin to see the light. I never understood what kind of a spell that woman conjured up to take him away from here. Don't know what it must be like for him, married to a bitch like her!"

"There's no accounting for taste, honey. Oh, and they have the girls with them. Dad said one has spiked hair and tats all over her body!"

"Well, that's what comes from growing up in California."

The two women spoke some more before Maggie hung up and returned to the kitchen to finish cleaning up the dinner dishes.

If Karen knows about my boy then I bet the girls will probably know, too. They might even want to meet him, seeing he's their half-brother. Oh God, why didn't I tell him about his father a long time ago? Guess I'll have to do it now. Don't want him finding out from a stranger.

Shaking her head, she put the last dishes in the dishwasher, dried her hands, and walked to the living room. Sitting down in her rocker, she made a decision.

Tonight, after dinner. Yes, tonight I'll tell Billy all about his dad. It's time he knew.

WKZTV NEWSROOM, PORTLAND, MAINE

SUSAN LEVEQUE WAS SITTING at her desk, going over her notes for the evening news when the phone rang.

"LeVeque speaking," she answered.

"Hey Susan! It's Dr. Harve Specks. Remember me?"

Susan searched her memory. "Can't say as I do, Harve. Want to fill me in?"

"You interviewed me eight years ago, remember? When that guy was found on Puffin?"

The reporter was silent for a minute. *That was my big break - getting the lead on that story.*

"Yes, now I remember. You were the attending doctor when the poor guy was brought in to the ER, right?"

"Yes, that's the ticket. I was an intern at the hospital in Portland back then. I'm at Bangor State now."

"So, what's up, Harve? Got another shipwrecked guy for me to try to interview?"

Dr. Specks laughed. "Think you're going to like this one."

31

Susan waited impatiently for him to continue. "Let's get to the point, Harve."

"Sure, right. You remember John Doe? The guy they found on Puffin Island eight years ago?"

"Yes, I remember. And, Harve, I don't have all day."

"Okay, I'm getting there. After he was stabilized, he was transferred to Bangor State and he's been here ever since. No one's ever claimed him. And he's been mute and amnesiac all this time."

"Yes, go on."

Dr. Specks paused for dramatic effect. "Well, Susan, last night, out of nowhere, he began to speak!"

The reporter leaned forward in her chair, her interest more than a little bit piqued. "That so? And what's he saying? Does he remember what happened to him? Or who he is?"

"Unfortunately, no. He has no memory of being on Puffin or his true identity, but he's talking."

Susan sighed, deflated. *Not much of a story.*

"So, why are you calling me about it, Harve?"

"I thought you might want to do a retrospective piece - bring the public up to date as to what happened to him. Something like that. Might be a good human-interest story. And maybe he'll remember something or someone might recognize him. He looks a lot different now than when they found him."

Susan thought for a moment. *Mmmmmm, it would make a good piece. Worth looking into. Who knows - maybe he will remember. It'd be a feather in my cap to get an exclusive if he did.*

She glanced down at the phone in her hand as she pulled up her calendar on the computer. "When can I come out there and interview you both? Soonest I can get it together would be Saturday."

"Saturday will be great. You bringing a whole crew?"

Susan rolled her eyes. *This guy is really is a piece of work!*

"Yes, I'll be bringing a crew. You just make sure you clear it with Dr. Todd. Don't want him raising a ruckus. And I'll want to interview him, too, seeing he's the senior medical officer there.

Okay? We'll plan to be at the hospital around ten. That work for you?"

They spoke for another minute or two then Susan hung up abruptly. She sat at her desk thinking, then picked up the phone again and began arranging for the crew that would accompany her to the State Hospital on Saturday. When she finished, she searched through her computer files for the story she'd filmed eight years before. As she reviewed the film, she smiled to herself.

If I get lucky, this could be something good. Maybe even award material.

Pleased with herself, she began to flesh out questions and mentally rehearse for the interview on Saturday.

EXPLANATIONS AND EXCUSES

THEIR RIDE TO THE rented house was a silent one. Terri and Sophie, in the backseat, were well aware of their mother's anger and wanted no part of it. Dex kept his eyes on the road, letting Karen stew.

I should have told her before - made her listen. And the girls should have known, too. If I'd fessed up, we might have made this trip sooner.

He sighed to himself. *Well, there's no use crying over spilt milk - what's done is done. I'll just have to make the best of it. Maybe some fresh lobster and good wine will help mellow her out a bit.*

He put the evening ahead out of his mind and concentrated on the scenery. *God, it's good to be home. The California coastline is nice, but it has nothing on Maine. Can't wait to get back out on the water.*

"Here we are," he announced as he pulled in the drive. He turned his head to address his stepdaughters. "You're in for a treat here, girls."

"This used to be yours, didn't it?" asked Terri. "Mom said once that you built it yourself."

"Ayup, with a little help from my friends, of course. Now let's get our stuff inside. Wait'll you see the view."

Working together, they lugged all their belongings and groceries into the house. Karen, obviously still angry, began exploring the kitchen while the girls put the food away. Dex took their suitcases to their rooms; his and Karen's to the loft upstairs and the girls to the guest bedroom on the first floor. Then he walked to the kitchen where the women were working.

"I'm going to run out and see if I can rustle us up some lobsters and clams for dinner," he said as he grabbed his windbreaker. "Anyone want to go with me?"

Karen didn't look up when he spoke, but Sophie and Terri, glad for the opportunity to leave the tension-filled room, looked at each other and nodded.

"We'll come," said Terri. "If that's okay with you, Mom?"

Karen was silent for a moment, as if thinking, then she turned toward her daughter. "Go. I can take care of this myself."

Terri leaned over and gave her mother a kiss on the cheek. "You're the best, Mom! Come on, Sophie. Dex is waiting."

After they left, Karen quickly finished up in the kitchen. Feeling tired and depressed, she opened a bottle of wine, poured a glass, and took it to the living room. She stood quietly for a time, gazing out at the sea as she sipped her drink.

Maggie has Bill's child, she thought as she sat down in one of the captain's chairs that faced the window. *How could Dex have kept that from me? And the house - I would never have sold it to that girl. I'd have burned it down first.*

She stared at her glass of wine as memories of ten years ago washed over her, then she lifted her head and gazed out the window. It was early evening and the moon was beginning to rise in the night sky. She could hear the wind whistling in the trees as wave after wave crashed against the rocky shoreline. Feeling tired, she put her wine glass down, closed her eyes and, soon the sounds of the sea and the rustling of the wind lulled her to a restless sleep.

She opened her eyes. She was no longer sitting by the window, but somehow had been transported outside. She was standing in the middle of an old gravel road, the shoulders of which were shrouded in darkness and shadows. She glanced to her left and then to her right, but nothing seemed familiar.

Where am I? And what am I doing here?

Frightened, she began to jog down the road, not knowing exactly where she was going, but hoping she'd see the house around the next bend. She glanced down at her feet finding it difficult to see what lay on the path beneath them and worried that she might fall. The night was ominously quiet and the air hung heavy around her. She gazed ahead and was heartened when, in the distance, she saw a faint light begin to glow. Wanting desperately to reach it and put the shadows behind her, she picked up her pace, fueling her body with adrenalin.

As she neared the brightly shining light and what she thought was safety, she was startled by the soft hoot of an owl coming from somewhere close behind her.

"No!" she cried as panic and fear threatened to paralyze her. She peered desperately into the darkness on the side of the road, hoping to find a place to hide, but there were only shadows. She began to run again toward the light, with its promise of sanctuary, which was now glowing even more brilliantly. Beginning to feel a sense of relief, she forced herself to run harder, her lungs close to bursting from the exertion.

I'm almost there. I'll make it. I know I will.

Concentrating all her energy on the light and certain she was only a heartbeat away, she began to relax and slowed her pace a bit, breathing more easily. Then, from above her, she heard and felt the beating of wings and knew she was too late.

Desperately, she picked up her pace again trying to reach some safe haven, but the light that had seemed so close was now receding far into the distance, threatening to flicker out and leave her in total darkness. The sound of the wings came closer, echoing in her ears, and the draft they created ruffled her hair. Unable to help herself, she looked up, horrified to see the creature's talons, strangely illuminated in the dark, descending upon her. Then all light went out and she screamed.

Jarred abruptly awake and trying to swallow the scream that was building in her throat, Karen tried to catch her breath. Drenched in sweat, she looked around, unsure of where she was. For a moment, she thought she was back in California at the beach house, and a sense of peace began to settle over her. But that feeling didn't last. She looked out the window and recognized the rocky coast of Maine and she knew where she was. She rubbed her eyes, trying to erase the terrifying dream from her memory as Dex and the girls came laughing through the front door.

"Got you four fine hard shells, princess," he said as he placed the bag of lobsters in the sink. "One-and-a-half pounders. And a peck of clams. We're going to be eating fine tonight!" He walked over to where she stood and kissed her lightly on the cheek.

When she didn't respond, he looked at her, frowning. "Now, you're not going to stay mad at ole Dex, are you? Not after I went to all the trouble to get you fresh lobster?"

Karen, still trying to recover from the nightmare, didn't answer. After a moment, she turned and looked at him.

He noted the perspiration on her forehead and recognized the remnants of fear in her eyes. Worried, he took her hands in his. "Are you all right?" he asked gently, putting his palm on her forehead. "You feel warm."

She shook her head and gave him a shaky smile. "Just a bad dream."

"I hope it wasn't my fault," he whispered, putting his arms around her. "You know I would never do anything on purpose to hurt you. We'll talk after dinner, okay?"

Karen nodded and smiled, trying to force some enthusiasm. "And speaking of dinner, I hope you know I expect you to do all the cooking. And I'm not cleaning up either!"

Dex chuckled. "For you, my love, anything. I'm your knight, remember? I'd walk over hot coals if you wanted. Steaming some lobsters and clams is a no brainer! But I hope you'll allow me to enlist the help of these two scullery maids in the prep and cleanup?"

"They're at your disposal," she laughed. "Now, before you get started, why don't you pour me another glass of wine?"

After dinner, Dex pulled a pint of gelato from the freezer and took it to the table along with four spoons. As they passed the ice cream around, Dex began to speak.

"Okay," he said. "There are some things you girls need to know before you go around talking to people here on the island. And some of the stuff may be pretty unpleasant. There are things your mom never told you because I'm sure she didn't want to tarnish the memory of your father. But, now that we're here, you have to be aware of what went on back then."

Terri and Sophie leaned forward in their chairs. "What is it, Dex?" Terri asked. "What about Dad was so bad?"

Karen took her daughter's hand. "Honey, as I told you before we left home, your dad and I weren't getting along that well when we moved here. You remember all the fighting? I was very unhappy and I blamed your dad. So it was probably my fault as much as his when he reached out to someone else."

"What do you mean by 'reached out'?"

Karen took a deep breath. "He had an affair with your teacher, Maggie Maguire."

"What?" Sophie asked incredulously. "The redhead?"

Karen nodded. "When I found out, he broke it off. But there was still a lot of tension between us. The affair was only one symptom of something much larger that had been eating away at our marriage for a long time."

Terri leaned back in her chair. "Okay, so he had an affair. I get it. Is there more?"

"Yes, honey, there's more," replied Dex. "You know I've kept in touch with my friends here, right, Karen?"

She nodded as he continued. "Well, Rusty, Maggie's dad, let me know what was going on a few months after we left and I can tell you he was not a happy camper. It seems Maggie was pregnant and she said it was Bill's child. I don't think she ever had a chance to tell your dad about it though. She'd just found out a few days before he died."

Dex paused for a moment, watching his stepdaughters' reactions. Finally, Terri spoke up.

"Did she go through with it? Have the baby, I mean?"

"Yes, Terri, she carried the baby to term. You have a brother - I mean, half-brother. His name's Bill and he'd be about nine years old now."

Sophie stared at him. "You've got to be kidding! All these years and you never said anything about it? Don't you think we had a right to know?"

Dex bowed his head. "From what I hear from his grandpa, he's a real nice kid. Shy, but good-hearted."

Terri glared at Dex. "You had no right to keep this from us. Once we were old enough to understand, you should have told us. And, Mom, did you know?"

Karen shrugged. "No, honey, I didn't. At least not until we docked here this afternoon. The boy was on the wharf. He looks just like Bill except for the red hair. It wasn't hard - I just put two and two together. And, that's why I was so mad."

Terri turned from her mother and stared angrily at Dex. "That was bogus, Dex, totally bogus! You should have told Mom years ago. You had no right to keep information like that to yourself."

Dex responded apologetically. "I know and I'm sorry. But I just could never find the right time. I did try to talk to your mother, but, you know, she doesn't like to talk about Mateguas and..."

Karen cut him off mid-sentence. "Don't you go blaming me for your shortcomings, Dexter Pierce. You should have told me and you know it! There's no excuse for not letting me know."

Dex sighed. "You're right, princess. And I apologize to all of you. I hope you can forgive me. I just wanted peace in the family and I never thought we'd be coming back here. But circumstances have changed so now I'm coming clean."

Sophie reached over and squeezed his hand. "It's okay, Dex. I forgive you. Now tell us, is there anything more we should know?"

Dex looked at his daughter gratefully. "Yes, there's more. Maggie bought the house you lived in. It's just she and the boy; she never married. It was pretty rough for her when news of the affair with your father got around. Islanders don't cotton to someone poaching what's isn't theirs. But when they found out she was with child, opinion turned and they supported her. Your dad became the bad guy since he was from away and all. So, you may run into some harsh words about him when you're asking around. I just want you to be forewarned."

Karen bristled at his remarks. "That's not fair. That slut went after Bill. He was vulnerable and she took advantage of that. He was a good man and a very good father. The affair was as much my fault as it was his. I didn't support him like I should have. And, I know you don't want to believe it, but he *was* despondent and that's why he went out into that storm. He just couldn't take another failure."

Dex watched Karen out of the corner of his eye as she tried again to convince her daughters that their father had committed suicide. *She's not telling them everything. She's just telling them a version of the truth that she thinks they can live with and one that will keep them from digging any deeper. What's she hiding that's so important?*

Knowing there would be no easy answers, he turned back to his stepdaughters.

"Maybe your mother's right and Bill did go into those woods with a purpose in mind. But for now that's neither here nor there. I know you girls want to find out things for yourselves, so if you want to visit your old house or walk on that property, you're going to have to have Maggie's permission since she's the legal owner. And you might want to meet your brother. Like I said, I hear he's a good kid."

Terri nodded. "Sure, I'd like to meet him and I'd like to talk to Maggie. Seems she might know some things about Dad that you don't, Mom. Given that you and he were so estranged and all."

Karen forced a smile. "Okay. Go see her. Doesn't bother me in the slightest. But for me, I think I'll pass on that walk down memory lane."

"All right, that's settled," said Dex getting up from the table. "You girls want me to talk to Maggie first? She and I have been friends for a long time and it might help."

"That'd be great, Dex," said Sophie as she began to clear the remnants of their dinner from the table.

Karen rolled her eyes then glanced at her watch. "It's going on ten," she said, "and I, for one, am beat. It's been a long day. Remember your promise - you're cleaning up, right?"

"You go on up to bed," laughed Dex. "I'll be there as soon as I dump the remains of our dinner down on the rocks. The smell of lobster shells that sit overnight can be pretty gruesome. Gotta recycle the bugs."

Karen kissed the girls goodnight and went upstairs to the loft. Terri and Sophie remained at the table as Dex took the lobster shells outside.

"Holy crap," said Terri. "Dad having an affair, us having a brother - it boggles the mind."

"Yeah," agreed her twin. "Glad Mom eased off Dex, but she was right. He should've told her. I can't believe Dad was fucking around with our teacher back then."

Terri nodded. "Yeah. Doesn't seem like the Dad I remember at all. But, if memory serves me, she was quite a babe! I'm surprised Mom didn't toss his ass out."

"Yeah, me, too," replied Sophie with a grin.

"Okay, so what's our plan? I'd like to see the house as soon as possible and maybe Maggie knows something we don't seeing she was so *close* to Dad."

Sophie laughed, then turned when she heard the door open. Dex was back.

Yawning, he bent down and gave each of the girls a kiss. "I'm going to bed now, kids. If you want, I'll stop by Maggie's tomorrow morning and see if she's willing to meet with you all. She should be home seeing it's Saturday. Okay?"

The twins nodded. "Thanks, Dex," said Sophie. "We appreciate all your help. And that was a great dinner tonight!"

Dex laughed. "Happy to oblige. Don't stay up too late."

"We won't. Tomorrow's hopefully going to be a big day. What do you say, Soph, ready to get some shut-eye?"

Her twin stood up and stretched. "I'm actually bushed, too, and sleep sounds very appealing right now."

Smiling, Dex mounted the stairs to the loft to join Karen. Terri and Sophie headed for their room, tired, but also full of anticipation for what the next day might bring.

 **PATERNITY**

"I'VE GOT HOMEWORK TO do, Mom," said Billy taking his dinner plate to the sink and rinsing it off.

"Not just yet, honey. Mom has something she wants to talk to you about."

The boy smiled and came back to the table and sat down. "What's up? This about school? You look real serious."

Maggie smiled. "No, sweetie, it's not about school. It's about your father."

A surprised look came over the young boy's face. "My dad? What about my dad?"

Maggie leaned across the table and took his hands in hers. "I know you've always wondered about your father. And I've probably been remiss in not telling you about him sooner and for that, I apologize. My only excuse was that I was waiting for the right time and now circumstance has dictated that the time is here."

The boy sat quietly, his eyes filled with hope and anticipation, waiting for her to continue.

"Now where do I begin?"

Maggie hesitated for a moment, thinking, and then she looked back up at the boy and smiled. "Let me tell you first off that your dad was a great guy. He was smart - had an advanced degree - and had a good sense of humor, too. Oh, and he was very good-looking. I think you've got his looks and when you're a little bit older, you're going to have to beat the girls off with a stick!"

Billy blushed. "Aw, Mom. Don't say that. I hate girls!"

Maggie laughed. "You'll grow out of that, sweetie. You'll see. Okay, now where was I?"

"My dad is smart, funny, and good-looking, right? But who is he? Is he a lobsterman?"

"No, honey, he's not. Be patient. Let me tell this my own way. Okay?"

The boy nodded.

"Okay. Now he wasn't an islander like you and me. No, he moved here from California with his family."

"His family? You mean his mom and dad?"

"No, honey, he was married - had a wife and two little girls, twins. They lived right here - in this house."

"How come they lived in our house?"

"Oh, he'd inherited it from his aunt. I bought it later on after they'd moved out."

Maggie stood up, walked to the cupboard and pulled out a bottle of wine. After pouring herself a glass, she sat back down at the table.

"Okay, I met him right after he'd moved here - right down on the beach across the street. I liked him straight off and could tell he liked me, too. But he was out of bounds, you know, being married and all."

Maggie paused, trying to find the right words to explain her affair to her son. *He's still so young. I have to get it just right.*

"So, we became friends, but it wasn't long before I discovered his marriage was falling apart."

"Falling apart?"

44

"Yeah, you know, like Cecil Putnam's parents."

"Oh, you mean, he moved to town like Cec's dad?"

"No, they were like Cecil's folks before his dad moved away. Fighting all the time and stuff. You remember."

Again, the boy nodded.

Maggie took a deep breath and then smiled at him. "Okay. So, his marriage was in a bad way and it was like that before he got to Mateguas, mind you. I didn't break anything up. He was only staying with his wife because he loved his children and was afraid she'd take them away from him. So, like I said, we were friends, but over time, it became more than that - we fell in love. I know it was wrong, 'cause he was married, but we shared a physical relationship, too. And, out of that came you. I'd just found out I was pregnant and was going to tell him when he had an accident."

"Accident? What happened?"

"There was a very bad storm and he got caught out in it. I'm sorry, Billy, but he drowned in the swamp behind this house."

"You mean he's dead?" the boy asked, disappointment apparent in his tone. "My dad's dead?"

"Yeah, honey, he died. I'm sorry this is so hard. But, think on this. You've got two half-sisters, his kids from his marriage, and they're here on the island visiting right now and I'll bet they'll want to meet you."

The boy sat quietly, digesting this information. "How old are they?"

"Oh, they're old," she answered, laughing. "Probably seventeen or eighteen now. And they're twins! What do ya think of that?"

Billy paused, then smiled at his mother. "I'd like to meet them. It might be fun to have sisters."

The boy got up, walked around the table and put his arms around his mother. "Do you miss him, Mom? I mean, my dad?"

Maggie pulled out of his embrace and looked at him, her eyes softening. "Oh sweetie, of course, I miss him. I wish he were here to see what a fine young man you're becoming. He would be so proud."

45

The boy hugged her again. "Thank you, Mom. Thank you for telling me."

Maggie smiled and hugged him back. "Now you run upstairs and do your homework. I'll be up to tuck you in later when you're ready for bed."

Billy kissed her then ran up the stairs to his room.

Watching him go, Maggie poured herself another glass of wine. *Now that wasn't so hard, was it? Now all I have to do is make sure those girls come by to meet him. And, I'm sure they will. Once they know about him, it will be only natural for them to want to see what he's like, if only out of curiosity. And won't that be a thorn in that woman's side!*

 **FORGIVENESS**

KAREN WAS ALREADY IN bed curled up around a pillow, feigning sleep, when Dex got upstairs,

She's still angry with me, he thought as he stripped off his clothes. *But she'll come around.*

Sliding under the covers, he reached for her. She resisted at first, but then curled herself up next to him, warming to his embrace. He nuzzled her neck, holding her close, murmuring her name.

"I love you," he whispered. "I'm sorry I hurt you today."

She turned in his arms until she was facing him. "I love you, too. And I know you didn't do it on purpose. You were only trying to spare me pain by not telling me earlier. But, Dex, you have to be honest with me about anything that goes on in this place. It's important."

"I know. And I will from now on. I promise."

He pulled her to him and kissed her. Not breaking the embrace, she rolled on top of him, straddling him as he entered

47

her. They made love slowly and generously, each secure in the bond they felt for one another. Later, he put his arms around her and they curled up tightly together, like two pieces of a puzzle, and soon drifted off to sleep.

Feeling warmly wrapped in the cocoon of his love, Karen slept peacefully, untroubled by any nightmares.

But as she lay content and safe in her lover's arms, somewhere on the mainland, a man sat at a computer, his hands swiftly typing endless code while his mind tried desperately to remember what he had forgotten.

SATURDAY MORNING

"PRINCESS, GET UP!"

Karen rolled over and glanced at her watch. "What? It's not even six o'clock yet."

Dex laughed. He was standing at the side of the bed dressed in jeans, sweatshirt, and topsiders.

"Shake a leg, girl. It's time for you get outta bed and face the dawn!"

Karen pulled the covers up over her head. "Go away. I've faced enough dawns already."

"Not like this," he said, roughly pulling the blankets down off the bed.

Reluctantly, admitting defeat, she sat up as he tossed her a pair of jeans and a sweatshirt.

"Underwear?" she asked as she picked up the clothing.

"No time. Just throw these on and slip on your tennies. You can get dressed properly later. Now hurry."

Karen sighed and quickly pulled on the clothes. "Now what?"

Dex laughed again, reaching for her hand. "You'll see."

49

Once downstairs, he led her out the backdoor on the seaward side of the house. They followed a short path over the rocks until finally they stood on the sandy shore. They were facing east and the sun was just beginning to peek up over the horizon.

"Oh my," exclaimed Karen as beams of sunlight sparkled off the shiny, wet seaweed and tiny birds swooped up and down dancing over the water in celebration of the dawn. Dex stood behind her, his arms wrapped around her waist as they watched the spectacle unfold.

Too soon, it was over. Karen, feeling content, rested her head back on his chest.

"Worth it?" he asked.

"Yes, it was worth it. Thank you for sharing with me." She turned in his arms to face him, suddenly serious. "If Maggie agrees to see the girls today, you'll make sure she doesn't do or say anything that will hurt them? Won't you?"

Dex nodded. "Yes, I'll try. It may be unpleasant for them hearing about their dad from his one-time girlfriend, but I'll make sure she doesn't over-embellish. You know I think of them as my daughters, Karen. I won't let anyone harm them."

She nodded and smiled as he took her hand and led her back up the short path to the house. Once inside, he headed for the kitchen while she went upstairs to shower.

When she came down a short time later, Sophie and Terri were already sitting at the kitchen counter watching Dex whisk together the ingredients for a lobster omelet with the leftovers from the night before.

"Here," Karen said taking the whisk from his hands. "You shower, I'll cook."

After breakfast, Dex grabbed his windbreaker and headed out the door. He drove the short distance to what had once been Karen and Bill's home, parked the car, and walked up the hill toward the main entrance. He no sooner got to the porch when the door opened and his old friend came running out and leapt into his arms.

"Dex!" she cried, hugging him. "Oh God, I've missed you."

He laughed as he pulled out of her embrace and looked her over. "Now you haven't changed one bit, Red. Still drop-dead gorgeous. How is it that none of the eligibles here on the island, or for that matter, on the mainland, haven't snatched you up yet?"

Maggie blushed at the compliment. "Oh, Dex. No one wants an old spinster schoolteacher. And especially, not one with a young son. Let me take a look at you."

She stood still for a moment, running her eyes over him. "You look pretty darn fine, too; a little silver creeping in, but it suits you. California must be treating you right. Gotta tell you, when word got out that you were coming back, all the girls were suddenly lined up at the beauty parlor gettin' their hair and nails done. Some even went and got a bikini wax, just in case, if you know what I mean. So if you're lookin' for a little something extra to spice up your visit, I don't think you'll have to look very far!"

Dex laughed. "Thank you, but no thank you. Karen takes very good care of me in that department."

At the mention of Karen's name, Maggie scowled. "Let's not spoil this by talking about her."

"Now, kitten, she's my wife and I love her. And I won't hear any bad talk about her, you hear?"

Maggie frowned, then laughed. "Okay, Dex. I'll be good. Now, come on inside. I've got a fresh pot of coffee on the stove."

Sitting down at the kitchen table, Dex glanced around the room. "Where's your boy?"

"Oh, he took off early this morning. He's sterning with my dad this season."

"At his age?"

"Well, not exactly sterning. He's too young. But Dad lets him think he's doing the job and that's what matters. How about you? Any little Dex's around or on the way?"

Dex sighed. "No, unfortunately. Not that we haven't tried. And are still trying. We've had all the tests and there's nothing wrong with me or with her. Don't know what the problem is but somehow we just can't catch. But I have the girls. You remember them - the twins. They're my daughters now and I wouldn't trade them for anyone."

Maggie smiled as she sat down across the table from him. "I remember them. They were real cuties. Must be all grown up now."

Dex nodded as he sipped his coffee. "They're the reason we're here."

Maggie looked puzzled. "How so?"

"Well, as you said, they're grown now and will be going off to college in the fall. But before they go on their separate ways, they want a little closure about their dad. Terri especially doesn't believe that he would have just gone waltzing off into the woods the night of the storm. She thinks there has to be more to it than that and hopes by talking to people here, she'll uncover the real reason he disappeared."

Maggie sat still for a moment, thinking. "So, that's why you're here. They want to talk to me."

Dex nodded.

"You've told them about me and Bill?"

"Ayup. Told them last night."

"And about Billy? You told them about their brother, too?"

Dex nodded. "Came clean about everything. They want to meet him, you know."

Maggie smiled. "He wants to meet them, too. I hadn't told him about Bill before. Thought it would just be too confusing for him. But when I heard you all were coming back, I had to."

"How'd he take it?"

"Real well. I don't think he completely understands about Bill and me. But he seemed happy to learn about his father, even if it ended up he was dead and all."

"I've heard good things about your boy. Seems like you're doing a real fine job raising him. But what about you? Don't you long for some masculine companionship sometimes? You could have your pick, you know."

Maggie blushed. "There's really been no one for me since Bill. Think he was my 'one and only,' if you know what I mean."

Dex leaned back, studying her.

She caught his look. "Oh, but don't you go thinking I've become a dried-up old maid. On occasion, I've been known to go to town and hang out at The Sternman and I usually don't leave alone. But that's all it is - getting my itch scratched. I have Billy and he's pretty much my life now. And, that's not a bad deal, you know."

Dex smiled. "You're right. How about some more coffee?"

Maggie grabbed the pot from the stove and refreshed Dex's cup. "When do they want to come by, Dex?"

"They were hoping to stop by this afternoon, if that's all right with you. I know it's short notice, but they're anxious to talk to you. Think you might have some insight as to what was going on with their dad."

Maggie nodded. "Well, Billy and his granddad should be back in around noon. Why don't you tell them to come by for lunch at, say, one o'clock?"

"That'd be great. Mind if I tag along?"

"As long as it's just you - I don't want that woman anywhere near this house or my boy."

Dex chuckled. "I don't think you have any reason to worry in that regard. She feels just the same way about you. I, personally, don't understand it. Ten years have gone by. Let bygones be bygones is what I say. But you women - you really know how to hold a grudge."

Maggie stood up, frowning, and walked over to the sink to rinse out her cup. "You just don't understand." She was silent for a moment, then turned back to him. "Okay, so I'll see you and the girls here at one o'clock, okay?"

Dex brought his cup to the sink and handed it to her. "Sure, kitten, we'll be back later. Anything we can bring?"

Maggie smiled. "No, Dex. Just bring your bad self. That'll be treat enough for me."

Laughing, she took his arm and led him to the door.

He leaned down and kissed her lightly on the cheek. "Good to see you again. I've missed you."

"I've missed you, too. Hope we have time to catch up while you're here. I'll see you all later." She gave him a quick hug and went back inside.

Dex walked slowly down the hill to his car. Standing by the door, he turned and stared at the house as if trying to will it to talk.

What secrets do you hold? What really happened here that night? What is it Karen's not telling anyone?

He got in the car, shaking his head in frustration, and backed down the driveway.

His examination of the house, however, did not go unobserved. Maggie watched him silently from the second story window, smiling to herself. *And so it begins. Yes, indeed, the game has begun and I think the next move is mine.*

FILM AT ELEVEN

SUSAN LEVEQUE HELPED HER cameraman load their
equipment into the WKZTV news van. When all was secure, she
hopped up into the passenger seat and put on her seatbelt.

"Now, James," she said to the cameraman as he backed the
van out of the station's parking lot. "I'm going to give you an
overview of what I want to happen today."

James nodded. "This is about the Puffin man, isn't it?"

"The Puffin man? Is that what everyone calls him?"

The cameraman laughed. "Yeah, as in 'Have you seen the
Puffin Man, the Puffin Man, the Puffin Man.' You know, that old
kids' song."

Susan was quiet for a moment, obviously not appreciating his
humor. "How'd you hear this story was about him anyway? Only
people that are supposed to know are me and the station manager."

James chuckled. "Station manager has loose lips, Susan. But
don't worry. Its been kept in-house. Nothing will spoil your
exclusive."

Susan breathed a sigh of relief. "It better not."

She waited as James merged the van onto the freeway and headed toward Bangor.

"So, you were going to tell me how this all is supposed to go down?"

"Yeah. The guy who tipped me off on this, Harve Specks - *Dr. Harve Specks* - is a bit of a publicity hound. So, even though he's a certifiable idiot, I'm going to have to interview him. Probably will spend about twenty minutes' airtime. "

James looked at her questioningly. "Twenty minutes? That's a lot."

Now it was Susan's turn to laugh. "It's all going to end on the cutting room floor, but we have to do it anyway. The guy in charge, Dr. Horace Todd, is the one we really want on camera. He's been the primary on the Puffin man's case since he was brought in. And, unlike Specks, he has a brain."

"Okay, got it. But what about the Puffin man? They say he's talking now, right?"

"Yeah. But he still doesn't remember anything about what happened to him, how he got to Puffin, how long he was there, yadda, yadda, yadda."

"So where's the story, Susan?"

"I'm going to play it up as a mystery. You know, who is this man? Is there anyone out there who can identify him? Etcetera. So, I'm going to want you to get some real good close-ups, full face and profile, as well as full body. Probably be good to get a shot of him next to something or someone that can give some perspective so John Q. Public will know how tall he is and what his body build is like. I don't know if you remember - you were just a kid - but when they brought him in eight years ago, he was barely recognizable as a human being. But now, who knows? Maybe there's someone out there who will come forward and claim him."

"Sounds good. Not too complicated."

"Yeah. At the end of the piece, I'm going to give the public a hotline number just in case we get lucky."

"Very neat, Susan."

Smiling, the reporter leaned back in her seat and pulled out her cell phone. "I've got to make some calls now, James. You just drive, okay?"

REMEMBERING

AFTER BREAKFAST, SOPHIE AND Terri decided to go for a walk, leaving their mother home alone. Karen tried reading but found she couldn't concentrate so she went out back and sat on a rock overlooking the sea.

Maggie ... God, I wish that girl had left this island long ago. I'm sure she hates me as much as I hate her. Lord only knows what she'll tell Sophie and Terri about me. I'll probably come off as the villain of the piece, complete with black hat and moustache. But Dex will be there - maybe that will keep her in line. He won't allow any bad mouthing - not from me or from her.

She reached around behind her head and undid the barrette that held her ponytail in place, then leaned over and shook it out, letting her hair fall gently on her shoulders.

I wish we were back in Monterey. Everything was so good there.

She smiled, remembering how it was when they'd first arrived at the beach house. Dex had given up everything and come with them at her invitation. It was pretty much a spur-of-the-moment decision on both their parts, with little thought as to how they were going to handle things, especially with her daughters. But, true to form, Dex knew instinctively the right thing to do.

He took his own stuff directly to the den, where he took up residence. And he was so careful when the girls were around not to show me any undue affection. He helped them so much to heal from the loss of their father - something it was so hard for me to do. He became a part of our lives - like a good friend who'd stopped by for a visit and decided to stay. But it didn't remain like that forever, she thought, remembering the day everything changed.

It was around noon and she'd been out to the beach. When she came home, she jumped right into a hot shower to wash the salt and sand from her body. Dex was working on his new boat and she didn't expect him until much later. But for some reason he had to knock off early.

She laughed softly to herself as the memory played at the corners of her mind. *When he got home, he called out for me but I couldn't hear him because of the noise of the shower. When I didn't answer, he must have assumed I was still at the beach.*

Full of grease and grime and anxious to clean up, he'd stripped off his shirt, thrown it in the hamper and opened the bathroom door just as she was stepping from the shower, naked except for a towel wrapped loosely around her body. They'd stared at each other, neither knowing what to say or do. Just the sight of his bare chest made her knees go weak and she was about to fall when he closed the distance between them and pulled her roughly to him.

I wanted him so badly. I just threw my arms around his neck and that damned towel, the only thing that was keeping me decent, dropped carelessly to the floor.

She blushed remembering what happened next. He'd held her tightly against him as he ran his hands all over her body. She could feel the force of his arousal through his jeans and, unable to stop herself, she unbuckled his belt and unzipped him as they sank to the floor.

We made hot, sweaty love on that bathroom floor, she giggled to herself. *Gosh, it was almost pornographic.*

Afterwards, when they were sated, they'd showered together and then went upstairs to her room and made love again, this time more properly.

It was so wonderful. He made me feel like I was seventeen again. All bright, shiny, and brand new. And whole. Yes, he made me feel whole again. And from that moment on, he has shared my bed and my life.

She sat looking out at the sea, smiling, the memory bringing her a sort of peace. But her reverie was short-lived. The sound of a car in the driveway brought reality thudding back and the moment of serenity she'd managed to capture was lost. Sighing, she pulled her hair into a ponytail, clipped it in place, and started on the path back to the house.

It must be Dex ... back from Maggie's. Can't wait to hear what that slut had to say.

STATE HOSPITAL, BANGOR, MAINE

THE MAN THEY CALLED John Doe stood at the window, his arms folded tightly across his chest, tension apparent in his stance and expression.

"But what if I don't want to do it, Hod?" he asked, his voice still raspy and hoarse from years of disuse. "It'll bring all the loonies out again, just like before."

Dr. Todd sat at his desk, silently drumming his fingers against the mahogany surface. He waited, choosing his words carefully. "It might be your only chance, John. You know, now that your talking, I won't have a reason to keep you here much longer. I'll have to discharge you. You'll be out in that cruel world anyway. Wouldn't it be better if there was someone, anyone, who knew you; who could help you make the transition?"

John laughed sarcastically. "I haven't seen my picture on any milk cartons lately. Have you? Don't you think that if someone were searching for me they would've at least filed a missing persons' report way back when? Come on, Hod. You and I both know that there's no one out there looking for me. I was left to die on Puffin and whoever took me there sure doesn't want to adopt me now."

Dr. Todd nodded. "I know, I know. But I think you have to take this chance. Maybe, just maybe, there is someone out there who will recognize you. You look a whole lot better now than you did back when they first brought you to me."

John nodded. "You're right about that." He stared out the window then turned to face the doctor. "God, I wish I could remember. I try so hard and it's like everything's right there waiting for me, just around the corner. But when I get close and think it's all going to come back, it fades away, out of my reach. Why is it, Hod? Why can't I remember?"

"Mayhap it's the blow to the head that you sustained. From the scar, it looks like it was a pretty lethal one. You might have lost some brain tissue, causing permanent memory damage. Or maybe, it's psychological - you just need some sort of trigger to get it going. This interview may provide that."

John stood quietly for a moment, thinking, then he smiled. "Okay, you win. I'll go along with it. But when all the loonies come out of the woodwork, don't be surprised if I say 'I told you so.'"

Dr. Todd laughed, getting up and moving toward the window to stand beside his patient. "I won't. But I've got my fingers crossed that something good will come of it. Okay?"

John turned to him and smiled. "Don't you get tired of being right all the time, Hod? Guess I'd better go clean up before they get here. And, thanks. Thanks for everything. Without you, I don't know what kind of shape I'd be in. And, if you have to let me go, it'll be okay. I think I'm strong enough now to take on anything the 'cruel world' throws at me."

He allowed Dr. Todd to give him a manly hug then sauntered out of the room.

The doctor watched him go then sat back down at his desk to document the conversation they'd just completed. He was about to begin typing when something distracted him. He stood up and walked to the doorway, listening.

Return to Mateguas Island

In the distance, he could see John walking down the corridor, his bathrobe flapping as he moved, but it was the sound of his flip-flops, echoing strangely down the corridor, that caused the doctor to take pause.

How unusual, he thought. *It's almost like the remnant of some forgotten melody or maybe a half-remembered dream.* Shaking his head, Dr. Todd smiled to himself, crossed his fingers on both hands, and returned to his office.

SATURDAY AFTERNOON

KAREN AND DEX ENTERED the house at the same time

"Hi, princess. I got it all set up for the girls," he announced, glancing around the room. "Hey, where are they anyway?"

"They went out for a walk. Call Terri on her cell if you need them back soon."

Dex glanced at his watch. "Well, we're supposed to be at Maggie's for lunch at one o'clock. It's only ten now. I'll wait. If they're not back by eleven, I'll call."

Karen nodded, sitting down on the sofa. "So what did Mateguas Island's paragon of virtue have to say for herself?"

Dex frowned. "I thought we were going to quit with the name-calling. I didn't let her say anything bad about you - and you know she was more than happy to. So, I'm not going to let you do it to her either. If you want to know what she said, ask me nicely."

Karen sighed. "I'm sorry. Okay, what did that sweet young woman have to say? Is that better?"

"I can't win, can I?" he laughed, sitting down beside her. "Okay, to start with, she looks good and seems content. I know that doesn't mean much to you, but I'm glad for her. Her life hasn't been easy. And her son, Billy, knows about his father. She told him last night. The boy is eager to meet his sisters. He's out fishing with his granddad right now. They'll be done by noon. That's why the luncheon invite."

"And that's it?"

"Just about. She hasn't changed much. Maybe put on a pound or two but she wears it well. Still runs the school and doesn't have any serious entanglements romantically. Seems in her mind, Bill was her one true love."

Karen shook her head. "She's delusional. All Bill ever saw in her was a hot piece of ass. Their liaison was just a passing thing."

"Be that as it may, to her it was love with a capital 'L.'"

"Well, you'll be there when she talks to the girls, right? So you can set them straight if she tells them anything off base."

"Yes, I'll be there. And what are you going to do while we're waltzing down memory lane with Maggie?"

"I have it all planned out. Before you head over to the house, you can drop me at the boatyard. I'll spend some time looking for glass and grab lunch at the store if I get hungry. You can pick me up on your way home."

"Sounds like a plan."

He stood up and kissed her lightly on the top of her head. "Think I'll give Terri a call. Make sure they get home in time. We don't want to be late for this lunch."

Later, Dex dropped Karen off at the boatyard then drove with the girls to the house on the hill. Just before he arrived at the driveway, he pulled the car to the side of the road.

"Now, Terri, Sophie, I know you've heard all the stuff your mother's been saying about Maggie, but I have to tell you I've known this girl all my life and at worst she's just an island girl who exhibited some pretty poor judgment with regard to the men in her life. But besides that, she's smart and good-hearted. And don't think it didn't take a bit of courage for her to go ahead and have that child, your half-brother. This is a close-knit community and lots of folks are pretty religious. Having a baby out of wedlock didn't set well with some. But she toughed it out and earned their admiration and respect.

"She's a good person and I want you to treat her properly. Also, you'll want to know that she likes your mother about as much as your mother likes her. So, weigh carefully whatever she might say about your mom and her relationship with your dad. Okay?"

Sophie smiled. "Thanks, Dex. Don't worry."

"Good. Now let's get this thing over with."

Smiling, he pulled the car back on the road and turned up the driveway. Maggie was on the porch waiting to greet them. She gave Dex a quick hug then stood back and stared at the girls. "Now don't tell me. Let me guess. On the right, you're Terri? Am I correct?"

Terri laughed. "Yes, you got it. It's good to see you again, Maggie."

Maggie smiled. "Give your old teacher a hug then."

Once inside, Maggie gave them a brief tour of the downstairs.

"The house looks pretty much like I remember. Maybe smaller, but that's probably cause I'm bigger." said Sophie.

Maggie laughed. "I didn't change much. The house came furnished when I bought it and I'd been living with my folks so I didn't really have much of my own stuff. I like all these antiques anyway. Gives the place a homey look."

"Where's Billy?" asked Terri, anxious to meet her new half-brother.

"Oh, he just got home from fishing with his granddad. He's upstairs washing off the smell of bait. He'll be down directly.

Come on into the dining room and have a seat. Can I get you all anything to drink? Soda? Beer? Tea?"

"I'll take you up on a beer, Red," said Dex, sitting down.

"Tea would be great," said Sophie.

"Same for me," answered Terri.

"Okay, you all make yourself comfortable. I'll be back in a minute."

Maggie walked toward the kitchen, stopping by the stairway to call to her son. "Billy, we have company. Now shake a leg and get on down here."

Dex and the girls sat quietly at the table, waiting for her to return. She came back shortly with their drinks and soon they heard the thunder of a young boy's feet running down the stairs. He stopped at the bottom and shyly entered the dining room. Maggie stood up and put her arm around his shoulder.

"Billy, I'd like you to meet your sisters - half-sisters, I mean. Terri and Sophie, this is my son, Bill."

The girls smiled at the boy and said hello. He nodded shyly and gave them a barely audible greeting as he sat down at the table. Maggie, shaking her head, returned to the kitchen to finish preparing lunch.

It was quiet at the table for a few minutes, no one knowing quite how to begin, until Dex asked the boy about his morning's fishing. Billy broke into a big grin and began to animatedly describe his day on his grandfather's lobster boat. By the time Maggie came back carrying a large casserole dish, the table was alive with conversation.

"Hope you all like lobsta-mac 'n cheese," she said, placing the dish in the middle of the table.

Later, when they finished eating and the table was cleared,

Maggie steered her son over to Dex. "Why don't you two go outside for a while? The girls and me need to talk and it's going to be 'girl talk' so it would just be boring for you all. Dex, you can fill Billy in on your fishing exploits seeing you're a local legend and all."

Dex laughed. "Sure, kitten, if it's okay with the girls?"

"Go on, Dex," replied Terri. "We'll be fine."

Nodding, Dex and Billy went outside to the porch. When she heard the door slam, Maggie came back and sat down at the table with the girls.

"Okay, you wanted to talk to me about your dad - right? So, ask away."

Terri and Sophie looked at each other, suddenly at a loss for how to begin. Silent for a moment, Terri turned her head to Maggie.

"We know you and Dad had an affair and, obviously, Billy is the result. He looks a lot like Dad. But how did it start?"

Maggie sighed, then began to speak.

BEACH WALKING

KAREN LEFT THE BOATYARD and walked the rocky coastline, head bowed, searching for unique pieces of sea glass. Back in Monterey, she found this activity soothing - almost a form of meditation. However, today her thoughts kept returning to memories of Maggie, Bill, her daughters and Dex.

If it weren't for that girl, Bill would still be alive, I know it. His connection to her somehow tainted him - made him easy prey for that evil being, the Mskagwdemos. But if he were still alive, where would I be now? With him? Or would I have left him for Dex?

Sighing, she forced herself to concentrate on the sand and rocks beneath her feet. However, try as she might, she was unable to shake the vague sense of unease and fear that that had been plaguing her mind ever since their return to Mateguas.

Searching among the myriad small rocks and debris left by the tide, her eye was caught a piece of glass, shining up at her. Bending down to pick it up, she was surprised by its beauty. It was a small piece, smooth and oval-shaped. That in itself was not unusual - no, it was the color. The glass was aquamarine, uncommonly clear and vivid and, rolling it over in her hand, it felt remarkably soft and pliant.

This would make a lovely pendant, she thought, holding it up to the light to see it better.

As she lifted the tiny piece of glass, the sun moved from behind a cloud and cast its gaze upon it, causing the color to change from pale blue to deep purple and then to a vibrant red. Delighted, Karen laughed as the glass moved through the color spectrum. Resting the piece in her hand, she was surprised at how warm it felt. She rolled it over, studying it, and noted that it was just large enough to cover the small crescent-shaped scar that sat in the middle of her palm. Somewhere, in the back of her mind, a warning bell went off, but it was faint and she could not tear her eyes from the shard - its beauty overwhelmed her. Oblivious to everything but the glass, she didn't notice the shoreline and the beach take on a shimmery glow and begin to fade slowly away. In a heartbeat, the once-sandy shore was filled with tall trees, their gnarly branches dark and menacing, obliterating the sun and its warmth. Suddenly, the glass in her hand turned cold and black. Startled, she looked up.

Oh no! It can't be! she thought as her eyes darted back and forth, searching frantically for the beach and the ocean beyond. Finally, recognizing where she now stood, her mind shuddered. *Oh, my God, no - it's the trail - the one behind the house - the one that leads to the swamp!*

As if reading her thoughts, crows began to shriek in the treetops above and a strong odor of decay surrounded her, causing her to gag. Frightened, she whipped her head back and forth, unsure which way would lead to safety.

The soft hoot of an owl pierced the stillness.

Terrified, Karen began to run blindly in what she hoped was the direction of the house. Panting with fear, she made her way down the winding trail, pushing aside dark branches that seemed to be reaching out to block her. Without warning, a twisted root sprang out of the dirt and snaked itself tightly around her ankle.

Losing her balance and unable to stop her forward momentum, she fell heavily to the ground. When her hands hit the forest floor, she screamed in pain as something sharp pierced her palm. Looking down, she was surprised to see she was no longer holding a smooth piece of glass, but instead, her hand was wrapped tightly around a sharp shard that looked like a remnant from a broken mirror. Wincing, she unwrapped her hand from the glass, noting how it pierced her skin in the center of her palm.

It's cut me right where the scar is - the crescent moon that the blessed boy left on my hand.

Breathing heavily and bracing herself for more pain, she pulled the shard from her flesh. Blood immediately welled up and began flowing freely, dripping to the forest floor. As the drops soaked into the dirt, the scenery around her again began to shimmer and fade.

As the landscape shifted and changed, she was overcome by a strong sense of vertigo and forced her head between her knees in an attempt to regain her equilibrium. When she finally looked up, she was no longer in the forest but was back on the beach, kneeling in the wet sand. The sun was again shining warmly above her and, resting next to her hand was a small, rather ordinary, piece of sea glass. She glanced at the wound in her palm but it was already beginning to heal, leaving just the small scar shaped like the moon in the center.

Gathering herself together, she took a deep breath and stood up. Her jeans were now wet and uncomfortable from the damp sand. Looking around, she noted that her tote, which she always kept with her, now sat at the far end of the beach. Slowly and carefully, she retrieved it and headed back to the safety of the boatyard. Once there, she went into the store, bought a cup of coffee, and took it to one of the picnic tables that sat outside.

Sipping the warm liquid, she puzzled over what had just happened. Something was gnawing at the back of her mind. Something was missing.

There was no rabbit! The rabbit was always there, guiding and protecting me, when these things happened.

She sat quietly remembering the terror she'd lived through ten years before and how the spirit of the blessed boy, son of Mateguas, God of the Dead, had been able to shape-shift into the form of a rabbit, his father's totem.

If the rabbit isn't around that could mean the blessed boy isn't around either! And, without his protection, what will happen to us?

She pondered this for a while, but unable to make sense of it, decided to think about it later. *Yes, you'll have to be Scarlett again, girl. Maybe later it will come clear.*

Feeling bone-weary, she gazed seaward, trying to blot the experience from her consciousness. Looking down at the rough-hewn table before her, she noticed someone had carved a heart on its surface. Lovers unknown to her had placed initials inside the heart and she smiled as her thoughts wandered back to other times sitting in this place - times with Dex when they were young and falling in love. The warmth of these memories overshadowed the fear she felt and brought a sense of peace to her mind. Confusion tucked away for a time, she stared out at the sea - remembering.

 THE AFFAIR

THE GIRLS LISTENED INTENTLY as Maggie described her first meeting with their father on the beach in front of what once was his house. Speaking almost reverently, she told them of the trip to Little Glooskap, a small island not far from Mateguas, where the affair began in earnest.

Terri struggled to keep her expression neutral as her former teacher went on about the love she and Bill had shared. She knew, deep down, that her mother was her father's only true love, and that Maggie had never won his heart.

Nonplused, Maggie continued to describe in less vivid detail the progression of the relationship, up to the point when Karen forced him to break it off.

"She was going to take you two away from him, back to California, and that was something he just couldn't accept. So, he opted to stay in a loveless marriage with her. It broke my heart, I can tell you. But I accepted it."

She paused, taking a sip of her tea. "But then he contacted me and asked me to meet him at the boatyard. I went, not knowing what to expect. He said to me, and I remember his exact words, 'I love you and I want to take you back to Little Glooskap - make love to you again. Will you go with me?' Naturally, I said 'yes' and we went back to that beautiful island and made love. Afterwards, we talked of a future together but he said he needed to make sure he didn't lose you girls first. So, he asked me to be patient and not to contact him - that he would be in touch with me. I agreed. Shortly after, I found out I was pregnant, but I couldn't tell him."

She hesitated for a moment, a tear slipping down her cheek. "That was the last I spoke to him. He died about a week later. I tried to go to the house to help search for him, but your mother threw me out. I'm sorry, but she's a cold, heartless woman and I blame her for his death."

Sophie looked at Maggie indignantly. "My mother is not a heartless person. She loved our father and the fact that he betrayed her hurt her terribly. And I don't believe that he planned on a life with you. His writings from that time indicate that he was going to take us to live on the mainland after he got his promotion. What he had with you was just physical. It wasn't love."

Maggie smiled, expecting this. "I'm not surprised you don't believe me and that's okay. I know the truth and that's enough for me. But, what about your mother and Dex? Do you really think they were just friends? They spent an awful lot of time together back then, alone on his boat or at his house. And your dad - did she tell him about her new *friendship*?"

Maggie paused, letting this sink in. "No, she didn't. But he knew about it - the gossip was all over this island. And then, conveniently, your dad dies and Dex just up and sells everything and moves to California with you. Doesn't that seem a little odd? How long was it after you got there that they started sharing a room? Think about that."

Sophie started to rise from her seat, an angry look on her face, but Terri reached out and stopped her. "Sit back down, Soph. This isn't a surprise. We've talked about this before."

74

Sophie reluctantly sat back down, her back rigid with emotion. Terri turned to Maggie.

"I believe you when you say there was something between my mom and Dex back then. But I don't believe it would have progressed any further if my father had lived. My mother believes strongly in marriage and would have done anything to preserve her union with our dad. You have your memories and I'm sure that to you they ring true, but we have ours, too, and they are of a family committed to staying together."

Maggie smiled again. "I meant no harm, girls. Only telling you the way it was, at least to me. Talk to others here on the island - maybe that will give you a better perspective."

"Who would you suggest?" asked Terri.

"Oh, folks who knew your parents: Pete and Louise, my parents, Amy Hassler who used to work at the boatyard. That's where I'd start. And you're welcome here anytime - to see Billy or me or even just to sit on the porch and remember. Just give us a call before you come. I'm in the Island Directory. Okay?"

Terri nodded. "Thanks, Maggie. I'd like that."

Standing up, she turned to her twin. "Guess we'd better get going now. Dex might be running out of tall tales to tell young Bill."

Sophie, still not pleased, stood up. "Thank you, Maggie, for taking the time to see us," she said stiffly.

"My pleasure, Sophie."

Outside, they found Dex and Billy in the backyard with fishing gear, discussing bait and other salient aspects of the sport. Dex looked up when he heard the girls approach.

"Have a good talk?" he asked, glancing at his watch. "Think it's time to go. Your mom is probably all beached out by now."

As he spoke, his cell chimed. Pulling it out of his pocket, he smiled. "That's her now."

He turned and talked briefly with Karen, then said his goodbyes to the young boy and walked over to where Maggie and his stepdaughters were standing.

"All set, kids?"

Terri nodded as Sophie walked quickly over to the car and got in the front seat. Terri turned to Maggie, thanked her again, and gave her a brief hug. Dex also gave Maggie a hug and sauntered over to the car.

Once out on the road, Sophie turned angrily to her twin, who was sitting in the back. "How could you sit there and let her malign Mom like that? I don't understand you. She's awful. Just like Mom said."

Terri gave her twin a hard stare. "Sophie, let's talk about this later, okay?"

Listening to the exchange, Dex glanced back at Terri. "What's so bad that you can't say it in front of me, Ter?" he asked.

Terri sighed. "She said some nasty stuff about Mom, Dex. Called her heartless and blamed her for Dad's death. That made Sophie pretty mad and I didn't like it much either. But, if we want to get information from her, we need keep our options open and try not to piss her off. I'd like to know my stepbrother a little better and make sure he knows the truth about his father. I also may want to go over there and take a walk in those woods to see what my dad saw the night he died. So, I made nice and that's what Sophie is ticked off about."

"Sounds like you did the right thing. I don't know why those two women can't bury the hatchet. Bill's been gone a long time. I mean, they don't have to like each other, but, for Christ's sake, you'd think they could be civil to one another."

"You're right, sis," said Sophie contritely. "Sorry I got so pissed. We do need to keep the door open."

Tension eased, they rode in silence until they got to the boatyard. Karen was sitting at the picnic table and stood up as they drove in. Dex parked, hopped out of the car, and walked over to her.

"Have a good afternoon, princess?" he asked taking her tote from her. "Doesn't feel too heavy - not a good day for prospecting?"

Karen shook her head. "No, it wasn't. Just ordinary glass. I'll have to try another beach. How'd things go with you all?"

"Apparently, Maggie called you 'heartless,' which ruffled Sophie's feathers a bit, but Terri kept her cool. The boy's a real nice kid. I think the girls really liked him. All in all, it went pretty good. No one came to blows."

"Okay, well, I'm glad that's over with. Let's go home. I'm tired and wet and would like a nice hot shower."

Dex smiled and bowed low. "Your wish is my command, princess."

Laughing and content with each other, they walked arm in arm back to the car to head home.

 WKZTV

SUSAN LEVEQUE SAT IN the film editing room at WKZTV NEWS going over the piece just filmed at the Bangor State Hospital. She was pleased with her work. John Doe had turned out to a much better subject than she'd anticipated.

Damn good-looking man, she thought. *Got that sixties aura about him. Articulate, too. Funny how he just started talking out of the blue. Says he doesn't know why. Just felt the urge. Mmmmm, I bet if we don't find him some family, we'll at least get him a girlfriend or two out of this.*

Having done her best to show off "The Puffin Man," she turned to the interview segments with his doctors. Dr. Specks she put right where she felt he belonged - on the cutting room floor. But Dr. Todd was another matter altogether.

Another good one, she thought. *Intelligent, sartorial, and soft-spoken. All those things we want a doctor to be. Yup, that's our Dr. Todd.*

When she finished with that segment, she reviewed her work. Satisfied with the piece, she saved the final cut and left the room.

She had convinced the Station Manager to air the piece on their Sunday afternoon magazine show, *What's Happening, Maine!* The show had good ratings, especially this time of year when there wasn't too much going on in sports that competed in its time slot. If all went well, she hoped to air it again on the evening news later in the week.

If we can get this guy ID'd, it might mean a Cronkite for me and who knows where that could lead. Maybe national prime time news or even anchor.

Smiling to herself, she decided to leave the station early and go shopping for a new outfit to wear on the air on Sunday.

AN AFTERNOON IN FRONT OF THE TUBE

THE NEXT MORNING, KAREN was cleaning up the breakfast dishes when Dex walked into the room, tucking his cell into his back pocket. "Who was that on the phone?" she asked.

"Pete McKinney."

"We're going to their place for dinner tonight, aren't we? Is that still on?"

"Ayup. But he's asked us if we want to go out on the boat with him and Louise this afternoon. What do you say? It's been a while since we've been out fishing together."

Karen smiled. "Sounds good. Ask the girls if they want to go, too."

Dex kissed her on the cheek and walked to the living room, where Terri was busy on her laptop and Sophie was reading.

"Got an invitation to go fishing with Pete and Louise this afternoon. Your mom and I are going. You guys want to tag along? See if you can land a big one?"

Terri laughed. "Been there, done that. Think I'll pass."

Sophie nodded. "You know I can't stand the smell of bait. Gives me a headache. You and Mom have fun."

"Your loss, kids," said Dex, pulling out his cell to call Pete back.

Later that afternoon, bored with her book, Sophie turned on the television. Scrolling through the channels and not finding much, she settled on a local news magazine show.

"Hey, Terri, check this out. Local color. Maybe there'll be something on Mateguas."

Terri put down her computer and moved over to the couch to see what Sophie was watching. The show's anchors chatted for a few minutes then introduced the first segment, "Do You Know the Puffin Man?"

Curious, Sophie turned up the volume.

An attractive woman in her mid-thirties took over the screen and began to speak.

"Eight years ago, a group of graduating seniors from Mateguas Island decided to party down on Puffin Island. Puffin, as most Mainers know, is a small island about five miles from Mateguas and was once owned by multi-millionaire, Richard Whitely. Whitely built a large summer home on the island and for a while it served as a playground for the rich and famous."

As she spoke, pictures from another era flashed across the screen showing a large manor house, docks, yachts, and people dressed in tuxedos and evening gowns.

"But that all changed in 1929 when the stock market crashed. Whitely lost everything and was forced to abandon Puffin and put it up for sale. It remained on the market for decades, the house falling into ruin, until the 1970's when it was deeded over to the State. Having no real use for the island, the State let the elements take over - the wind, sea, rain, and snow destroying what was left of the house, docks and all other man-made structures.

"Being small and remote, it was rare that anyone ever stopped there - that is until this group of Mateguas teenagers ventured out on the evening of June seventeenth, eight years ago."

The screen now showed a young man, wearing jeans, sweatshirt, and a baseball cap being interviewed by a younger version of the same reporter.

"Tell us what happened," she asked.

"Well, we all came over here for a lobsta bake to celebrate graduation. My younger brother and his girlfriend tagged along. They were off exploring in the ruins when we heard a scream. Thinking maybe she'd fallen through the floor of the house or something, we all ran over there. That's when we saw him. He was lying in the sand. Thought he was dead at first, but Josh, he's a volunteer paramedic with the fire department, said he was still breathing."

The interview cut to a film of a man, emaciated and barely recognizable as human, lying on a gurney. Then they cut back to the teenager.

"We jerry-rigged a stretcher from the blankets we'd brought and got him over to the bonfire. I went out to the boat and called the Coast Guard."

The screen focused back on the reporter as she continued speaking.

"The Puffin Man as he became known as, survived - amnesic and mute - but despite the fact that he gained national recognition, no one ever claimed any knowledge of him. Because of his poor health, he was transferred to the Bangor State Hospital where he remains to this day.

"But last week, something extraordinary happened. The Puffin Man began to speak. When we come back, we'll take you to Bangor State Hospital for the first interview with this man, who the staff calls John Doe, in the hopes that this time someone will come forward and identify him."

The show went into a commercial break as Terri and Sophie sat on the couch stunned.

"How come we never heard of this?" Terri asked.

"Think, Terri. We were in California and were only about ten years old. Mom and Dex were getting married. We didn't watch the national news."

"But what about them? Didn't they question this? A guy found only five miles from Mateguas. You'd think...."

Sophie hushed her as the show came back on. The same reporter was now standing in front of a large institutional-looking building.

"This is Bangor State Hospital which has been home to John Doe these past eight years."

The scene shifted to inside and the reporter standing with nice-looking older man wearing a white coat.

"This is Dr. Horace Todd, Chief Medical Officer at Bangor. He has been John's physician since he was transferred to this facility. Dr. Todd, what can you tell us about these new developments in John's case?"

Dr. Todd smiled gently. "John has begun to speak. I don't know what triggered it, but he is regaining full use of his vocal faculties. Unfortunately, his memory has not come back with his speech. He still has no recollection of who he is or why he was on Puffin. We're hoping that this broadcast will bring someone forward who knows or knew him. We want to find his family."

"Do you have any guesses as to why his memory hasn't returned, Doctor?"

"Yes, I do. It could very likely be organic. When he was brought to us seven or eight years ago, he had a large scar at the base of his skull. The margins had not healed properly and thus I assumed that the wound had never been treated. Loss of brain tissue from this injury could have caused his amnesic state."

"Could you tell from the wound how old it was?"

The doctor nodded. "It was not a new wound. I would say it was one to two years old."

The reporter smiled. "So, assuming John got this wound either directly before or after he arrived at Puffin, that would put him alone on that abandoned island for one to two years. Is that correct?"

"Yes, that is a valid assumption."

"Now you said that it could be organic, but you're not sure? What other cause could there be?"

"Psychological, of course. Being alone on that island for two years - who knows what that could do to a man. The fact that he functions at all is a miracle and you'll see when you interview him that he has adapted very well to his condition. He is an intelligent man, very well versed in computers. He takes care of all of ours here at the hospital. He's even been to my home to help out there when ours went on the fritz."

The camera left the doctor and focused on a man standing by a window. He was tall and thin with long silver-streaked hair tied back in a ponytail. He wore wire-rimmed glasses that gave him a serious look. The camera rested on his profile for a moment and then the station broke away for a commercial.

Terri turned to her twin. "How old do you think he is?"

Sophie shook her head. "You know I'm not good with ages. And with what he's been through, he could look way older than he is."

"I think he looks in his mid-forties, just like Dad would be."

"Terri, you don't think....?"

"Soph, it could be him. You heard what they said about computers."

"I know, but how would he have gotten to that island from here? And what about that wound the doctor talked about? How could that have happened?"

Terri shook her head. "Don't know. But I do know we have to find out more."

The twins sat silently, each alone with her thoughts, waiting for the series of commercials to end. After what seemed to them to be a lifetime, the screen returned to the reporter, who was now sitting at table across from the man called John Doe.

"John, how are you doing?"

"Quite well, Susan," he replied, his voice raspy and hoarse from years of dormancy.

"Is it true you still have no memory of who you are or why and how you got to Puffin?"

"That's correct. At times, it seems the memories are right there - just around the corner. But when I look, they're gone and all that's left is a blank wall."

The interview continued for several more minutes - the reporter asking him mundane questions about his life at Bangor State. As the segment came to an end, the camera again focused solely on the reporter.

"And there you have it. John Doe, "The Puffin Man," still hoping his family or friends will come forward and open up his memory. And we want to help him. At the bottom of your screen is a number. If anyone has any knowledge whatsoever about the identity of this man, we urge you to call our hotline. All calls will be kept confidential. Again: if you think you know this man, please come forward. Thank you. This is Susan LeVeque reporting."

The show then returned to its anchors who chatted inanely for a minute or two about the broadcast before going to another commercial break.

Terri got up and walked to the bedroom. She came back a minute later, her cell in her hand. "I'm calling them. Going to tell them about Dad. Maybe we can go see this guy and find out for sure."

Sophie stared at her sister, thinking. Then she nodded. "Go on. This is why we came here. We can't leave any stone unturned."

Terri smiled as she looked at her cell and began dialing the station's hotline number.

Dex and Karen arrived home late afternoon full of stories about their day on the water. After relaxing for a while, they retired upstairs to shower and change for their planned dinner at the McKinneys'.

Terri and Sophie also began getting ready for the evening out, but they found it hard to concentrate on their appearance.

"So, when do you think the station will get back to us, Ter?"

"Don't know. I hope I left a credible message. I gave as much detail as I could. They may wait until tomorrow to review what they've gotten. Probably will get a lot of crank calls and they'll have to sift through them to find what's actually real."

"Yeah, you're probably right. You sure you don't want to tell Mom?"

"Soph, we've already talked about this. What if it's all a big nothing? If we tell Mom, we'll just upset her needlessly. Dex, too. No, we need to see this guy in person. If he's not Dad, then 'no harm, no foul.'"

Sophie shook her head. "I guess you're right again. But how are we going to explain going to Bangor or wherever this hospital is?"

"We'll just say we want to do some sightseeing. If the station doesn't take us, we'll rent a car. Don't make such a big deal out of it. There won't be any problem."

Sophie nodded, then stuck out her lower lip in a pout.

Terri laughed seeing the expression on her sister's face. "Just chill, Soph. You worry too much. Now, what are you going to wear tonight for this big evening at the McKinneys'?"

Later, after dinner, the McKinneys and their guests sat outside on the porch enjoying coffee. The conversation was casual, centered on fishing and local politics.

Beginning to get bored, Terri turned to their host. "Hey, Pete," she said. "Since we've been away, have there been any other spooky happenings related to all that old Indian legend stuff?"

Pete laughed. "You remember that? All my stories?"

Terri nodded. "Yeah, made me a little afraid of those woods back then. However, now I think I want to take a walk there - see what my dad saw before he died."

Pete studied her for a moment, becoming serious. "Not much has changed in them woods as far as I know. There are a lot of footpaths leading to the swamp. They come from all corners of the island. But not too many people venture back there. Too much history, I guess. You sure that's what you want to do?"

Terri nodded.

"Well, if you're determined, don't go alone. Some of the trails intersect and, since they all look pretty much the same, you could get lost. And if you think you can depend on your cell's GPS for guidance, think again. Woods are so thick in places, you can't get a signal to save your soul."

Karen, a frown on her face, looked at her daughter. "I don't want you going in those woods, Terri. It's too dangerous."

Terri smiled indulgently at her. "I'm not eight years old anymore, Mom. I think I can take care of myself. And it's not like I'm going to go for a walk at night or during a storm or anything. Just a stroll in the woods in broad daylight. What can happen?"

Remembering the owl and the horror of the swamp, Karen shuddered. "I don't care. I don't want you in those woods. I forbid it!"

Dex, alarmed by his wife's distress, put his hand over hers. "Karen, if she's determined to walk in her father's footsteps, how about I go with her? Will that help ease your mind?"

Karen was silent for a minute and then she stood up. "No, I don't want either of you in those woods and nothing you can say will change that. It's just too dangerous. I think I want to go home now. It's been a long day."

Dex nodded and indicated for the girls to get ready to leave. He spoke for a minute with Pete and Louise, apologizing, then went inside and grabbed their jackets.

Karen walked stiffly to the car and got in the front seat, fear and anger beginning to overwhelm her. When her daughters were seated in the back, she turned to them.

"I meant what I said, Terri. I don't want you in those woods. All this about walking in your father's footsteps is just a bunch of crap and I've about had enough of it. You've had your little interview with Ms. Maggie and seen the house again. What more do you want? Your father is dead! He's not coming back. Can't we just let it lie?"

Terri sat mute, listening to her mother's almost hysterical outburst. She glanced over at her sister then back at Karen. "Okay, Mom, don't have a cow. I won't go in the woods. That make you happy?"

Karen stared at her, then nodded. "Thank you."

Once back at the house, the girls excused themselves and went to their room to begin getting ready for bed.

As she pulled her nightgown down over her head, Sophie turned to her sister. "Did you mean it? What you told Mom? You won't go in the woods?"

Terri was sitting on her bed, staring at her cell, deep in thought.

"Terri, did you hear what I said?"

"Huh? Oh, sorry, Soph. It's just that I turned my cell off while we were at the McKinneys' and just switched it back on now." She took a deep breath. "We have a message from the TV station."

 **THE HOTLINE**

SUSAN LEVEQUE ARRIVED HOME a little after eight in the evening. She'd been out with some of her co-workers celebrating her Sunday magazine piece and had had just a tad too much to drink. Tired, she grabbed a bottle of water from the refrigerator, slipped into her pajamas, and was just pulling the covers up over her head when the phone rang.

Groaning, she leaned over to the nightstand and picked it up. "LeVeque here and this had better be good."

"Susan - sorry to disturb you. It's Arnie down at the station. I think we've got a live one."

Frowning, she stared into the phone. *What in God's name is this fool talking about?* Struggling to keep her anger under control, she waited several seconds before replying.

"Arnie, what do you mean 'a live one'? Explain it to me and do it fast."

"The hotline, Susan. Saw the light blinking and thought I'd take a listen to hear what we got. There were quite a few

90

messages, but most of them were junk. You know, the loonies coming out of the woodwork. But there was one that I think you'll want to follow up on."

Susan was suddenly fully awake and completely sober. "Go on, Arn, tell me."

"It was from a teenager from California, visiting here now. Seems she lived on Mateguas ten years ago. Her father went missing one night during a storm. Local authorities claim he drowned in a swamp behind their house, but his body was never recovered. The girls - the caller and her sister - saw the magazine piece. The Puffin Man generally fits their father's description - height, age, body build, hair color. They want to see him in person. What do you think?"

Susan had a hard time keeping her excitement in check. "Give me her name and number. And thanks for calling me. This could be big. I won't forget you if it works out."

Jotting down the caller's information, Susan got out of bed and grabbed her robe. She picked up her cell and quickly dialed the number but was disappointed when she was transferred directly to voicemail. Leaving her name, number, and a quick message, she hung up and walked to the kitchen to start a pot of coffee. As she waited, she pulled out her laptop and logged into the station's back files. Searching for 'Bill Andersen' and 'Mateguas', she located all the news stories on his disappearance and presumed death ten years prior. Making note of all the salient facts, she then switched to her search engine and Googled for any and all information she could get on the Andersens' background and their lives in California. In a short time, she uncovered a surprising amount of data.

As she sifted through websites and old newspaper clippings, she was startled by her cell's ringtone. Checking the time, she noted she had been at it for almost two hours. A brief glance at the caller ID told her this was the call she'd been waiting for. Taking a deep breath, she answered.

"Susan LeVeque."

"Ms. LeVeque, this is Terri Andersen. I'm returning your call. I called you earlier about the man found on Puffin Island."

"Yes, I know, and you think he might be your father?"

"That's right. It's a long shot, but my sister and I feel it's worth checking out."

"That's your twin sister, right?"

Terri was silent for a moment, surprised. "How'd you know that?"

Susan laughed. "Since I got your message, I've been doing some research. Looked into all the old newspaper stories about your father's disappearance. One of them mentioned you were twins. Strange stuff happening on Mateguas back then. From what I can see, it looks like not much of an investigation was done. Seems the authorities took the easiest way out by just assuming the worst. Now what makes you think 'The Puffin Man' could be your dad?"

Terri took a deep breath and again related what she and Sophie remembered of their time on Mateguas ten years before. She gave a detailed description of her father's appearance and uploaded a couple of photos of him from that time and sent them to the reporter. Finally, she talked about his computer expertise, explaining that he was a software engineer with an advanced degree.

Nothing that Terri said was news to Susan. She already had all this information from her online research. However, hearing the girl actually describe what happened, the reporter got a sense of the young woman's sincerity and heartfelt desire to find out what happened to her father. Convinced that this was no crank call or quest for publicity, she made a decision.

"Thanks, Terri. I spoke with Dr. Todd at the State Hospital before I called you. He's amenable to having you and your family come by tomorrow to meet John. I assume your sister will be joining you. What about your mother?"

Terri hesitated. "Our mom's here, but she remarried eight years ago. If this turns out to be a wild goose chase, then we'd be upsetting both her and my stepfather unnecessarily. Just coming back here was hard enough for her."

Susan was quiet for a moment. "So, your mother's remarried? Someone from California?"

Terri again hesitated. "No, he's from Mateguas. He and my mom were friends when we lived here. He actually moved to California the same time we did."

The wheels in the reporter's head began to spin. *Oh boy, the plot thickens. Maybe if the Puffin Man turns out to be Andersen, I'll have an attempted murder mystery to solve and that could really get national attention.* A vision of herself sitting in Diane Sawyer's chair passed through her mind as a smile played on her lips.

"Ms. LeVeque, are you still there?"

The sound of Terri's voice brought Susan back to reality. "Yes, sorry, I was woolgathering. So, is tomorrow - Monday - okay with you?"

"Yeah, we can work it out."

"Good. Now you have to take a ferry to get over to the mainland, right?"

"Yes."

Quickly Susan pulled up the ferry schedule on her computer. "Can you get the nine a.m.? I'll have our van pick you up. It's about a two-hour drive to the hospital."

"Yeah, I think we can do that."

"Okay then. I'll see you at the terminal around nine-thirty. Bring pictures of your dad with you. And, Terri, I hope this works out for you. John - the Puffin Man - seems like a good guy who got a raw deal. I'd like to think there's someone out there who cares for and misses him."

Hanging up, Susan sat quietly, lost in thought. Again, the vision of herself sitting in the anchor chair floated before her eyes. *This could have everything - raw sex, violence, betrayal, love ... all the stuff that makes for good TV. If this works out - wow, I could really score. Yes, I think I'm going to enjoy this.*

 **BANGOR STATE HOSPITAL**

THE NEXT MORNING, THE girls got up at six, not wanting to miss the morning ferry. By the time Karen came downstairs, they were washed, dressed, and seated at the table having breakfast.

"Well, you two are up early," she said with a frown. "What's on your agenda today? More islander interrogations?"

Terri laughed. "No, Mom. We decided that maybe you were right and we're going to give it a rest for a day. We're going to the mainland to do some sightseeing. We'll probably mess around in town for a while, shopping, and maybe visit a couple of the museums. But don't worry, we plan on being back in time for dinner."

Karen smiled. "That sounds like fun - maybe Dex and I can tag along?"

Sophie and Terri exchanged looks. "Don't take this wrong, Mom," said Sophie. "But we'd like to be on our own. We've been hanging out with you old folks quite a bit lately, you know. Some of the places or stores we want to visit might not suit you."

Laughing, Karen sat down opposite them. "Okay, I get it. You kids have fun. We old fogies will find something to do here."

On the mainland, outside the ferry terminal, the girls easily identified the WKZTV van parked at the curb. Susan LeVeque hopped out, recognizing them from pictures she had found online. They spoke briefly then got into the van for the long drive to the hospital. During the trip, Susan questioned them in detail about their father and his alleged death. She also queried them about their life in California trying to draw them out about their mother and her relationship with their Mateguas-born stepfather.

When they arrived at the hospital, Susan and her cameraman set up for a shot outside.

"We're here again today at the Bangor State Hospital to see the man they call John Doe. With us are Sophie and Terri Andersen. These young ladies lived on Mateguas ten years ago and their father, Bill Andersen, allegedly died there, drowning in the swamp behind their house. However, his body was never found ..."

The reporter went on to describe the girls' crusade to find out more about their father's last days, culminating in their viewing of the Sunday broadcast. Susan had the cameraman focus in on pictures of Bill Andersen and his family taken in the weeks before his death. Finished with her introductory piece, she escorted the girls up the steps to the hospital entrance. At the front desk, she had the clerk page Dr. Todd as they sat down to wait.

About fifteen minutes later, the doctor arrived in the reception area. Susan introduced him to the girls and, smiling, he led them down a corridor to a large room that served as a recreation area for the hospital's patients. People in bathrobes and lounging pajamas were scattered about, playing cards, talking, or watching TV. Dr. Todd indicated for the girls to sit down at one of the vacant tables.

"You all just sit tight here," he said. "I'll go talk to John. I have to warn you - he's pretty nervous about all this. So please, be gentle with him."

The girls watched as he walked to the far end of the room and began speaking to a tall man who was standing looking out the window.

"That's him over there," Susan said, pointing to where two men were talking. She watched the girls intently for a minute, trying to gauge their reaction to their first glimpse of the man who might be their father, then she stood up and, with the cameraman, began preparing for the next segment.

Terri stared at the man talking with Dr. Todd, then pulled out her iPad and opened her photo file to the album she'd labeled "Daddy."

Heads together, the girls studied pictures of their father from ten to fifteen years before, glancing up occasionally to gaze at the man across the room.

"He's tall like Dad," said Sophie, "but thinner."

"Yeah, but remember Dad was a runner. He was always pretty lean and fit."

"Shit, I almost wish Dad had had a tattoo or a scar on his face or something else unique. Then it would be easy to ID him."

Terri laughed. "You've got to be kidding. I can't imagine our father with a tat! He was way too conservative for that."

The reporter laid her hand on Terri's shoulder, startling her. "They're coming over now. I'm going to be filming all of this. We'll edit it later and you'll get to see it before it goes on the air - if it goes on the air. Good luck."

Terri smiled at her then turned back to watch the man as he crossed the room.

Dr. Todd took a deep breath. "Okay, John. This is it. Let's go see if we've found your family."

The man called John Doe laughed. "Probably just an exercise in futility. Two girls from California? Looking for the father that drowned ten years ago? Hardly seems to fit my scenario."

"Give it a shot, John. Stranger things have happened."

The man nodded. "Okay, Hod. Let's get this over with."

Smiling, he turned from the doctor and began to saunter over to where the twins sat. Dr. Todd, staying close to his patient, silently crossed his fingers behind his back.

John slowed as he approached the girls. Staring at them, a puzzled look came over his face. They seemed somehow familiar, but that was impossible - he'd never seen them before. But there was something - something nagging at the back of his mind that he couldn't quite put his finger on. He stopped about ten feet away, his formerly relaxed posture becoming rigid.

Suddenly, his head seemed to explode as a vivid memory flashed across his consciousness.

A woman standing on the beach, waves gently lapping at her bare feet, her face turned away from him.

As he gazed at her with his mind's eye, he was overcome by an intense feeling of desire and joy.

Then slowly she turned around, smiling, her palms resting on her huge belly. She reached out toward him and took his hand. "The girls are pretty active today, hon. Want to feel them?"

Staggering, John let out a groan as the force of the memory washed over him. Dr. Todd, alarmed, reached out to steady him, but John brushed his hand aside. Regaining his equilibrium, he closed his eyes and began to relax as he let memory after memory stream into his consciousness as what once had been his life passed swiftly before his eyes.

Unsure of what was happening, Terri turned to her twin and was surprised to see tears sliding down her cheeks. "Soph, what's the matter?"

"Look, Ter. Look."

Terri turned back toward the man. His face was now a mask of pain and longing as he stared at the young women in front of him. He reached out with one hand, his mouth barely forming the words. "Smaller - you were so much smaller."

Sophie gasped, stood up, and rushed around the table to face him.

"Daddy?"

A tear slipped down his cheek as his unbelieving eyes gazed upon her. "Sophie? Is that really you?"

Sophie nodded once, then moved forward and wrapped her arms around him, hugging him tightly.

Terri stared at her sister and the man embracing. After a minute, he looked up at her.

"Terri-bug?" he asked. "Won't you come and give Daddy a hug?"

Slowly, unable to fully comprehend what was happening, she rose out of her chair. "Are you really my dad?" she asked, wanting to believe but afraid to at the same time.

The man nodded, then turned to look at Dr. Todd, who was standing close behind him.

"Hod, you were right. Thank you for making me do this."

"No problem, John," replied the doctor, marveling at the scene taking place in front of him.

"No, Hod. Not John. My name's Bill - Bill Andersen. These are my daughters, Sophie and Terri."

Now it was Terri's turn to cry as she launched herself into his arms.

Some time later, the girls and their father sat in the hospital cafeteria, talking.

"My parents," Bill asked. "How are they?"

Sophie looked down at the table then back up into his eyes. "I'm sorry, Dad, but Granddad passed away last year. Heart attack. Grammy's still alive though. She lives with Uncle Bob and his family. We'll have to call and let them know you're okay."

Bill took a sip of his coffee, nodding. "Yeah, we'll do that."

They all sat without speaking for a few minutes, then Bill looked up again at his daughters. "Okay, there's one subject you've been avoiding, and we all know it. Your mother. Come on - tell me. I'm assuming she has someone else. Is that right?"

Terri and Sophie looked at each other, then Terri nodded. "Yeah, Dad. She remarried about eight years ago. And she's happy. It's a good marriage."

Sophie watched her father's reaction carefully. "You know him, Dad. He's from Mateguas. Remember Dex Pierce? He and Mom became good friends after we thought you were dead. He traveled to California with us when we left Mateguas. They got married about two years later."

Bill's face hardened. "She married that fisherman? Dex Pierce? Is that what you're telling me?"

Sensing the change in their father's mood, Sophie sat quietly again staring at the table, unable to meet his eyes.

Terri, observing her father's anger, weighed her words carefully. "Yes, Dad. Dex is our stepfather and he's been a good one. He loves Mom and us. You have to remember - everyone thought you were dead. Mom was devastated. And, yes, Dex did come with us to California but they were just friends then."

Bill laughed, raising his voice. "I'll bet it didn't take long till she was sharing his bed. You guys wouldn't know - you were too little to understand what was going on."

As he spoke, he slammed his fist down on the table, upsetting a glass of water.

Alarmed, Sophie turned to her sister, her eyes questioning. Terri reached over to right the glass, using her napkin to wipe up the spilled liquid. No one looked at Bill.

His fists still clenched and his jawline set, he stood up and walked over to the cafeteria counter to get more napkins to wipe up the spilled water.

Standing nearby, Dr. Todd was witness to his patient's outburst and now approached him.

"John - sorry, I mean Bill - anything the matter? You look upset."

Bill turned and saw the concern on his old friend's face. Knowing he was out of line, he took a deep breath, trying to get his temper under control. "I guess I got a bit out of hand, Hod. Just found out my wife has remarried and the guy is one I don't like at all. It's hard to take it all in. Guess I lost my temper."

Dr. Todd nodded. "You going to have to make a lot of adjustments. This is just the first. But think about your family. You have one now and they look pretty darn nice to me. Don't blow it."

Bill nodded. "Again, you're right. I have to apologize to the girls. Why don't you come on over and sit with us a bit? Might make things easier."

Dr. Todd smiled. "Be happy to. Just let me get some coffee and I'll be right there. Got some questions for you myself."

Bill nodded then walked slowly back over to the table and began wiping up the spilled water, avoiding eye contact with his daughters. When the table was cleaned, he tossed the napkins in the waste bin and sat back down.

"I'm sorry, girls. It's just a lot to digest. Your mother ... I love her and thinking of her with that ... I mean, Dex ... it's just hard. But I shouldn't take it out on you. Can you forgive me?"

Terri smiled and reached for his hand. "I think given the circumstances, you're doing remarkably well. I don't know how I'd feel if I was in your shoes. It's like coming out of a coma after ten years. Everything's changed, but for you, for your emotions, it's still the same. You have to play catch-up and you have to do it too quickly. I'd probably be screaming and tearing my hair out. No, Dad, we don't need to forgive you. Being upset is perfectly understandable."

"Sophie, are you okay with me, too?"

"Dad, I'm just so happy you're alive. I couldn't be mad at you if I tried."

Bill forced himself to smile, wanting to regain his good mood, but the picture of Karen and Dex together somehow would not leave his consciousness.

Terri and Sophie looked up as Dr. Todd approached the table. "Mind if I join you all for a few minutes?" he asked, putting his hand on Bill's shoulder.

Bill turned to look at him, grateful for the interruption. "Sit down, Hod. Girls, this man saved my life - or at least my sanity. I was in pretty bad shape when I first got here. I don't know what I would have done without his support."

Dr. Todd blushed slightly at the compliment then chuckled. "Well, I got free computer expertise out of it, didn't I? Think that makes us even, Bill."

PRIME TIME NEWS

SUSAN LEVEQUE SAT IN the viewing room at the WKZTV newsroom with her station manager. They had just finished watching her segment at Bangor State Hospital and she was waiting for his reaction.

"This might get you a Cronkite, Susan," the manager said softly. "This is good stuff. I want it on at five tonight. We'll repeat it on Sunday with a recap of your previous piece. And, I assume you are going to follow-up with an in-depth interview with Andersen after he settles in with his family. Great work, Susan. I'll make sure the Network is watching."

Susan nodded and smiled, unable to find words. She checked her watch. It was almost five. *I promised those girls they would see it before it went on,* she thought. *Well, no time for that now. I'll text them. There's nothing in it they could object to anyway. They signed all the releases.*

Her conscience eased, Susan got up and hurriedly left the room to get the 'on air' crew up to speed on her segment.

Back at Bangor State, Dr. Todd's appearance at the table had lightened the atmosphere considerably. After chatting amiably with the girls about themselves and then about the hospital in general, he felt the mood was convivial enough for him to pose the questions that had been praying on his mind.

"Now, Bill, " he began, "I have a couple of questions that I hope you won't mind answering."

Bill smiled at his friend. "Shoot away, Hod. My life's an open book."

"Okay, I know you now remember your life with your family back ten years ago, but do you remember Puffin and under what circumstances you got there?"

Bill paused for a few moments, thinking. "Sorry, but that's still a blank. Last thing I remember before coming to the hospital is grabbing a lantern, kissing Karen - that's my wife - and going out into the storm. Everything from then on is still a mystery."

"Do you remember why you went outside, Dad?" asked Sophie. "Mom says you went for a walk before the storm hit. Is that what you recall, too?"

Again, Bill was silent. "Kids, like I said, I remember kissing your mother, grabbing a lantern and going outside. I don't know why I went out or what happened after I left. I think it must have been at least raining - I remember I was wearing my slicker. And, that's it."

Terri was about to speak when her cell chimed. She looked down and noticed she had a text from Susan LeVeque. Reading it, her mouth fell open.

"Holy crap, they're airing the segment tonight!" She looked back at her cell to check the time. It was already ten after five. "And they're doing it right now! And we haven't told Mom!"

Bill looked at her quizzically. "Your mother doesn't know you're here?"

With a hint of panic in her voice, Sophie responded. "No, Dad. We didn't tell her anything about it. We thought it probably wasn't going to pan out and didn't see any reason to upset her. Oh, Terri, if she's home, she always watches the five o'clock news. What will we do?"

"I'll call her," her twin replied, hitting speed dial on her cell. "Fingers crossed she's not home."

# A SHOCKING DISCOVERY

ON MATEGUAS, KAREN AND Dex had just returned home from a day on the water. Dex rented a boat and they'd motored out to sea, stopping for lunch at Elliot's Island at a five-star hotel. After enjoying a leisurely meal, they rented bicycles and spent the afternoon exploring. It was close to five when they got home and Dex went upstairs to shower and change. Karen grabbed herself a glass of wine and sat down to watch the evening news, wanting to catch the weather segment.

Turning on the TV, she noted it was tuned to WKZTV and that the news was just coming on. She slipped off her shoes, put her feet up on an ottoman, and relaxed as the anchor opened the show.

"And tonight we have breaking news - John Doe, also known as 'The Puffin Man,' has been identified. We turn you over now to Susan LeVeque who has been the lead on this story from its beginning eight years ago."

The camera shifted to an attractive brunette who Karen guessed was in her mid-thirties. The woman briefly recapped who

"The Puffin Man" was and the piece that had aired about him the previous evening. "Last night, we received a call on our hotline from a young woman looking for her father."

The camera again shifted and, to Karen's surprise, she was now watching Terri and Sophie standing in front of a hospital as the reporter began to interview them. Gripping her wine glass tightly, Karen leaned forward in her chair and listened. When the scene again changed and the camera focused on the man called 'John Doe,' she dropped the glass.

"Dex," she screamed. "Get down here now!"

Unmindful of the red wine that was soaking into the carpet, Karen watched as her daughters embraced their once-dead father.

Dex, hearing his wife's scream, came running down the stairs, a towel wrapped loosely around his waist. "What is it? What's happened?" he asked as he ran over to where she sat perched on the edge of her chair.

"Look," she said in a whisper as she pointed to the TV screen. "It's Bill. Oh, my God, Dex, it's Bill. He's alive!"

Dex stood behind her chair, staring at the television. Karen turned to speak to him but was silenced when she saw the stony expression on his face. He stood rigid, the muscles in his chest and back tense, his jawline set and his hands balled tightly into fists.

A look of concern crossed her face as she reached out and laid her hand lightly on his chest. "Dex?"

Feeling the warmth of her touch, he began to visibly relax. After a moment, he looked down at her. "Are you sure that's Bill? Looks like him, but ..."

Karen nodded her head. "Yes, that's him and the girls would know. Apparently, when he saw them his memory began to come back. He remembered his name. How would he know that if he weren't Bill? And I recognize him, too. Sure, he's changed, but underneath ..."

Her thoughts were interrupted by the sound of the phone. Dex strode over and picked it up.

"Hello?"

Terri grimaced and mouthed the words "They're home" to her sister.

"Hi, Dex," she said hesitantly.

There was silence on the line.

"Dex, are you there?"

"Yes, I'm here. And thanks for the heads up, Terri," he retorted, anger apparent in his tone. "You almost gave your mother a heart attack. How long have you know about this?"

Terri mouthed "Dex is pissed" to her sister.

Catching the communication, Bill leaned back in his chair and smiled.

"I'm sorry, Dex," she said into the phone. "We didn't want to alarm you or Mom unnecessarily. And the reporter told us we would be able to see the piece before it went on the air. We just found out a few minutes ago that it was going to lead the news at five. Can I speak to Mom?"

Without replying, Dex held the phone up toward Karen. "It's Terri and she wants to speak to you."

Karen got up and walked over to him.

"You okay?" he asked, handing her the phone.

"Yes," she replied. "Why don't you finish getting dressed while I speak to Terri? After, we'll sit down and talk."

Terri spoke with her mother for a few minutes, then passed the cell over to Sophie. "She wants to talk to you."

Sophie took the phone, spoke a few words of greeting, then got up and left the table.

Bill leaned back in his chair. "Well, how'd it go? Does she want me to pack my bags and get on the next boat back to Puffin?"

Terri smiled. "No, Dad. But she's upset. It was quite a shock for her. She asked how you were. I think she might want to talk to you when she finishes reaming out Sophie."

Bill laughed. "Hasn't changed much has she? Still a control freak when it comes to you two?"

"You got it!"

Sophie returned and sat down, looking pale and upset, the cell still in her hand. She slid it across the table toward her father. "She wants to talk to you, Dad."

Bill stared at the phone. As he reached for it, his hand began to visibly shake and the beginnings of a tremor moved up his arm.

Dr. Todd, always observant, saw his patient's distress and quickly reached out and took the phone from the table.

Standing up and turning away from the girls and Bill, he spoke into the cell. "Mrs. Andersen?" he said, "Let me introduce myself. I'm Dr. Horace Todd, your husband's physician. I'm afraid all this may have been just a bit too much for my patient and I think it might be wise to put this conversation off for a bit. Your daughters are going to remain here in Bangor overnight - the TV station has booked them rooms at a very respectful bed and breakfast not far from the hospital. They have also arranged to send a van in the morning to bring them back to the city. John, er, I mean, Bill, will be coming with them. The plan is for him to spend the afternoon tomorrow on the island with his family. If all goes well, he will be discharged from the hospital and move into a halfway house down your way so that he can visit with his children as he returns to a more normal life. And I've found him some temporary employment. I hope all this meets with your approval."

Dr. Todd paused for a minute or two then spoke with Karen briefly again, hung up, and returned to the table.

"She's amenable to our plan," he said, handing the cell back to Terri.

Bill looked at him and smiled, visibly relieved. "Thanks, Hod. Just the thought of speaking with her scared the crap out of me. Don't know why, exactly. Maybe because she's moved on and I haven't. But thanks for getting me this space to get my act together."

Dr. Todd smiled. "No problem, Bill. I hope this all meets with your approval, too, girls?"

"You're a godsend, Dr. Todd," said Terri, laughing. "Thanks for your help. Now, it's going on six o'clock. Is there somewhere nice around here where we can take our father out to dinner? I think it would be good for him to get a taste of non-hospital fare tonight."

"I know just the place and it's within walking distance. It's Italian, small and very quiet. Let me write down the directions. Bill has to be back at the hospital by nine, though. He's still a patient here and we must follow the rules."

"No, problem, Dr. Todd. You ready, Dad? Or do you want to freshen up first?"

"Give me a couple of minutes to change and I'll meet you in the lobby."

Later that evening, Karen sat in the living room watching the eleven o'clock news. She leaned forward, listening intently, as the station replayed the segment shot at the hospital. Susan LeVeque was recapping the history of "The Puffin Man" and details of how he was discovered on that remote island. Dex stood at the window, staring out at the sea.

When the station went to a commercial break, she turned toward him. "Dex, I know you've kept in touch with people here. Did you know about this?"

He glanced over his shoulder to look at her. "Know about what?"

"About finding Bill on that island - it was kids from Mateguas that discovered him. Didn't any of your friends ever mention it? Seems like it would have been pretty big news for this place."

Dex turned back to look out the window. He was quiet for a few minutes.

"Dex?"

He shrugged his shoulders and continued gazing seaward. "Yeah, someone told me about it. Why?"

"Well, you never told me. Didn't you make the connection or think just maybe it could have been Bill?"

He muttered something under his breath, ignoring her.

"Dex, I'm talking to you. Trying to have a conversation. We need to discuss this."

He turned from the window and walked over to where she was sitting and stood between her and the television. His eyes were cold and his mouth was set in an angry scowl.

"No, I didn't make the connection. Why would I think it was Bill? He was dead and gone. And you never wanted to talk about Mateguas anyway, so why would I tell you about it? This is as much a surprise to me as it is to you. Can't you cut me some slack here? What are you accusing me of anyway?"

Karen stared at him, surprised by his apparent anger. "I'm not accusing you of anything. I'm just trying to understand." As she spoke, she reached out and took his hand in hers. "Why are you so angry? Are you mad at me? Or, mad because Bill's alive?"

Dex pulled his hand away and walked to the kitchen. He came back a minute later with a glass holding two fingers of Jack Daniels. Sipping, he sat down on the couch next to her.

"I'm not angry at you, but I am upset. Jesus, your husband's alive - don't you think that I have a right to be a little pissed off? How is this going to affect us - you and me? He's going to want you back - you know that, don't you?"

Karen sighed and reached out again for his hand. "You and I are just fine. Nothing is going to change that. I love YOU. Bill will just have to adjust. But, I am glad he's alive - he didn't deserve to die in that swamp or on that island."

Dex eyed her carefully. "Thought he committed suicide? Or, at least that's the line of malarkey that you tried to feed the girls."

Karen blushed. "I was just trying to keep them from coming here, you know that. But now, I'm sorry I did. If we hadn't come, Bill might never have remembered who he is. The girls now have their natural father back and that's a good thing."

Dex nodded. "Yeah, but he's been in the State's care for the past eight years. Who knows if he's all right in the head."

Karen sighed. "Well, we're going to find out, aren't we? He'll be here tomorrow." She stood up. "I'm going to go to bed. Try to get some sleep. We've a big day ahead of us. You coming?"

"I'll be up in a minute. Just let me finish my drink and lock up."

He leaned over and kissed her briefly, then walked to the window again.

Karen watched him for a minute, then, shaking her head in frustration, went up to the loft to bed.

Dex waited quietly for a minute while Karen ascended the stairs. Then he took his drink and walked outside, down to the beach. He stood motionless for a time, staring at the dark sea, sipping, and then, without warning, turned and threw the glass with all his might against the rocks, watching as it shattered into a million tiny shards. Taking a deep breath, he ran his hands through his hair, nodded, then turned again and walked slowly back to the house and up the stairs to Karen.

REUNION

THE NEXT MORNING, DEX drove to the wharf alone. Karen argued that it was her place to go, but he insisted she stay home. With Bill and the girls arriving on the ferry, Dex was sure there would be more than a few curious islanders hanging about and he wanted, more than anything, to avoid an emotional reunion in public that was sure to get their tongues a-wagging.

Arriving early, he parked the car and walked over toward a lobster boat that was loading traps.

"Hey, Rusty, how's it going?"

Maggie's father turned around. Recognizing Dex, he hopped out of the boat and strode over to him.

"Dex Pierce, you old rascal, you! Heard you was back. What ya doin' down here this morning? Meeting the ferry?"

Dex frowned. "Now you wouldn't have seen the evening news last night, would you?"

Rusty laughed. "Yup, 'fraid I did. Andersen showing up on the boat?"

Dex nodded. "Him and my girls. Maggie see the broadcast?"

Rusty immediately became serious. "Yeah, and she was ready to grab the boy and head straight on over to the loony bin to see him. Emma and me finally convinced her to stay put. Let him come to her, if he's got a mind to. But it's hard. She never really let go of him, you know. And the boy, well, she's got to think of him."

Dex nodded again. "Going to be interesting, that's for sure."

"Yeah. Can't imagine how that city boy survived two years on Puffin. Fucking unbelievable."

"You're right about that. And, I can tell you, I'm not looking forward to spending the afternoon with him - especially since I think he still feels he has a claim on my wife."

Rusty nodded. "Boat's comin' in now. Best you skedaddle down over there. Put your best foot forward for your kids."

"You're right, Rusty. I'll just suck it up and lay on the charm!"

Clapping each other on the back, the two men separated as Dex walked over to the gangplank to wait for the girls and their father.

At home, Karen could not sit still. Pacing the floor, she kept looking at her watch. *What's keeping them?*

Deciding to check her appearance again, she walked to the powder room.

This makes it about the fiftieth time I've combed my hair. If I keep this up, by the time they get here, I won't have any left. She took a deep breath, reached for her lip gloss, and began to reapply it. Her hand stopped mid-air as she heard a car pull up the drive.

Dropping the lipstick, she looked at herself in the mirror one last time, turned, and walked back toward the living room. She got there just as the door opened.

Dex came in first, followed by the girls. Bill stood just outside the door, seemingly unable to move, his eyes locked on her, a hard expression on his face. No one said anything. Then Bill smiled and walked inside.

"Hi, Kar. Long time, no see."

After an awkward pause and hug, Karen and Bill sat down in the living room for a quiet talk. Dex and the girls left them alone, moving over to the kitchen breakfast bar. Terri could see that Dex was visibly nervous, his eyes constantly darting over to the living room where his wife sat with her first husband.

"It's okay, Dex," Terri said. "They're just talking."

"Yes, I know, but is he all right? He's been in the State Hospital for years. If he's okay, why didn't they let him out?"

Terri sighed. "Dr. Todd worried about him. He didn't start speaking until very recently. He was actually going to be discharged next month even if they didn't find any family. But now he has us."

Dex grimaced. "Yeah. He has you girls. But does he think he has your mother, too?"

Unsure of how to respond, Terri glanced over at her sister, who was sitting next to her.

"Dex, Dad knows Mom's with you now. We told him she was happy and that it was a good marriage. It might be hard for him to accept it, but he's trying. You gotta cut him some slack after all he's been through."

Dex was about to respond when Karen walked into the room. "Girls, could you please put a salad together for lunch? Your dad and I are going to take a short walk on the beach. We'll be back in about a half hour."

When Sophie nodded, Karen turned to Dex. "I know you're worried, but it's all right. He and I just need a few minutes to talk and I think he'll feel more comfortable if we're totally alone. Okay?"

Reluctantly, Dex nodded then leaned over and kissed her lightly on the lips. "If you need me, you holler, okay?"

Karen laughed, kissed him back and left the room.

Once away from the house, Karen and Bill walked side by side down the beach. They were physically close, but the emotional gulf between them was enormous.

Stopping to pick up a piece of sea glass, Karen looked up at him. "You really don't remember, do you?"

"Remember what?"

"You know, what happened that night. Why you went out into the storm and what happened in the woods."

Bill stopped and sat down on a rock. "No, I don't. Last thing I remember is kissing you, putting on my slicker and boots, and leaving the house. Next thing I know I'm waking up in the hospital, half dead. Don't know how I got to Puffin or who dumped me there, either - although, I may have a suspicion."

Karen eyed him closely. "You don't mean Dex, do you?"

Bill just stared at her, his expression neutral.

"If you do, you're way off base. He was with the search party and stayed at it for two days. And why would he abandon you at Puffin anyway? It makes no sense."

Bill smiled. "Well, he got what he wanted, didn't he? You and my family. Hell, he got my life. Am I supposed to be grateful?"

Karen sighed. "Oh, what can I say? You're going to have to accept it. He's my husband now and I love him. Doesn't mean I won't always have special feelings for you, but it's not like it used to be and it can't be that way again. You'll always have the girls - they love you. And there's something more - something they haven't told you."

Bill looked at her, puzzled. "What?"

Karen took a deep breath. "Maggie - she's still on the island and ..."

"What about her? You think I still want her?"

"No, it's not that. When you got lost, well, she'd just found out she was pregnant. She has a son - a boy she says is yours."

Bill could only stare, stunned. "I have a boy? A son? You're sure?"

Karen smiled. "Yes, he looks just like you except for the red hair. Dex says he's a nice kid. The girls met him a couple of days ago and they liked him, too."

"And you? Did you like him?"

"I didn't meet him. Maggie has our old house and I just couldn't go there and see her lording over it all. Sorry, I'm just not the forgiving type."

Bill stood up and stared out to sea. He leaned over, picked up a rock, and tossed it, skipping it across the water. "Well, that changes things, doesn't it? Guess I'm going to be spending quite a bit of time over here now. You'll have to get used to seeing me around. You are here for the summer, aren't you?"

"Unfortunately, yes. And now that you've been found, I know the girls will want to spend as much time as they can with you before we go back home. So, I guess I'm stuck." She glanced at her watch. "We'd better be getting back. It's time for lunch."

She turned to go but Bill reached out and took a hold of her arm.

"I still love you. You have to know that."

She looked at him, pity in her eyes. "I know. But it can't be. And you have to accept that. Now let's head back."

They stared at each other for a moment, then Bill dropped her arm and put his hands in his pockets. Nodding to her, he turned and they walked silently back to the house.

Later, after lunch, the girls and their father went for a walk until it was time for him to catch the ferry back to the mainland. They made plans for him to return the following Friday afternoon. Sensing that Dex would not want him staying in the same the house with Karen, Bill told them he would look for a room to rent on the island, making it sound like it was his choice.

Ready to leave, Karen insisted that she drive him to the wharf alone. Dex reluctantly agreed.

Arriving early, Karen parked the car. They sat for a moment and then she turned her face toward him. "Well, Bill, it's been quite a day."

Expecting him to say goodbye and just leave, she was surprised when he remained immobile staring at her, his face a mask. She cocked her head quizzically. "Is there something else? You don't want to miss the ferry."

He smiled. "We've got time. It doesn't leave for another ten minutes."

As he spoke, he reached out and took her hand. He held it softly in his for a moment then leaned toward her, attempting to kiss her.

Startled, she pulled away abruptly. "Bill, don't. We've talked about this. It's been ten years. I'm married to Dex now. What you and I had once is in the past. It's over."

Bill took her hand again, this time holding it tightly. "Kar, you have to understand," he said emphatically. "To me, the last ten years don't exist. My feelings and memories are just a heartbeat away from when I went out into that storm. I still love you; I never stopped."

Upset, she tried to pull her hand away, but he was holding it too tightly. "Bill, let me go."

He looked down at their hands, hers white from the pressure he was applying. Finally, with some effort, he relaxed his grip, letting her wiggle her fingers away.

She rubbed her hand, staring at it, and then she looked back up at him. "You can't just turn back the clock. It doesn't work that way. I'm glad you're alive, believe me, but things can't - no, they won't - go back to where they were ten years ago. That's over and done with and you have to accept that. And remember, things weren't all that rosy for us then. We were on the verge of breaking up."

Slowly, he nodded. "You're right, but we were trying to put it all back together. Don't you remember? We made love that night. God, that memory is so fresh and new - I can still smell you and feel you - so warm and wet."

Seeing the look of reproach on her face, he sighed and took a deep breath. "But, okay, so that's over with and you're with Dex. But tell me, Karen, how long did you wait?"

She looked at him quizzically, surprised. "What do you mean by 'wait'?"

He smiled again. "What I mean is how long after I was declared dead did you wait to hook up with that ... that fisherman? I know he moved back to California with you. The girls told me all about it. So, what is it? How long did you play the role of the grieving widow?"

Shocked by the bitterness in his voice, she bowed her head, unable to respond. He was right. She didn't wait all that long to fall into Dex's arms.

He has good reason to be angry. I didn't wait. I really didn't grieve for him and he deserved so much more from me.

Neither of them spoke. She sat quietly staring down at her hands feeling his eyes boring into her. *But he strayed first. I didn't do anything wrong. He betrayed me with Maggie long before Dex and I got together.*

She raised her head up and met his eyes, defiantly, and was about to speak when they were both startled by the sound of the ferry's horn signaling last call to get on board.

"Well, I guess I've got to be getting along," he said lightly. "I'll be back on the weekend to see the girls. I hope that's okay with you?"

"They're your daughters and they're adults now," she said, tersely. "You can see them whenever you like."

"Thanks," he replied as he leaned over and kissed her chastely on the cheek. "Good seeing you again, Kar. Till Friday, then." Without waiting for a response, he hopped out of the car, jogged down the wharf, and boarded the ferry.

Watching him, Karen sat stiffly behind the wheel as the deckhand untied the boat. When, at last, it began to move out to sea, she slumped in her seat. *Thank God, that's over. Hopefully, next time will be easier.*

She took a couple of deep breaths, sat up straight, and, without another glance at the retreating ferry, started the car and headed home to her husband and family.

On the boat, the man formerly known as 'John Doe' stood in the stern watching as the lights of Mateguas faded in the distance. His face was a study in concentration and his hands gripped the railing tightly, knuckles white with tension. Then, as the last light seemed to twinkle and disappear, he visibly began to unwind, hands now resting lightly on the rail, the color returning. As the tautness in his facial expression melted away, he nodded once as if he had come to some sort of decision. He looked one more time toward the lights of Mateguas, then turned away and moved to go inside the cabin, the corners of his lips turning upward in the beginnings of a small, but not too pleasant, smile.

KAREN

HER MIND A CONFUSED jumble of thoughts, Karen veered off the main road and pulled down a dirt lane that was marked as a "Right of Way to the Shore." Parking the car at the end, she got out and walked to the beach

She stared at the sea before her as the moon made its way from behind a cloud. Gazing up at it, she nodded. *Yes, it's almost time again. But does that damned ritual I promised the God of the Dead I'd perform every month really mean anything? Bill's alive - he wasn't devoured by the Mskagwdemos back on that horrible night ten years ago. So, was any of it real? Have I been mutilating myself for years for no reason? And if that's the case, am I insane? Is all of this nonsense really just in my mind?*

She let her thoughts travel back to that night ten years before when she'd stood, facing the sea, a protective circle of blood powder around her, reciting the prayers - prayers she believed would bring her family home safe to her. Silently, she relived her mistake; that slight turn of her head away from the east - the turn that she thought had sealed the fate of her husband.

But he wasn't killed. Someone must have taken him to Puffin, someone human. But who? I know Dex was in love with me and wanted me, but would he go that far? No, it's not in his nature. But someone must have wanted Bill out of the way. But who?

She picked up a stone and skipped it across the water.

And now, we're back here and it's starting up all over again. That vision I had on the beach - was that real? Or is my mind playing tricks on me?

Unsure of anything, she tried to shake the doubts from her mind, hoping to hang on to some semblance of sanity. Standing quietly, she was startled when her cell began to vibrate, bringing her back to reality.

"Yes?"

"It's me. Is everything okay? You should have been home by now."

Karen smiled. "Yes, Dex, I'm okay. I just stopped on my way back to get some air. I'll be home directly."

She spoke to him for a few more minutes, then, hanging up the cell, gazed again at the moon. It seemed to be shining too brightly, as if calling to her. Shaking her head, she tore her eyes away. She put the cell back in her pocket and walked slowly to her car, her mind still a mass of tangled threads, none of which seemed to lead her home to her family and to what she thought was safety.

OLD FRIENDS

THE NEXT FEW DAYS went by swiftly for Karen and her family. Mid-week, the twins went to town to have lunch with their father, who was now working in a soup kitchen that was sponsored by a local church. The employment was menial but it was all that Dr. Todd could arrange for him on short notice.

They ate at a restaurant located on the wharf where they could sit outside by the water.

"I spoke with Pete," said Bill. "You remember him, Pete McKinney? He said I could stay at their cottage this weekend. They're not expecting family till later in the summer, so it's vacant and I told him I would help with any repair work that needs to be done."

"That's great, Dad," replied Sophie. "What boat do you expect to take on Friday?"

Bill was about to respond when Terri's cell phone chimed. Pulling it from her purse, she looked at the caller ID, puzzled.

"It's the TV station. Maybe it's about the follow-up interview. I'd better take it."

Opening the phone, she answered the call.

"Hi, Terri? It's Susan LeVeque. How are things going?"

"Great. We're actually having lunch right now. Is this something that can wait?"

"Oh, I'll be quick. I just called to get a message to your father. We had a communication here at the station from a man who said he used to work with Bill - a Gerry Davis. Davis wants to get in touch with him, but I wasn't about to give out your number to just anyone."

"Hang on a minute." Terry put the call on hold and looked at her father. "You had a call at the station - a Gerry Davis - said you worked with him?"

Bill's face brightened. "Yeah, yeah. Gerry. He was head of R&D at Omicron - the place I worked here in Maine. I was going to move into his division in the fall. Get his number, so I can call him back."

Terri returned to her call from Susan. "Dad knows him. Did he leave his number?"

The reporter passed on the phone number, spoke briefly with Terri about the follow-up interview, then hung up.

"What do you think he wants?" asked Sophie.

"Maybe just to say hello, but it could lead to a job."

Terri passed him the cell. "Call him."

Bill stared at the phone then took it from his daughter. Dialing the number the reporter had given them, he waited as the call went through. A minute later, he hung up and handed the phone back to Terri.

"It went to voicemail. He's out of the country. Left this morning. Won't be back till next week."

"Why didn't you leave a message?" asked Sophie.

Bill shook his head. "What would I say? I don't even have a phone he can call me back on. And look at me - would you even considering hiring a guy who dresses like this and works in a soup kitchen?"

Bill leaned back in his chair showing off his threadbare shirt and stained jeans. Terri and Sophie sat quietly for a minute, then Terri again handed him the phone.

"Call the church. Tell them you're sick and can't come in this afternoon."

Bill looked at her questioningly. "Why?"

"Cause we're going shopping!"

Bill shook his head. "I can't let you do that. Pay for me. That's not the way it's supposed to work."

"You can pay us back later. What do you think, Sophie, how about some nice jeans, a couple of shirts and a sport coat?"

Sophie looked at her father appraisingly. "I think some socks and a good pair of shoes, too - topsiders or Nikes, and a cell phone so you can call Gerry back and call us when you want to. And how about a shave and a haircut?"

Bill laughed. "A shave, yes, haircut, no. I like my hair long."

"Okay, but how about a trim - neaten it up a bit?"

Bill leaned across the table and took his daughters' hands in his. "What did I ever do to deserve you two? I will pay you back - that's a promise I won't forget."

REUNION NUMBER TWO

ON FRIDAY, BILL TOOK the evening commuter ferry over to the island. The girls met him at the dock and drove him over to the McKinneys' guest cottage where he would be staying. He brought with him some groceries and offered to fix dinner for them all. After eating, they sat outside on the patio enjoying the cool ocean breeze.

"So, what do you want to do tomorrow, Dad?" asked Sophie. "Maybe we can do some island exploring?"

"Sorry, honey. Can I take a rain check? There's something I have to do on my own tomorrow. We haven't talked about it, but your mother told me about Maggie and the boy. I think it's time I go see her and talk to her about him. If he's my kid - well, I need to take some responsibility."

"You want us to go with you?" asked Terri.

"No, honey. This is something I need to do alone. I'll call you later though. Maybe we can grab a bite at the Burger Shack or something."

The following morning, Dex suggested to Karen that they take an early ferry to the mainland and spend the day shopping and sightseeing. Karen happily agreed - she had been dreading the possibility of another emotional encounter with Bill and a day away from the island would keep her at a safe distance from him.

Bill, however, was not thinking about Karen that morning. Waking early, he walked the mile and a half to what once had been his house, inherited from his late aunt. When he reached the driveway, he stopped and stared at the place for a moment. It hadn't changed much in ten years. Taking a deep breath, he walked up the hill, relishing the experience of being on the property again. When he reached the porch, he knocked on the door and waited, but there was no answer.

After peering in the windows and seeing no one inside, he strolled around to the back and was surprised to find a young boy stacking firewood. The boy looked up as he approached.

"Hi," he said. "Can I help you, sir?"

Bill smiled, appreciating the boy's politeness. "I'm looking for your mom. Is she coming back soon?"

Young Bill nodded. "She just went to the dump. Should be home in about a half an hour."

"Well, is it okay if I wait? Maybe I could help you with your chores?"

The boy looked at him skeptically. "I can stack. Mom won't let me split though. Says I'm too young."

Bill eyed the hatchet that lay next to a large tree stump that was apparently used for splitting the wood. Several logs were piled next to it. "Well, how about I split while you stack? Got any protective eye gear?"

The boy nodded. "Yeah. I'll get it for you."

He started toward the garage then stopped and turned. "Who are you anyway, mister?" he asked.

Bill laughed. "Oh, I'm an old friend of your mom's. Haven't seen her in a long time. Thought I'd surprise her."

The boy nodded again then got the goggles for him. Smiling, Bill put them on over his glasses and hefted the axe. After a couple of practice swings, he looked at the boy, who grinned, apparently satisfied that this man knew what he was doing. Smiling again, Bill began to split the wood in earnest as the boy returned to his stacking.

It was a warm day and the work was hard. Bill paused for a moment and took off his shirt, hanging it on a fence post. "Could use a drink," he said to the boy. "Mind if I get some water from the hose?"

Young Bill smiled, indicating that it was okay. Bill walked over to where the hose was coiled next to the house, turned on the water, and drank deeply. Then, with a grin on his face, he returned to the woodpile and continued swinging the axe.

About fifteen minutes later, they heard the sound of a truck pull up the driveway. Maggie was home.

She drove slowly toward the garage, but was surprised when she saw a stranger in the yard with her boy.

Who the hell is that? she thought, beginning to feel a bit anxious. The man had long hair he wore tied back in a ponytail, but some of it had pulled free and hung down obscuring his face. He had his shirt off and though his body was lean and angular, she could tell by the way he hefted the axe that it was all muscle.

When he heard the truck, the man turned and stared at her. He put down the axe and reached for his shirt. She watched him closely as she opened the door to get out. *There's something familiar about him, but I can't place it.*

Then he smiled.

Her mind reeled as recognition set in. *Oh my god, it's him!* Her heart began to pound violently as he walked slowly toward her. Feeling her knees go weak, she clung to the truck's door for support, willing herself not to faint. His smile grew as he neared her, lighting up his face and erasing the ten years since she had seen him last. She tried to let go of the door but began to fall in a swoon. Quickly, he closed the distance between them, putting his arms around her, giving her support.

"Hi, Mags," he said, laughing. "You act like you've seen a ghost."

She struggled to catch her breath. *Oh God, don't let me fall*, she thought as she tried to steady herself. She was suddenly conscious of her appearance - wearing old faded jeans torn at the knee and a plain denim workshirt. Her face was devoid of makeup except for a little lip gloss and her unruly red hair billowed around her face. She reached up and tried to tidy it a bit with one hand.

He pulled away from her and took a step back, his eyes slowly traveling up and down her body. "You look beautiful, Mags. You haven't changed one bit from when I last saw you. Remember?"

There was a twinkle in his eye and she recalled the last time they were together. It had been on that small island, Little Glooskap, a couple of days after he'd broken off their affair. She felt her face go red at the memory of the passion and violence of their lovemaking. He laughed again when he saw the blush creep into her cheeks.

"Did you know I was back?" he asked.

She nodded, struggling to find her voice. "Yes, I saw it on TV and Dex called, too."

At the mention of Dex's name, Maggie thought she saw a flash of anger in Bill's eyes. She began to say more, but was silenced when he reached out and touched her face with his fingertips, tracing a line along her cheekbone, across her lips, down under her chin, and finally resting his palm on her neck in a gentle caress. Shivers ran down her spine and she felt she might swoon again.

Get a grip, Maggie, she commanded herself, trying to stand on her own.

"Now Mags," he said, reaching for her hand. "Don't you think it's time you introduced me properly to my boy?"

A big smile broke out on her face and, for the first time, she felt steady. Nodding vigorously, she squeezed his hand. "Yes, Bill, yes. It's time you met my son."

He looked at her reproachfully. "*Your* son?"

She frowned, puzzled, then realized what he was asking of her. "No, that's wrong," she laughed. "Not my son, Bill - *our* son."

Bill grinned and put his arm around her. She rested her head on his shoulder and together they walked up the hill to where the boy stood waiting for them.

 THE BIRDS

WHILE BILL BECAME ACQUAINTED with his son, Karen and Dex were enjoying their day off the island. As soon as she'd stepped onto the mainland, Karen's mood visibly lightened and she and Dex spent the morning exploring shops and other attractions on the busy downtown wharf. At lunchtime, they found a small bistro overlooking the water and enjoyed a nice meal. Afterwards, they followed a series of paved jogging trails to one of the many municipal parks that ringed the city.

Leaving the path, they climbed up a grassy knoll where several other couples were having picnics or just admiring the view. The sun was hot and Dex laid his jacket on the ground and gestured for Karen to take a seat.

"I saw an ice cream vendor over yonder on the way up here," he said. "How about something sweet to top off that meal?"

"That would be just about perfect!" she replied, smiling up at him. "And make it really nasty - whipped cream, sprinkles - you know, the whole enchilada!"

Laughing, Dex bent down and kissed her lightly. "Your wish is my command. I'll be right back."

Karen watched him until he was out of sight. Leaning back on her elbows, she kicked off her shoes, closed her eyes, and tilted her face toward the sun, letting it warm her. There was a cool, soft breeze blowing her hair about her head and she felt invigorated, inhaling the fresh, salty air. After a few moments, she opened her eyes and looked around. She was now alone on the knoll. The few people who had been there before had disappeared. Puzzled, she began to get up but was overcome by a wave of dizziness. Putting her head between her knees to keep from passing out, she took several deep breaths until the vertigo passed. Then she looked up again.

The landscape around her was changing, everything suffused by a vague shimmering light. She felt herself begin to panic as the grass and open space around her began to fade and disappear. Suddenly, the warmth of the sun was gone, replaced by a cold dampness that caused her to shiver uncontrollably.

She squeezed her eyes tightly shut, hoping to shake off the hallucinogenic quality of the world around her. *Please, please, make it go away! Don't do this to me. Don't!*

Gingerly, she opened her eyes and gasped. Tall trees now stood all around her as she knelt in the dirt on an all-too-familiar trail leading deep into the woods. Slowly, she looked around, knowing that somehow she was back on Mateguas, on the path behind the house she had once lived in. But now it was different. Dark and twisting, the trail was shrouded in fog and seemed even more threatening than before.

Carefully she got to her feet, trying to get her bearings. She wrapped her arms around her body in an attempt to ward off the chill caused by the pervasive dampness of the heavy fog. Trying to locate the position of the sun, she gazed skyward, but all was dark and dismal. A cold breeze wafted over her and she shivered violently as the wind whispered eerily through the branches. Then she heard a rustling of wings in the canopy above.

Her fear now escalating, she made a conscious effort to control the pounding of her heart. *I've got to find my way out of here,* she thought desperately. *But which way? Which way is safe?*

Struggling with indecision, she turned her head left and right, trying to sense the way home. Again, she heard movement in the branches above and several leaves fell, landing on her shoulders. Unable to help herself, she looked up toward the sound.

A large owl was perched directly above her. A scream threatened to burst from her throat as she recognized it and she froze in place, unable to move. The creature, locking eyes with hers, began to stretch out its wings as a soft menacing hoot emanated from its chest.

Overwhelmed by sheer terror, Karen's first instinct was to run headlong into the woods - run anywhere to get away from the raptor - but she knew, deep down, that that would be a fatal mistake. She could not leave this path - if she did, she would be lost.

The owl began moving its wings again and, as it did, a murder of crows began shrieking in the forest all around her. Knowing that time was running out, she finally willed herself to make a decision. Slowly and purposefully, with one eye on the owl, she put her foot out on the path in front of her. She could feel the bird watching her intently, and she was sure it meant to dive-bomb her as soon as she began to run down the path. She leaned forward, hoping to give the impression that she was about to sprint, but when she heard the bird move above her, she pivoted sharply and began to run in the opposite direction.

The raptor, caught off-guard, lost precious seconds as Karen sprinted down the trail as fast as she could. The shrieking of the crows ceased and the wind evaporated as the forest became cloaked in deathly silence for several moments. Then the eerie stillness was pierced by a loud and angry screech from the owl as it began its pursuit in earnest.

Praying that she was headed in the right direction, Karen ran on. The crows once again began their horrible chorus as the owl gained on her. She turned a sharp corner and, seemingly from out of nowhere, a jagged rock appeared in the middle of the path. Unable to stop in time, she tripped over it, losing her balance. Screaming, she fell to the earth as the owl swooped down at her, its talons grazing her arm, opening up a vicious wound.

Trying to catch her breath, she watched her blood drip to the forest floor and she thought she could almost hear the earth sucking at it greedily, wanting more. The crows screamed in triumph, their loud caws deafening to her ears. She started to rise, but when she got to her knees, the flock of scavenger birds descended upon her, tangling in her hair and scratching at her face and torso.

Using her arms to protect her eyes, she fought her way to her feet and again began to run. Heart pounding in her chest, she rounded a bend and saw the end of the path in front of her, the trailhead marked by a strange, evil-looking bush. Powered by a strong burst of adrenalin, she sprinted toward the bush, unmindful of the wounds its thorny barbs might inflict. Throwing herself into its embrace, she pushed her way through and fell panting on the soft grass that lay beyond.

For several seconds she lay pressed to the earth, trying to catch her breath and calm the rapid beating of her heart. Then she looked up. She was back on the knoll, the waterfront spread out before her. The picnickers, who had disappeared, were now back as were the sun worshipers. Everything was peaceful and serene. There was no owl, no murder of crows, no trail - nothing to indicate the terror she had just experienced. Confused and unable to comprehend what had happened, she curled herself into a ball, hugging her knees to her chest, and retreated into herself, losing consciousness.

Dex, gone only about fifteen minutes, climbed the knoll, an ice cream in each hand. As he rounded the crest, he was surprised to see Karen curled up on the grass, her knees tucked tightly to her chest. Thinking she might be asleep, he walked silently toward her. As he approached, he became alarmed when he saw that her blouse was torn at the shoulder and that there was drying blood on her arm. He dropped the sundaes and knelt down in the grass beside her, whispering her name.

"Karen, it's me. What happened? Karen wake up."

He reached out and took her in his arms, noting that her hair was tangled and knotted and there were grass stains on her shirt. A strong sense of déjà vu washed over him as he remembered finding her in a similar state ten years before in the yard behind her house on Mateguas. But this time it was different. This time she actually *had* been attacked by something or someone, scratches on her face and arms giving testimony to that.

A soft moan escaped her lips as she opened her eyes. Not acknowledging him, she began to thrash about wildly as if trying to ward off something that was attacking her face.

Holding her tightly, he willed her to look at him, to focus on him, and when she realized who he was, her struggles ceased. Burying her face in his chest, she began to sob uncontrollably.

"Hush, now, Karen," he crooned. "I'm here. You're safe now. Hush."

Slowly, her sobbing abated and Dex began to examine her, trying to assess how badly she was hurt. When he saw the wound on her arm, he became alarmed.

"How did this happen, Karen? We have to get you to the hospital. It's going to need stitches."

"The owl, oh, Dex, the owl ... and the crows; they came at me, too." She gripped him tightly as a new round of tears began. "Why? Why are they doing this to me? I don't understand."

Wrapping his handkerchief around her torn arm, he again soothed her. When she relaxed, he pulled out his cell and dialed 911.

THE EMERGENCY ROOM

THE AMBULANCE ARRIVED AT the knoll about fifteen minutes after Dex called. Karen weakly protested, saying she was all right and didn't need any help, but Dex hushed her, telling her to relax. On the way to the hospital, he rode in the back holding her hand as the EMTs evaluated her.

When they arrived at the Emergency Room, Karen was whisked away to a cubicle while Dex was left to navigate the insurance paperwork. When he finished and located her, he was distressed to find her close to panic, her eyes darting around the room as if looking for something that meant to harm her. A young physician was attempting to examine her, but was having difficulty because of her demeanor.

"Mrs. Pierce, you will have to stay still," admonished the doctor. "I have to examine your wounds. If you don't settle down, we'll have to sedate you."

Dex introduced himself then sat down at Karen's side, trying to calm her. "Take deep breaths, princess," he instructed. "You're safe now. I'm here. Nothing is going to happen to you on my watch. That's it, breathe."

Observing that his patient was starting to relax in her husband's presence, the doctor continued with his examination. Looking at the jagged wound on her arm, he frowned. "Now you say an owl did this? Is that right, Mrs. Pierce?"

Karen nodded.

"The other scratches and cuts, you say they're made by crows?"

"Yes, crows. They were in my hair, pecking and scratching. I know it sounds crazy, but it did happen."

"I'm not doubting you, Mrs. Pierce," the doctor replied, calmly. "The wounds are consistent with those that could be made by a bird's feet and beak. And the damage to your forearm could certainly have been done by an owl's talon, but it is very unusual behavior for birds. You know, to attack a human that way. Sort of Hitchcockian, don't you think?"

He glanced at Dex, questioningly.

"If Karen says she was attacked by birds, then she was attacked by birds, doctor," he said adamantly. "Now it looks to me like her arm needs stitches; all the other wounds are superficial - just need to be cleaned up to prevent infection. Right?"

The doctor nodded to Dex. "Yes, you are correct. Now I'm going to need to work on the laceration on your arm, Mrs. Pierce. Do you need to be sedated? I can't have you jumping around while I'm working, you know."

Despite Dex's presence, Karen's anxiety had returned, her eyes flitting around the room and her body jerking spasmodically at any unexpected sound or movement.

"I think a light sedative might be in order, doctor," said Dex. "I'll okay it."

"But I don't want -," Karen cried. "I just want to go home."

"Now, princess, you know I'm right about this. Let the doctor give you a Valium or something and stitch up your arm. We'll be home before you know it."

She was silent for a moment, then sighed with resignation. "Okay. I'll cooperate. Knock me out, doctor."

BILL AND MAGGIE – ON MATEGUAS

BILL SPENT THE AFTERNOON at Maggie's getting to know his son. They were sitting inside the house talking when he received a text from his daughter.

"It's Terri. Wants to know if I'm going to meet up with them for dinner. Karen and her husband are still in town."

Maggie smiled. "Why don't you invite the two of them over here? I can call Dad and get us some lobsters and I've got the makings for a big salad. What do you say?"

"Sounds good to me. I'll text her back."

Later, after dinner, they were sitting in the living room talking when Terri's cell buzzed.

"It's Dex," she explained, getting up and walking to the dining room.

"Hi," she said. "You guys ever going to come back?"

There was silence on the line for a moment. "Terri, we're on the boat now. Your mom's had an accident. She's okay, but I need to get her home. Can you meet us at the wharf?"

"Sure, but what happened?"

"I'll explain everything later. Just be there."

Terri started to say something more but the line was dead. Worried, she walked back to her sister.

"Sophie, we have to go now. Dex and Mom are on their way home and we need to pick them up. Maggie, thank you so much for the dinner. It was great. And, Dad, can you find your way back to Pete's by yourself? Apparently, Mom's had some sort of accident and I think we'll be needed at home."

A look of concern passed over Bill's face. "Accident? What kind? Is she okay?"

"Dex says she is, but he sounds upset. I'll let you know later, okay?"

Bill nodded. Sophie said her goodbyes and the girls quickly left for the wharf.

COMING HOME

TERRI DROVE DIRECTLY TO the dock, not wanting to make her mother and Dex walk to the parking lot. As soon as the boat was tied up, Dex emerged, his arm wrapped protectively around Karen's shoulder. Quickly, he walked her to the car and got in the back.

"Thanks, girls," he said. "Let's get home."

Sophie turned in her seat as Terri drove away from the wharf. "Mom, what happened? Are you all right?"

Karen smiled briefly. "I'm okay, honey. Just a little zonked out from the medication they gave me. I'm not really hurt. It was more frightening than anything, actually."

"But what happened?"

Karen was about to explain when Dex cut her off.

"Let's just get home first, okay? I'll explain everything once we've gotten your mother to bed."

Karen looked up at him and smiled, them leaned her head on his shoulder and closed her eyes.

Sophie turned back around and glanced meaningfully at her twin as they drove silently home.

In no time they were back at Dex's old house, and he told the girls to wait for him in the living room as he ushered Karen upstairs.

"Now, let's get you out of those messy clothes and get you straight into bed," he instructed as he began to unbutton her shirt.

"No, no, I want to take a shower. My hair's all dirty and I need to wash," she protested, but he insisted that she wait until morning. Finally, too tired to fight him, she acquiesced to his wishes and slipped under the covers, closing her eyes. With the effects of the sedative from the hospital still working on her, it wasn't long until she was fast asleep. Convinced she was resting comfortably, Dex turned out the light and went downstairs to where the girls were waiting.

Pouring himself a drink, he sat down opposite them on the couch.

"Okay, there's a lot I have to tell you and it includes more than what happened today." He took a sip of his drink. "This all started ten years ago - back before your father went missing. You were too young then to understand and I thought it was all over with. But now, after what's happened today, I think you need to know."

Terri and Sophie looked at each other then back at Dex. "Go on," said Terri.

"Back then, your mom was having a rough time. As you know now, your dad was messing around with Maggie. I don't think your mom knew on a conscious level, but I do think somewhere deep inside she was aware of what was going on. But that knowledge was so hurtful to her, she couldn't admit it to herself. The result was an undue amount of stress and anxiety and all those hidden emotions translated for her into hallucinations or some kind of visions. She claimed she was being harassed by an owl and rabbits."

"What?" exclaimed Terri. "You've got to be kidding! Our mom? That doesn't sound like her at all."

"I know, I know. But it's the truth. She told me about it one day after she nearly drowned herself in the bathtub - an attempt at suicide. That's how serious all this was. Then, a few days later, I found her in your backyard, passed out. I thought she was having seizures so I took her to a doctor I knew for tests."

"And?" asked Sophie. "What was the result?"

"Everything came back negative, leaving us with only one possible cause - psychological disturbance."

He paused for a moment, sipping his drink. "But everything seemed to go away after your dad disappeared. No more owls or rabbits; no more visions."

"Does this have anything to do with that weird Wiccan thing she does once a month?" asked Terri. "You know, when she goes out at dawn and raises her arms to the sky and intones some prayers?"

Dex looked at his stepdaughter appraisingly. "You know about that?"

Both girls laughed. "We've known about it for a long time, Dex," explained Sophie. "I think I was about ten when I first saw her doing it. I asked her about it but she basically told me to mind my own business."

"Yeah," agreed Terri. "Same thing happened to me. MYOB! I told some friends at school about it and they said she was probably a white witch and that she was praying to the Goddess. There's a lot of that sort of hocus pocus going on back in California, you know. It's a real religion."

Dex got up and poured himself another scotch. "You may be right, but I believe the 'ritual' has its roots here in Mateguas and what happened to your dad. It all dates from then. She was getting herself involved in some of the old Indian legends that surround this place, delving into the history of the property and its former occupants. She was meeting with an old lady on the mainland, Madge Parker, who, I think, convinced her all that malarkey was real."

"Okay," said Terri. "But what happened today? She's all scratched up and her arm's in a sling. How did she get hurt and how bad is it?"

Dex sighed and went on to explain about the park and Karen's claim that an owl and crows attacked her.

"But you gotta understand, girls, she was sitting in a municipal park. There were people all around. None of them saw anything actually go after her. And there were no big trees nearby - no place for an owl or a bunch of crows to perch."

"So, what are you saying, Dex?" asked Sophie. "That it's like stigmata? Or, that she did it to herself?"

"I think the latter is a definite possibility. Maybe your dad's reappearance has brought back all that stuff from ten years ago and, in a way, she reliving everything again. In any case, I think we need to watch her carefully; make sure she doesn't do any more damage to herself. That doctor I told you about, the one she saw back then; he's still at the hospital here and I'm going to give him a call. Maybe he can recommend her to someone who can help."

Again, Terri and Sophie looked at each other. Then Terri turned back to Dex. "You think Mom's nuts? Is that what you're saying?"

Dex shook his head. "It's not a simple as that. Think about what I've told you, then come back to me and we'll discuss it further. Right now it's late and it's been a long day. I'm going to go up and check on your mom then go to bed. Think about what I've said."

Yawning, he kissed the twins goodnight, put his glass in the sink, and headed up the stairs to the loft.

Terri and Sophie stayed in the living room, trying to absorb and understand what Dex had told them, wondering if it was true that their mother was losing her mind.

BILL AND MAGGIE

AFTER THE BOY HAD been put to bed, Bill helped Maggie clean up the dinner dishes. When the last plate had been put in the drainer, he folded his towel and placed it on the rack.

"Guess it's time for me to hit the road, Mags," he said, walking over to the closet and grabbing his jacket. "Thanks for dinner. It was great."

Maggie stood quietly with her back to him. She seemed outwardly calm, but inside she felt like she was dying. Her heart was racing and she knew she could no longer keep up this "just friends" facade. Making a decision, she turned to look at him, desire and longing etched across her face.

"Don't go. Stay - stay here with me. Please." Her voice broke and a tear slipped down her cheek.

Bill stopped mid-stride, watching her, his face a mask.

"Please, stay. I ... I need you here. I don't know what I'll do if I lose you again."

Slowly, he moved toward her, a small smile playing on his

lips. Unable to stop herself, she closed the distance between them and threw her arms around him, pressing her body tightly to his.

"Hey, hey, Mags," he whispered. "Take it easy. What's the rush? I'm not going anywhere."

He pulled away from her and gazed into her eyes - eyes that were full of pleading and passion. With infinite patience, he put his hand under her chin, tilted her head back, and leaned down and kissed her softly.

Moaning, she parted her lips to allow him to probe her soft mouth with his tongue. Their kiss deepened and he began to move his hands delicately over her body, teasing her with his touch.

They played at this game for a time, their desire for one another escalating as each second passed. Moving his hands purposefully between her thighs, she cried out his name and he lifted her to him. His hands moved over her buttocks as he carried her, fingers probing the cleft between.

She wrapped her legs tightly around his waist as he moved to the dining room and set her down on the edge of the table. Sweeping the candles and centerpiece to the floor, he pushed her flat on the surface. He stood smiling down at her for a moment, then slowly and deliberately opened his jeans and released himself. Reaching under her skirt, he ripped off her panties and entered her roughly.

When she felt him inside, she began to cry out, but he covered her mouth with his hand. Looking at her intensely, he mouthed two words, "The boy," then silenced her again with a kiss. She raised her hips to meet his thrust as he slowly brought her to orgasm. When he felt the pulsing of her flesh against his, he could hold back no longer and he let himself go, once more spilling his seed within her.

Later, upstairs, Bill and Maggie lay in bed, both exhausted from another bout of lovemaking. After cleaning up the dining room from their first encounter, Bill grabbed a bottle of bourbon and they retired to her bedroom. There, they made love again, taking their time, exploring and tasting one another.

When they were sated, Maggie sat up and poured them each another shot of the liquor.

"Can I ask you something?" she said tentatively.

"Sure," he replied. "Shoot."

"Well, you were in that hospital an awful long time and I was wondering what you did ... I mean, how long has it been since you ..."

"Had sex? Is that what you're asking?"

There was a twinkle in his eye as if he were relishing her embarrassment. She took a deep breath. "Yeah, that's what I'm asking. I mean, eight years is a long time to be celibate."

Bill laughed. "I wasn't the only one in that hospital, you know. Yeah, for the first year, I was pretty damn sick; sex was the last thing on my mind. But, later, when I was well - sure, I got horny."

"So, what did you do about it? Did you do it with some of the female patients?"

Bill smiled at her. "There was one patient - a nice-looking woman. She was catatonic ... you know, you could move her limbs about at will, put her in any position you liked. That was a hoot!"

Maggie's eyes widened in shock. "You did that? You did it with her?"

Bill looked at her straight-faced for a minute, then burst out laughing. "Got ya!" he exclaimed. "No, of course I didn't. I'm just fooling with you. But there's a lot of other people in a hospital other than the patients - nurses, doctors, receptionists, secretaries, pharmaceutical reps - and there's nothing sexier to most of them than a man who can re-configure their computer or show them how to use their new smartphones. No, Maggie, I did not lack for female companionship at Bangor."

Maggie smiled. "You had me going there for a minute. Well, you won't lack for companionship here on Mateguas either, not if I have anything to say about it!"

Bill studied her for a minute, suddenly serious. "You know, Maggie, tomorrow I'm going over to see Karen."

For a moment, her eyes flashed with anger, then she looked down at her drink. "Why?" she asked. "She's got Dex now. Why do you still want her?"

Bill sighed. "I didn't say I wanted her. But she's been hurt and I do still care for her. You have to accept that she's a part of my life and always will be. Okay?"

Reluctantly, Maggie nodded, "I'll try."

Bill smiled then kissed her and lay back down on the pillows. "Let's get some sleep now, okay? We can talk about this some more tomorrow."

Maggie smiled, nodded and reached over to turn out the light. She laid her head on his chest and closed her eyes, feeling loved and content.

Later, as the moon shone brightly through the bedroom window, Maggie lay fast asleep, snoring softly. Bill, however, wasn't lying next to her. Instead, he stood naked at the window, fists clenched at his sides, his face hard and unyielding. He gazed silently at the night sky, alone with his thoughts, until finally, nodding to himself, he turned and walked back to the bed. Hesitating before getting in, he stared at Maggie's soft form. Then, smiling to himself, he pulled the covers back, got in, and put his arms around her.

Stirring when she felt his touch, Maggie pushed her body back into his, snuggling closely, a smile of happiness blossoming on her face.

KAREN AND BILL

KAREN WOKE UP, ROLLED over and checked the clock. It was four a.m. and her head was pounding. Carefully, she got out of bed, not wanting to wake Dex who was slumbering peacefully beside her. She padded down the stairs to the kitchen, downed a couple of ibuprofen and started a pot of coffee. Removing the sling the hospital had forced her to wear, she examined the laceration on her arm. As usual, like the wounds she inflicted upon herself monthly, the lesion was healing at an uncommon rate, as were the scratches and peck marks inflicted by the crows. As she waited for the coffee to perk, she thought about the experience in the park.

The owl got to me. That never happened before. And the crows ... they were always in the background, but now they can attack me, too. What does this mean?

The coffee pot beeped, breaking her train of thought. She poured herself a cup and walked over to the window. The moon was beginning its descent toward the horizon and she stared at it intently.

It's almost time again. Tomorrow it will be in its waning crescent phase and I'll have to make sacrifice. But will it be of any use? I was always protected in some way before, but now? And if I'm not protected, what about Dex and my girls? And, I have to worry about Bill, too? Something's changed and I need to find out what. But how?

She sat down in the chair by the window still watching the moon as if by doing so she could persuade it to give up its secrets. But the orb refused to cooperate. She sighed, took a sip her coffee, and closed her eyes. *The answers will come; they have to.*

She sat quietly for a time, not moving, deep in thought, until she was startled by a sound behind her.

"Mom, are you all right?"

Karen smiled. "Hi, Soph. What are you doing up so early? I hope I didn't wake you."

"I think I heard the coffee pot, but don't worry about it, and, more importantly, how are you this morning?"

"I'm good. Come sit with me. I'm sorry I was such a mess last night, but the medication they gave me at the hospital threw me for a loop. Did Dex tell you what happened?"

Sophie hesitated for a moment. "He told us a little. Why don't you tell me in your own words."

Karen cocked her head to the side, thinking for a minute. "Okay. We were in a park and I was sitting on the grass. Dex had gone to get ice cream. I was enjoying the sun when out of nowhere this owl, or some kind of raptor, swooped down out of the sky and raked my arm with its talons." As she said this, she held up her forearm for her daughter to see.

Sophie examined her mother's arm carefully, wondering what the big deal was - it didn't look bad enough to warrant the stitches or the visit to the ER.

"Okay, but where did it come from? The owl. Were you near the woods or someplace it might nest?"

Karen smiled. "No, honey, I wasn't. It just came out of the blue. I had been gazing at the sun and was a bit blinded. So, no, I didn't see it coming."

"What about the crows? Dex said there were crows, too."

Karen looked at her daughter closely. "He doesn't believe me, does he? He thinks I did all this to myself?"

Unable to meet her mother's gaze, Sophie looked down at her hands.

"Honey, I'm not going to get mad at you. Now, tell me exactly what Dex told you. Don't leave anything out."

Sophie finally looked up and, seeing only kindness in her mother's eyes, began to relate what Dex had told them the night before.

When she finished, Karen leaned back in her chair, nodding. "So, he thinks Bill's reappearance has triggered some emotional disturbance in me. Is that right?"

Sophie nodded. "Yes, that's what he told us."

Karen smiled. "Thanks for telling me. For the record, I didn't do these things to myself. It did happen, just as I told you. But Dex is a rational man and sometimes he can't see beyond the end of his nose. But don't you worry about that - I'll talk to him. Now, I think I could use another cup of coffee and maybe a Danish. What about you?"

At the house on the hill, Bill was also up early and, leaving Maggie in bed asleep, threw on his jeans and shirt and went downstairs to start a pot of coffee. Once it was brewed, he took a cup and walked outside, across the road, to the beach.

Sitting on a rock waiting for the sunrise, he was reminded of other times, years past, when he had done the same thing. Relishing these memories, he closed his eyes and let them wash over him.

Karen - it always comes down to her. She's the only one who can make me whole again.

Return to Mateguas Island

He thought about his life with her back in California before he lost his job, and how they were going to start over - try to recapture that magic - just before he went out into the storm. Picturing her in his mind's eye, he recalled the feel of her skin - so soft and warm - and how she always clung to him in the afterglow of lovemaking.

Then, a picture of her with Dex came flashing into his mind and his reverie was shattered. He took his cup and smashed it against the rock, spraying coffee on his shirt and jeans and slicing open his thumb. Ignoring the blood dripping to the sand at his feet, he stood up.

That damned fisherman. What does he have that she wants so? He's just a redneck with no sense of class. And where was he the night of that storm? Did he want her so badly that he would dump me on Puffin? Yes, I think he did. But what about her - was she a part of it? Did she want him that badly, too? No, I can't believe that. It had to be just him. But how do I prove it?

He pulled his handkerchief out of his pocket and wrapped it around his bloody thumb. Silently he stared at the horizon before him, his mind whirling in turmoil. Finally, taking a deep breath, he calmed himself, turned, and began the short walk back to the house, a frown etched on his face and a dangerous hint of steel in his eyes.

KAREN, DEX, AND BILL

WHEN DEX WOKE UP, he found the bed beside him empty. Wondering where Karen had gone, he tossed on his sweats and hurried downstairs where he was surprised to see Karen and her daughters laughing and enjoying some sweet rolls. He stopped in the doorway and watched them for a minute. Karen was no longer wearing a sling on her arm and her demeanor seemed calm and happy. This perplexed him. He had been sure that, given the state she was in the night before, she would still be agitated and upset. In anticipation of this, he held in his hand the bottle of sedatives the doctor had prescribed for her. Seeing her sitting with her daughters, obviously unperturbed, he quickly put the pills in his pocket before entering the room.

"Morning, all," he said with a smile as he walked over to Karen, leaned down, and planted a kiss on her cheek. "Glad to see you're feeling better. Let me take a look at that arm."

Karen dutifully held out her arm for examination.

Dex gazed at the wound and shook his head. "You heal so rapidly. Wish I knew your secret. If I did, I could bottle it, sell it, and we'd all be millionaires."

Karen laughed. "It's easy: clean living, plenty of fresh veggies, and red wine every night. No, seriously, I'm just blessed with an awesome immune system. Probably hereditary."

Dex laughed and walked to the kitchen and poured himself a cup of coffee. "Well, what's on the agenda today? Want to go clamming?"

Karen was about to respond when there was a sharp knock on the front door. She started to get up but Dex put his hand on her shoulder, stopping her. "I'll get it, " he said.

Opening the door, he was surprised to see Bill standing on the steps, a bouquet of wildflowers in his hand.

"Hey, Dex," he said with a smile. "How's Karen? Just came by to see if she's okay and if I can bum a ride to the wharf from one of my daughters. Mind if I come in?"

Dex nodded slowly. "Sure, Bill. Come on in."

Still smiling, Bill walked over to where Karen and their children sat. Proffering Karen the bouquet, he sat down in an empty chair next to hers. "Thought some posies might make you feel better, but you don't look like you need them. You look beautiful. What kind of accident was it anyway?"

Karen smiled, taking the flowers from him. "Thanks. Want some coffee?"

"Sure, I got time."

Karen got up and poured him a cup, then put the flowers in a vase. "I was attacked by a raptor of some sort - I thought it was an owl. Came swooping down and raked my arm with its talons. And then a bunch of crows got tangled in my hair, scratching and pecking. I know it sounds bizarre, but that's what happened."

Placing the cup in front of him, she sat down again. Bill stared at her, absorbing what she'd said. "Birds? Well, that's unusual."

He sat quietly for a moment, thinking about this, then began to laugh.

"What's so funny?" asked Dex, raising his voice. "She had to go to the ER for stitches. I don't see where there's anything to laugh about."

Karen put her hand on her husband's arm, attempting to calm him while Bill put his head down, trying to control himself. Wiping away tears of laughter, he looked back up at Karen.

"Sorry, I'm not laughing at what happened to you, Kar. It's just that what you said triggered a memory. Remember when we went to the Rialto to that Hitchcock festival? *'The Birds'* was one of the pictures we saw and it came back to me how later we joked about the blonde in it. Can't remember her name - it wasn't Grace Kelly, was it?"

Karen grinned, enjoying the memory, too. "No, it wasn't Grace Kelly ... It was Tippi someone. And, yes, I remember. We had fun that day."

Bill smiled at her. "Yeah - we had a good time." Becoming serious, he reached out and lightly touched her cheek where a remnant of one of the crow scratches was scabbed over. "Is this what one of the birds did to you?"

As he waited for her reply, he glanced up at Dex, who was obviously angry, a scowl on his face. Slowly removing his hand, Bill leaned back and sipped his coffee, pleased with the reaction he had elicited from his rival.

"Yes, that's one of the scratches. And my arm here," Karen replied, showing him her stitches.

He leaned forward and gently traced the wound with his fingertip. "It looks almost healed," he said, amazed. "That must have been pretty scary, an owl coming at you like that. I'm glad you're okay."

Dex, his anger escalating, walked behind Karen's chair and put his hands on her shoulders, glaring at Bill.

Getting the message, Bill smiled, patted Karen's arm, then turned to his daughters. "I've got to take the next boat back. I'm due at the Mission at ten. Can one of you give me a ride to the wharf? Oh, and I'm going to try to get in touch with Gerry. He's supposed to be back in the country by now."

Karen looked puzzled. "Gerry? Who's Gerry?"

Smiling, Bill turned his attention back to her. "You remember him - Gerry Davis from Omicron? He was the head of Research and Development there. We socialized with them - even had them out to the house."

A vivid memory of a toddler running toward the woods after a rabbit flashed through Karen's mind and she shuddered thinking about what might have happened to the boy if she hadn't been there. But outwardly, she remained calm.

"Yes, now I remember. You were going to move into his division. He called you?"

"Not exactly. He must have seen the segment on TV and called the station. They called Terri. But when I tried to get back to him, he was out of the country."

"Any idea what he wants?"

"Don't know. Maybe just to say 'hello.' But, hopefully, it's something more." Bill checked his watch. "Well, we'd better get going. Terri, Sophie, who's up to driving me?"

"We'll both go," replied Terri. "Afterwards, we can go to the beach. Just give us a minute to get ready."

Bill nodded and stood up. "Well, till next weekend then. Glad you're not badly hurt, Karen. I'll let you know what Gerry says. Good to see you again, Dex."

He leaned down and kissed Karen lightly on the cheek, enjoying the expression he saw pass across Dex's face. Then, he walked to the door to wait for his daughters.

THE KNIFE

LATE THAT EVENING AS the crescent moon shone brightly on the water, Karen, the bone knife in her hand, carefully made her way down the path to the beach. Her mind was still confused - was this sacrifice really necessary? And would it provide her family with protection? She didn't know, but was unwilling to take a chance and leave her family's safety up to fate.

Standing on the beach, she took a deep breath, faced eastward, and raised her arms to the sky. The moon, as if recognizing her, began to glow eerily, its light illuminating her slender form. She gazed at it intently for a moment and then she began to speak, *"Oh, Mateguas, Great Father of the Dead, hear my prayer ..."*

Dex rolled over, reaching for Karen, but she was not in bed beside him. Wondering where she had gone, he sat up and gazed around the dark room.

"Karen?"

He waited, but there was no response. Beginning to feel alarmed, he got out of bed, turned on the light, and checked the bathroom, but it was empty. Worried, he made a brief tour of the house, but she was nowhere to be found.

"Karen!" he called, hoping somehow he had missed her, but, again, he was met with only silence.

Walking to the window, he gazed out at the beach. The moon shone brightly on the sand and the rocks below. In its glow, he could see her standing at the water's edge. She was facing the sea, her arms upraised, a knife in her hand.

"Enough!" he cried angrily. "This stops now!"

Turning away from the window, he strode purposefully toward the door, yanking it open and letting it slam behind him on his way out.

Outside, Dex made his way down the beach unaware that his actions were being observed.

Unable to sleep, Terri had gone to the living room to read. She was interrupted by the sound of her mother rushing down the stairs and then out the back door to the beach. Curious, Terri moved to the window and peered out, wanting to see what her mother was up to. Shortly afterward, Dex came down the stairs, agitated, and, without thinking, Terri followed her instincts and hid in the shadows, watching as he gazed out the window looking for her mother.

Alarmed by his angry outburst, Terri pressed herself tightly against the wall, not wanting to be discovered. Silently, she watched as he rapidly made his way to the door and left the house.

Emerging from her hiding place, she returned to the window, curious to see what was going to happen between her stepfather and her mother.

Dex quickly navigated his way down the narrow path to the beach and walked toward Karen. Her back was to him and he could tell she was about to use the knife on herself in some sort of grisly sacrifice. Unable to stand seeing her hurt again, he roughly grabbed her shoulder.

"This stops now, Karen!" he commanded. "I won't let you hurt yourself again! Give me that knife."

Startled, she whirled to face him. "You have no business here. Leave me! Let me do what I have to do!"

Dex reached up and grabbed her wrist, trying to wrest the knife from her grasp, but she resisted. Silently they struggled in the moonlight, neither one willing to give in. Karen, determined to maintain control of the little bone knife, fought him with all she had, but in the end, he prevailed. Wincing in pain, she dropped the blade and it fell harmlessly to the sand by her feet.

Angry, she screamed at him and tried to claw his face with her fingernails. "You don't know what you've done! You've ruined everything - everything!"

Dex grabbed her wrists again, subduing her, and then lifted her in his arms. "This ends here, Karen. No more cutting. You need help and I'm going to make sure you get it."

With his words, all of the fight drained out of her. Exhausted, she let her body go limp as he carried her back to the house and upstairs to their bedroom.

Terri watched transfixed as her mother and stepfather confronted one another. She could tell they both were yelling, but was unable to make out the words. Watching intently as they fought on the beach, she gasped when she saw the bone knife fall from her mother's hand. Unable to take her eyes off the small blade now lying harmlessly in the sand, she was surprised when she heard the door open.

Shrinking back again into the shadows, she watched as Dex took her mother upstairs to their bedroom. When she was sure they couldn't hear her, she slipped quietly out of the living room to the backdoor and down the path to the beach. When she reached the sandy shore, she knelt down, searching. After a few minutes, she found what she was looking for - the small bone knife.

In the moonlight, it began to glow and she was mesmerized and surprised by its beauty. Slowly, she reached out and took the hilt in her hand. As soon as she touched it, the blade began to pulsate with light and the shaft became warm to her touch.

It's mine now, she thought.

Smiling, she carefully put it in her pocket. Then, with one last glance at the moon above, turned and went back to the house.

Inside her bedroom, she quietly wrapped the little knife in a clean handkerchief and hid it away under her mattress. Then, suddenly exhausted, she lay down and was instantly asleep.

 **BROKEN PROMISES**

THE NEXT MORNING, DEX was up early, leaving Karen asleep upstairs. Knowing that she would be angry with him for interfering with her bloodletting the night before, he thought he might soften the blow by making breakfast. He prepared an omelet and, while it was cooking, pulled out his cell and dialed the hospital in town. After asking to be connected to Dr. Joshua Rosen's office, he waited patiently as the call was put through.

"Hi," he said to the secretary who came on the line. "My name's Dex Pierce and I'm an old friend of Dr. Rosen's. I'm in town and am hoping you can have him give me a call. Tell him it's about my wife - he may remember her as Karen Andersen. She was a patient of his ten years ago. Here's my number."

The secretary promised to get the message to the doctor before the day was out and Dex thanked her, hung up, then returned to the stove to check on his eggs.

As he busied himself in the kitchen, Terri and Sophie emerged from their bedroom and joined him at the breakfast bar.

"Morning, girls," he said, pouring them each a cup of coffee. "I gotta warn you, there may be some fireworks around here this morning. Your mom and I had a bit of a set-to last night and I think she might still be angry."

"What happened, Dex?" asked Sophie. "Was it about the other day in the park?"

Dex sighed. "No, it was her ritual. She went outside late last night or early this morning to cut herself again. I'm sorry, but after what happened in town, I just couldn't let her do it. I have a call in for doctor I know here. She needs to see someone - someone who can get to the bottom of this self-destructiveness of hers."

As he spoke, Karen walked into the kitchen. Ignoring him, she poured herself a cup of coffee and left the room.

Dex watched her go, then turned to the girls. "Why don't you two go sit with her. I'll finish up here and bring breakfast in for you all."

Terri looked at Sophie, then nodded and left with her twin to find their mother. Karen was seated at the dining table, sipping her coffee, her expression unyielding.

"Are you okay, Mom?" asked Sophie as she sat down.

Karen bit her bottom lip, then smiled at her daughter. "I'm fine, but there are going to be some changes around here soon and I don't want either of you interfering. Understand? This is between Dex and me. If you feel the need to put your two cents in, don't. Okay?"

The girls nodded and sat quietly, waiting to see what was going to happen. In a few minutes, Dex strode in the room carrying a tray laden with eggs, bacon and toast. As he placed it in the middle of the table with a flourish, he turned to Karen.

"A small token of my regard, m'lady, in the hopes that you can forgive me for last night."

Karen glared at him silently for a minute, then stood up. "I want you GONE! You broke your promise and you knew what the consequences would be. GET YOUR THINGS AND GET OUT!"

Dex was shocked by the vehemence in her tone. "Karen, be reasonable. I only did it for your own good."

"I SAID GET OUT NOW! I WANT YOU GONE! You have no idea what harm you've done!"

Dex stared into her cold blue eyes, waiting for her to explain, but she said nothing. Terri and Sophie sat mute, astounded by their mother's anger and her pronouncement.

Finally, Dex nodded his head, turned and left the room.

As soon as he was out of sight, Karen sat back down and reached for a slice of bacon. Nibbling at it, she smiled and looked up at her daughters. "Now I know you're confused. But, it's necessary that he leave. I'm not going to explain to you why, so don't ask me. This is just the way things need to be, at least for a while. Okay?"

The girls nodded, surprised at the sudden change in their mother's mood.

A few minutes later, Dex returned to the dining room, his leather satchel in his hand. He stood silently by the table for a minute then looked at the girls.

"I'll be staying down by the boatyard, if you need me. It's the Houghton cottage. Just ask at the store for directions. You have my cell number."

Then he turned to face Karen. "You know I only did what needed to be done. You need help, Karen, and I just want to see that you get it. I love you and hope you'll come to your senses. But I'm not about to stay where I not wanted."

He waited for a moment, giving her a chance to respond, but she refused to look at him. Sighing, he nodded once to his stepdaughters, then turned and walked out the door.

CHARLIE

LATER THAT MORNING, KAREN and Sophie went on a hunt for sea glass down at Eagle Point. Terri, claiming a headache, remained at home. Once alone in the house, she retrieved the little bone knife from under her mattress, opened the handkerchief, and studied it. It looked strangely familiar, but she was unable to say why.

It looks like an Indian relic, she thought.

She sat staring at it, enthralled by its beauty. Finally, she tore her eyes away and wrapped it carefully again, putting it in her purse. She pulled out her laptop and did some research online and then, having found what she was looking for, printed out a map and wrote a hasty note that she tacked on the refrigerator.

Taking one of the bicycles that was stored in the garage, she made her way to the wharf in time to catch the noon ferry. In town, she followed her map until she came to an old two-story building about a mile from the downtown area. The sign outside read: **Native American Museum of Southern Maine.**

163

This is the place, she thought, opening the door. Once inside, she walked around through the exhibits, then approached the docent who was sitting at the front desk.

"Hi, I'm hoping I can get some help identifying an artifact I that I think could be Indian, maybe Abenaki."

The woman smiled indulgently. "Where did you find it?"

"On the beach at Mateguas," Terri replied, pulling the handkerchief from her purse. "It's a knife with carvings and I think it's made of some kind of bone."

Carefully, she unfolded the cloth, revealing the small blade.

The woman's eyes widened in surprise. "Hmmmm," she murmured. "I think you probably should speak with our antiquarian. I bet he'd like to see this."

She indicated for Terri to rewrap the knife as she picked up the phone. After speaking briefly, she directed Terri to a room in the back. "He's in there. You just go right on in. He's expecting you."

Terri thanked her, walked to the door, and lightly knocked.

"Come on in."

As she opened the door, an old man sitting at an antique roll-top desk, swiveled in his chair to greet her and motioned to her to take a seat across from him.

"I am called Mekwi Mikoa by The People," the man said, smiling at her, a twinkle in his eyes. "In your English this means Red Squirrel. But you may call me Charlie. Now how may I help you, young lady?"

Terri grinned, instantly feeling a connection with this man. "I have an artifact I found on the beach on Mateguas Island. It looks quite old and the woman at the front desk said you might be able to tell me something about it."

As she spoke, she pulled from her purse the handkerchief that concealed the bone knife. She laid it gently on the antiquarian's desk and slowly unwrapped it.

Lying on the white cloth, the little knife appeared quite ordinary and unassuming, but the man who called himself Charlie peered down at it intently, his face alight with wonder.

"You say you found this on the beach?" he asked, his tone full of disbelief.

Knowing that this was only a half-lie, Terri nodded. "Yes, I found it at low tide a couple of days ago."

Slowly, Charlie reached into his desk and took out a pair of latex gloves. Once he donned the gloves, he picked up the knife examining it closely in the light of a magnifying lamp on his desk.

Terri watched as he ran his fingers almost reverently over the symbols carved on the handle and then seemed to weigh it in his palm as if checking its balance. When he was finished, he placed it back down on the cloth, nodding solemnly.

"This is a sacred knife," he said softly, "and it is very, very old. Did you notice how it warms when you touch it?"

Terri nodded, surprised that he, too, felt the heat of the blade.

"And the symbols: do you see the moon, the thunderbolt, and the teardrop? These, child, are the symbols of Mateguas, God of the Dead, and they contain very powerful magic."

Terri looked at him questioningly. "Magic? What magic? What is it used for?"

The man smiled. "It is the magic of the first creator. But before we talk about magic, let me tell you a story. This tale I'm about to relate to you has been passed on from generation to generation and is at the center of my tribe's belief system."

The man got up, walked over to a table in the corner of the room, and poured himself a cup of coffee. "Can I get a cup for you, child?" he asked.

Terri shook her head and smiled as he sat back down, sipping the dark brew.

"Ah, that's good. Strong black coffee is an elixir of the gods, my dear."

He looked back down at the knife and then continued with his tale. "The Abenaki call the creator spirit, Tabaldak. This name means 'The Owner' and, out of the dust of his body, he created Glooskap and his twin brother, Malsumis. Glooskap was endowed with the power to create a good world but his brother had no such intention. No, Malsumis - whose totem was the wolf - was the destroyer."

Terri looked at him, puzzled. "The destroyer? How so?"

The old Indian smiled. "I'll give you an example. Wanting to give his human brethren a thing of beauty, Glooskap created the rose bush with its magnificent blossoms. But as soon as soon he gave this gift to The People, Malsumis adorned it with wicked thorns that would scratch and tear at the skin. Understand?"

Terri nodded.

The antiquarian again smiled. "And there was great rivalry between the brothers. Glooskap tried to bring peace and harmony to the world but Malsumis often perverted his brother's creations in an effort to cause pain and suffering.

"Into this mix, Tabaldak brought a third son, Mateguas, a younger brother to the two. At the time of his birth, his father gave him the gift of mysticism, and when he was grown, Mateguas became the very first shaman of The People - the one from whom all other shamans are descended.

"But Malsumis was always jealous of his brothers and one day dared Mateguas to demonstrate his mystical powers by flying off the top of a mountain. The taunts of his older brother emboldened the younger son and, foolishly, he leapt off a cliff only to fall to his death. Glooskap, grieving for his younger brother, proclaimed Mateguas to be 'God of the Dead', the ruler of the Underworld. From then on, Glooskap relied on Mateguas' knowledge of things beyond the grave to enrich the lives of his human adherents."

"But how does all this relate to the knife?"

"Patience, child, I'm getting there," he chuckled. "So Mateguas flourished as God of the Dead but he still hungered for a greater connection to the earth he had once walked. Thus, he demanded that The People provide him with an acolyte, a human woman. She was to be dedicated to his service at the time she approached her womanhood, her menses. No human man could ever know her and she would be mandated to live a solitary life as Mateguas' disciple and keeper of the sacred land and its secrets.

"The first such acolyte was commanded to make a knife out of the bone of the sacred moose and on that knife to carve the God's symbols - the crescent moon, the thunderbolt and the teardrop. With this knife, she was to make sacrifice each month, letting her blood soak into the earth thereby ensuring its fertility."

Terri stared down again at the little knife. "Is this that knife? Is that what you're telling me?"

"No, I don't think so. That knife was made centuries ago. It is by now long gone. This knife is a replica, perhaps carved when the first or second knife disintegrated with age. But it still holds great magic. Be very careful with it, child, as it is much sharper than it looks. And above all things, do not cut yourself with it!"

"Why? What would happen if I did?"

"Bloodletting with this sacred knife would bind you to Mateguas. You would become his servant; in effect, his wife."

Terri thought for a moment, picturing in her mind's eye her mother standing on the beach preparing to cut herself.

"And what would happen, say, for example, to a woman who cut herself regularly with this knife over a period of years?"

The old Indian looked at her with great interest. "I'm afraid she would be lost, her soul forever bound to the God of the Dead. And it might not stop there - he might try to take her earthly body, too."

He gazed at the knife once more then placed it back on the handkerchief and carefully re-wrapped it. Taking off his gloves, he handed the package back to Terri.

"I fear you are not being totally honest with me, child, about how you came to be in possession of this knife and how it is connected to you. But that may be as it should be. It is not for me to judge.

"I do not know what you plan on doing with this artifact, but please be careful and do not involve yourself in magic that you will be unable to control. This knife requires a person of great strength to wield it and it will spell doom to any other who tries to do so. Hide it; tuck it away someplace far from you so you will not be tempted. For, to be sure, it will try to lure you, to trick you into thinking it is benign. Don't be fooled, child."

Nodding, Terri held the wrapped knife in her hand, careful to grasp it by the hilt and not the blade when she placed it back in her purse.

"Thank you so much for your time, Charlie. You've been a great help to me. I hope you won't mind if I come back again so we can talk some more after I've had time to think about all you've said."

The old Indian smiled. "You are always welcome in my wigwam. And remember what I told you: be careful!"

Terri arrived back at the house just in time for dinner. Curious, Sophie and Karen questioned her about her day and the sudden trip to town, but Terri fielded the interrogation with ease.

Later, as she climbed into bed, she could swear she could feel warmth emanating from the little knife, which she had again hidden underneath her mattress. Curling her body around a pillow, she forced her mind to go blank and, finally, fell into a dreamless sleep.

ISLAND NEWS

BY WEDNESDAY, NEWS OF Dex and Karen's break-up was common knowledge on the island. Bill, however, was working on the mainland and unaware that anything had happened. Louise McKinney, assuming that this was a difficult time for Karen and wanting to help, called and invited her and the girls to a dinner/dance that was being held at the Hall that coming Friday. As usual, it was a benefit for one of the island charities and Karen accepted the invitation, volunteering to bring a dessert.

Terri's mind continued to be plagued by the little bone knife that was still hidden under her mattress. She found that whenever she was near it, she was overcome by a strong desire to touch it. She resisted this as best she could, remembering what Charlie had said about the blade's power. However, it was getting harder and harder to ignore the knife's pull.

On Thursday night, Bill called his daughters to let them know that he had connected with Gerry Davis. Gerry was now living in Boston, having left Omicron several years before to start his own consulting firm. He and his wife, Samantha, were divorced but she still lived in the Portland area with his son, Little Gerry, now a teenager.

The two men had a long conversation and, as Gerry was going to be in Maine to see his son over the weekend, made plans to get together Saturday night. Gerry, recently remarried, was bringing his new wife along and Bill, figuring Karen was out of the question, planned to bring Maggie but needed a babysitter for his son.

"So, Terri, think you and Sophie could stay with young Bill on Saturday? We'll be leaving around five and will be back on the ten o'clock boat."

Terri asked him to hang on a minute while she relayed his request to her twin, who smiled and nodded. "Sure, Dad, we'd be happy to. Can you pick us up? I don't want to leave Mom alone without a car."

Bill hesitated. "Alone? Where's Dex?"

Terri sighed. "He's not here. He and Mom had a fight and he moved out. He's staying at a cottage down by the boatyard. But I think it's only temporary - they'll get back together."

Bill's heart leapt. The fisherman was gone! "Yeah, sure, Terri," he replied, trying to keep the excitement out of his voice. "They'll get back together."

They talked a bit more, making the necessary plans for the weekend. After he hung up, Bill sat down on his bed, angry with himself.

Return to Mateguas Island

I should have taken a chance and called her. It would have been so perfect - Karen by my side at dinner. She would have impressed the hell out of Gerry's new wife. As it is, I'm stuck with Maggie - beautiful, yes; but classy, no. He sighed to himself. *Well, what's done is done. I'll take Maggie on Saturday, but that will be the last time. With Dex out of the picture, I'll have a chance to get Karen and my family back.*

Smiling to himself and full of confidence, he lay down on the bed and closed his eyes.

Late that night, Karen rolled over in bed. In a state of semi-consciousness, she reached across to the other pillow for the man who had shared her life for the past ten years. But his side was cold and empty. Waking up, she remembered that she had forced him to leave.

I should beg him to come back, she thought, sitting up. But then she recalled the struggle on the beach and how he had prevented her from doing what she had to do to protect her family. *No, I can't ask him back. I still may be able to keep my children safe. They are my blood. But could I save him?* She thought for a moment. *No, I don't think so. He would be so vulnerable, just like Bill was. It's better he's not with us for now.*

She stood up, running her fingers through the knots in her hair. *But I miss him so. Oh, God, why did we have to come back here?*

She walked into the bathroom and stood for a moment, staring at her reflection in the mirror. *And what about Bill? I know he wants me back. He's only with Maggie by default, probably because of the boy. But I can see the longing in his eyes when he's here. Is there any love left inside of me for him?*

She shook her head, the answers eluding her. Returning to her bed, she lay down and pulled the extra pillow to her chest, hugging it. *Maybe I'll see Dex at the dance tomorrow. I could talk to him and let him know that the door is open for him to come back when we leave this place.*

Nodding to herself, she closed her eyes and let her mind wander back to another event at the Hall she'd attended ten years before and the dance she'd shared with the man who was to become the love of her life.

THE DANCE

ON FRIDAY MORNING, KAREN instructed her daughters to go down to Eagle Point, where there were many wild blueberry bushes, and collect berries. She was making a pie for the dinner that evening and she told them not to come back until their bucket was full.

Around five o'clock, the Andersen women began getting ready for the evening ahead. The event was casual and Terri dressed in torn jeans and a silk gypsy blouse. Borrowing her mother's gold hoop earrings, she turned to her twin.

"How do I look?" she asked twirling around.

Sophie, who was dressed in a mid-calf-length skirt and matching top, eyed her sister carefully. "If you had a peg-leg or a parrot, you would be a dead ringer for Long John Silver. Maybe you should tuck a treasure map in your back pocket. That would probably attract all the local talent."

Terri stuck out her tongue at her sister. "Hey, I wouldn't mind meeting up with a younger version of Dex. I'm getting pretty tired of this 'all women society' we've been living in. I sure could use a little testosterone about now."

Sophie laughed. "Let's go see what Mom's wearing."

Karen, who was sipping a glass of wine in the living room, was dressed much like she had for that dance ten years before - jeans and a sweater adorned with her southwestern turquoise jewelry. She even French-braided her hair.

Hearing her daughters come into the room, she stood up. "Let me look at you," she said. "You both look great. How about me?"

"You're beautiful, Mom," replied Sophie. "I love your hair that way."

They arrived at the Hall at little after six. As expected, Karen was commandeered by the kitchen crew and gamely donned an apron to help. Terri and Sophie, hoping Dex would show for the dinner, were disappointed he wasn't in the dining room.

"Maybe he'll come later, for the dancing," suggested Sophie.

"I hope so. Somehow, we have to get them back together. I can tell already that Mom misses him, but her pride will probably keep her from apologizing."

"Yeah, you're right. Hey, there's Dad and Maggie. Let's go say hello."

The twins chatted with their father for a while but soon it was time to eat and they rejoined their mother and the McKinneys at the table.

After the meal was finished, they moved into the barroom, found a table, and chatted as the local band set up on the stage.

Terri half listened to the conversation, her attention diverted by the activity at the bar. A young man who looked to be in his early to mid-twenties was acting as bartender. He wasn't especially tall or handsome, but there was something intriguing about him. He had dark curly hair and a ready smile and seemed to be having a good time, laughing and joking with all the islanders queuing up for libations. She watched him for a while, waiting for the crowd to thin out, trying to ascertain what it was about him that she found so attractive.

"I'm going to get a drink. Mom, you want anything?"

Karen looked down at her wine glass, still half-full. "I think I'm okay for now. You go ahead, though."

"Sophie?"

"I'm good, too."

Terri smiled, stood up, and strode over to the bar, which was now deserted, the crowd having moved over to the dance floor.

The bartender was sitting on a stool reading a book and did not look up as she approached.

"Hey, cowboy, can a girl get a drink around here or are you just there for show?"

The boy put down his book and raised his head, an easy grin blossoming on his face. Standing up, he stretched then walked over to where she was leaning on the other side of the bar. "Now what can I get for you, sugar?"

Terri laughed. "Just a beer, please."

He pursed his lips and studied her for a minute. "Methinks you might not be over the legal limit. Drinking age here in Maine is twenty-one. Got some ID?"

Terri blushed. "No, I'm afraid I don't. I thought it was eighteen."

She turned to go but felt his hand on her arm stopping her. "Well, how about a ginger beer? You're old enough for that!"

Terri smiled and turned back to the bar. "What's a ginger beer? I've never had one before."

The young man laughed as he placed a cold, frosty bottle in front of her. "You're new around here, aren't you?"

Terri nodded, taking a sip.

"Good?"

"Yeah. It's good," she replied.

He studied her for a moment, then reached out for her hand. "Hey, let me see if I can tell your fortune."

When she nodded, he turned her hand over so it was palm-side up and began to lightly trace the lines with his fingers, all the while keeping his eyes locked on hers. His touch sent goose bumps running up her arm.

"Now, before I tell you the future, I think I need to know who it is I'm talking to."

"You can't get my name from my hand? You're not much of a fortuneteller. I think maybe you're just a charlatan."

"Aw, come on. Names are hard to tell from the creases in your palm. Give a guy a break."

Terri laughed. "Okay, I'll give on this one. I'm Terri - Terri Andersen. And you are?

"Shawn O'Dwyer," he responded, a frown on his face. "Andersen? I know that name."

He was quiet for a moment, thinking. Then he began to laugh. "Say, I know who you are. You're the Puffin Man's daughter."

"Jesus, The Puffin Man? Is that what everyone here calls him? I know they called him that on the broadcast, but I thought that was just for TV."

The young man smiled and nodded. "Yup, just like in that old kids' song, *The Muffin Man*. Is he your dad?"

Terri nodded, laughing. "Yeah. We used to live here years ago for a brief time. My dad got lost in the woods and was declared dead - drowned. His body was never found. We, my sister and I, actually came back here to try to find out more about happened to him and, voila, we find him alive. Crazy, huh?"

"Crazy good, you mean. You know I was there on Puffin eight years ago when they found him."

Terri leaned forward, suddenly serious. "You're kidding? You were? Tell me about it."

The boy laughed. "Sure. It was in late June. My brother was graduating from high school and he and a bunch of his buddies got it into their heads to go party down on Puffin. You know - no adults around to spoil the fun. He and I were pretty tight back then so he let me and my girlfriend tag along. I was fifteen.

"We took his boat. Told the folks we were going to the mainland. Just piled a bunch of kids aboard with a couple of coolers of beer, some bugs - that's lobsters to you - clams, a couple of ounces of weed, and some blankets. You know - all the fixins to have a regular lobster bake.

"We were all pretty high by the time we got there. Jason, my brother, got a big old bonfire going then we dug a pit and started cooking the lobsta' and all. Everyone was sitting around, drinking and smoking, just having a good ole time.

"I grabbed Marcy - my girlfriend - and dragged her off over by the ruins of the house. I was a bit of a horndog back then and was hoping I'd get finally get lucky with her."

Terri laughed. "Go on."

"Yeah, I was hot to trot. But she wasn't having any of it. She put me in my place and started walking back to the fire. She almost tripped over your old man. He was lying on the ground, half naked and skinny as a jaybird. When she saw him, she screamed bloody murder - thought he was dead.

"Jason came running when he heard her. Boone, one of Jason's pals, came too. He was on the volunteer fire department back then and knew CPR and all that shit. He said your dad was just barely alive.

"We Jerry-rigged a stretcher out of the blankets and moved him over to the fire for warmth while my brother went to the boat and called the Coast Guard. The rest of us got rid of the beer and weed and tried to clean up the empties, if you know what I mean. And that's about it. The rest of the story you probably already know."

Terri sighed. "Yes, we know all the main facts about his recovery and his time at the hospital. But his memory doesn't start until he woke up there. He has no recollection at all of Puffin or how he got there. "

"Well, he musta pissed someone off royally to have them go to all he trouble of dumping him way out there. How about another ginger beer? It's on me."

He turned and pulled another frosty bottle out of the cooler and placed it in front of Terri.

"You know, I could take you out there on Sunday, if you're interested."

"Out where? To Puffin?"

The young man nodded. "Ayup. I got some traps I want to set out that way."

"Traps?"

Shawn laughed. "Lobsters, girl. Boy, you are going to take some educating. You think I do this for a living? No way. I've got my own boat. I just bartend occasionally to help out my mom 'cause she's on the Hall Committee."

Terri laughed. "Will you have time to spare to go to Puffin? I mean, actually walk around there and all?"

"Can't do any haulin' on Sunday. So, we'll have the whole morning to go exploring and, maybe, this time when I'm there I will get lucky."

Terri shook her head, smiling. "Don't count on it, cowboy. But I'd love to go and see the place where Dad was abandoned. Get an idea of what he went through, you know. What time?"

"Now, this you may not like, but I've got to go when the tide's running. So, I'll pick you up at six-thirty. That way we'll be off by seven."

Terri frowned. "That is early, but I guess you're the captain. Six-thirty it is."

Shawn smiled. "Where you stayin?"

"At my stepdad's old place. Dex Pierce's."

"Oh yeah," he replied, grinning. "Your mom married the island legend. All the lobstermen talk about him. Best fisherman to ever come out of Mateguas. Maybe best in the whole region.

And a cocksman, too. All the ladies wept crocodile tears when he up and took off with your mom. Hear they've split, though."

Terri frowned.

Shawn reached out and took her hand. "Sorry, that was rude of me; but this is a gossipy place. Ain't no secrets here."

"That's okay," Terri said. "You're right, she and Dex are apart - for now."

"She going back with your dad? Heard he was shacked with the schoolmarm?"

Terri thought for a moment. "About my mom and Dex - I think it's just temporary. They'll get back together. They had a fight and my mother can hold a grudge for a while. But they love each other. And about my dad - yeah, he's staying at Maggie's when he's on the island. Don't know how long that's going to last though. I think it's more about the boy than her."

Shawn laughed. "Your family's just a regular *Days of Our Lives*, isn't it?"

He shook his head then leaned over so his face was just inches from hers. "I'll pick you up on Sunday at six-thirty sharp. Dress in layers - you can never be sure about the weather. I'll take care of lunch. You just bring your sweet self."

Terri was about to reply, but he silenced her with a kiss. Their lips lingered against one another for a minute, pressing softly, then he pulled away.

"It's about time for me to take a break. What say we step out on that dance floor?"

"Sure," Terri replied, smiling, as he came around the bar and took her hand.

Back at the table, Karen excused herself to go get some air. She knew that many of the unattached males congregated on the porch and she was hoping she would find Dex there. He had been absent at dinner, but she suspected he would show up once the music and dancing started.

She stood quietly by the steps, watching as some of the young people headed down the path to the beach. Suddenly, she heard male voices followed by raucous laughter coming from the far end of the porch beyond the wicker swing, but was unable to discern the actual words or identify the speakers. Another round of laughter followed and she thought she heard Dex's voice.

Slightly embarrassed and not wanting him to see her standing there alone, she stepped back into the shadows, still listening. *He seems to be having a good time*, she thought. *Of course he is - he's back in his element with all his friends and people he grew up with. How he must have missed this. Yet, he gave it all up for me. Do I have a right to try to take him away again?*

She heard the scraping of a chair being moved and saw a figure leave the group of men, walking her way. Pressing herself farther into the shadows, she watched as her husband entered the Hall. Not knowing what else to do, she waited another ten minutes, then followed him.

Inside, Dex spied Sophie sitting alone. "Hey, sweetheart. How about a dance?"

Sophie grinned. "Dex! I'd love to."

Smiling, he took her hand and led her out to the dance floor.

As he whirled her around, he caught sight of Karen, now standing just inside the entrance from the porch, watching them. To his eyes, she looked exactly as she had ten years before when they first met in this same Hall. Catching his eye, she smiled at him and, when the number was over, he sauntered over to where she stood.

"Hi," he said. "You look beautiful."

Karen blushed and stammered her thanks.

The band began to play a slow number and Dex held out his hand. "How about it, princess? Just one dance for old times' sake?"

Karen smiled shyly. "I think I'd like that."

They danced wordlessly, neither of them wanting to break the spell cast by the music and their movement together. But the song was over too soon and awkwardness again enveloped them.

"Well," said Karen finally. "I think it's about time we should be going. It was good to see you, Dex."

"It was good to see you, too, Karen. You know where I am. If you've a mind to, stop by. We could talk."

Not knowing what to say, she nodded and turned to go, but he stopped her with a hand on her arm.

"Anytime you're ready. Okay?"

Again, she nodded, smiled and walked back over to the table where Louise, Pete, and Sophie sat watching.

"Where's your sister?" Karen asked, reaching for her sweater and purse. "It's time to go."

Sophie nodded in the direction of the bar. "Over there. I think she's found a friend."

Karen turned to see Terri and the young man she had been dancing with in animated conversation by the bar.

"Well, go get her. I'm bushed."

Sophie obediently walked over to the bar and tapped her sister on the shoulder. "Hey, Ter. Mom says it's time to go. You ready?"

Terri frowned and was about to answer when Shawn interjected.

"I've got to get back to work anyway or my mom will ream me out for sure," he explained. "Sunday, six-thirty, sharp. Right?"

Terri smiled and nodded. Then she turned to her sister. "I'll be right there, sis. Just give me a minute. Okay?"

Sophie grinned and headed back to the table.

Terri turned back at Shawn. "Well, looks like I've got to go. See you Sunday, bright and early."

She looked up into his eyes, waiting. With a grin on his face, he reached out and pulled her to him. As their lips met, Terri was surprised by the sudden pounding of her heart and had to resist the urge to throw her arms around his neck and press her body tightly to his.

Feeling a similar response, Shawn pulled back and gazed longingly into her eyes.

"Till Sunday, then," he whispered hoarsely.

He squeezed her hand then made his way back behind the bar and began talking with some of the islanders who were waiting for drinks.

Pulling herself together, Terri walked back over to where her mother and sister sat waiting impatiently.

"Who was that young man?" asked her mother.

"Oh, just a guy. He's a lobsterman. He's going to take me out on his boat on Sunday. Take me to Puffin Island to see where Dad was abandoned."

Sophie leaned forward. "He's taking you to Puffin? I want to go, too. Can I come along?"

Terri laughed. "Sure. I planned to ask you anyway. What about you, Mom?"

Karen stood up, ready to leave. "I think I'll pass. One island is enough for me. Okay, let's get going. I'm feeling a bit exhausted."

As they gathered up their things and said their good-byes, Terri glanced back over to the bar. A heavy-set middle-aged woman with short gray hair was standing next to Shawn, obviously giving him an earful. When he saw Terri looking his way, he rolled his eyes and smiled. The woman caught his look and turned to stare at Terri for a moment, a frown on her face. Obviously irritated, she shook her head, looked back at Shawn and continued her harangue.

Bet that's his mom, Terri thought as she gave him one last smile and turned to join her family as they left the Hall.

MEMORIES AND MOONLIGHT

MUCH LATER, WHEN ALL was quiet inside the house, the moon snuck out from behind a cloud, shining brightly, its reflection sparkling off the water. Seaweed on the exposed rocks shimmered in its glow like a field of precious gems, dazzling to the naked eye. But Terri saw none of this.

She stood unaware on the sandy shore, the frigid seawater lapping at her bare feet. Unmindful of the cold, she wore only her sleep shirt and in her hand, she clenched the old bone knife that she had tucked away for safekeeping under her mattress. She and her twin had gone to bed shortly after returning home from the dance and she had fallen asleep easily. But sometime in the night, the knife had called to her and now, in a half-conscious state, she stood alone in the moonlight.

Slowly, with unseeing eyes, she moved the pointed edge of the knife toward the palm of her hand and, without hesitation, slashed savagely down with it. The blade cut deeply into her flesh, moving as if through softened butter. Blood welled up from the wound, dripping down her arm to the wet sand and rocks below. As it soaked into the ground, her mind was brought to a strange sense of wakefulness, visions of long ago rising up before her eyes.

She and her twin sitting on their beds in the L-shaped room at the house on Mateguas - Sophie playing with three cornhusk dolls while she saw herself pantomiming with an old bone knife.

As these memories resurfaced, she began to shiver violently. One after another they came back, skipping across the edge of her barely conscious mind. She saw herself as a little girl hunkered down in the L-shaped room's closet, discovering the hidden panel in the wall that held the ancient box. Reliving this moment, she almost smiled, but then the scene changed to her mother's ravaged face and bruised wrists and she felt her knees go weak as she sunk down to the sandy shore. Again, the memory faded and another took its place - this time it was of her father holding them close, saying over and over again that he would never leave them. She wanted to call to him and ask him why? Why had he broken his promise when another memory flashed vividly into her mind.

They were in the woods, she and Sophie, and her father was telling them to run - to run as fast as they could home to their mother.

Tears began to stream down her cheeks as a hideous image rose up before her now blind eyes and she remembered how she and her sister were held captive in the woods. The creature that had lured them there was female - tall and muscular, its naked body covered with damp, rotting moss. Snakes writhed between its thighs and a strong odor of decay emanated from its very pores. She wanted to cry out for help but, in an instant, the creature was gone and, again, she heard her father's gentle voice, urging her to run and telling her that he loved her.

As hard as she tried, she could not keep any one memory static in her mind for long. As soon as she began to focus, the scene changed and now ... now they *were* running through the woods, home to their mother, but unreasonably, they stopped on the path and turned back, not wanting to leave their father alone with that monster.

Seeing now through the eyes of her younger self, Terri's body began to jerk as if consumed by a seizure. So vivid, the memory seemed more real than the beach she now knelt on. Her eyes widened in horror when saw the creature, that unclean thing, open its mouth and somehow absorb him ... her beloved father ... stealing him away from her.

Unable to control the violent movement of her body, she let out a plaintive moan as the worst memory of all played at the corners of her mind, building to a crescendo of fear and pain. It was the sound of her father screaming.

Involuntarily, she cried out, her scream echoing his. At the same moment, her fear was so intense that she could not help herself; her bladder let go and warm urine ran down her thighs to mix with the cold seawater that was soaking her sleep shirt. Then her mind went blank.

It was almost dawn when she awoke. She was surprised to find herself lying in the sand, her shirt soaked with urine and cold saltwater. At first, she didn't know where she was. The beach seemed alien to her. She sat up and looked down at her hands. In one, she still clenched the little bone knife. The other was now covered with drying blood. As she stared at it, the memories from the night before came rushing back and she leaned over and retched quietly into the sand.

Afterwards, she sat still for a time, reliving the memories one by one. When she felt calm and in control, she stood up, her limbs crying out in protest from the night spent on the cold, damp beach.

I'm lucky the tide was going out, she thought. *I might have drowned otherwise.*

She turned and looked back at the house. All was dark and quiet. *Thank God, they're still asleep.*

She gazed again at the palm of her wounded hand. Amazingly, the savage cut she had inflicted upon herself was almost healed. *Sweet Jesus, that can't be,* she thought, her mind reeling. *It should still be open and bloody. I cut too deeply for it to heal so fast.*

Confused and frightened, she wrapped her arms around her body for warmth and quickly made her way back to the house. Once inside, she tiptoed to the bedroom she shared with her sister and stripped off her sodden sleep shirt. Being careful not to wake Sophie, she made her way to the bathroom, closed the door, and turned on the shower. As the water heated, she surveyed her appearance in the mirror, trying to brush the sand and drying salt from her hair and skin. *Christ, I'm a mess!* Shaking her head, she stepped into the shower letting the hot spray warm her. As the sensation of the water pounding on her weary body soothed her, she let her mind wander back to the memories that had consumed her on the beach. While some were still horrific to her, they now seemed like distant recollections of a time long ago instead of the violent reliving of the night before.

Her thoughts clarified as she stepped from the bath and wrapped her body in a soft terrycloth towel. *I have to find that box. I think it may be the key to everything that happened back then and to what's happening now. But what was inside? There were the dolls, the knife, of course, something in a jar - a powder I think, and the prayers in French. But there was something more.*

She stood staring at herself in the mirror, trying to remember. Then she smiled. *The parchment! Sophie and I never really studied it. It told a story in pictures. But what story? Maybe Charlie can decipher it. Yes, he'll know.*

She rubbed her body vigorously, still trying to erase the cold and fatigue that had possessed her. *That box - I bet it's still in its hiding place. I'll have to look for it tonight when I'm babysitting Billy.*

She nodded to herself, resolved. Then she dried her hair and opened the door that led to the bedroom.

When Terri came back into her room, Sophie was sitting up in bed. "You're up early," she said. "Do we have something to do this morning I forgot about?"

Terri forced a laugh, trying to sound natural. "No, sis. I just couldn't sleep. That's all. Too much going on, I guess."

Sophie yawned and lay back down, pulling the covers up over her head. "Well, in that case," she mumbled. "I think I'll go back to sleep, at least for a little while."

"I'll wake you when breakfast's ready," said Terri as she quickly picked up her soiled nightshirt and tossed it into the hamper. Then, with one eye on her sister, she reached over to the dresser to where she had left the bone knife. Careful to lift it by the hilt and not the blade, she wrapped it in a clean cloth and tucked it into her purse.

She was zipping the handbag shut when Sophie moaned, pushed the covers back, and sat up again. "I think sleep's a lost cause now," she said with a tinge of regret. "Listen, Ter. I'm worried about tonight."

Surprised, Terri looked up at her twin. "Why?"

"Well, if we both go to Dad's to sit Billy then Mom will be left alone, and with Dex gone, I'm concerned about her getting depressed."

Terri's heart leapt. *How perfect. Now I can be alone in the house to search for the box.*

"Did you hear what I just said?" Sophie asked impatiently.

Terri tried to suppress her excitement. "Yeah, I heard. I was just thinking. How about I go alone to watch Billy and you stay home with Mom? It isn't like Billy needs two sitters. And I don't want to let Dad down. You know he's counting on this meeting with his old boss."

"Yeah, I know. I think that'll work and we'll have both bases covered."

"Sounds like a plan. I'll sit Billy and you sit Mom!"

Both girls laughed. Then Terri became serious. "I wish to Christ she'd take Dex back. That was all so bizarre - her kicking him out. I know she misses him. I can see that look in her eyes when she thinks no one's watching."

Sophie stood up, heading for the bathroom. "Yeah, but she's not the only one who misses him. I miss him, too."

Terri nodded in agreement. "Okay, you take a shower and by the time you're done, I'll have breakfast ready. Or, at least, a cup of coffee!"

Sophie laughed as she turned on the hot water. "You're on! Only, I want the whole enchilada - eggs, toast and coffee!"

Terri smiled. "You'll get what you'll get! Now hurry up!"

Terri was surprised when she found her mother already up and sitting at the breakfast bar with a cup of coffee.

"Hi, Mom. Sleep well?"

"Yes, I did for a change. Took one of those pills the doctor at the ER prescribed. They make you sleep like the dead."

"Well, you needed it. It's been a rough week. Did you talk to Dex last night? I saw you two dancing."

Karen looked down into her coffee, not wanting her daughter to see the tears that sprang into her eyes at the mention of his name.

"No, but I know where he's staying. And I believe he's been going out fishing with Pete every day."

"I'm glad he's doing something he loves. But, Mom, don't you think you ought to reconsider? I mean, what could have been so bad you had to kick him out? I know you miss him."

Karen stiffened. "That's between Dex and me, Terri," she said flatly. "It's none of your business." She stood up, poured herself another cup of coffee, and abruptly changed the subject. "Now what are you girls up to today?"

Terri sighed. "I don't know. I'm sitting Billy tonight. Dad and Maggie are going to the mainland for dinner with Dad's old boss, Gerry. Sophie decided she wants to stay home."

"They're quite the little item now, aren't they, your father and Maggie? Hope that slut doesn't screw things up for him. She's not the classiest girl in town."

"Mom! Give it a rest! Can't you be a little more generous? Maggie's nice and what happened ten years ago is ancient history. You don't want Dad back, do you? Is that what all this is about?"

Karen looked sharply at her daughter. "No, I don't want him back. That's not going to happen. But I do want what's best for him. That girl, Maggie, she's trouble, plain and simple. No good will come from that relationship."

Karen turned her back, indicating to Terri that the conversation was over, and walked to the window looking out at the sea. "I think I'll do some sea glass hunting today. Maybe go over to the boatyard, look around, and then have lunch. You interested in tagging along?"

Terri thought for a moment as she began making breakfast. *I don't have anything pressing to do today. Maybe it would be good to spend some time with her. Maybe I can soften her up a bit, so she'll forgive Dex for whatever it was he did.*

"Sure, that sounds good, Mom. If it's a nice day, Soph and I can go swimming. I don't have to be at Maggie's till five."

BILL

HE STOOD ON THE beach, cell phone in hand, waiting for his call to connect. He stared intently out at the sea. *A bit rough today*, he thought. *Good thing we're taking the ferry tonight.*

His thoughts were interrupted when a voice came on the line. "Gerry Davis here."

"Hey, Ger, it's Bill."

"Hey, bro, good to hear your voice. You're not bailing on me tonight, are you?"

Bill laughed. "No chance. You're stuck with me. Just wanted to firm everything up."

"Yeah, okay. We'll meet you and your date at the terminal at five-thirty? That work for you? And who is this mystery date anyway? I assume it's not Karen."

Again Bill laughed. "No, it's not Karen, although she just split with her husband. Don't know if it's temporary or if it's the real thing. If it is, maybe next time I'll have her on my arm. But tonight, I'll be bringing this island chick that I've been keeping company with."

"Oh really? An islander? Sounds intriguing. Anything serious going on?"

"Come on, Ger - you know I'm trying to get back with my wife. No, Maggie's just this drop-dead gorgeous babe who's been helping me keep visions of Karen with that fisherman at bay. Thought she deserved a night on the town. Hope you don't mind?"

"No way, bro. Bring her along. When I lived in Maine, guys were always talking about the island girls and now I get to meet one in the flesh, so to speak."

The men laughed and talked shop for a while. Then Bill shut down his cell, put it in his pocket, and gazed at the sea in front of him, his mind on Karen and what it might take to get her back. Then he thought about Maggie. Yes, he'd keep her around for a while. But as soon as he was sure Karen was his again, that would be it. He wanted his family back and he wasn't going to let anything or anyone get in his way.

Feeling confident that everything he wanted would soon be within his grasp, he turned and sauntered back to the house.

BABYSITTING
AND THE BOX

AT FOUR-THIRTY, BILL ARRIVED to pick up his
daughter. He exchanged pleasantries with Karen and Sophie,
who were playing cards in the living room. Resisting the
impulse to just forget about the evening ahead of him and join
them, he hustled Terri out of the house and drove back to
Maggie's.

"Got a fire in the woodstove in the family room for you," he
said. "How do I look?"

He was dressed in chinos, a madras shirt, and beige sports
coat. His hair was neatly tied back in a ponytail.

"You look great, Dad. Where's Maggie?"

"Oh, you know women! She's still getting ready. Billy's
upstairs in his room. Why don't you go on up and say hello?"

Terri kissed him on the cheek, then bounded up the stairs.
When she reached the landing, Maggie walked out of the front
bedroom. She was wearing a short black sheath with matching
stiletto heels. Her abundant red hair, which she usually pulled

back haphazardly into a scrunchie, was carefully coifed. Her jewelry was understated and sophisticated.

She's dressed herself a lot like Mom would for this kind of evening, Terri thought as she took in Maggie's appearance.

"Well?" asked Maggie, acknowledging Terri's scrutiny.

"You look fantastic. You and Dad are going to really 'wow' them tonight."

"Thanks, honey. That means a lot to me. This is an important dinner for your dad and I don't want to screw it up for him. So, I'm going to try hard tonight not to be the 'island girl,' if you know what I mean."

Terri nodded. "Well, you look great. And don't worry, you'll do fine."

Maggie smiled at the compliment. "Billy's in his room playing some violent video game or something. See if you can get him focused on a more educational pursuit. Oh, and dinner's in the fridge. There's a pot of venison stew and some veggies. All you'll have to do is heat them up in the nuker."

"No problem," said Terri. "You and Dad have a great time."

"Thanks, sweetie. We're taking the ferry tonight - no punt for me in these heels. So, we'll be home on the last boat. That work for you?"

"Sure."

"And get Billy to bed by nine, okay? He'll try to play you into letting him stay up, but be firm."

Terri laughed. "I'll take care of it. You better get going now or Dad might leave without you."

Maggie smiled. "Fat chance - I've got the car keys. See ya later, kiddo."

Terri watched as her father's girlfriend descended the stairs, her hips swaying as she moved. *She sure is a piece of work! Hope things go well for them tonight. If she messes up, it might be the end for her and Dad.*

Turning away from the stairs, Terri knocked lightly on her half-brother's bedroom door. *This was our room once upon a time,* she thought. *Maybe after dinner I can get him occupied with the TV so I can slip back up here to look for the box. But first, I have to try to find that key ring - the one to the island car. It's been ten years and it might be long gone. If it is, I'll just have to force the box open.*

Her thoughts were interrupted when the boy came to the door, smiling shyly. "Have they gone?" he whispered.

Terri looked back down the stairs. "Yeah, I just heard the car. We're on our own. What do you want to do?"

"Grandpa gave me a new video game. Wanta play?"

Terri laughed. "Sure. Let's give it a whirl. Bet I beat the pants off of you!"

Later, before dinner, Terri broached the subject of the island car. "Hey, what ever happened to that old car that came with the house? You know, the Civic?"

Billy looked at her puzzled. "Why do you want to know about that?"

"Oh, just curious. It was our car, you know, when I was your age and we lived here."

Billy smiled. "That old heap's out behind the garage. Grandpa uses it for parts. Mom says it costs too much to haul it to the dump. It's kinda creepy - you wanna see it?"

Terri grinned. "Yeah, I like creepy! Let's go take a look."

Once outside, Billy led her around to the back of the garage where the old Civic, barely recognizable, sat perched on blocks, its tires long gone.

"Wow, it sure is a mess," she said as she walked around the rusted-out vehicle.

Peering inside, she noted that the key was not in the ignition. Glancing around the interior, she smiled when she recognized the old beaded bracelet that she and her sister had "borrowed" from their parents' dresser ten years before, now dangling from the rearview mirror. One key still hung from it. Knowing that this was what she was looking for, she sought to distract the boy and turned her head toward the woods.

"Hey, Billy, is that a deer?"

The boy turned to look and, in that instant, Terri grabbed the bracelet and tucked it in her pocket.

"I don't see anything," the boy said.

"Ah, it was just probably a shadow. Why don't we go back inside for dinner? I'm hungry."

After cleaning up the kitchen from dinner, Terri and Billy sat down in the family room to watch TV. Terri tuned the set to a program that she was sure would interest the young boy and when she could see he was wrapped up in the plot, excused herself to use the bathroom.

Leaving the room, she grabbed her tote and quickly ran up the stairs and into what once was her bedroom. Searching her memory, she ran her fingers across the floor and located the floorboard with the knothole that once contained one of the keys to the box. Pulling the compartment open, she smiled when she saw a small key lying in the interior. Putting that key in her pocket and replacing the board, she stood up and walked to the closet.

It looks just like I remember. The back wall is still lined with shelves.

Now, as she had done when she was a little girl, she knelt on the closet floor. Slowly and purposefully, she ran her hands along and between the shelves, trying to find the secret compartment that she hoped would hold the box. Not locating it easily, she sat back on her haunches and closed her eyes, trying hard to remember. *I was putting my shoes away - lining them up on the shelves.*

Mentally picturing her younger self, she reached out and ran her hand again along the closet wall, pressing lightly against the wood. Suddenly, she felt one of the boards give way. Opening her eyes, she pushed harder and, with some coaxing, a panel slid open.

She took a deep breath. *Oh, God, let it be here.* With hands shaking slightly, she reached inside the dark recess and pulled out the ancient box.

"Yuck!" she exclaimed, noting the box was covered with fresh mouse droppings and spider webs. Grabbing a T-shirt from one of the shelves, she quickly ran it over the ancient relic, and then wiped her hands on her jeans. Eager to get back downstairs, she reached again for the box, but stopped when she felt a sudden compulsion to run her bare fingertips over the symbols carved on the top. One by one, she traced them, the crescent moon, the thunderbolt, and the teardrop, her hands caressing each one reverently. As she continued to stroke the arcane artifact, she was unaware that her other hand was reaching into the tote, searching for the small knife that lay within.

Staring blindly at the box, she pulled the little bone knife from its resting place and raised it in the air. As she moved, the details of the closet began to grow vague and an ever-thickening fog obscured her vision. Heat, generated from within the blade, traveled up her arm as the knife began to pulsate and glow.

Suddenly her sight cleared and she was surprised to find she was no longer in the closet, but was outside, somewhere deep in the woods. Kneeling in the grass and dirt, she unthinkingly lifted the knife to the sky and her lips began to form the prayer - the prayer that she and her sister had tried so hard to translate ten years before.

"Oh Mateguas, great God of the Dead, hear my prayer..."

Slowly, as the words slipped from her mouth, she moved the blade of the knife purposefully toward her palm.

"Hey Terri! You're missing the best part!" the boy yelled from the bottom of the stairs. "What's keeping you?"

Terri shook violently when her name was called, breaking the spell cast by the knife. Pulling herself together, she was shocked to see she was holding the blade aloft, apparently ready to cut herself again. She took a deep breath and forced her arm down as she tossed the artifact into her tote, and stood up.

"I'm coming, Billy," she yelled. "I'll be right down."

Carefully, but quickly, she picked up the box, placed it in the bag along with the knife, and zipped it closed. Glad the blade was out of sight, she took another deep breath and, feeling relieved, left the room and headed downstairs to join her half-brother.

DINNER IN TOWN

BILL AND GERRY WERE sitting at the table, sipping brandy while the ladies freshened up. The dinner had been an unqualified success - Maggie, surprisingly, playing her role to perfection.

"So, Bill, what say you come down to Boston in a week or so. I'd like you to meet my team. I've got a sweet deal going on down there. You're going to love it."

Bill smiled. "I'd really like that, Ger. I don't want to be presumptuous, but are you thinking of bringing me on board?"

"There's nothing I wouldn't like better, but I've got to tell you, a lot will depend on what my folks in Boston think. I know you're still playing catch-up, but I'm impressed with how you've kept yourself current despite what you've gone through. And I think we make a good team. So, if you're willing to put yourself on the line with my people, we'll see if we can make something happen."

Bill took a deep breath. This was more than he expected. "Yes, I'm willing. No, I'm more than willing. And, thank you,

Gerry. Not many people would put their trust in anyone who's spent eight years in the State Hospital. Even if things don't work out, your belief in me means worlds."

Gerry held up his brandy snifter and clinked it against Bill's. "To the new old team. I think this is going to be great."

"Okay, what are you boys toasting to?" asked Gerry's wife as she and Maggie returned to the table.

"Just plans for the future, babe. I think Bill just might join us down in Boston."

Maggie beamed at Bill. "Oh, that's wonderful! I love Boston."

Bill gave her a hard stare. "We can't count our chickens yet, Mags. A lot can happen before any decisions are made. Let's just enjoy the evening, okay?"

Maggie, chastened, gave him a shaky smile and sat down at the table, her head bowed.

Bill smiled indulgently at her. "Okay," he said lifting his glass. "I think we have time for one more before we need to leave for the last ferry."

Gerry laughed, waving for the waitress. "You're on!"

Bill and Maggie didn't arrive home until close to eleven o'clock as the ferry was running late. They found Terri in the living room working on her laptop and Billy safely tucked away in bed. Bill dutifully drove his daughter home then returned to the house on the hill. Maggie was seated in the rocker, a glass of wine in her hand. She did not smile.

"I think that went well tonight, don't you?" Bill asked as he entered the room. "I'll probably be going down to Boston in the next week or so to meet Gerry's team. I'm going to have to work my ass off before then, though, to get current on things. I don't want to go there and end up looking like a fool."

Maggie just stared out the window, not acknowledging him.

"You okay?" he asked.

Slowly, she turned her head to face him. "What was that all about after dinner?"

"Huh? What are you talking about?"

"You know what I'm talking about: that *look*, the one you gave me when I said I loved Boston. Like I was dog shit. As if you'd never think of taking me with you."

Bill stared at her, surprised by her anger, then laughed. "Mags, you're over-reacting. I just didn't want you to get your heart set on it. It might not happen - in fact, it probably won't. Gerry has a hotshot team down there. You think they're going to jump at the chance to take the 'Puffin Man' on board? Gerry's just being kind. Maybe I'll get some kind of a job out of it, but it won't be big time in Boston."

Maggie's face softened, hearing the bitterness in his voice. She smiled sympathetically and reached out to him. "You'll convince them. I know they'll take you on. Just you wait and see. And it will be 'big-time Boston.' After all you've been through, the tide just has to turn in your direction."

Bill leaned down and kissed her softly on the cheek. "Thanks for believing in me. Well, I don't know about you, but I'm bushed. Think I'm going to hit the hay."

Maggie nodded. "You go on up. I'll be there in a few minutes - just want to finish my wine."

Bill nodded and headed up the stairs as Maggie turned back to gaze out the window at the night sky.

I love him, that's for sure, but do I trust him? Is he going to dump me as soon as he doesn't need me anymore? And what about Karen? What if she wants him back? She and Dex have split. Maybe that's all because of Bill. Would he go back to her?

Maggie sighed and downed the rest of her wine. *Well, I'll just have to make him stay with me. I can do it - I know I can. I just have to be on my guard - not get complacent. It'll be him and me in Boston one day. I'll make sure of that.*

Smiling to herself, she stood up and, leaving her empty glass on the side table, stretched, then turned and headed upstairs to join her lover in bed.

VOYAGE TO PUFFIN ISLAND

SIX-THIRTY IN THE MORNING came too soon for Terri and Sophie, but they gamely forced themselves to get up, determined to be ready when Shawn arrived. Karen also was up early, wanting to meet the young man who was taking her daughters out on his boat.

Shawn was prompt, pulling into the driveway at six-thirty sharp. The twins, dressed in jeans, sweatshirts, and slickers, answered the door together, their mother waiting in the background.

Nodding, Shawn grinned as he walked inside. "Take it your sister's coming along? How about Mom, she coming too?"

Terri laughed. "No, just my sister. Shawn, this is Sophie."

"Hi, Shawn. I hope you don't mind me tagging along, but I really want to see where Dad was marooned for so long. I promise not to act like a third wheel."

"Hey, no problemo. The more the merrier. I kinda figured something like this would happen. So, are you all ready to go? Gotta make the tide."

"We're ready, but I think our mom would like to meet you first."

Shawn grinned again, a sparkle in his eye. "Oh, so now I'm going to get the third degree? Have to pass inspection?"

Terri laughed. "No, just say hello and we'll be on our way."

Shawn winked at her as he walked over to where Karen was sitting at the dining room table, enjoying a cup of coffee.

"Shawn O'Dwyer, ma'am," he said offering his hand.

Karen smiled, shaking his hand. "Karen Pierce. Nice to meet you. Now, tell me briefly just how you're related to all the other folks on this island."

Shawn laughed and launched into an abbreviated family tree. Karen listened politely then nodded. "Okay, thank you. Now you take good care of my girls today, Shawn. I understand that some parts of Puffin may be hazardous because they're in ruin. I don't want to have to sic their stepfather on you. Got it?"

Trying to keep a straight face, Shawn nodded. "Yes, ma'am. You can be sure I'll take good care of them."

"Have them home in time for dinner. And, Shawn, you're welcome to join us, if you want."

"Thank you, ma'am. I think I might just take you up on that."

Karen nodded. "And one more thing - enough with the 'ma'am' business - my name is Karen. Feel free to use it."

"Thank you, m..., Karen, I will." he replied, smiling at her. Then he turned and looked at Terri. "Ready?"

"Yes, sir! Mom, we'll see you later. Have a good day."

The first couple of hours on the water were spent working and the girls got a good lesson in what a lobsterman's life was like. Since it was Sunday, Shawn was prohibited from hauling any of his traps, but he could set new ones. Terri gamely tried to help as he put off several new stringers while Sophie watched. It was chilly out on the water and Terri was glad she'd followed Shawn's instructions and dressed in layers. By ten o'clock, the sun began to warm them up and they were on their way to Puffin.

"That's it straight ahead," said Shawn, pointing to small island that had just come into view. "See where the manor house was? On top of that knoll. Not much left of it now."

"This was quite the place once, wasn't it?" asked Sophie.

"Yeah, playground of the rich and famous. But that's long gone now. Mother Nature has taken it all back."

He turned to Terri. "I'm going to cruise around the island first - let you get an idea of the size and all. Then we'll anchor and take the punt in to what's left of the dock. The piers are still there so we can tie up. Last I was here, you could still find a dry way to get to land, but that might have changed by now. Could be we'll get a little wet. You still want to go?"

Terri smiled. "Of course. A little seawater won't kill me - or my sister. Right, Sophie?"

"Sure," her twin replied a bit reluctantly, glancing down at the new pair of Adidas that she wore.

Shawn laughed. "Don't worry. If I have to, I'll carry you ashore. Okay, now see over there?" He pointed to what once was a structure off to the side of the ruins of the main house. "That's the place where your dad holed up."

"But there's nothing there that I can see," replied Terri, puzzled. "Maybe part of the foundation is left. But that's all. How could that have provided Dad with any kind of shelter?"

"You'll see when we get ashore. I'm going to take us in now. You girls ready to go exploring?"

Shawn anchored his boat and helped the girls into the small punt that was tied to the stern. He motored them into what once was a large elaborate dock now fallen into ruin. Luckily, it had been well made and enough still stood to give them a place to tie up to and get ashore without having to wade through the cold seawater.

Silently, the girls stood on the beach, gazing at the ruins of the house on the knoll above.

"I can't believe Dad spent almost two years here," said Sophie. "How did he ever survive?"

"I have to hand it to him," replied Shawn. "He must be a pretty wily character. Knows a lot more about living in the wild than most city boys. Come on, let's go on up to the house. I'll show you where we found him."

They made their way up what once was a road or driveway to where the ruins of the manor house stood. Shawn pointed out the spot where his girlfriend had practically stumbled over Bill's emaciated body. Then he carefully led them through the underbrush to what appeared to be the remains of the foundation of a smaller outbuilding.

"Figure this must have been the servants' quarters," explained Shawn. "When we was here eight years ago, still was a stone wall standing. Looks like Mother Nature's taken it back now."

"Is this the place you showed us from the water?" asked Terri. "Where you said our dad holed up?"

"Yup, this is it."

"But where?" asked Sophie. "There's no cover at all here."

Shawn laughed. "Come over here and lookee see."

He gestured to what once was the far corner of the building, away from the manor house. "This was the kitchen. And here...." He pointed down to what looked like a heavy wooden trapdoor set in the stone floor.

"What is that?" asked Terri, kneeling down.

There was a metal ring in the middle of the heavy oak door and Shawn knelt beside Terri and pulled on it. It took some doing and some muscle, but finally the door opened. The hinges having rusted away, Shawn was able to pull the oak slab off and push it aside, revealing a hole in the foundation large enough for a man to fit in.

"It's a root cellar," said Shawn. "Your old man found this place and this is where he rode out the worst of the winter." He pulled a flashlight out of the backpack he'd brought from the boat and shone it down into the hole.

"A few days after we found your dad, I came back out here with my brother and we scouted around the place. Back then there were still stairs going down to the cellar, though they were pretty rotten. My brother put a rope around me in case I fell and I went down there. Nice and cozy. Could see where your dad made a bed and stored firewood to keep it dry. Lots of clam and mussel shells down there - that's probably what he subsisted on for the most part. Yeah, I'd say he was a pretty wily guy."

"But he was half-dead when you found him, wasn't he?" asked Sophie. "Doesn't sound any too swift to me."

Shawn smiled and turned to her. "We had a bad winter that year. And, most likely, since he was eating them all, the clams were disappearing and mussels were scarce, as well. Come on, I'll show you the rest of the place."

They spent another hour or so walking around the island, getting a feel for the place their father had been marooned on for almost two years. When it was lunchtime, they returned to Shawn's boat.

"You guys hungry?" he asked as he pulled a cooler out from a compartment in the wheelhouse. "I liberated a couple of lobsta' rolls from the stash my mom made for the Ladies' Aid luncheon."

Opening the cooler, he handed a sandwich each to Terri and Sophie, then pulled out one for himself.

"How'd you know to bring three?" asked Terri, curious since she had not informed him that Sophie would be joining them.

Shawn smiled at her, his eyes dancing with mischief. "Figured you would be a might nervous coming out alone with a handsome bloke like me. I expected either your sister or your mother would tag along. Now, how about something to drink to go along with that roll?"

As he spoke, he pulled a six-pack of beer from the cooler and handed one to each of the girls. They sat quietly eating for a while, enjoying the food and the warm sunshine.

When she was finished, Terri leaned back and looked at Shawn.

"What was it like for Maggie when the islanders found out she was pregnant? Couldn't have been too pleasant."

Shawn thought for a minute. "No, it wasn't. You gotta understand, her dad - Rusty Maguire - he's got a temper. My mom said she was sporting a black eye and split lip right around the time your dad got lost."

Sophie looked up incredulous. "Her dad beat her?"

"Not beat - just popped her a good one. Like I said, he's got a temper and Maggie, well, she was always a wild one. At least that's what my mom says. Hung out with the summer crowd against her parents' wishes. Mom says that when she was a teenager, it wasn't unusual for her to show up at school with a bruise or two. Rumor was that Emma threatened to leave him over it, so Rusty had to keep his temper in check. Then, there's what he said about your dad."

Terri leaned forward. "What did he say?"

Shawn took a deep breath. "Well, this comes from my mom. She said she heard that Rusty told some of the guys that it was a good thing your dad drowned 'cause if he hadn't, he was going to come after him with his twelve-gauge and finish the job himself."

Terri's eyes widened in surprise. "Do you think he might have had something to do with my dad's disappearance?"

Shawn shook his head. "No, Rusty's an islander. He wouldn't do anything so sneaky as to hijack your dad to Puffin. He's a man, and to defend his daughter's reputation, he would have confronted him face to face."

Terri nodded.

"Well, it's about time we should be heading back," said Shawn, gathering up the remains of their lunch and putting the trash in the cooler. "You all just relax and enjoy the ride."

KAREN AND DEX

AROUND TEN IN THE morning, Karen took the car and drove in the direction of the boatyard. Once there, she parked and walked to the little store where a teenager was sitting by the register reading. She looked up when Karen came in.

"Can I help you with anything, ma'am?"

Karen smiled. "Yes, I'm looking for the Houghton cottage. I understand it's nearby."

The teenager grinned. "Oh, you must be Mrs. Pierce."

When Karen nodded, she continued. "The cottage is just down the road on the right. It's the little blue house with the white shutters. Has a cutout of a lobster nailed to the side. You can't miss it."

Karen began to thank her and turned to leave when the girl stopped her. "But Dex isn't home right now. He's out fishing with Jim Taylor."

"Jim Taylor? Who's he?" Karen asked.

"Oh, he's one of the summer people. Owns that big white house down on Eagle Point. He has an awesome boat. They went out early this morning. Should be back in soon with their catch."

Karen sighed and looked at her watch. "Well, maybe I'll have a little lunch and wait for him."

Smiling at the clerk, she picked out a sandwich and an iced tea, paid, and walked outside to sit at one of the little picnic tables beside the store.

It's just like ten years ago, she thought. *Here I am sitting at this table, waiting for him - hoping he'll come along to save me.*

Alone with her memories, she opened her sandwich and took a bite. She wasn't really hungry, but eating would help pass the time. She was about halfway done when she noticed a yacht coming in to the dock. It was, she guessed, a fifty or so footer and it gleamed in the early afternoon sun. She recognized Dex immediately as he off-loaded two coolers from the boat. Carrying one of them to a black truck parked nearby, he noticed her sitting at the table and walked over.

"Hey, princess, what you doin' down here?"

Karen grinned. "Actually, I came to see you. Thought I'd take you up on that talk you offered."

"Okay," he said, a big smile breaking out on his face. He dug into his pocket, pulled out a key, and handed it to her.

"Here's the key to the cottage. You know where it is?" When she nodded, he continued. "You go on up there and let yourself in. There's white wine in the fridge and a bottle of red on the counter. Make yourself comfortable. I'll probably be about a half an hour. That work for you?"

"That'll be fine. Good day fishing?"

"Yeah, it was a real treat to be out on that yacht. Jim's a good guy. I'll have to help him fillet everything tonight. Gotta get back to work now. I'll see you in about thirty."

He gazed at her for a moment, then turned and strode away. Glancing down at the key in her hand, Karen picked up the remains of her lunch and tossed them in the trash barrel that sat beside the store.

She found the cottage easily and let herself inside. Walking into the living room, she was pleasantly surprised at what she saw. The room was tastefully decorated, Maine Cottage style. Hardwood floors gleamed in the sunlight and braided rugs in shades of cornflower blue and pale yellow adorned them.

We should have had a place like this, she thought. *With a place like this, I wouldn't have minded half so much being on this God-forsaken island.*

She gave herself a tour of the cottage, delighting in its ambiance. When she was done, she walked outside onto a deck that was furnished with two Adirondack chairs with a small table in between. The view was spectacular, looking out over the rocky shore below.

Smiling, she went back inside, poured herself a glass of white wine, and took it out to the deck to wait for Dex.

Why didn't we ever get a place of our own? The beach house in Monterey, well, that was mine. And the house here - that was his. We should have had our own place. Someplace special that we could have called 'ours'. Maybe if we'd done that long ago, we wouldn't be in this situation now.

Her thoughts were interrupted by the sound of the front door opening.

"Karen, you here?" called Dex as he walked inside.

"I'm out on the porch," she replied, turning in her chair to greet him.

He was standing in the doorway, the smell of fish strong on his body. "Listen," he said. "I'm going to grab a quick shower. I know I stink pretty bad right now. You just stay where you are; I won't be long."

"No problem," she replied. "I'm enjoying the view."

Smiling, he nodded and went back inside the house.

About twenty minutes later he reappeared, wearing clean jeans and a T-shirt, drying his hair with a towel.

"Let me get you a refill, princess," he said.

A few minutes later, he was back with the bottle of white wine and a glass for himself. He refilled her glass and sat down in the chair beside her. "Okay, you wanted to talk. Well, I'm here and I'm listening."

Karen took a deep breath. This was not going to be easy. "First, I need to apologize. I should never have spoken to you that way, especially not in front of the girls. I hope you can find it in your heart to forgive me."

She paused, waiting.

"That's water under the bridge, now. You were upset. Sometimes things like that happen. But, if you need me to, I'll forgive you. Now, go on."

Karen nodded. "Okay. I want to try to clear the air, but you have to understand, there are things I can't tell you or explain to you. Things that happened ten years ago - promises I made - vows I took. It's not black and white, Dex. Everything's a murky shade of gray, and I don't know if you can understand that."

"Are we getting into all that old Indian legend hooey, again? You're an intelligent woman, Karen. What happened to make you buy into all that old crap? I think you need help, can't you see that?"

Karen sat still for a minute, staring at the rocks below. How was she going to convince him that she wasn't crazy?

"I know you think I did all those things to myself - the cut on my arm, the scratches. But I didn't. It happened. Maybe not exactly as I told you, but it happened. An owl and a bunch of crows attacked me. I *didn't* do it to myself. And the thing I do every month on the beach, well, I can't explain that to you, but it is necessary. Your interference ... well, I don't know what the consequences will be, but there will be fallout from it."

"Princess, just listen to what you're saying. What consequences? So you didn't maim yourself; I think that's a good thing and if I had to do it all over again, I'd still stop you."

211

She leaned over toward him, speaking softly and calmly. "I know I sound crazy, but I'm not. Didn't you ever wonder why with all the cutting, my hand is still just fine? No infirmity at all. Look at my palm. Where are the scars? There aren't any, are there? Just that one little one in the middle. And what does that look like to you? Tell me."

She held her hand out for his examination. He stared at her palm for a minute, using his finger to trace the small sickle-shaped scar that sat like a bad omen in the middle. Then he looked back up at her.

"Okay, you got me there. It looks like the moon - like the moon that hangs in the sky every time you cut yourself. Are you trying to tell me that it was put there by some kind of magic? That some old Abenaki gods have marked you? Karen, be reasonable. I admit, I don't know why you heal so rapidly and so completely, but there's gotta be a rational explanation for it. Not some sort of mystical malarkey. No, Karen, I'm not buying it."

He sipped his wine, waiting for her response. Again, she gazed at the rocks below, her mind trying to find a way, any way, to make him understand.

"What if I agreed to see someone - a shrink, a counselor, or someone? Would that satisfy you? I'll do it if that's what it takes."

"You'd do that? And I could come home?"

She looked at him, biting her lower lip. "Yes, I'd do that, but I think that as long as we're on this island, we should stay apart. We can see each other, yes, but not live together. Please understand, I need time. And, maybe, when all this is over and we go home, we can start again. The girls will be off to college and it will just be us, Dex. We've never been really alone. I was thinking ... maybe it's time we got a place of our own - someplace new where we can rebuild our lives."

Staring into her eyes, he reached out and took her hand, leaned down and gently kissed her palm. "Okay, you need your space. I can give you that. And about a place of our own - I'd like that. Yeah, that could be good. Just give me the go ahead to contact Josh at the hospital and set you up with someone to talk to. Is that okay?"

Karen nodded, smiling. "Yes, you set it up. Now, how about just a teensy bit more wine?"

Dex laughed, stood up, and poured them each another glass, emptying the bottle. "I love you, princess," he said. "And I don't want to lose you."

She smiled up at him. "You won't. There's nothing on this earth I wouldn't do to keep you with me. I love you, too. We'll get through this, you'll see."

She stood up and reached for him. In response, he put his arms around her, pulling her close. They embraced silently, each wanting nothing more than for this moment to go on forever.

However, as they clung to each other, hopeful for their future together, the sea below began to churn - cold, salty spray shooting into the air. And somewhere within the dark forest, an owl sat perched high in the branches above them, watching and waiting.

 ## DINNER WITH KAREN

"HOW ABOUT YOU COME with me to a lobster bake on Saturday?" asked Shawn as he helped Terri out of his truck back at the house. "A bunch of the island kids are going to be there."

Terri smiled. "I think I'd like that, now that you've proved yourself to be trustworthy."

Shawn laughed, putting his arm around her. "Okay, girl. Saturday night it is. Now, did your mother really mean it? You know, about inviting me to dinner tonight?"

"She wouldn't have asked if she didn't. She's a pretty straightforward person."

Grinning, Shawn nodded. "Okay, I'll be there. What time do I show?"

"Try six, six-thirty. And be on your best behavior or Mom might decide to lock me in my room on Saturday."

At six sharp, Shawn was at the door with a small bouquet of wildflowers for Karen. Smiling warmly at him, she escorted him into the house, where he was surprised to find another guest.

"Shawn, this is my husband, Dex. He's joining us for dinner, too."

Dex stood up and offered his hand. "So, this is the young man who shanghaied my daughters this afternoon. Lucky for you, they seem to be none the worse for wear."

Shawn blushed and stammered a greeting, obviously in awe of meeting one of the island's local legends in the flesh.

After dinner, Shawn thanked Karen and shook hands again with Dex, then grabbed his windbreaker and prepared to leave.

"I'm going to walk Shawn out," said Terri as she joined her young man at the door. They held hands as they walked slowly to his truck, which sat at the end of the driveway. Standing by the driver's side door, Shawn turned to her before getting in.

"Hope I didn't make a fool of myself jabbering on like that about my boat and all."

Terri smiled and leaned forward on her tiptoes and kissed him softly. "No, you didn't. You were great."

Responding to her, he put his hands on her waist, leaned in, and kissed her gently, then turned his head and whispered in her ear. "Saturday, girl. You, me, and a couple of lobsters. Okay?"

"You're on," she replied, reluctantly pulling away from him.

He gave her one last quick kiss then jumped into his truck and, smiling, backed out of the driveway.

Inside, Dex was alone in the kitchen with Karen, helping with the cleanup. Tired from the long day, Sophie had excused herself and gone to bed. When the last dish was safely tucked away in the dishwasher, Karen turned and smiled at him.

"Thanks for coming tonight. I think the girls really enjoyed it."

"I hope they weren't the only ones," he replied, staring at her with longing in his eyes.

Karen paused for a moment, her gaze shifting down to her hands, not sure how to reply. Finally, she looked up at him.

"No, they weren't. I enjoyed it, too. I've missed talking to you and just being with you. And what did you think about Terri's young man? Should I be worried?"

Dex laughed. "He seems like a good kid. He's about the same age I was when I started my fishing business. I liked him and Terri's got a level head on her shoulders. No reason I can see for either of us to be worried."

Karen nodded as they walked from the kitchen. Standing in the entryway, Dex reached for her, wrapping his arms around her and pulling her close. Unable to help herself, Karen melted into his embrace, relishing the feel of his strong body so close to hers. They clung to each other for a moment, then she pulled away.

"I wish you could stay," she said sadly. "But I just don't think it'll work right now. Please try to be patient with me."

Dex sighed, frowning. "I'm trying to understand, Karen. Really I am. But you remember your promise. I'm going to call Josh tomorrow and find someone for you to talk to. That's still okay?"

Karen nodded. "I said I'd do it and I will. Mind you, I don't think there's anything wrong with me. But, for your peace of mind, I'll do it."

Dex reached into the hall closet for his jacket. "Okay. I'll call you when I have it set up. And thanks for inviting me tonight. It was good to be with my family again."

As he opened the door to leave, he leaned down and kissed her chastely on the cheek and then, with a sad smile, left the house.

Karen stood staring blindly at the door for a few moments, then moved to the windows and looked out at the night sky.

If only things were different, she thought. *If we hadn't left home, we'd still be together. But I can't keep him close now. There's too much danger and he's better off far away from me.*

Sighing, she turned from the sea and headed upstairs to her empty bed.

THE KNIFE

AFTER SAYING GOODNIGHT TO her mother, Terri, exhausted, slipped under the covers. Closing her eyes, she thought about Shawn and how she felt such a connection to him. She smiled to herself, looking forward to Saturday and the chance to be alone with him. Then her thoughts turned to the box, secreted in the tote under her bed. She decided to call Charlie in the morning, hoping he could help her make sense of it.

Rolling over on her side, she hugged her pillow and willed sleep to come. But something she couldn't place was nagging at the corners of her mind, causing her to toss and turn restlessly.

As she struggled with insomnia, she felt a dull aching sensation begin at her temples. At the same time, an eerie tingling began to spread across her abdomen and, without warning, a vision of the little bone knife exploded in her mind. Head now pounding with excruciating pain, she gasped for breath. Suddenly, she felt a strong sense of vertigo and squeezed her eyes tightly shut as a wave of nausea overcame her. When she opened her eyes again, she was shocked to find her perspective radically changed. It was as if her conscious mind had been ripped from her physical being and was now suspended somewhere above the empty shell of her body lying on the bed below.

She watched in horror as the bone knife materialized out of nowhere, its blade hovering over her body as if suspended from the night sky, glowing hotly. It stayed motionless for a moment, and then down it moved between her breasts, its molten tip leaving a crimson trail of blood behind. It lingered momentarily above her stomach, the intense heat searing her tender skin. Feeling impotent, she saw herself try to cry out but somehow her voice had been rendered mute.

The blade circled above her once, twice, then continued on its journey down her body and settled in the cleft between her thighs. Slowly and sensuously, the little knife began to pulsate, moving back and forth against her soft skin. No longer was the warmth or sharpness of the blade painful to her, and she watched as her body arched to meet it as it moved. Aroused, despite her fear, she saw her hips begin to circle involuntarily in time with the blade's erotic beat. As the pulsation intensified, the sensuous heat coming from the knife became almost unbearable and she watched her hand move purposefully down to her mound.

Her mind, overcome by terror, watched helplessly as her fingers, now alien to her, began to probe and stroke in time with the rhythm created by the knife. A soft moan escaped her lips as she saw herself give in to the sensation that was enveloping her. Again, her hand responded, moving with greater urgency and she knew that, soon, the heat generated by the knife would somehow devour her.

Suddenly and violently, without warning, her perspective changed again and she found herself back in bed, her body consumed by desire. Above her, the little knife glowed hotly, its heat merging and becoming one with her mind. She bit her bottom lip fiercely to keep from screaming as the sensation intensified, blotting out everything else. Then, as if consumed by a fiery light, she found herself writhing in a silent and mind-blowing orgasm.

Then as swiftly as the image of the knife had appeared in her mind, it was gone and she was left tangled in her bedclothes, drenched in sweat, her head aching horribly. Feeling as if all the warmth of her body had been stolen, she shivered violently and staggered into the bathroom. She stripped off her soaked nightshirt and dried her body with a towel, rubbing it vigorously trying to bring back some warmth. When she no longer felt the cold, she stared at her reflection in the mirror. Her lip was swollen and bloody where she had bitten it and dark circles stained the delicate skin beneath her eyes. Gently, she tended to her cut lip, then splashed some water on her face, downed three aspirin to quell her headache, and returned to bed.

Resisting the strong temptation to remove the knife from the tote, she pulled the covers up to her chin and curled her body into fetal position. Again, hugging the pillow, she willed her mind to go blank and soon fell into a dreamless sleep.

CHARLIE AND THE BOX

ALARMED BY WHAT HAD happened to her during the
night, Terri knew she had to talk to someone. Her mother
would have been her first choice, but Karen was always so
guarded and secretive about everything to do with Mateguas,
Terri decided to seek help elsewhere. She phoned the **Native
American Indian Museum** first thing Monday morning and
made an appointment to see Charlie on Tuesday. Worried that
the episode with the knife might repeat itself, she moved her
tote to the back of the closet, farther away from where she
slept.

On Tuesday, telling Karen and her sister that she wanted to
do some mainland exploring by herself, she biked down to the
wharf and, with the tote in hand, boarded the ten o'clock ferry.
Once in town, she made her way to the museum for her
appointment with Charlie.

The old Indian greeted her warmly, again offering her a cup
of strong black coffee, which this time, she accepted.

They sat without speaking for a moment, then Terri launched into the events and thoughts that had been plaguing her since she'd found the knife on the beach. The memories the small blade had awakened tumbled out of her mouth like so many grains of sand, one after another in random order.

Seeing the panic in her eyes, Charlie reached out and took her hand in his. "Slow down, child. Take a deep breath and remember, most stories are best started at the beginning."

Feeling the warmth of his large hand holding her smaller one, she nodded and took several breaths, trying to slow her heart rate. Calmed, she began again, this time telling her story chronologically, starting with the trance on the beach and the memories that had surfaced - memories of that night ten years before, when her father was lost.

"I know what I saw, Charlie. That thing, that monster, she ate him - somehow absorbed him. I saw it! How can he still be alive?"

Charlie nodded and took a sip of his coffee. "Remember, your memories are those of a small child - a very frightened child - and are probably prone to exaggeration."

Terri nodded. "Yes, but, still...."

"Hush, now. Let me explain. For I have studied the lore of the Mskagwdemos and I believe I know what it was you actually saw."

Terri nodded again. "Okay, tell me."

The old Indian smiled. "Contrary to many local legends, the Mskagwdemos is not a flesh eater. No, child, she forbears the flesh of her victims for her appetite is much more heinous. It is not the blood and bones she desires. No, it is the human soul she craves." He paused for moment, letting his words be absorbed by the confused young woman who sat before him.

"The soul? She wanted my dad's soul? Are you telling me she's a soul-sucker?"

Charlie laughed. "A soul-sucker. Ah, you modern young people have such a way with words. Yes, what you saw was her eating, not his flesh, but his soul - or part of it. You see, it is the human soul that she longs and hungers for since she lost hers so long ago."

Terri sat quietly for a moment, digesting this. "But what about the other disappearances? If she just takes the souls, why weren't any of those other people ever found?"

"Ah, child, don't you see? Without the soul, the body cannot sustain itself; it quickly withers and dies. And once that happens, the Great Mother takes back what was once hers to begin with and the remaining husk becomes a part of the earth and the cycle is complete."

"But my dad - he's still alive. Are you saying he has no soul?"

Charlie smiled. "No, I would guess that only a part of his soul was consumed. This may be because the Mskagwdemos took pity on him for the sacrifice he willingly made to save you and your mother. Or perhaps, she just wasn't very hungry and only ate a little, that part that contained his memory, saving the rest for later. However, your father wandered off and I fear may have stumbled into some human mayhem."

"Human mayhem? I don't understand."

"Think, child. Somehow, he got to Puffin Island, and that would not be the doing of the Mskagwdemos. No, some human who may have wished him harm, found him wandering and by some means coerced him into a boat then motored him there. Once on the island, he was apparently left for dead - to die of starvation and exposure to the elements. But your father survived and, through his strong and abiding love for you, regained his memory."

"Makes sense. But, did he regain the part of his soul that she took, too?"

The old Indian sat still, staring at his hands for a moment, thinking. Then, he looked deeply into Terri's eyes. "I'm sorry, of that I do not know. Only your father will know that."

They sat for a time just sipping their coffee as Terri mulled this over. "Okay," she finally said. "I think I'm beginning to understand."

Charlie smiled. "Good. Now, how about some more coffee?"

When she nodded, he stood up and slowly walked over to the table in the back and picked up the pot. After pouring another cup for himself and for Terri, he returned and sat back down, handing the cup to her.

"Now, I believe you have something else to tell me."

"Yes, I do," Terri answered, as she pulled the ancient box from her tote and handed it to him. "I found this at our old house. It's the box that my sister and I discovered in our closet ten years ago. The one the knife was in, before my mother took it with us to California."

Putting on his glasses and pulling out his latex gloves, Charlie examined the exterior of the box carefully before opening it.

"This is very old," he mused. "I'd say it dates from sometime in the nineteenth century."

Nodding, he slowly opened it up and gazed at its contents with obvious reverence. "Come to the table with me," he said standing up. "So we can get a better look at these relics."

He took the box over to a large table that stood against the wall. The table was empty except for two lamps, equipped with magnifiers that were situated at either end. Charlie turned on the full-spectrum lighting of the lamps then took a large, very clean white cloth out of the table's drawer and spread it on top. In the middle of the cloth, he placed the box.

The knife lay on top of the other artifacts and Charlie carefully removed it and placed it on the far corner of the white cloth. Then he removed the cornhusk dolls.

Examining them closely, he laid them next to the knife. "These are also very old," he said, turning to Terri. "But they look like they've been handled quite a bit. Do you know how?"

"Yes," she acknowledged apologetically. "When we were kids, my sister liked to play with them. I, well, you know, I liked to play with the knife."

Smiling, Charlie nodded. "These figures represent the concept of family and familial bonds which extend beyond the nuclear to the family of all mankind. This acknowledgement of the relationship between man, his fellow man, and nature is inherent in the belief system of The People, the Abenaki."

Reaching back into the box, he extracted the little bottle of blood powder. Placing it under one of the lamps, he examined it closely using the magnifier. "This bottle has been opened," he stated. "Did you and your sister play with this, too?"

Terri shook her head vehemently. "No. We thought it was yucky. It was sealed last time I saw it. Someone else opened it, but not us."

Charlie removed the stopper from the bottle and poured a small amount of the powder it contained onto the white cloth. "Blood powder," he whispered. "I have heard of it, but I never thought I'd actually live to see it."

"What is it?"

Charlie sighed. "Powerful magic. It is made from the blood of the sacred moose, much like the knife is made from the same animal's bone. Most likely, the powder and knife came from the same creature - this would give them both even more power."

"But what can the powder do? I mean what kind of power does it have?"

"This talc can render a human person invincible, child. It can form a barrier around a person ... keep them safe from all the elements and render them immune to the forces of the natural world. It is very strong magic and, like all strong magic, can only be controlled by someone ordained to do so by the gods."

Carefully, he returned the loose powder to the bottle, put the stopper back in, and placed it to the side along with the knife and dolls. He then replaced the soiled cloth with a clean one and spread it out on the table before returning his attention to the remaining objects in the box.

Satisfied that no dust or dirt would sully the relics, he removed an envelope from the box. Taking out the papers it held, he examined them briefly, then placed them next to the dolls. "These writings are not old, but the prayer cited in one of them, is. Who do you think it was that wrote down this prayer? Do you know?"

"I think it may have been Lisbeth Boucher. She lived in the house before we did and I think I heard someone say once that she was part Abenaki. She was from Quebec."

Charlie nodded. "That makes sense. Many of The People moved to Canada when they were forced from their homes by the whites. It could be that her ancestor was an acolyte of Mateguas and, therefore, knew all the ancient rituals. Yes, it makes sense."

"But what is it a prayer for, Charlie? I remember it a little, but not much."

"It is the prayer to be made to Mateguas, God of the Dead, and it has the power to save a family from the Mskagwdemos. It is meant to be recited by the Mother, as she is the only member of the family who is immune to the lure of the hag. Could it be that your mother said such a prayer? That it was she who wielded the knife and used the blood powder as protection? Tell me, child. Tell me the truth."

Terri hesitated and then nodded. "I don't know for sure, but I think she did. Something happened when we were in the woods that freed my sister and I from the spell that hag put on us. Something that allowed us to run with our dad. I think that it was Mom. I remember her hand being bandaged and bloody after Dad got lost. Then, suddenly it was all healed."

Charlie smiled at her. "The Mother is the protector of her little ones. Knowing you were being lured to your death by the Mskagwdemos, she recited the prayer and gave sacrifice by cutting herself. Mateguas, acknowledging her bravery and strength, healed her wounds."

Once again peering into the box, Charlie removed the last item - the parchment. Slowly he untied the blood-red ribbon and unrolled it onto the white cloth. He secured the corners with special weights then bent down and began examining it, using the magnifiers attached to the lamps. He was silent, taking his time, trying to interpret the artifact. Terri sat patiently at his side, waiting. Finally, he raised his head and turned to her.

"This is the most important relic in the box and is older than all the rest combined. It is the 'source' and it is crucial that it be interpreted correctly. I could tell you what I think it means, but if I am mistaken, I could send you on the wrong path - a path that could lead to your destruction and that of your family. I am sad to tell you that you are in great danger - that your family is in danger - and I must be certain that what I tell you is the truth. Do you understand?"

Terri sat silently for a minute, hearing the anguish in the old man's voice. "Yes, I understand. But how can I find out for sure what it says, if you won't tell me?"

The old Indian nodded. "Our tribe has a shaman, Harry Three Feathers. He is much more learned than I am about the portents and omens that are displayed in this parchment. With your permission, I would like to show this to him. He is old - much older than me - and is in a nursing home not far from here. I could go see him on my day off, Wednesday, if you allow it."

Again, Terri nodded. "Okay. If you think he can interpret it."

"If anyone can, he can," answered Charlie as he re-rolled the parchment and tied it again with the ribbon. "And be assured, I will take good care of it. No harm will befall this document while it is in my possession."

Terri smiled at the old man. "I know it's safe with you, Charlie."

"Thank you for your trust," he replied, smiling.

He leaned down and opened a drawer, pulling out a white cloth bag, into which he carefully placed the parchment. He returned the other relics to the box and handed it back to Terri. He placed the bag containing the parchment in his briefcase, which stood beside his desk.

Standing up, he opened his arms to Terri. With tears in her eyes, she gladly embraced this man who had shown her so much kindness.

When they separated, he looked down at her, his eyes full of compassion. "And remember, child, don't let that knife lure you. It will become your undoing if you do. Perhaps it and the other contents of that box should be returned to their rightful owner."

Terri looked at him, puzzled. "Rightful owner? Who would that be?"

"Why your mother, of course. She has wielded them, harnessed their power. Who else would they belong to? Think about it. You will see that this is the only solution."

Terri's eyes widened in shock. "My mother? But you said ..." She hesitated before finishing her sentence, thinking back to their first meeting. "You said whoever used that knife would be lost. And my mom, she's used it over and over again. Why would I give it back to her?"

Charlie looked with sympathy and compassion at the young woman who stood before him. "Yes, she is lost. She has unwittingly surrendered her soul and now belongs to Mateguas. But, you must understand, there is a trade-off. In exchange, she has been given great power and only she can safely wield the contents of this box. What her fate will ultimately be, I cannot say now. Perhaps, after I speak with Harry Three Feathers, I will have a better idea."

Nodding, Terri embraced him once more, then picked up the box and returned it to her tote. "You'll call me after you see Harry Three Feathers?"

"Yes, as soon as I am clear on the interpretation of the document, I will be in contact."

"Okay - I'll give the box to my mom and I'll tell her what you said about being lost. Maybe she'll understand."

The old Indian smiled and walked Terri to the door. "Be careful, child. You were never meant to touch that relic and, by doing so, you may have altered the course of this story. Be wary, for there are evil portents in the air and they will seek to harm you. Stay strong within yourself. Do not doubt, and you will triumph over them."

Again, Terri, not really comprehending what he was saying, nodded and smiled at him. Then she walked out the door.

 KAREN

WITH TERRI IN TOWN and Sophie, a bit miffed at her sister's defection, holed up in her room reading, Karen found herself at loose ends. Again, she was drawn to the beach, scouring the sand in vain for a sign of the little bone knife.

After searching for about an hour, frustrated, she sat down on a rock and gazed at the horizon, hoping to find answers to the questions rolling around in her mind. She calmly watched the sea for a time, then looked down at the palm of her hand. The little crescent moon scar seemed to pulsate, growing warm and then cool, as if trying to tell her something. She gently traced the scar with her finger, hoping to soothe it.

I could cut you with a kitchen knife, she thought. *But I'm afraid that would end up just being a normal cut and it would take a long time to heal. No, I need the bone knife and I'm afraid that's lost forever now.*

As if taken aback by her thoughts, the little scar began to ache and she rubbed her hands together to try to abate the pain. Then she turned her thoughts to Dex.

He's going to call me today with the name of a shrink or something. Christ, am I going to have to sit down and talk about all this with a stranger? No, I'll make something up; I can't tell the truth. But I have to go through the motions to appease him, to keep him.

She considered possible lies to tell the shrink ... things that might explain her behavior. Normal things. But her thoughts kept returning to Dex.

Is he at his little cottage now, thinking about me? No, he's in his element here. He's probably out fishing or hanging out with old friends. And I doubt he's lacked for female companionship since I kicked him out. There's probably a whole lineup of women bringing him casseroles, offering to do his laundry and other more enticing things. Would he succumb? Maybe I should call him. We could have lunch down at the yard like we used to. And then, maybe we could ...?

She smiled to herself, all thoughts of the little bone knife gone as she immersed herself in a daydream of being with Dex and making love in that adorable little cottage, his strong arms wound tightly around her ...

Her reverie was broken by the sound of footsteps coming down the path behind her. Turning her head, she smiled when she saw Sophie.

"Come sit with me," she said, patting the rock beside her.

Sophie sat down, a frown on her face. "Do you know what's going on with Terri, Mom?"

"What do you mean? She just went to town by herself, that's all. Has something else upset you?"

"No, it's not that she went out by herself - it's the way she did it. Sort of secretive - like she's hiding something."

Karen patted her daughter's hand. "Maybe she's meeting her young man? You think?"

Sophie shook her head. "No, she's got a date with him on Saturday. She's got no reason to sneak out to see him. It's something else. I know it. Maybe it's the twin thing, but I feel there's something wrong."

Karen studied her daughter carefully. Sophie and Terri did have strong intuition about each other and often picked up on things that Karen would never notice. Was there something going on with Terri? Something to do with Mateguas?

Sophie picked up a rock and skipped it across the water. "And how about you, Mom? What's up with Dex? Are you two getting back together?"

Karen smiled. "We're not really apart, sweetie. We both just need some space right now. Everything will be okay ... "

Her words were cut off by the ringtone of her cell phone. Pulling it from her pocket, she checked the caller ID. "That's him now. I need to take this - do you mind?"

Sophie smiled and nodded. "No problem, Mom." She stood up and began to wander down the beach, giving her mother the privacy she requested.

Watching her daughter walk away, Karen answered the call. "Hi."

"It's me. I just got off the phone with Josh. He recommends a Dr. Sylvia Petrie. She has an office near the hospital. I hope you don't mind, but I called and took the liberty of making an appointment for you."

Karen sighed. "When?"

"Tomorrow. At eleven. Thought maybe we could go over together - I could hang out with Josh for a bit while you're with the doctor. Maybe we could have lunch after?"

Karen smiled. "That sounds good. And about lunch - I was thinking maybe we could have lunch today down at the boatyard?"

There was silence on the line for a moment, then he spoke. "I'd like that. Like old times. Meet you at noon?"

"Sure. See you then."

Hanging up the cell, she watched her daughter who was standing at the far end of the beach skipping stones across the water and her mind traveled back to their conversation about Terri. *I hope she hasn't gotten herself involved in any of this stuff. Going to Puffin Island, wanting to walk in her father's footsteps. What if the magic wears off and she remembers? How will I keep her safe then?*

Again, she stared down at the little wound in the center of her palm, looking for answers. But now, the scar was just a scar and apparently did not intend to give up any of its secrets.

 **STREET PHANTOMS**

LEAVING THE MUSEUM, TERRI began the long walk back to the ferry terminal. Her mind was troubled as she desperately tried to internalize everything she'd learned from Charlie, especially his final warning.

What does all this really mean? she asked herself. *If I give the box back to Mom, will it eventually destroy her? I can't let that happen. But what else can I do?*

As she walked, the box seemed to grow heavy in her tote and, unbidden, visions of the small bone knife surfaced to plague her mind. Waiting at the curb for a traffic light, she suddenly found herself overcome by a wave of dizziness and the ordinary street scene in front of her began to blur and shift out of focus. She closed her eyes tightly, willing the vertigo to stop. When she opened them again, all was back to normal and the light was now green. As she stepped into the street, she checked her watch.

I need to eat something, she thought. *I haven't had anything since early this morning. Maybe I should stop and grab something quick.*

She glanced around but there were no fast food places close by. Determined to make the next boat, she put her hunger aside and continued walking but was unable to shake off a vague feeling of unease.

Concentrating on the activity around her, she stumbled when she was, once again, hit by sense of disequilibrium, this time accompanied by a sharp pang of nausea. She stopped and leaned against a lamppost, desperately trying to regain her balance and keep herself from vomiting in the gutter.

What's happening? This can't be just hunger.

Confused and a little frightened, she closed her eyes and tried to focus her mind. When she began feeling steady and in control again, she took a deep breath, opened her eyes and looked around.

Oh my God! What's happening?

Turning her head left and right, she stared in disbelief as the shops that lined the street begin to shimmer and change. She clung to the lamppost, her sense of fear escalating as everything that made up the real world suddenly started to liquefy, melting slowly away and disappearing into the pavement beneath her feet.

She closed her eyes again in a desperate attempt to make reality return, but when she opened them, all she saw before her was a barren landscape. The people and buildings were gone and what remained was only scorched earth, reeking of desolation.

As she stared at the scene around her, shadowy shapes began to pull themselves from the raw earth, hovering strangely above the ground, their soulless eyes staring at her, their mouths gaping.

She shrank back as their foul breath assailed her nostrils and she fought to keep from vomiting in the street. Suddenly, the shapes reached out for her, whispering her name. Frozen in sheer terror, she watched as the strange phantoms grew larger and began to sinuously drift toward her, their arms stretching out as if wanting to enfold her in some sort of foul embrace.

She opened her mouth to scream, and as she did, the busy downtown street came rushing back, appearing before her eyes in sharp and vivid detail. The shadows were gone - vanished!

Uncomprehending, she stood still for a moment, rubbing her eyes and trying to wrap her mind around what had happened. Shaking her head and breathing deeply, she was about to continue on toward the terminal when the street in front of her again began to shimmer, fading away like a bad dream - and then the shadows were back and closing in on her.

Filled with terror, she began to run, unmindful of what direction she was going, but determined not to let the darkness reach her and swallow her soul like it had her father's.

Panic fueling her body, she wove her way through the empty streets, her heart beating wildly. Feeling the hot, decaying breath of the shadows close behind, her adrenalin surged and she picked up her pace.

But it was all to no avail. They were gaining on her and there was no way to elude them. Praying desperately for a miracle, she stopped running and turned to face the darkness.

KAREN AND DEX

KAREN MET DEX AT the boatyard as planned. They purchased sandwiches and drinks at the store, then sat down at one of the picnic tables outside. While the day was sunny, there was a stiff breeze coming off the water and Karen hugged herself, feeling chilled.

"Cold, princess?" Dex asked. "We don't have to stay out here. The cottage is just up the street."

Karen smiled at him. "I think I'd like that. It wasn't this cold at the house and I didn't bring a jacket."

"Okay, come on," he said, gathering up their lunch items. "We can leave your car here - it's just a short walk."

At the cottage, they sat down at the dining room table and

resumed their lunch. Conversation was minimal, as they were both a little nervous about being alone with the other again so soon since the breakup.

Finishing his sandwich, Dex leaned back in his chair, staring at her.

"Did I just grow a third ear?" she asked, noting how intent his gaze was. "Is there something wrong?"

Dex shook his head, smiling. "No, nothing's wrong. I'm just trying to memorize you again so I can see you in my mind's eye anytime I feel lonely."

Karen reached across the table and took his hand. "You don't have to memorize me. I'm right here. And I always will be here."

They sat quietly, holding hands for a time, then Dex got up and walked around the table toward her. As he approached, Karen stood and faced him.

"I've missed you," she whispered. "I don't feel whole without you."

Dex responded by putting his arms around her and pulling her tightly against his body.

"I've missed you, too. There's no one and nothing that can replace you for me. It's all empty without you."

She reached up and took his face in her hands. "Kiss me."

Leaning down, he kissed her passionately and then lifted her in his arms and carried her to the bedroom.

Later, as they lay tangled in the sheets, Dex gently traced the outline of her body with his fingertips.

"I won't beg," he whispered. "But, if you ask, I'll be glad to come home."

Karen pulled away, sitting on the side of the bed, her back to him. "Nothing's changed, Dex. I still don't think we can be together - really together - on this island. It's not safe."

Dex looked at her quizzically. "Safe? What do you mean by safe? Do you think some harm is going to befall me if we're together? That makes no sense. Is that what this separation is all about? My safety?"

Karen reached down to the floor for her underwear and began to get dressed, refusing to make eye contact with him. "You don't understand. There is danger - very real danger - for you, if you're near me. I won't have what happened to Bill happen to you."

Dex sat up, a look of exasperation on his face. "Karen, would you listen to yourself. How in God's name would what happened to Bill happen to me? I'm not about to go traipsing about in the woods late at night, and even if I did, I can take care of myself a whole lot better than Bill ever could. All this mumbo jumbo about danger on this island is in your mind. It's not real and it never has been. Can't you see that?"

He stared at her as if willing her to turn and face him. But when she didn't, he got up off the bed, pulled on his jeans, and stood in front of her. "You're not going to bail on me tomorrow, are you? You're going to see this doctor?"

Karen stared at her feet for a moment, feeling his eyes boring into her, then slowly raised her head to meet his hard stare. "I'm sorry. I just can't do it. I called and cancelled the appointment."

Anger flashed across his face. "Jesus, Karen. What were you going to do? Go to town tomorrow and just pretend that you saw the doctor? Lie to me?"

"Dex, I ... Don't you understand? There's nothing wrong with me. I don't need a doctor. Please, believe me."

"Believe you? Yesterday you promised. Now you've lied to me and broke your promise. And you were going to lie again tomorrow, weren't you? Why should I believe anything you say? We've been together for ten years and I've never lied to you. Don't I deserve better than this? Christ!"

Without waiting for a reply, he turned and walked over to the closet and pulled out a clean shirt. Buttoning it up the front, he walked to the bathroom, splashed water on his face, and began to comb his hair.

"I'm going to town," he said, flatly. "You better finished getting dressed if you want a ride to your car."

Karen frowned. "To town? Why?"

He turned from the bathroom mirror to face her. "Why am I going to town? I'll tell you why. I'm going to sit in a bar, most likely The Sternman, if it's still there, and get drunk. And, maybe, just maybe, some sweet young thing will join me and tell me I'm the greatest thing since sliced bread and help me forget all about you and your lies for one night, at least. Now get a move on."

Karen stared at him for a moment, suddenly angry. "You're going to WHAT? Find a cheap piece of ass just to spite me? Is that what you're telling me?"

Dex shot her a cold look, then turned his back on her again.

With tears of outrage welling in her eyes, Karen grabbed her clothes and quickly finished dressing. They walked silently to the car and drove to the boatyard. Dex put the car in park and gestured for her to get out. He didn't look at her, just stared straight ahead.

"Look at me, Dex," she demanded, as she opened the car door. "I didn't mean to hurt you or lie to you. I don't need to see a shrink. Can't you even try to have some faith in me? Don't our ten years together mean anything?"

He turned his face to her, his jawline still set in anger. "I can't talk to you now. I've got some serious thinking to do. We'll discuss this later."

Stiffly, she nodded to him, got out, and closed the door. Without further ado, he put the car in reverse and backed out of the parking lot, then floored it as he turned down the road to head toward the wharf.

Defeated, Karen walked slowly to her car and got in. Silently, she sat staring out the window at the sea before her.

I've really fucked things up this time, she thought. *Maybe, irreparably.*

Shaking her head in frustration and sadness, she started the car, turned around, and headed for home.

TERRI AND SHAWN

AS TERRI PIVOTED AROUND to face the shadows that were menacing her, reality came rushing back with the sharp sound of a car's horn and she found herself in the middle of a busy intersection, seconds away from being run down. Quickly she jumped back to the sidewalk and leaned against the wall of the nearest building, trying to slow her rapidly beating heart and regain some control. People were staring at her as if she had lost her mind.

I need help, she thought as she pulled her cell from her pocket. Rapidly scanning her contacts, she dialed. The phone was picked up on the first ring.

"Hey, girl! Didn't think I'd hear again from you so quick. What ya up to?"

"Shawn, I'm in trouble. Can you come get me?"

"Trouble? What do you mean? And where are you anyway?"

"I'm on the mainland, on the wharf. I'll explain when you get here. Can you come?"

Recognizing the panic in her voice, Shawn became serious. "Yeah. I'm about fifteen minutes away. Go to pier fifty-two; that's the one south of the terminal. I can pick you up there. Can you do that?"

"Yes, but please hurry, please."

"I'm turning the boat now. You just make it to the pier and sit tight."

Finding it hard to keep her footing, her grasp on reality fading in and out, Terri lurched and stumbled her way to the pier. Afraid she might fall into the water and drown, she sat down far away from the edge, her head in her hands, trying to hold off the visions that kept attacking her mind. In an attempt to thwart them, she focused on Charlie's last words and tried to hold herself to them. *"... there are evil portents in the air and they will seek to harm you. Stay strong within yourself. Do not doubt, and you will triumph over them."*

Focusing her mind completely on those words, she started and almost screamed when she felt a hand on her shoulder.

"Whoa, girl. Take it easy. It's me."

Shawn knelt down and took her face in his hands, willing her to recognize him. When her eyes focused on his, she sobbed, leaning forward into his embrace. He wrapped his arms around her and held her tightly.

"Hush now. You're safe. I'm here."

Breathing easier, she pulled her face back from his chest and stared into his eyes.

"You're here? You're real? I'm not imagining this, am I?"

Shawn smiled. "Don't worry, I'm real. Now let me help you get up," he said, keeping his arm around her as he gently pulled her to her feet. "You're safe now, Terri. I'm not going to let anything happen to you."

She rested her head on his chest, her breathing slowing as her panic subsided.

"Thanks," she said weakly. "I don't know what I would have done if you hadn't come."

"It's okay now. Let's get you aboard the boat and then we can talk."

He helped her on board and sat her down. Then he pulled out a bottle of water from the cooler and handed it to her.

"Drink this and try to get your bearings."

Terri dutifully drank the water, gulping it down. She took several deep breaths, then looked up at him.

"You look better now," he said, nodding. "You were pale as a ghost when I saw you on the pier. Tell me what happened."

Terri hesitated for a moment, then tried to explain the phenomena she had experienced; how the world around her kept changing as reality faded in and out, each time becoming more elusive than the last.

Shawn listened quietly trying to keep his expression neutral.

"And that's about it. I thought it was 'cause I hadn't eaten, but now I think it was something more than that."

"You sure someone didn't slip you something in a drink somewhere? There are a lot of nefarious types that hang out by the wharf. You don't do drugs, do you?"

Terri looked at him indignantly. "No, I don't. And the only thing I had to drink was coffee at the museum and I don't think the antiquarian, who's about eighty years old, wanted to date-rape me."

"Okay, okay, don't get sore. You said you thought what happened was 'something more.' What did you mean by that?"

Terri again took a deep breath then reached down and pulled the box out of her tote. "I think it has something to do with this and with Mateguas and what happened to my dad."

Shawn reached out and took the box from her hands. He studied the carvings on the top then opened it, examining the contents carefully.

"Looks like a bunch of old Indian shit to me, Terri."

He picked up the cotton cloth and unwrapped the knife, weighed it in his hand, and then held it up to the light.

"Be careful with that. It's very sharp."

Shawn laughed. "Sharp? You gotta be kidding." By way of demonstration, he grasped the knife in one hand and ran the blade swiftly across the palm of the other.

Terri gasped, then looked up in surprise as he held his palm for her examination. "There's nothing there. Why didn't it cut you? Are you playing some kind of trick on me?"

Shawn laughed, tossing the knife aside. "No, honey. It's just a very old, dull blade. And the rest of this crap - it's just a bunch of stuff someone put together as a joke."

Terri paused for a moment, then slowly stood up. She leaned over to where Shawn had thrown the knife and picked it up. She took hold of it lightly by the hilt, careful not to touch the blade and rewrapped it in the cotton cloth.

"It is sharp, Shawn. At least to me it is. And the rest of this stuff has meaning, too. It's not just crap."

"Sure. And I'm the Easter Bunny. What is it about you people from away? Always gotta make some sort of mystical shit out of everything."

Terri sat back down. "You're a lot like Dex, you know. So deeply rooted in reality. I think that's why Mom and he split - he couldn't accept anything not fully of this earth. He couldn't understand that there are things out there ... ancient things that defy explanation."

Shawn started to speak but she silenced him with a wave of her hand, pointing to the box he had so carelessly dismissed.

"There is great power in all this 'shit.' I know it and my mother knows it. She thinks she can control or channel that power into some sort of protection for her family. But she's wrong. The power in that box, in that knife: it controls her. Actually, it owns her in a way. And now that force or spirit or whatever it is wants to own me, too. It scares me, Shawn, but I'm not my mother and I think whatever it is may have made a mistake and underestimated me."

She sat quietly for a minute letting him digest her words before she continued.

"I like you, Shawn, maybe too much. I feel we have some sort of connection. But right now, I have a path laid out for me and I don't think you're willing or able to join me on it. Thanks for the rescue this afternoon. I was floundering and lost and don't know what I would have done if you hadn't been there. Maybe when this is all over, we can start again, fresh."

"Terri, I ..."

Again, she silenced him, then picked up the box and gently laid it in her tote and stood up.

"I think it's time to go home now, Shawn. Back to Mateguas."

She leaned over and kissed him lightly, smiled, and turned her gaze from him, toward the sea. Confused, he found himself feeling like a boy of fifteen, frightened by a mere girl. He knew that in actual years, he was the elder and was supposed to be the adult, but somehow, she had reversed things, making him feel he was the younger one - imperfect and horribly wet behind the ears.

Shaking his head, he stood staring at her as she serenely gazed at the horizon, her face now calm and full of confidence. Slowly, he turned toward the wheelhouse to motor them home, for once in his life feeling terribly unsure of himself.

And, looking back over his shoulder at her, another alien emotion began to play at the corners of his mind and he knew that maybe - just maybe - he was falling in love.

BILL

THAT SAME MORNING, BILL sat on the commuter train to Boston going over his notes. The meeting with Gerry's team was scheduled for ten a.m. and he wanted to be prepared. This was his one chance and he was determined not to blow it.

A car was waiting at the train station to take him to Gerry's office downtown. Upon arrival, he was escorted to a conference room where Gerry and his team were waiting. The younger man greeted him warmly, introduced him, then took a seat away from the table in a far corner of the room. It was obvious then to Bill that Gerry only meant to observe, not participate, in this interview.

Bill took a seat midway down the table, smiling at the six young people who were already there. He noted, with some dismay, that he was the oldest person in the room and that some of the team members didn't look much older than his daughters. Continuing to smile, he waited.

The young people seemed nervous, as if they didn't know how to proceed and Bill wondered if Gerry had set this up as a sort of test, not only for him, but for them. The silence in the room was becoming deafening and lacking a better idea, Bill stood up and walked to the chalkboard that was mounted at the far end of the room. Picking up a piece of chalk, he wrote two words on the board, "Puffin Island."

Smiling, he returned to his seat. "Okay, see those words," he said, pointing to the board. "That's the elephant in this room. I don't remember much about being there, but if you all have any questions, fire away and I'll try to answer them."

One young man, seated across the table from him, laughed. "Yeah, man, how did you survive it? I've been there and it's like the pits. You must have had some real heavy-duty survival skills to last that long."

Bill laughed. "I was a Boy Scout and my family used to go camping all the time during summer vacation. That's how I learned to make fire. But that's about the extent of my prior knowledge. The rest, well, I must have learned by trial and error."

The tension in the room now eased, the questions came fast and furious and Bill fielded them as best he could. When the subject of his abandonment on Puffin was exhausted, the interview began in earnest.

About two hours later, when it was approaching noon, Gerry stood up.

"I think that's about enough, guys. I'm getting hungry. Thanks for taking time from your busy schedules to meet Bill."

Bill shook hands all around as the young people filed out of the room. When they had all gone, he gathered up his things and turned toward Gerry. "Well? How'd I do?"

Gerry laughed. "As I expected - you did great! Let's go get some lunch and talk about the future."

TERRI AND SHAWN
& MAGGIE AND BILL

THE BOAT RIDE BACK to Mateguas was a silent one for Shawn and Terri, both young people alone with their thoughts. Upon arrival at the wharf, Shawn loaded Terri's bike into the back of his truck, helped her up into the cab and drove her home. Parked in the driveway, Terri finally broke the silence.

"Thanks again for rescuing me today. I needed help and you were there. You didn't hesitate and that means a lot to me. I'm sorry about the other stuff, I probably should have kept my mouth shut."

She started to get out of the truck but he stopped her with a hand on her arm. "I'm the one who should be sorry. I had no business making fun of you and what you believe. It was out of line."

Terri smiled. "And I shouldn't have been so defensive. It *is* weird stuff and I don't know if I really believe it all. But I do feel *something* is coming. Something's going to happen, and happen soon, and there will be danger for a lot of people when it does.

247

You may think I'm crazy, but, somehow, I know that I've been chosen to be an instrument in all this - to keep someone or something safe. I can't give you anything concrete to back this up. It's all just intuition and feeling."

Shawn nodded then pulled her to him, wrapping his arms around her. "Well, girl," he whispered. "If you're keeping someone else safe, then I guess it's my job to make sure that nothing happens to you."

She leaned away from him and looked into his eyes. Recognizing the emotion in them, she reached up and pulled his face to hers.

They kissed and then Shawn leaned back against the driver's side door. "You going to be okay?" he asked. "Are we still on for Saturday?"

Terri smiled and nodded. "Yes, to both." She leaned forward, kissed him lightly then jumped out of the truck and started toward the front door.

"Terri."

She turned to find him leaning out the driver's side window. "What?"

"Let's talk some more about that box and all that stuff on Saturday. I promise to keep an open mind. Maybe, just maybe, I'll learn something."

Terri laughed. "Okay. I hope by then I'll know more. See you Saturday." She turned away and started up the steps to the front door, her fears abated for the time being, a smile on her face and a lightness growing around her heart.

Later that evening, Maggie drove slowly to the wharf to pick up Bill, a nervous frown on her face. She was worried about how his day in Boston had gone. The text he'd sent her had said nothing other than what boat he would be on. She feared his silence meant that things had gone badly. She parked the car and sat watching the ferry as it approached the island.

What if he blew it? she asked herself. *He'll be stuck in that dead-end job in town, washing dishes and cleaning up after the homeless. That'll kill him. But what if he got the job? And, if he did, why didn't he tell me? You'd think he'd be excited. Yeah, if he got it, his silence means something. Something bad. And as much as I need to know, I have to be careful. Not over-reach. That'll just push him away.*

Sighing, she opened the car door, got out, and walked down the wharf to meet the boat that was now pulling up to the dock. She smiled at the deckhand as he tied it up and began letting passengers off. Bill was one of the last.

Smiling, he strode down the gangplank. "Thanks for coming to get me, Mags," he said, putting his arm around her and kissing her lightly.

"No problem," she replied. "How was your day?"

Bill shrugged. "It was okay. Boston's a neat city."

Maggie pursed her lips. *He's not going to tell me. He's going to make me tease it out of him. Well, I won't rise to his bait.*

Once back at the house, Bill excused himself to go upstairs and wash. Even though it was late, Maggie had saved supper for him.

"You hungry?" she yelled to him. "I saved you a plate. Won't take a minute to heat it up."

She waited at the foot of the stairs for his reply. After a minute or two, he came to the landing. "Naw. I grabbed something before I left. Think I'll just hit the hay. But thanks for offering."

She frowned as she watched him turn and walk to the bedroom they shared. Back in the kitchen, she unceremoniously dumped his supper into the trash but restrained herself from throwing the plate against the wall. Angry, she poured herself a shot of bourbon and walked outside. It was an unusually warm night for early summer and she headed to the edge of the lawn, where she had strategically positioned two Adirondack chairs so they faced the ocean. Plopping down in one, she stared at the night sky as she sipped her drink, trying to dispel her irritation.

Upstairs, Bill stood at the window, watching her. He knew she was angry and that she had every right to be. He should have shared his news with her, even though he knew she would never be a part of his now-rosy future. No, in his mind, he would always be with Karen and, with Dex out of the picture, it appeared more and more certain that he would get what he wanted.

Shrugging, he turned from the window, pulled off his shirt and trousers and climbed into bed. He'd tell her in the morning. Not everything - not Gerry's offer of partnership - but just enough to satisfy her so she didn't do anything rash before he was ready to leave.

Smiling smugly to himself, he turned out the light, closed his eyes, and settled in for a good night's sleep.

KAREN, TERRI, AND THE BOX

AT CLOSE TO MIDNIGHT, Terri, who had been feigning sleep, slipped out of bed. She tiptoed to the closet, put on her robe and left the room, taking with her the tote that contained the ancient box. She moved toward the stairs, intending to go up to the loft where her mother slept, but was surprised to see that Karen was still up, sitting in the shadows of the living room, gazing out at the sea.

"Hey, Mom," she said softly as she approached. "Am I disturbing you?"

Karen turned toward her, her face illuminated by the moonlight that was streaming through the windows. It was obvious she had been crying.

"What's wrong, Mom? Are you okay?"

Karen smiled a shaky smile and reached for her daughter's hand. "Oh, it's nothing. I just messed up again with Dex. Seems to be becoming a pattern. Don't worry about it. It's my problem. Now, what's up with you? Why are you up so late?"

"Actually, I wanted to talk to you alone. I was going to wake you up."

Karen cocked her head, puzzled. "What about? Is it about that boy?"

Terri laughed softly. "No, it's not about Shawn. It's about you, me, Sophie, and Dad and what happened ten years ago."

Karen sighed, exasperated. "Are we going to have to do this all over again? Terri, we've been through this a dozen times. You know what happened."

"No, this time it's different. 'Cause you see, Mom, I *remember*."

Karen stared at her, surprised. "Remember what?"

Terri reached out and took her mother's hands. "I remember what happened that night. Soph and I went into the woods and Dad came after us. And ... and I remember what happened to him. I remember that thing ... that horrible creature that tried to take him."

Karen studied her daughter's distraught face, trying to stay composed. "But how? How is that possible? I don't understand."

Terri leaned over and pulled the box from her tote, placing it in her mother's lap. Karen stared at it for a minute, then slowly opened it. On top lay the little bone knife and she gasped when she saw it.

"How? Where did you find this?" she demanded.

Embarrassed, Terri gazed down at her feet. "I was up that night, here in the living room. I was watching you outside. Then Dex came down the stairs and I hid. I don't know why, but I did. I saw you and Dex fighting. After he brought you back in, I went out to the beach. I found it there, lying in the sand."

"But why didn't you tell me? Why did you keep it?"

"I don't really know, except that it seemed to have a hold on me. Back when I was a kid, I handled it - played with it. I know this may sound crazy, but I think that it remembered me."

Karen stared at her daughter, then nodded. "Go on. Did everything come back to you when you touched it?"

Terri shook her head. "No, it was a couple of nights later. I was asleep and I think the knife kind of possessed me and I found myself outside on the beach and all the memories came rushing back. It scared me and I passed out. I came to in the morning. Are you angry with me?"

Karen hesitated for a moment. "No, I'm not angry. But you should have brought it to me right away. It's dangerous, as I think you now know."

Terri nodded and, seeing only kindness and love in her mother's eyes, smiled. "I know. But I felt that I needed to find out more about it. So I took it to the **Native American Indian Museum** in town."

Karen listened intently as Terri went on to tell her about meeting Charlie and all that he had told her about the little knife.

"I see," said Karen. "But, the box? Where did you find it?"

"After talking with Charlie, I looked for it. It was right where Soph and I found it the first time. And I'm giving it to you because Charlie says it belongs to you. But it frightens me, Mom. He said you were lost, your soul bound to Mateguas, and that the power of the knife now controls you."

Karen laughed a sharp, bitter laugh. "Don't you worry about me. I can take care of myself. Haven't I proven that all these years? And you were right to bring this to me. Hopefully, it won't have to be used. But it would have been dangerous for you to keep it. And don't you fret. I'm not 'lost.' That knife doesn't control me."

Karen noted the look of skepticism on her daughter's face. Nodding, she closed the box and stood up. "Does Sophie know any of this? Does she remember what happened that night?"

Terri shook her head. "She didn't touch the knife much when we were little. I cut myself with it once and I think that's why it knows me."

Karen nodded her head. "Strange as it seems, that makes sense. I'm glad, though, that Sophie's out of the loop. Let's keep it that way. It will only upset her. Now, I'm going to put this box away in a safe place and go to bed and I suggest you do the same."

Not knowing what else to say, Terri nodded, kissed her mother lightly and walked back down the hall to her room.

Karen watched her daughter leave, a worried look on her face. Clasping the box firmly in her arms, she went upstairs and sat down on her bed. Slowly, she again opened the lid and stared at the little knife.

"You don't own me, do you?" she asked as she reached out and grasped the blade in her hand. At her touch, the hilt began to glow and grow warm, the heat radiating outward and up her arm. The warmth moved across her chest and seemed to settle just above her heart, bringing with it a strong sense of peace and serenity.

I need this knife, she thought. *It doesn't own me but it's part of me now and always will be. I'm not whole without it. Maybe Terri's Indian is right. Maybe I am lost.*

She gazed down again at the small artifact laying in the palm of her hand and she could swear that the glow that encircled it was not actually coming from the blade, but from the tiny crescent moon scar in the middle of her hand.

Yes, the magic of this blade has possessed me and it fills me with power. Without me, it becomes just an old knife, dull and useless.

Nodding to herself, she replaced the blade in the ancient box and secreted it in the back of her closet under some old blankets. Satisfied it was well hidden, she moved to the bathroom, where she washed up and got ready for bed. She stood naked at the window for a moment, staring at the moon, lost in thought. Then she turned, slipped under the covers, and closed her eyes. The feeling of confidence remained, but there was something else tugging at the back of her mind. Something was missing. She went over the contents of the box in her mind's eye but could think of nothing that wasn't there.

Shaking off her doubts, she curled herself around the pillow, let her body relax, and drifted off to a peaceful sleep.

Downstairs, Terri lay in bed, wide-awake.

I should have told Mom about the parchment. She thinks she's in control, but she's not. And I didn't tell her about my visions either and how I'm sure I'm a part of all this. She thinks it's just her, but she's wrong. It's all of us. But how can I convince her when I'm not sure of anything myself?

Confused, she rolled over, hugged her pillow, and tried to sleep. But unlike her mother, her slumber was fitful, punctuated with dreams that seemed like dark omens of the days to come.

MALSUMIS

KAREN WOKE A LITTLE before dawn. She'd slept soundly but didn't feel refreshed. Noting the time, she stood up and reached for the clothing she had discarded carelessly on the floor the night before. Slipping into her jeans and sweatshirt, she padded silently down the stairs to the kitchen to make herself a cup of coffee.

As she waited for the dark brew to perk, she pulled out her phone to check for messages. Somewhere in the back of her mind, she was hoping and praying that there would be something from Dex. She didn't believe he really planned to cheat on her. No, that was just talk, bravado. He was angry and wanted to hurt her. She hoped that he'd had time enough to think things through and contact her. But she was disappointed. There was just a message from Bill from the day before.

Sighing, she opened Bill's email and began to read.

Hey Kar - I'm on the train back from Boston and wanted to let you know how my meeting with Gerry and his team went. Don't really know if you're interested, but you're the only person I really want to share this with. So, here goes.

The meeting went great! It was weird though - the members of his team are all just kids, not much older than Ter and Soph. It reminded me of myself, ten years ago - young, cocky and so very foolish. If only I could turn back the clock. There are so many things I'd do differently. But, what the hell, there's no use crying over spilt milk! In any case, he's going to take me on! I'll start with clients up here, then eventually, move to Boston, and, if all goes well, Europe.

You'd love Boston, Kar. A lot like San Francisco, only colder.

Okay, I'm rambling and I'll stop. I know you've moved on - you're with Dex now and I get that. But I just had to tell you. Okay?

Be back on the island tonight. Maybe I can stop by sometime and tell you all about it?

Luv u,

B.

Karen poured herself a cup of coffee, shaking her head. She was happy for Bill. He had gone through so much. It was about time he got a break. But she knew he still harbored hopes that she would accept him back and that they could start over again as a family. Sipping her coffee, she texted him back.

Glad things went well. Stop by when you're back on the island. You can tell us everything then.

K.

Shutting down her phone, she walked to the closet and grabbed a jacket. She refilled her cup and headed out the back door, down the path to the beach.

The tide was coming in, so she sat on a rock close to the walkway to wait for the sunrise. The moon peeked out from behind a cloud and winked at her, as if acknowledging her presence. Its light sparkled off the water for a moment before it swiftly retreated again behind its dark curtain. As it disappeared, a faint glow began to shimmer on the horizon to herald the start of a new day.

Karen stared at that glow, remembering only a few days before when Dex had awakened her to witness the dawn. As she tried to relive in her mind the feel of his strong arms around her, she was startled by a rustling sound coming from the tall grasses that lined the path behind her. Her reverie broken, she turned her head to see what was moving in her direction.

Probably an animal, she thought. *Maybe a fox or a raccoon. Probably saw me and took off.*

She stared at the path for a few more seconds, but all was quiet. Satisfied that whatever had been there was gone, she turned back to the sea and warmed herself with the hot coffee. The glow on the horizon was stronger now and she could envision the sun beginning its climb up into the sky.

Again, there came the rustling sound behind her, seeming closer this time.

Feeling a little alarmed, she turned again to see what might be on the path. But, as before, there was nothing out of the ordinary. Shaking her head, she decided go back inside, not wanting to confront some wild animal alone on the beach. She reached down for her coffee cup, but as she did, she sensed another movement, this time directly behind her. Inhaling sharply, she stood and whirled around, ready to hurl the half-full cup at whatever was moving in the grasses above. But again, there was nothing.

A soft breeze ruffled her hair and she laughed to herself. *It was only the wind. God, am I jumpy.*

Trying to relax, she turned seaward again, ready to greet the sun, but was shocked to find her view was now blocked. Before her, standing on a rock, was what she at first thought was a large gray dog, its teeth bared and hackles up. Vicious-looking saliva slowly dripped from its maw to the sand below and she heard a soft growl emanate from its throat.

Sweet Jesus! That's a wolf! Where did it come from?

Frozen in fear and indecision, she stared at the predator before her. Its sharply defined muscles were taut as it leaned forward, giving the impression it could spring at any moment. It was so close, she could feel its warm, fetid breath on her face.

Time seemed to stand still as the light from the sun, now halfway over the horizon, sparkled and glinted off the beast's shiny hairs, creating a kaleidoscope of color that, even in her terror, she found breathtaking. She was sure she was going to faint when a drop of hot spittle from the beast's jaw landed on her ankle, sizzling as it touched her soft flesh.

Reacting to the intense pain, she squeezed her eyes tightly shut and waited for the inevitable. Seconds passed.

Nothing happened.

Slowly she opened her eyes and was surprised to find the creature gone. It had simply vanished. She looked around the beach but there was no sign of movement anywhere. Carefully, she crouched down and examined the sand around the rock, searching for paw prints that would show her which way the animal had gone. But there were none.

That can't be! The sand is dry. It had to have left tracks. The only way it couldn't would be if it could fly and I don't think there's any way that animal had wings!

Her fear abating now that the wolf was gone, she breathed a sigh of relief and began to wonder if it had ever really been there at all.

Did I just hallucinate that?

She shook her head as she stood up. *Maybe Dex is right. Maybe there is something wrong with me.*

But as swiftly as that thought came into her mind, she shook it off. *No, I'm not going bonkers. It's this island that's somehow wrong ... somehow insane. Not me.*

Feeling calmer, she gazed out once more to the sea, watching as the sun hovered gently over the horizon, promising another bright and placid summer day.

When Karen returned to the house, Sophie was busy preparing

breakfast and chatting with Terri who was sitting at the breakfast bar. Pouring herself another cup of coffee, Karen motioned to Terri to join her in the living room.

"What's up, Mom?" she asked as she sat down on the couch.

"When you spoke with that curator at the museum, did he mention anything about a wolf?"

Terri gave her mother a puzzled look as she searched her memory for details of her first meeting with Charlie.

"Yeah, he did, I think. It was Mateguas' brother or one of them. Why?"

"One of them? I thought he just had one brother, Glooskap."

"According to Charlie, there were two and they were twins, symbolizing the duality of nature. Glooskap was the good and the other, Malsumis, I think his name was, was evil. I think Charlie said that the evil twin's totem was a wolf. Why are you interested in this?"

"Just curious, honey. Now, another thing. I don't want you messing around anymore in this stuff. Okay? It's dangerous and I want you to promise that you'll let it drop."

Terri hesitated before responding, knowing that she was about to lie to her mother. "Sure. If that's what you want. I promise."

At that moment, before Karen could say anything further, Sophie walked into the room. "What's going on here? You two look thick as thieves."

"Oh, nothing, honey," said Karen, smiling. "I'm just giving your sister the third degree about that young man."

"Well, breakfast's about ready and I hope you two are hungry."

"I could eat a horse, sis!" laughed Terri, getting up to follow her sister back to the kitchen.

Karen stood silently for a moment, watching them. *Twins,* she thought. *Is it just coincidence? Or are my girls in trouble?*

A worried look on her face, she gazed out the window. Everything was serene with the sun shining boldly down on the water giving no indication of the menace that surrounded them all.

"Mom, are you coming? Breakfast is getting cold!"

Karen sighed and tried to shake off her growing apprehension as she turned from the sea and went to join her daughters for their morning meal.

 ## HARRY THREE FEATHERS

ON WEDNESDAY MORNING, CHARLIE gathered up his gloves and other items needed to examine the parchment and put them in the trunk of his car. He drove north, his destination the nursing home where Harry Three Feathers was a patient. He had known Harry for decades and, in fact, had studied shamanism under him for a while before turning his back on tribal customs and opting for university life instead. However, as time passed by, Charlie rediscovered the wisdom and beauty in all that he had forsaken and returned to the study of his tribe's folklore. He considered Harry to be the wisest, most learned man he had ever met and he was sure that if anyone could interpret this parchment, it would be him.

At the nursing home, the staff greeted Charlie warmly and led him to a conference room in the back of the building. Harry was seated in a wheelchair at a small table in the middle. The wizened old man smiled when he saw his friend.

"Greetings, Mekwi Mikoa," the old man said. "It has been too long since I gazed upon your face."

Charlie smiled as he walked over and embraced his old friend. "You look younger than you did when I was here last. Have you found the fountain of youth, old friend?"

Harry laughed and gestured for Charlie to have a seat next to him. The two old friends talked for a few minutes catching up, but then the ancient shaman became serious.

"What have you have brought to me? You were very guarded on the phone."

Charlie nodded, then explained to Harry the substance of his meetings with Terri, his examination of the little bone knife, and the contents of the ancient box. "In the box was an artifact; a parchment, the meaning of which I am not able to fully decipher."

As he spoke, he leaned down and pulled the cotton bag from his valise. With great care, he donned his gloves and laid a white cloth on the table. Then he unwrapped the parchment and spread it on the cloth.

The elderly shaman gazed at it for a few moments. "Tell me more about the other contents of this box. I must know everything."

"As I mentioned, there was the sacred bone knife, three cornhusk dolls representing the family, and a bottle of blood powder. There were also prayers to Mateguas but these were modern interpretations of the ancient ones."

Harry nodded, then turned his attention back to the parchment. He sat quietly for quite some time, staring intently at the drawings, his fingers moving back and forth as he translated in his mind.

Finally, he leaned back in his chair. "This is quite something you have brought to me, Mekwi Mikoa. What do you think it means?"

Charlie sighed. "I can read the parts about Mateguas and his acolyte, but there is another thread woven throughout that stumps me. The young woman who brought this to me is in danger: that, I can feel in my bones. But from who or what I am not sure."

The old Indian nodded. "You are right to fear for this woman, for the thread you speak of was woven by the wolf, Malsumis."

"The destroyer?"

"Yes. Look, Mekwi Mikoa," he said, pointing to one of the drawings. "Do you not see it? Malsumis has made a pact with the Mskagwdemos, binding her to him."

"A pact? What sort of pact? That evil hag bows to no one."

"That was once correct. But now, the wolf has promised her something she has lost and forever searches for."

"Tell me - what evil thing has he promised?

The old man chuckled. "Evil is right. He has pledged her a human child. One of her own making to replace the one she lost so long ago."

"A human child? But how is that possible?"

"By granting her the power to possess a human woman and seduce a human man, that's how. And I'm afraid these events have already occurred. The result of that joining is a boy child, born of a human, to be sure, but tied mystically to the hag. And, now the time is ripe for her to reclaim this child."

"But why now? Why did she not take the child at birth?"

"Mateguas' acolyte left the sacred land making it impossible. But now, she has returned and her return has set in motion all the portents laid out so long ago. If the hag is allowed to fulfill her desire, then her power will increase seven-fold and, with the aid of Malsumis, will seek to destroy everything good in the world. This must not be allowed to happen!"

Charlie frowned, trying to understand. "But what of Mateguas? Why does he let this happen? Does he not have power over the hag?"

The old man shook his head. "His mind is elsewhere, my friend. He has a purpose in all that he has done and his goal is now in sight. He will not let his older brother's plots and schemes get in his way. And, he cares nothing for the boy or your friend. No, you can expect no help from him in this."

"But what of my friend, the young woman? Will she be safe?"

"Ah, that is up to her. It may be that she is the unknown element in all this. If she were to keep the child safe - not let the Mskagwdemos have him - then all of Malsumis' schemes will be for naught."

Charlie nodded but looked troubled. "But how can I ask her to do this? She is just a child herself."

The old Indian sat silent for a moment, thinking. "She has already shown wisdom beyond her years by seeking you out. And somehow, through you, I sense that she is strong. But it will be by her choice. You must give her the interpretation of these signs. How she deals with them is, of course, up to her. If she chooses the path that will save the boy and, by doing so, the world as we know it, then it will be your job to act as her guide, teaching her what she needs to know to prevail."

Charlie sighed, shaking his head. "I will do as you say, Harry Three Feathers, and try to guide my friend. But I am frightened for her."

"You are right to be frightened and not only for her, but for all of us. If Malsumis is allowed to triumph, it will be the undoing of mankind and it may be that only your young friend has the power to stop him."

"How much time do I have to prepare her?"

Harry Three Feathers again turned his attention to the parchment, studying it intently. Finally, nodding, he turned to Charlie.

"When the moon is in its waning crescent phase, that is when the portents align. The hag will call to the boy, luring him to her lair. Your friend must be ready."

"But when is the next waning crescent? How much time do I have?"

The old man wheeled himself over to a desk that sat in the corner and consulted a calendar that was tacked up on the wall. "The waning crescent will appear a week from Friday, in nine days' time."

Charlie gasped, alarmed. "But how can I prepare her by then? It's just not possible."

The old Indian just smiled. "You will find a way, my friend. You must!"

 **DEX AND MAGGIE**

DEX WOKE UP WITH a fierce hangover. True to his words, he had planted himself firmly at the bar still known as The Sternman and stayed there until closing. However, Karen was right, he did not seek out the company of a young lady. Not that he didn't have the opportunity. More than one willing beauty had tried to catch his eye, but try as he might, he couldn't get Karen out of his mind, her face and voice haunting him. So, he just drank and now, at seven in the morning, was paying for it.

After downing a couple of aspirin and drinking several glasses of water to rehydrate himself, he took a cup of coffee out onto the deck and sat heavily in one of the Adirondack chairs. There was a cool breeze coming off the water and it felt good to be outside in the warm sun and salty air. He closed his eyes, breathing it all in, and was beginning to doze off when his cell phone rang. Picking it up, he glanced at the caller ID and smiled.

"Hey, Red, how you doing this morning?"

Maggie laughed. "I'm just fine, but I hear you may have slipped off the wagon last night. Need a little of the hair of the dog that bit you this morning?"

Dex chuckled. "Nothin' changes around here, does it? A man's got no privacy at all. Yes, I tied one on last night and, yes, I'm suffering this morning. But I'm drinking coffee now. No more booze for a while, young lady."

"Well, you up for some company? Billy's off with his granddad, Bill's in town, and I'm just about sick to death of summer school. So, if you've got an extra cup, I'd love to join you for some java."

Dex laughed. "I'll put on a fresh pot just for you."

"Okay - I'll see you in ten."

Tucking his cell back in his pocket, Dex got up and walked to the kitchen to start a fresh pot of coffee. *I wonder what she wants to talk about?* he thought as he filled the pot with water. *Mayhap it has something to do with Bill.*

Shaking his head, he walked to the living room and gazed out the window. It was not long before Maggie's car pulled into the driveway. She was wearing tight jeans and jersey top that accentuated her curvaceous form. Her voluminous red curls sparkled in the morning sun as she ran up the walkway.

He opened the door for her, gave her a hug, then walked with her to the kitchen, where he poured them both coffee. "Let's take this outside. The sea breeze sure does smell good this morning."

They sat quietly for a while, sipping their drinks and enjoying the salty air and morning sun.

"Okay, Red, I can tell the wheels are turning in the gorgeous head of yours. What's it that you want to run by old Dex this morning?"

Maggie sighed. "Gone ten years yet you still know me like the back of your hand." She laughed and shook her head. "It's Bill. I think he might be getting ready to dump me and I need to run it by someone - someone I trust - so I can get it all straight in my mind."

267

Dex reached out and took her hand. "Tell me what's going on. Why do you think he's getting ready to skedaddle? Looks from the outside like you and he are doing okay."

Maggie took a sip of her coffee. "It's this trip to Boston. He went down there to meet with Gerry Davis' people. I was really excited about it. I mean, BOSTON! Moving there would be great." She paused, a frown on her face. "But when he came back, he didn't say a word. Not one word about how it went. Just came home and went to bed. Then, in the morning, he says they took him on - oh, not to move to Boston; no, just to work accounts up here. He kept playing it down, like it was a dead-end job or something. It just didn't ring true, Dex. He's lying and I don't know why."

"He's been through a lot, sugar. Maybe he just doesn't want to put all his eggs in one basket. Once burned, twice shy and all that."

"I thought about that, but I don't buy it. You know what I think? I think he still thinks he can get it back together with your wife and I'm just a way station for him until that happens. Doesn't want to really piss me off, but wants to be ready to cut and run if she gives him the go-ahead. So, I need to know what's going on with you and her. Are you done? Or just taking a time out?"

Dex sat silently for a moment, thinking. He took a sip of his coffee and turned to face her. "You know it was good back in California. Real good. Just her and me and the girls. We were happy. Then we came back here and things began to just fall apart. You know that 'accident' she had?"

Maggie grinned. "You mean when she said she was attacked by birds?"

"Yeah, that's it. Do you believe that really happened? I don't. I think all the stress of Bill coming back got to her and, well, she did it to herself. That's what I think."

Maggie studied him before replying, her face once again serious. "How could that be, Dex? She had all sorts of scratches, didn't she? And a wound that needed stitches. How could she have done that to herself?"

Dex shook his head. "I don't know. Maybe it's like some kind of stigmata. But, you have to understand, I wasn't gone that long and there were people nearby. If birds had attacked her, someone would have seen it."

Maggie reached out and took his hand. "You think she's going bonkers or something?"

Dex laughed. "No, not bonkers. But I do think the stress of the situation has gotten to her. It happened before, back when you and Bill were having your affair. I found her passed out in her yard. She said an owl attacked her then, too."

"No shit! So what are you going to do now?"

"I made her promise to see someone, a therapist. I had it all set up for today. Then I found out she cancelled the appointment and was planning to lie to me about it. That's why I went on a bender last night."

"But you still want her, don't you?"

Dex stared straight ahead. "Yeah, I love her. Can't seem to get over that no matter what."

Not knowing what to say, Maggie stared out at the horizon, deep in thought. Sighing, Dex got up and went into the house. He came back a couple of minutes later with the coffee pot. He refilled Maggie's cup and then his own and sat down.

"Thanks," said Maggie. "I'm thinking maybe we can help each other out."

"How so?"

"Well, you know I don't like Karen very much, right?"

Dex smiled and nodded, returning his gaze to the sea.

Maggie hesitated for a second. "And I don't think you're too partial to Bill either. I know you weren't happy when he was found in that hospital. Am I right?"

When Dex didn't answer immediately, she turned her face toward him about to ask again, but something in his sudden silence stopped her. Watching him closely, she noted that his expression had become stony and his hands were gripping the armrests of the chair tightly, knuckles white with exertion.

He's hiding something, she thought. *Something about Bill.*

"Dex?" she asked finally, laying her hand softly on his arm. "Are you still with me? Is everything all right?"

With an apparent effort, Dex relaxed and turned his head and smiled at her.

"Sorry. I'm fine. Just woolgathering. Now what did you ask me?"

"I said I don't think you're too fond of Bill either. Are you?"

He thought for a moment. "As a person, I guess I'm neutral on him. But as a *man*, well, no, I don't like him. I don't like the way he took advantage of you back then. You were so young and he was married and should have known better."

Maggie grinned. "I knew what I was getting into, Dex. Don't fool yourself into thinking I was naive. And if I had told him I was pregnant, he might just have stepped up, you know."

Again, Dex's face hardened as he stared out at the rocks below. "If I'd a known he knocked you up, I just might have escorted him to Puffin myself."

Maggie watched him silently for a minute, surprised at the amount of animosity he was expressing toward her lover. "Well, that's neither here nor there now. Let's not rehash the past. What I'm talking about is the present - how he might still have designs on your wife."

Dex nodded, his face grim. "Yeah, you may be right. He may have some misguided notion that he can erase time and get his family back. And, no, I don't like the idea of that at all."

"Okay, so what I'm suggesting is that we help each other out."

Dex cocked his head, puzzled. "Okay, I'm listening."

"Well, it seems to me it might be to our mutual benefit to try to keep those two apart and keep each other informed about what's going on. That way there'd be no surprises for either of us."

Dex laughed. "I like the way you think, Red. Fine. You keep an eye on Bill and I'll try to find out what's going on with Karen and we'll pass along anything interesting. But don't think I'm going to do any real spying for you. I don't plan on getting myself involved in any island girl intrigue, if you know what I mean."

Maggie grinned. "Island girl intrigue? I like the sound of that. Yes, I am an island girl - always have been and always will be! Born and bred an islander and proud of it."

Dex smiled warmly at her. "Yes, that's what we are, kitten. We're both Mataguans with all the baggage that comes along with it, the good and the bad."

Maggie leaned back in her chair, laughing. She reached out and took his hand in hers and gave it a squeeze, then let go and picked up her cup and took a sip.

They sat silently for a while, each alone with their thoughts. She turned her head slightly to watch him out of the corner of her eye. He was staring out to sea again, his face a mask.

Yes, he's hiding something - something from back then - something about Bill and about Karen. Hmmmm, I wonder ... what could it be?

 **DATE NIGHT**

SATURDAY CAME AROUND QUICKLY and Terri was disappointed that there was no word from Charlie. She thought about giving him a call, but told herself to wait. He probably had good reason for being out of touch. However, thoughts of the little knife continued to plague her mind and she longed to understand its meaning.

I need to know more about it, she told herself. *In knowledge is power and I for sure need some kind of power over that damned thing!*

Trying to put her worries aside, she dressed for her date with Shawn. They were going to the beach for a lobster bake with a group of young islanders and she dressed carefully in layers. Even though it was warm now, it could cool off rapidly when the sun went down.

Shawn arrived promptly at seven p.m. and, after undergoing a brief interrogation from Karen, escorted Terri to his truck. They drove a short way and parked by the side of the road near a trailhead that led down to the beach. Several other cars were already there.

Taking a blanket and cooler from the back of the truck, Shawn guided Terri down the path to join the other young people.

After a time, when the lobster had been eaten and the remnants returned to the sea, Shawn motioned to Terri to come with him. Taking the blanket, they walked hand in hand down the beach. Reaching a spot far from the lobster bake bonfire, Shawn stopped and shook out the blanket, spreading it on the sand in a small nest created by the rocks. They sat down, leaning back against the boulders, and Shawn, with his arm around her, began to point out the constellations twinkling in the dark sky above them.

Silently, the moon, which had been hidden behind one lone cloud, peeked out, its sickle shape illuminating the sea and rocks below, sending a sparkling prism of color into the air before them.

It was a beautiful sight; but, to Terri, it seemed somehow too bright, too shiny and artificial to be real. She was surprised to feel a shimmer of fear begin to grow around her heart. Reacting to her apprehension, she turned in Shawn's arms to face him looking for some reassurance. In response, he leaned toward her and began to kiss her softly, his hands moving gently on her back as he pulled her to him.

Relaxing in his embrace, Terri once again began to feel safe, returning his kisses with controlled passion. They rested in each other's arms: two young people beginning an age-old dance that could possibly go on forever.

But without warning, everything changed.

Shawn moved his head down to nuzzle at her neck and, from out of nowhere, a vision of the small bone knife erupted in Terri's consciousness, blotting out everything else. The moon, as if sensing her unease, shone even brighter, its light so dazzling it hurt to look at it. Involuntarily, she squeezed her eyes shut to blot out its painful, probing glare.

In vain, with fear gripping tightly at her heart, she tried to warn Shawn, to stop what she knew was about to happen. But her voice was strangled as if something or someone had twisted a garrote around her neck, crushing her words before they could be spoken.

She gasped for breath as Shawn's hands, once so gentle, now began to roam her body forcefully, pinching and squeezing. She tried again to cry out, to tell him to stop, but her tongue was glued to the roof of her mouth and she felt like she was choking. She tried to twist her body away from his as panic began to overwhelm her, but he grabbed her arms with one hand and pinned them above her head and, using his knees, immobilized her legs.

With his free hand he pushed up her sweatshirt, tore open the cotton shirt she wore underneath and began to roughly massage her breasts. Becoming more and more aroused, he pushed her down into the sand and began to use his tongue and teeth on her as his knee forced her legs apart and his hand began to move downward, seeking entry into her tight jeans. His fingers felt like claws as they poked and prodded at the waistband of her pants, roughly seeking out the warmth she held within.

Again, she struggled to free herself, but the movement only seemed to intensify his desire. Her eyes, squeezed shut to avoid the burning light of the moon, now opened and her fear escalated sharply.

Shawn's face was changed - his features distorted by lust and violence. Acknowledging the fear in her expression, he laughed and his eyes began to glow with an unnatural light.

Terri's mind screamed as she realized that these were not the eyes of the young man she cared for. No, they were the eyes of a wolf, cunning and vicious.

As she stared at the beast that had somehow possessed Shawn, a soft growl began to emanate from his throat and his lips curled back in a snarl revealing sharp, rotting teeth. Vile, rancid spittle began to drip down from his mouth, burning her with its venom.

Realizing that much more than her virginity was at stake, Terri tried desperately to control the panic that threatened to overwhelm her. A vision of Charlie's kind face appeared in her mind followed by his gentle voice echoing throughout her consciousness, *"Stay strong within yourself. Do not doubt, and you will triumph over them."*

The words strangely calmed her and with her panic now under control, she tried once more to twist out of the beast's grasp, but failing, suddenly let herself go limp, feigning unconsciousness.

Believing she had passed out, the creature controlling Shawn's body let out a snort of triumph, then released her arms, sat back, and moved his hands to the front of his pants and began to unzip the fly.

Peeking out from half-opened eyelids, Terri waited precious seconds and, with her hands now free, slowly slithered her arm downward and braced herself for what was to come.

A loud crack resounded in the still night air as the flat of her hand connected with the creature's face. At the same time, she forcefully lashed out at his groin with her foot, causing him to fall over and cry out in pain. The moon, as if sensing its moment of triumph had been lost, scurried back behind the lone cloud and darkness enveloped the young couple once more.

Shawn backed away, doubled over in agony, his face a mask of confusion and pain. He looked up at her and was shocked by her appearance. She was standing about five feet from him, shielding her naked breasts with her arms, her shirt torn and in ruins. Angry red welts were blossoming on her chest and legs where his hands and mouth had abused her.

"I ... I don't know what happened," he stammered. "Oh, God, Terri, did I hurt you? I ... I didn't mean. I can't believe I did that. Are you hurt? Please tell me you're not hurt."

Terri moved farther away and stared at him. He was "Shawn" again. All traces of the evil being that had entered him were gone. She took a moment to gather her thoughts before she responded, rearranging her clothing and brushing the sand and debris from her body and hair. In her mind's eye, she could see his face again, leering hungrily at her, and she knew that the creature that had controlled him would have not have stopped at rape. Pushing that thought and the fear it engendered to the back of her mind, she finally turned to face him.

"I'm okay, Shawn. I'm okay."

On the verge of tears, the young man backed up, moving farther away from her. "I know this makes no sense, but I don't remember what I did. We ... we were kissing - everything was great - and then ... then it's all blank. What did I do, Terri? What happened? What's wrong with me?"

Taking a deep breath, she walked toward him. Instinctively, he backed away from her as if fearing that whatever had possessed him would return to harm her.

Shaking her head gently, she reached out for his hand. "It wasn't you, Shawn. Something took you over - possessed you. *You* didn't hurt me or try to hurt me. It was something else, something having to do with that bone knife. Something evil."

He stared at her, trying to comprehend, yet unable to grasp the truth in her words. He looked like a little boy, lost and alone, and her heart cried out for him.

Slowly, trying not to frighten him, she moved to his side, putting her arm gently around his waist.

"It's the magic, Shawn," she said softly. "The magic from that box, the magic that my mother's mixed up in. It all comes from ten years ago when my father got lost in the woods. It wants me now. It used you to try to get to me. But we stopped it."

He shook his head, as if forcing himself to believe. "I didn't. You did ..."

Terri smiled. "No, you stopped it, too. You're so much stronger than me. Do you think I could have fought you off if you were really determined? No, it was me and YOU - we stopped it. We were stronger - we prevailed."

Gingerly, he reached out and put his hand on her shoulder, afraid she might bolt at his touch, but she stood steadfast.

"It's okay, Shawn," she said as she moved into his arms and embraced him gently. "We're okay. It can't touch us now."

They stood together on the dark beach, listening to the sound of the waves lapping at the shore, each trying to understand and come to grips with what they had just experienced.

Finally, Shawn pulled away, gazing down into her eyes. "I think I'm falling in love with you," he said softly. "I don't understand what happened here tonight, but it won't happen again. I'll never hurt you. I'll keep you safe, if you'll let me."

Terri nodded and smiled as she leaned into his broad chest. "Yes, I know you will. But now, I think we'd better head home. It's getting late and we don't want my mother on your case."

For the first time in what seemed to be forever to him, Shawn relaxed and smiled. "No, we for sure don't want that!"

Moving out of her arms, he leaned down and picked up the blanket, shook it out, and folded it. Then he reached out and took her hand and together they turned and walked back up the beach to his truck.

As if sensing them go, the moon once again peeked out from behind its hiding place, shining with preternatural brightness, illuminating the young couple as they walked away. Then, as if summoned, came the sound of flapping wings and, with a soft hoot, an owl began to shadow them, following closely behind until they reached home.

Once there, it watched as Terri closed the front door and Shawn's truck pulled away. Then it perched in a tall tree, staring at the house, unmoving; content for the time being to just watch and wait.

At the same time, on the mainland, Charlie Red Squirrel was driving home from the Museum, his thoughts troubled. Since his visit with Harry Three Feathers, he had spent every waking minute studying and re-studying the parchment, hoping beyond hope he would find something that could dispute Harry's interpretation. But now he knew he could wait no longer. He had to contact his young friend and tell her that she was directly in harm's way and that, in his judgment, there was no way she could avoid the evil path she had been set upon.

Perhaps that's why he didn't see the truck that was backing out of the driveway ahead of him. Too late, he slammed on the brakes. As if in slow motion, he heard the awful sound of metal crunching and tearing and then came the shattering of glass as his head smashed violently into the windshield. His eyes fluttered briefly as blood trickled down his face. Then he lost consciousness.

HARRY THREE FEATHERS

AT FOUR A.M., TERRI was awakened from a deep sleep by the chiming of her cell phone.

"Get that damned phone, Terri," cried her twin as she pulled the covers over her head.

In response, Terri leapt out of bed, grabbed the phone, and took it into the bathroom. Closing the door, she glanced at the caller ID, but it was unfamiliar. Puzzled, she answered it anyway.

"Hello?"

"Is this the young one who is the friend of my friend, Mekwi Mikoa?"

The caller's voice was but a whisper and seemed so ancient that Terri wondered if she was hallucinating again.

Pulling herself together, she replied shakily, "Who is this? And who's Mekwi Mikoa?"

There was silence on the line and in the quietness she remembered: the caller was asking about Charlie.

"Are you still there? I'm sorry, I forgot Charlie's tribal name. Yes, I'm his friend. Who are you and how did you get my number?"

Again, there was silence and she was about to hang up when the caller began to speak. "The Red Squirrel gave me your number. I am called Harry Three Feathers and I fear something terrible has happened."

"Terrible? What do you mean? Has something happened to Charlie?"

"Yes, to our friend. The smoke spirits spoke to me in a dream and I saw twisted metal, broken glass, and rivers of blood. I fear there has been an accident and that our friend may be dying."

Terri sunk down heavily to the floor, trying to comprehend what this old man was telling her. Charlie dying?

Suddenly, she felt as if all the air had been sucked from the room and she began to hyperventilate. As she gasped for breath, she heard a faint chanting began to resonate from her cell phone. Concentrating on the rhythm and cadence of the chant, her fear suddenly abated and she was once again breathing normally and able to focus.

"Do you have any idea where he may be?" she asked.

"The smoke dream did not reveal this, but I sense that he had not left the city. Logic tells me that if he had an accident, he would be at the hospital."

The old man began coughing and she waited impatiently as he cleared his throat.

"Are you okay?" she asked.

"Yes, young one. When I heard you struggling for air, I asked the creator to pass your spasm on to me. But all is now well. I can breathe again."

"Was that what the chanting was for?" asked Terri incredulously. "To take my anxiety onto yourself?"

The old man chuckled. "Not a big deal. Now, what are you going to do about our friend?"

Terri hesitated for a moment, thinking. "I'll get the next

ferry to town. It's at five-thirty. I can take a cab from the terminal to the hospital. If I find him, how can I reach you?"

The old Indian gave her his number at the nursing home and said he would await her call. Then he said some words in a dialect she didn't understand and hung up.

Careful not to reawaken her sister, Terri washed her face, brushed her teeth, and got dressed. She left a hastily scrawled note for her mother tacked to the refrigerator and, grabbing her purse, headed through the house to the garage where her bike was stored. As she got on the bike, she checked her watch and then, moving swiftly, pedaled down the road to make the next ferry.

Karen arose early, awakened by the sound of the garage door closing. Her curiosity aroused, she threw on a robe and went downstairs. She cracked the door to her daughters' room and was surprised to find Terri's bed empty. Perplexed, she walked over to the kitchen and saw the note that her daughter had written and tacked to the refrigerator door.

A friend has been in an accident; gone to town. Will call later.

Karen stood staring at the note as her coffee brewed.

Now what 'friend' can she be talking about? The only person she knows in town is that curator at the museum. I wonder if she means him? God, I hope she's not getting involved in all this stuff again. She promised she wouldn't.

Feeling irritated, Karen crumpled the note into a ball and threw it in the trash. Then she poured herself a cup of coffee, sat down and pulled out her phone.

Terri was sitting on the ferry when her cell rang. Hoping it was Charlie or Harry with good news, she quickly answered.

"Hello?"

"So who's this 'friend' that's in trouble, Terri?" asked Karen, with a hint of irritation. "As far as I know, you don't know too many people around here."

Terri sighed, recognizing her mother's voice. "It's Charlie, Mom. The museum curator. I think he's been in an accident and I need to go see him, to find out for sure."

"Terri, you hardly know this man. What makes you think he's been in an accident anyway? Are you becoming clairvoyant?"

Terri smiled thinking how her mother would react if she told her about Harry's smoke dream, but then frowned as she struggled to find a way to answer.

"It's just a feeling, Mom. Listen, I can't talk now. We're docking. I have to go. I'll be home soon."

Without waiting for her mother's answer, Terri shut down the phone and tucked it away in her purse. Then she stood and got ready to debark and go into town.

It was close to six a.m. when Terri arrived at the hospital. Not knowing what else to do, she made her way to the Emergency

Room. After glancing around and seeing no sign of Charlie or anyone else who looked Native American in the waiting room, she approached the desk clerk.

"I wonder if you can help me. I got word that my uncle was in an accident and I think he might be here. He's a Native American Indian, about seventy-five years old. His Indian name is Mekwi Mikoa, but we call him Charlie - Charlie Red Squirrel."

The clerk stared at Terri's blonde, blue-eyed visage suspiciously for a moment, then turned to her computer screen. After typing in some information, she turned back to Terri. "Yup. He was brought here all right. Auto accident. He's been admitted to intensive care."

The clerk pulled out a hospital map and indicated to Terri where the unit was on the second floor. Terri thanked her and walked briskly down the corridor to the elevator.

Not wanting to interfere with Charlie's family if they were there, she glanced around the ICU waiting area, but it was empty. Taking a deep breath, she walked up to the duty nurse and repeated her story: Charlie was her uncle and she wanted to know how he was and if she could see him. The nurse led her down the corridor to a small room on the right. Inside, the old Indian lay in bed, hooked up to various monitors and machines, an IV attached to his arm. He appeared unconscious.

Terri pulled up a chair next to the bed and sat down. Reaching out, she took his hand gently in hers.

"Oh, Charlie," she whispered. "How did this happen? Somehow, I feel I'm to blame. Can you ever forgive me?"

Tears sprang into her eyes, blurring her vision, and she absentmindedly wiped them away with her free hand. She blinked her eyes and opened them again, aware now of a gentle fluttering of the old Indian's eyelids.

"Charlie? Are you awake? Can you hear me?"

The old man's eyelids moved again and she felt his hand squeeze hers weakly. She squeezed back just as his eyes opened halfway. "Child," he whispered. "You have come."

His voice was so soft she could barely hear him so she leaned closer to his face. "Yes, Charlie. I came. Harry Three Feathers told me. You have to get better, you hear? I won't stand for anything else."

"Come closer - I must ... I must tell you something."

Obeying the old man's wish, Terri leaned even closer. "Yes, I'm here. What is it?"

"The boy - it is all about the boy. You must safeguard him. Keep him from danger. Or all will be lost."

"The boy? What boy? Do you mean Billy? He's the only kid I know here. But what do I guard him from?"

The old man did not seem to hear her. "Keep him safe, child. Don't let him go into the woods or the world as we know it will end..."

Terri was about to question him again when suddenly his hand went limp and the monitors in the room began to shriek.

"Charlie!" she cried as a nurse came running in the room.

The words "code blue" echoed down the ICU corridor as the nurse hustled her out of the room and a team of doctors and nurses with machines rushed to his bedside.

The nurse escorted Terri back to the waiting room. When they arrived, the elevator opened and a group of people emerged. In the lead was a good-looking man about forty-five years old wearing a business suit. His features bore a striking resemblance to Charlie's.

"That's his real family, isn't it?" whispered the nurse. "You're not his niece, are you? Just a friend?"

Terri blushed and bowed her head, unable to meet the nurse's steady gaze. "He's important to me and I knew you wouldn't let me see him if I wasn't a relative."

The nurse nodded compassionately. "I know you meant no harm, but we have rules for a reason."

Terri nodded, not knowing what to say.

"Well, I have to speak with his real family now. But why don't you give me your number. I'll text you when we know his status."

Terri smiled gratefully, gave the nurse her cell number and thanked her. "You don't know how much this means to me. He's a very special human being."

The nurse smiled. "You don't know his family, do you?"

Terri shook her head.

"Well, I think to avoid any trouble you should go. Okay? I'll text you. I won't forget. Now scat."

Terri mumbled a quick 'thank you' and moved toward the elevators, passing Charlie's family as she went.

Leaving the hospital, she hailed a cab to take her back to the ferry terminal. The next boat would leave in about an hour and she planned to be on it.

 **MAGGIE**

MAGGIE SAT AT HER desk in the one-room island schoolhouse. It was Sunday and she didn't have any classes. This was summer school and while she was not very actively involved in teaching the students, she was still in charge and that meant overseeing quite a bit of paperwork.

Feeling tired and bored, she put her computer aside and walked over to the window. Outside, kindergarten-level students were working in the school gardens under the close observation of teachers' aides and volunteer mothers. She smiled as she watched them, remembering participating in the same class with her son when he was that age. Then she frowned, her thoughts turning to the other "Bill" in her life. He had come home late the night before after another trip to Boston. Again, he had evaded her questions about his time spent there and what the future held for him and for her.

He just waltzed right in, sat down, and ate the meal I warmed up for him and then, without so much as a 'thank you, Maggie', left and spent the

286

rest of the evening on his laptop! Then, when he came up to bed, out of the blue he expected me to be waiting for him, legs spread and all ready to go with stars in my eyes! The nerve of that bastard!

Her mood ruined, she walked back to her desk and sat down. *I wonder if that's how he was with Karen. Was he so wrapped up in his work that he left her feeling ignored and unappreciated? If that's the case, then I'm beginning to understand why she was always such a bitch to him. He may just have deserved it!*

However, as soon as those words crossed her consciousness, she began to regret them. *He's been through so much. Of course, he's intent on his work - he knows how much is riding on his success. But what about me? Is he really planning to leave me and our boy high and dry?*

She shook her head. No, he couldn't be. She would not let that happen. She had hung her star on him and, for better or worse, he was stuck. No, she vowed. He was not going to get out of this relationship easily - not if she had anything to say about it.

TERRI, KAREN, AND SOPHIE

IT WAS MID-MORNING WHEN Terri arrived back at the rented house on the island. Exhausted, she dropped her bike on the lawn and walked slowly up the path to the front door. Stopping before entering, she checked her cell phone once again to see if by some chance she had missed a message about Charlie. But there was none.

Shaking her head, she put the phone back in her purse and walked into the house. Her mother and sister were sitting at the breakfast bar drinking coffee and talking. When they heard the door shut, they both looked up.

Karen put her cup down, stood up, and faced her daughter. "Well, did you find out anything about *your friend*? Is he okay?"

Terri stood mute for a moment, trying to find the right words. "He ... he went into cardiac arrest while I was there ... I ... " She couldn't finish.

Seeing the look of devastation on her daughter's face and the tears that were welling up in her eyes, Karen immediately regretted her sarcastic tone. Her face softening, she crossed the room and put her arms around her distraught child. "I'm sorry, honey," she said quietly. "I didn't mean to sound so callous. Did he pass?"

Crying freely now, Terri shook her head. "I don't know. The nurse said she'd text me, but nothing's come through yet."

Sophie joined them, patting her sister on the back. "I don't understand," she said with a bit of irritation. "Who's this guy in town and why are you so upset? Mom says he the curator of a museum or something. What's he got to do with you?"

Karen turned to look at her other daughter, her face stern. "We'll talk about this later, Sophie. Your sister is clearly exhausted and needs some rest. Come on, Terri, let's get you to bed."

Shaking her head slightly at Sophie, Karen helped Terri to the bedroom. "You lie down and get some sleep, honey. Everything will look better once you're rested. If you need anything, let me know."

Thanking her mother, Terri closed the door.

Karen walked back to the breakfast bar and poured herself another cup of coffee.

"But Mom," complained Sophie. "She's become so secretive. Always sneaking off into town and lying to me. I'm worried about her."

Karen nodded. "Yes, I am, too. And that's why I've done something about it. Last night I booked us all on flights out of here. We're going home."

"Home? But I thought we were staying till August?"

"Think, honey. You've found your dad and that's more than you ever expected would come out of this trip. And now he's got a new job and is spending most of his time in Boston. So, you won't be seeing much of him here anyway. Also, you have school to think about and need to get ready for that. Terri will be in La Jolla at Scripps, but you're going to Yale and that means a completely new wardrobe for winter! And aren't you beginning to get just a little bored here?"

Sophie smiled. "Yeah, you're right about that. I miss California and all my friends. It is time to go. But what about

Terri? She has her new boyfriend and now this museum guy in town. And what's that all about anyway? You said you'd tell me."

Karen sighed. "Yes, I did. Remember all those old Indian stories Pete McKinney used to tell? Well, Terri's got it into her head they had something to do with your dad's disappearance ten years ago and she's trying to find out more about them. That's how she connected with the museum curator and now, for some unknown reason, he's become important to her. Hopefully, he'll weather this crisis and recover and she won't be so wrapped up with him anymore."

Sophie nodded. "Okay, that makes sense. But what about Shawn? She's not going to leave him easily."

Karen sipped her coffee, thinking. "He seems like a nice kid: steady and dependable. But she's too young to get serious with anybody and I don't want to see her end up wasting her life away here on this island. I'd like to nip this little romance in the bud and going home will do just that. You'll see. Out of sight, out of mind."

Sophie nodded. "Yeah, I don't see her hooked up with him for eternity either. But what about you, Mom? You and Dex? Will he coming with us or staying here?"

Karen sighed, knowing this question was coming. "I'm going to call him this morning and let him know our plans. Our flights are booked for a week from Friday. We'll fly from Portland to Chicago and then home to San Francisco. I'm hopeful he'll come with us."

Sophie stared down at her coffee cup, building up her courage to delve deeper. Finally, she looked at her mother. "Why did you kick him out anyway, Mom? Something about a broken promise? What was so bad you had to ask him to leave?"

Karen was about to issue a sharp retort but stopped when she saw the hurt look in her daughter's eyes. Softening, she reached out and took Sophie's hand. "Back ten years ago when we lost your dad so abruptly, I started saying these prayers - prayers to Mother Earth, the moon, just any deity I could think of that might keep our family together and safe. I asked Dex to promise that he wouldn't ever interfere with them. You see, over time I came to believe that the prayers *were* keeping us from harm. And, as part of that ritual, I cut myself in some notion of sacrifice."

Karen held up her palm for her daughter to examine. "It doesn't look like much, Mom. Just a tiny scar."

Karen laughed. "That's right. It was more of a symbolic gesture than anything else. But Dex ... after the incident in town with the birds, well, he thought I was hurting myself and he forced me to stop. That made me mad, so I kicked him out. And that's all there is to it, honey. I want him back and I think he wants me, too. I think once we get home, everything will work out. So, don't you worry about it, okay? You let me handle everything.

"Now, let's clean up the kitchen and go for a walk while you sister's sleeping. Maybe we can find some nice colored sea glass today. What do you say?"

Sophie laughed. "You're on, Mom."

SMOKE DREAMS

TERRI CLOSED THE DOOR and sat down on her bed. She was tired but didn't think she could sleep as long as Charlie's fate hung in the balance. She looked again at her phone as if by staring at it she could will it to ring. Nothing happened. Sighing, she reached out to put it down on the bureau. As soon as she let go of it, it chimed, indicating a text message.

Pulling it toward her eagerly, she read the text. *"He's stable, but there's been damage to his heart. He'll go to surgery this afternoon. His family is with him. I'll text when he's out."*

He's alive!

Breathing a sigh of relief, Terri opened up her "contacts" and quickly dialed the number Harry Three Feathers had given her. The phone was answered promptly.

"Yes, young one, you have news of our friend. He lives."

Surprised, Terri stammered, "Yes, Mr. Three Feathers, but how did you know?"

The old Indian laughed. "Do not question the spirits, my child. They are all around us and, if you listen carefully, they will reveal everything."

Terri laughed. "The nurse said he was going to surgery this afternoon and she'll contact me when he's out. Do you want me to call you when I hear something?"

"No, that will not be necessary. His son will call me. Now, what about you? Did our friend tell you what you needed to know?"

Again, Terri hesitated. "Yes, I think so. He told me I needed to protect the boy. I think he means my stepbrother, Billy. At least, he's the only kid I know of here on the island. But I have a question that I didn't have time to ask him."

"Go on."

"How will I know when to protect him? Is something going to happen that will let me know?"

"Oh, you young people - so impatient. Don't you see? The answers are all around you. You will find them if you stop and listen."

"I'm sorry, I don't understand."

"You, young one, are strong with magic. Can't you feel it all around you? You must relax and let the magic flow through you - it will come, trust me. Now let's try an experiment. Lie down. Keep the phone to your ear and close your eyes."

Confused, Terri did as the old man said. All was silent for a moment and then she began to hear soft chanting through the phone.

"Tankashila, mya kya,
Tankashila, mya kya,
Che wo kielo,
Wakan chelo heyo,
Ah hey wa hey cheyo,
Wachio hey hey."

Suddenly feeling incredibly sleepy, she turned off all her thoughts and fears and just concentrated on the soft voice of the old man. Within moments, she slipped into a deep sleep.

When her eyes opened again, everything around her was dark and hazy and she felt as if she were surrounded by a cloud of soft smoke. She reached out with her hands to try to find something familiar to hold on to, but there was nothing. Gingerly, she inched her way forward on the bed, trying to find passage out of the fog that encased her. She knew she should be afraid, but for some reason there was no fear present in her mind. The old Indian's words echoed across her consciousness, "... let the magic flow through you..."

Suddenly, in front of her, the haze was breeched by a bright flash of light, followed by a deafening clap of thunder. She looked around and was surprised to find that she was no longer in her bedroom. Now, impossibly, she was floating above the earth, suspended upon a cloud of smoke. She watched, amazed, recognizing the house on the hill - the one she had lived in when she was a child - as it came into view. She hovered over it for a second, then the cloud she sat upon moved to the backyard and she saw the woods looming below her.

The smoke cloud drifted effortlessly through the forest canopy and Terri could see a dark, twisted trail emerge beneath her. On that trail stood a girl, apparently frozen in indecision. Hard, cold rain flew out of the sky, drenching the girl within seconds, despite the slicker that she wore. Terri watched as the girl hugged herself to ward of the chill. Lightning again lit up the sky, illuminating the trail in front of the girl and Terri saw her nod and begin to move deeper into the woods. Crows began to shriek in the treetops and dark shadows loomed as the trail became narrower and more winding.

Out of nowhere, the root of an old oak lifted up out of the damp soil in front of the girl, opening up a large crevasse. The girl struggled to keep from being swallowed by the earth and, regaining her balance, finally managed to leap to safety on the other side. Terri could see the trail's end up ahead and the sight of it made her sick. It was the swamp, and, even from her lofty vantage point, the smell of it made her gag.

The smoke cloud now moved to hover above the tepid water and Terri could see a child sitting on a log, shoes and socks saturated with mud. The child was tethered to the log by the slimy tendrils of some noxious vine that wound tightly around his torso. Behind him stood another figure, one Terri recognized from long ago - and that vision struck fear deep within her heart.

She tried to call out a warning to the girl and the child, wanting to save them, but her vocal cords had somehow been rendered useless. Fear mounting within her, she squeezed her eyes shut, not wanting to see what would happen next.

Thunder roared again and she felt herself begin to fall as the cloud that had supported her quickly evaporated. Lightning flashed and she saw the swamp below coming rapidly closer as her body plummeted from the sky. It would be only seconds before she hit the poisonous water that she could now see was teeming with snakes and other vile creatures. Unable to help herself, she closed her eyes, whispered a prayer, and as her body hit the water, she screamed.

Terri jerked upright in bed, the scream caught in her throat, surprised to find she was back in her room, clothing and bedclothes drenched in sweat. The dream had been so real, she felt she could almost reach out and touch it. Shaking her head, she looked down at her hand. Her fingers still clutched the cell phone and only a few minutes had passed since she had closed her eyes.

He sent me a smoke dream, she thought. *He said the magic was in me and he was right. Now I know what I have to do. A storm is coming and I have to be ready.*

She glanced at the phone again and clicked on the weather app. Scrolling ahead several days, she saw the beginnings of some chatter about two low-pressure systems that might meet up in the Midwest and then collide with a large high settled over the East Coast. The result could be a monster storm. Nodding, she laid the phone on the dresser and walked to the bathroom, where she turned the shower on high. Then, stripping off her sodden clothing, she stepped in and let the heat from the water soothe and comfort her.

Yes, the magic is here, around and in me, and now I know what I have to do but will I have the courage to face the evil that hides in those woods? Oh, God, I hope I don't have to.

KAREN AND DEX

BACK FROM HER WALK with Sophie, Karen excused herself and went up to the loft. Sitting by the window, she stared at her phone. *I have to call him and let him know our plans to leave. Will he come with us? Oh God, I hope so. But he's still so mad at me.*

Sighing to herself, she knew that procrastinating further would get her nowhere. She had to know if he still loved her and wanted her despite everything she'd put him through. Reluctantly, she dialed.

The phone rang several times. She was about to hang up when he answered, his voice breaking up with static. "Hello? Karen? Listen hang on - the reception sucks - let me move the boat around."

She waited for what seemed forever, fearing he had hung up. Finally, he came back on the line. "Karen? You still there? I'm out fishing. Cell reception is lousy out here, but I think I've got enough for a short call. What's up?"

Relieved, she took a deep breath. "Dex, I called to let you know I've made a decision. It's time we went home - all of us. I

297

booked us flights back to San Francisco for a week from Friday. That should give you time to clear up any commitments you have here. We need to go home."

The phone was silent. Afraid she'd lost him, she checked the connection, but he was still on the line - just not answering. Then she heard him take a deep breath.

"I think we need to talk about this," he said. "I've got a couple of full days of work ahead of me this week. Maybe we can get together Thursday or Friday. We'll discuss *our* plans then."

Hearing the emphasis he put on the "our," she knew she may have made a mistake by making a decision without talking to him first. Not wanting to alienate him further, she chose her words carefully.

"Sure, Dex. We can talk about it. But understand I did this mainly for the girls. I think Terri's getting in a little too deep with that O'Dwyer boy and, well, both girls have a lot to do to get ready for college."

Again, there was silence.

"Dex, are you still there?"

"Yeah, I'm here. We'll talk about it, okay? Look, I have to get back to work. I'll call you."

"Sure. You have a good day. And, Dex ... I love you."

Afraid he would not answer in kind, she didn't wait for a reply but hung up the line.

Dex stood at the helm, fists clenched around the steering wheel, knuckles white with anger. She'd done it to him again - making decisions without consulting him. What in God's name was he to her anyway? He was her husband and lover for sure, but was he her partner?

Angry with himself, he knew his day's fishing was ruined, so he turned the boat around and headed back to the island.

California ... yes, he knew it was time to go back. His business needed him. He'd spent the better part of the morning on the phone with Brad. The boat needed repairs and he knew he had to be there to make sure the work was done properly. But why couldn't she have talked to him before going ahead and making plans? He shook his head, thinking back to when he'd first met her.

She was a bit of a spoiled princess then, for sure. But I watched her grow over that summer and with her maturity came a deep and abiding love. Yes, we're separated now, but it won't last. We're bound together. She'd call it mystical or some such bullshit. But, I have to admit, it is a bond - one neither of us would or could willingly break.

He looked out over the water, seeing the island in the distance.

God, how I love this place! The west coast is good, but it can't compare with this unspoiled beauty.

Watching as the coastline came into view, his thoughts strayed back to Karen and their life together. Bitterly, he acknowledged he was complicit in the problems that were having. He had backed down too many times.

But we lived in her house and the girls are her children - so what right did I ever have to interfere with her wishes? But, on the other hand, if we truly are partners in life, I do have that right. I don't want to leave this place forever. I want to come back here - and, often. Next summer, for sure. If we had a place here ... but she'd never agree....

That thought played around in his mind as he secured the boat to its mooring. When he was done, he stood for a moment, gazing at the shore. *I could do it. I could make it work.*

A smile on his face for the first time since Karen's call, he took the punt back to the wharf and jogged to his truck. He was in a hurry - he had some calls to make.

TERRI

TERRI EMERGED FROM THE bedroom after her shower feeling surprisingly well rested and refreshed. Her mother and Sophie were sitting in the living room. Karen was reading and her twin was talking and laughing on her cell phone. Karen looked up when her daughter entered the room.

"Feeling better, honey?" she asked. "Did you hear any news about your friend?"

Terri smiled. "Yes, on both counts, Mom. Charlie's stable, but he has to have surgery. I believe it's scheduled for this afternoon. The nurse said she'd contact me again when he's in recovery."

"I'm glad, honey. Do you want something to eat? You slept straight through lunch."

"No, I'm fine. I'll wait for dinner. Who were you talking to, Soph?"

"Brenda from home. You won't believe what happened. Tiffany and Judd broke up! He caught her with some college guy

300

from San Diego State! I can't wait to get home and hear all about it!"

"Well, that'll be awhile since we're here through August, sis! You'll have to content yourself with phone calls and texts."

"No way - we'll be home in time for the Summer Frolic a week from Sunday!"

Terri turned to her mother, a look of puzzlement on her face. "What's going on, Mom? Want to let me in on it?"

Karen sighed. "Sophie's right. We're going home. I made reservations for us for a week from Friday."

"But, Mom, we planned to stay the summer! Why?"

"There's no reason to stay any longer. You found your father. His disappearance *was* our reason for coming back here, right? And he's spending more and more time in Boston now so you won't be seeing much of him anyway. Also, you and Sophie have a lot to do to get ready for school, especially Sophie since she'll be on the east coast. It just doesn't make sense to stay here longer."

Terri stared at her mother then at her sister. It seemed they had formed a united front against her and she, for once, was the outsider. "But what about Dex? Is he leaving, too?"

Again, Karen sighed. "I hope so. I spoke with him today and he wants to talk about it later this week. He's still a tad mad at me, but I think he'll come around. His business in Monterey needs him."

Terri, realizing she was outnumbered, nodded, then walked over to the landline phone that sat in the hallway. Finding the number she wanted in the Island Directory, she picked up the receiver and began to dial.

"Who are you calling, honey?" asked Karen, puzzled.

"Shawn."

Karen frowned and was about to say something when Terri turned away and began to speak into the phone.

"Hi, is Shawn there?" she asked as she moved into the hallway to avoid being overheard by her mother and sister, who were now staring at her. A few minutes later, she returned, hung up the phone and reached in the closet for her windbreaker.

"I'm meeting Shawn at the Island Burger Shack for dinner. I'll just be gone a couple of hours. It's just a short ride on the bike."

Karen was about to object when she saw look of the grim determination on her child's face. That look told her that, yes, Terri would come home with them but, no, she would not give up this evening with the young man she cared for. Understanding the trade-off, Karen nodded. "Have a good time. And say 'hi' to him for us."

Recognizing the falseness in the pleasantry her mother directed toward Shawn, Terri just nodded and left the house.

Shawn was waiting when Terri arrived at the Island Burger Shack. She unceremoniously dropped her bike on the grass, grabbed his hand, and pulled him toward the beach.

"Whoa, girl! What's going on?"

"Let's take a walk. I need to move. Get some crap out of my system."

Shawn smiled and squeezed her hand. "Okay. You're the boss."

They walked down a short path to the shore, then Terri pulled off her sandals, placing them on a rock. "Race you to the point?"

"You're on," he replied, pulling off his tennies.

Dropping her hand, he let her get a head start then quickly caught up to her as they ran in the surf to an outcropping of rock at the end of the sandy beach. When they neared the rocks, Shawn slowed, letting her get ahead of him and win the race.

Out of breath, she bent over, shaking her head. "You cheated! You let me win."

Shawn laughed. "My mother taught me to be a gentleman and a gentleman always let's a woman win in a footrace. Now, what is it that's got you so pissed off?"

Terri sighed, sitting down in the sand, hugging her knees to her chest. "We're leaving. Next week. My mother made a decision and when she makes a decision, everyone just better hop to it, or else!"

"She doesn't like it here much, does she?"

"No, shit! Though I have to admit, she makes some good arguments for leaving, but still, I want to stay."

Shawn sat down beside her and began searching through the sand for some good flat stones. "When next week?"

"Friday."

"Well, that gives us some time, doesn't it? What say we go to town this weekend? If that storm hits, it'll be over by Saturday night. We could go to a movie and maybe get a bite to eat?"

Terri grinned and turned to him. "That sounds like a plan. I'd like that."

Shawn smiled and began skipping stones across the water as they talked about movies and food and what they liked and didn't like. Then they stood up and ambled back to the burger shack, ordered, and sat down to enjoy their meal.

# KAREN AND DEX

ON THURSDAY, DEX CALLED Karen and asked her to meet him at his cottage by the boatyard. When she arrived, she was surprised to find him kneeling by the front porch, painting the lattice that surrounded it.

"My, you're making yourself busy. Are you trading rent for handy work?"

Dex turned and smiled. "Hi. No, but the place needs some fixing up before winter comes and with us leaving next week and a possible storm coming, I figured I'd better get at it now. But I can leave it be for a bit. Want some coffee or iced tea?"

"Coffee would be great," she replied.

"Okay," he answered, standing up and laying the paintbrush down. He wiped his hands on his pants and then escorted her into the house.

Sitting down while he poured the coffee, Karen gazed at him, still puzzled. "But why is it your job to do the painting? I thought you'd want to get in as much fishing as you could before we left. Why take responsibility for the repairs?"

Dex handed her the steaming brew and sat down opposite her. He was silent for a minute, staring at his hands, then he looked up and met her gaze. "It's my cottage now, Karen, and I'm the one responsible for the repairs."

She had just taken a sip of the hot coffee and gagged when she realized what he was telling her. Coughing and then clearing her throat, she wiped tears from her eyes and looked at him. "I don't understand. Your cottage?" She glanced around the room, then back at him. "Are you telling me you bought this place?"

Dex smiled. "Yes, that's exactly what I'm telling you. Old Doc Houghton has been moved to assisted living and won't be coming to the island anymore. He was planning to put the cottage on the market in the spring anyway. We talked and I made him an offer. He's happy its going into the hands of another islander. He hated the idea of someone from away getting this place."

Karen pursed her lips, silently digesting this new information. She took another sip of her coffee, thinking, and then she faced him again. "Have you signed the papers yet?"

Dex's eyes narrowed. "I gave him my deposit and shook the man's hand, Karen. Where I come from, that's a deal. The papers will be ready next week before we leave."

Properly chastised, Karen decided to take a different tack. "So, what are your plans? Are you going to rent this place out for the summer? Use it as income property?"

Seeing where she was headed, Dex's eyes turned cold. "No. I've talked to Brad. I'm going to make him a partner. He'll take over the business in Monterey for the summer months. I have my eye on a boat here and I'll work the east coast while he works the west. I plan for us to be here from June through September. The girls can come visit whenever they like."

Karen sat staring at her coffee, which was now turning cold and stale. He was going to make her spend every summer in this God-forsaken place!

She looked up and locked eyes with him. "Is this some sort of punishment? You know how I feel about this island."

Dex met her gaze icily, his hands clenched tightly around his cup. "Yes, I know," he answered flatly. "And you know how I feel about it. I've spent the past ten years living where you wanted to live, doing what you wanted to do. We've had a good life, yes. But now, I want more. All I'm asking is four months - the rest is yours. Is that too much? God, Karen, the things I've done for you..."

She saw the anger in his eyes and suddenly, her mind raced back to another time on this island when she was locked in verbal combat with her husband. But then it had been Bill and she shivered remembering how their argument had ended in violence.

Reliving that pain, she lowered her gaze to the kitchen table. She didn't want to fight with Dex. All she wanted was to go home, to return to the life they had left behind. She waited for him to speak, but he remained silent.

Taking of a sip of her cold coffee, she finally looked up. He was still staring at her, no warmth at all in his eyes or in his face. He was not going to give in on this. Realizing that the future of her marriage now depended on what she said or did, her mind told her to compromise. *Tell him you'll give him his four months. You'll have eight to change his mind.* But her heart told her to stand fast - that no good would come from giving in to his demands. Conflicted, she paused, holding her breath.

"Okay," she finally said, filling her lungs with air. "You have your cottage. I'll text you the particulars of our flight out next week. All right?"

Dex nodded, his face still frozen in a mask of anger. "You do that. And you'll see, Karen, this place can be good for us. If you'll just give it a chance."

Nodding slightly, she stood up. She stared at him for a moment then turned and walked away, leaving him sitting at the table, a cup of cold coffee embraced by his hands, alone.

KAREN

INSTEAD OF GOING DIRECTLY home, Karen drove to Eagle Point. She was agitated from the conversation with Dex and hoped that the serenity of the rocky shoreline would soothe her troubled mind. It was a beautiful day so she got out and walked along the shore.

He bought that cottage! Why? Where did that come from? He's still mad at me, for sure, but to go to that length just to show me up? Why?

She hunkered down on the craggy rocks, weaving her fingers in and out of the silky seaweed as if searching for something long lost. Tears streamed down her cheeks and blended with the salty spray that splashed against the shoreline as the waves rolled in.

He doesn't know what it's like for me here. Always waiting. Always having to be on my guard, wondering where the next attack will come from. And I can't explain it to him ... he won't believe me. Even when he sees I'm hurt, he thinks I'm doing it all to myself. He thinks I'm nuts. I could get Terri to tell him about the knife and remembering everything. But, no, he'd just think we're both bonkers, that insanity runs in my family. He's just too freaking rational.

Shaking her head in frustration, she stood up and began to climb on the rocks, moving purposefully as if by doing so she could find a way to make things right again. Reaching the top, she turned seaward, letting the warm sea breeze dry the salty tears that stained her cheeks.

And what was that he said? Something about the 'things he'd done for me.' What was that all about? The only real thing I ever asked him to do was come to California and that was his decision. I didn't pressure him. So, what else has he done for me that sounds so desperate - like he'd robbed a bank or something? I just don't get it.

She sat down again, letting her legs dangle over the edge of the rocks, her face tilted toward the sun.

So to keep him, I have to come here and be tortured for four months out of the year. God, I just don't get it. Life was good for us in California, but it's not good here. Can't he see that? And it's not all just me. He's changed here, too - different - not the same man I married. And the girls - now Terri's getting mixed up in all the magic. How can I explain that to him? I'm afraid for her, afraid of what's going to happen. I need to get her away from this place and away from that boy. He did something when they were on that date Saturday that frightened her. I know it. Yet, she went out with him again the other night. What's the allure? He's cute, for sure, but he's nowhere near her caliber.

Knowing there would be no answers forthcoming, she began to carefully climb back down the rocks to the beach. Once there, she kicked off her shoes and waded into the cool water.

I could just keep walking then swim until I'm too tired to come back. Then it would all be over.

Again, the tears came and she stood motionless as they fell and merged with the sea around her. Shaking her head slowly, she turned and walked back to the sandy shore. She leaned down and picked up her shoes, brushing the sand from her feet before putting them on. Glancing one more time out to sea, she finally headed up the path and back to her car. She hesitated behind the wheel for a moment, staring out at the jagged coastline. Then, sighing, she put the car in gear and headed home.

FRIDAY —
THE BEGINNING

THE NEXT DAY, THE pundits were still saying that they thought the so-called monster storm would shift out to sea, leaving New England with just the usual rain and wind. Sophie spent the morning reading and Terri worked on her laptop, while Karen cleaned the house in anticipation of leaving the next week. She thought about calling Dex, but couldn't bring herself to do it.

By early afternoon, Terri noted that the forecast had changed. Now, they were saying that southern Maine would take a direct hit.

"Hey, Mom. Do we have candles and stuff? They're now saying the storm's turning, heading for the coast and packing wind speeds up to forty knots."

Karen looked at her, puzzled. "How fast is a knot?"

"It's about forty-five miles per hour. We may lose power. Does this place have a generator?"

"I don't know, honey. Let's look around. Sophie, you look in the cupboards for candles, flashlights, and lanterns - anything that doesn't use electricity. Terri, you go outside and see if there's a generator hidden somewhere. I'll check the garage for gas cans. Oh, and Sophie, look for batteries, too. A lantern won't do us much good without them."

The girls dutifully followed their mother's orders. Terri came back soon, reporting that there was a generator stored by the side yard. There were instructions on how to use it attached to the wall behind it, but the paper they were printed on was old and faded.

"Sophie," ordered Karen, "take down the model number and see if you can find a manual online that will tell us how to use it. In the meantime, I'll fill it with gas."

Terri watched her mother empty the gas cans into the generator, trying to find some excuse to leave and go over to Maggie's. The storm was rapidly approaching and she knew she had to be there before it broke.

"Hey, Mom, we don't know if Dad made it out of Boston or not. I think I'll take the bike over to Maggie's and make sure they don't need any help. You should be okay here with Sophie and I'll bet Dex drops by to make sure nothing's amiss."

Karen looked up at her daughter, puzzled. "Maggie's? Honey, she's an island girl - she knows what to do. Why do you need to go over there?"

"Well, actually, with us leaving next week, I'd like to spend a little more time with Billy and this seems a perfect opportunity. He won't be out fishing with his granddad in a storm. Is it okay if I go?"

Karen sighed. "Go on. He's your brother and I applaud your wanting to make and keep a connection with him. Soph and I will do just fine right here."

Terri leaned over, gave her mother a quick kiss on the cheek, and ran into the house to get her slicker. In a couple of minutes, she returned, hopped on her bike, and took off for Maggie's.

Karen watched her leave then put the gas cans back in the garage and went to join Sophie in the house. They were poring over Internet files trying to find a manual for the generator when the doorbell rang. Hoping it was Dex, Karen swiftly moved to answer it, but was surprised to find Bill instead.

"Hi," she said. "You made it back from Boston! Come on in."

"Thanks. I got out just in time. Thought I'd stop by to make sure you had everything under control here. The weather is coming in pretty fast."

Karen laughed. "Well, we could use a little help. We found a generator stored out back and there were a couple of full gas cans in the garage. I got it filled, but how the damned thing actually works is beyond me. Sophie's trying to research it on the web, but maybe you can figure it out."

Smiling, he walked over and gave his daughter a brief kiss. "Where's Terri?"

"Oh, you probably passed her on the road. She's headed to your place on her bike. Thinks Maggie might need some help with storm prep and she wants to spend some time will Billy since we're going home next week."

"You're leaving? Going back to California?"

"Yes, it's time - the girls need to get ready for college."

Bill was silent for a minute, his mind racing. He wanted to ask if Dex was going with them, but was afraid he would be overstepping if he did so. Deciding not to bring it up, he smiled.

"I'll miss you all. But, you're right - the girls need to be prepared. Sophie's going to be in New Haven, right?"

Karen nodded.

"Good, I'll get to see a lot of her then."

He walked to the window, surveyed the darkening sky, then turned back to Karen. "Okay, where's that damned generator?"

Smiling, Karen led him outside to the side yard to where the generator sat. Rolling up his sleeves, Bill took a few minutes, looking it over.

"Looks in good shape. Let me test it out."

Once he was satisfied that the machine was in proper working order, he and Karen checked the rest of the house, making sure all the windows were securely locked and that the gutters were clear. They were just finishing up when thunder began to rumble and rain started to fall in earnest.

"Well, I guess everything's secure and I should be getting back," he said reluctantly as he pulled on his slicker. "Looks like I'm going to get wet!"

"Oh, don't go just yet, Bill. You deserve a reward. Stay and have a glass of wine with me. Maybe it'll let up."

Bill smiled broadly, removed his coat and hung it back in the closet. "Now that's the best offer I've had all day."

Karen opened a bottle of wine and they sat down by the picture window, talking about old times. The rain was heavy and the wind was beginning to pick up, turning the once-gentle waves into vigorous whitecaps. Sophie joined them as they watched the storm escalate.

"Well, thanks for the wine," said Bill, looking at his watch. "It's getting late." He stood up to leave but Karen, noting the reluctance in his voice, reached out and laid a hand on his arm.

"Don't go yet. Stay for dinner. I'm enjoying this."

Obviously relieved, Bill laughed. "You won't have to twist my arm. It almost feels like we're back in California - like when we were at the beach house on our honeymoon. Remember the night it rained?"

Karen smiled as she stood up. "Yeah, I do, and maybe this is not exactly the same, but it has been nice. Now you and Sophie sit and visit some more while I go upstairs and clean up. Then I'll start dinner."

A short while later, she came back downstairs wearing a loose-fitting sweater and long skirt. Her face was freshly washed and she'd applied just a hint of blush and lip gloss. Bill smiled appreciatively.

"You look beautiful," he said, standing up as she entered the room.

Karen blushed. "Thank you. Now why don't you open another bottle of wine while I get some food together? I don't know about you, but all that hard work today has given me an appetite."

FRIDAY –
AT MAGGIE'S

TERRI ARRIVED AT MAGGIE'S just after the rain began. Shaking off her slicker in the mudroom, she entered the house.

"Maggie? Billy?" she called.

Maggie walked into the room, wiping her hands on a dishtowel. "Hi, kiddo. What are you doing out in this weather?"

"Oh, I just thought I run over and see if you all were okay. Did my dad get back from Boston?"

Maggie nodded. "Yeah, he took the train this morning. Got here around four. He's actually over at your place right now. Seems he's afraid Karen might not be able to handle storm preparations by herself. I'm working on dinner. Want to come help me?"

"Sure. Just lead me to it!"

Maggie laughed. "You know, you're an awfully nice kid. I'm glad Billy has a sister like you. Now, tell me what's up with you and that O'Dwyer boy. He's quite a looker! Got to tell ya, quite a few island girls were pretty pissed when he hooked up with you!"

Terri blushed. "Oh, it's really nothing. We just get along."

"Okay, you don't want to talk. I get it. Now, go ahead chop up those veggies for a salad. I expect your dad back soon. Why don't you stay and have supper with us? I know Billy would love the company."

Two hours later, fed up with waiting for Bill, Maggie finally sat them all down at the table. She'd tried calling him several times but he apparently had his cell turned off, either by accident or on purpose. The meal was eaten mostly in silence, Maggie's foul mood hanging over them like a shroud.

Only picking at the food on her plate, Maggie abruptly got up and left the room halfway through the meal. Terri tried to lighten the atmosphere, attempting to draw Billy out asking about the latest video games, but the boy seemed troubled and upset by his mother's bad temper.

A few minutes later, Maggie returned wearing her slicker.

"Listen, Terri, can you watch Billy? I need to go out for a bit."

"In this storm? I can hear the wind from here. You sure you want to drive in this?"

Maggie smiled. "Hey, kiddo, I've been through lots worse living on this island. I won't be gone long. You two finish dinner. There's ice cream in the freezer for dessert. Okay?"

Terri nodded as Maggie leaned over and kissed her son then ran outside into the rain.

AT KAREN'S – THE MIDDLE

AFTER DINNER, SOPHIE CLEARED the table and excused herself, complaining of a sinus headache brought on by the weather. She went to her room, took a decongestant, and was soon fast asleep.

Bill and Karen took their wine and again sat by the window, watching the storm.

"It is pretty majestic, isn't it?" she asked.

"Yeah, as long as you're nice and cozy inside, it is. But I wouldn't want to be out there right now. Hope you don't mind if I hang around a bit longer?"

Karen smiled. "You're always welcome here, Bill. You should know that. What happened to you on that island, well, that wasn't your fault and what happened between me and Dex, well, that wasn't anyone's fault either. It's just how things are. Now, you're with Maggie, so it all sorta worked out, didn't it?"

Bill frowned. "I wouldn't say I'm really 'with Maggie,' Kar. To me, she's just a consolation prize, if you know what I mean.

315

You ... to me, you'll always be the real prize. Unfortunately, I'm just about ten years too late submitting my entry form."

Karen leaned back and stared at him trying to see if there was any pent-up anger or jealousy hidden behind his words. But his facial expression seemed benign and maybe just a bit wistful. For reasons she couldn't fathom, this pleased her. She didn't want to be in an adversarial relationship with him; they had too much history for that. And, she had to admit that since Dex's departure, she'd missed the company of an intelligent male counterpart.

"More wine?" he asked.

"Sure, why not?"

He walked over to the table and picked up the half-empty bottle. When he brought it back, he sat down on the floor, leaned over, and poured her a glass.

"Toss me a pillow, Kar," he said, making himself comfortable on the carpet.

Karen threw him a couple of cushions, and sipped her drink, studying him. "You really don't remember anything about being on that island, do you, Bill?"

He shook his head. "No. My memory starts sometime after I got to the hospital. Guess I was pretty messed up when they found me. It took a while for me to recover. I didn't remember anything about you or the girls until I saw Terri and Sophie. Then it all came rushing back."

"They said you didn't speak for years, not until right around the time we came back here. Was that a conscious choice?"

Bill looked down at his wine, remembering. "When they found me, Dr. Todd said I was actually more animal than man. I'd been living alone, foraging for food and shelter like a wild dog. I had no need to talk, so I guess I just forgot how. I don't know why the words came back when they did. Maybe it was just coincidence. Or maybe it was something else. Fate, perhaps. I don't really know. All I know right now is that I'm grateful to be sitting here, drinking wine, and talking to you."

Karen was silent for a minute. Then she slipped down to the floor next to him, reached out and gently tugged on his ponytail.

"The hair, Bill. What's that about? You never wore your hair long before."

He reached up and pulled off the rubber band that held his hair in place. Then he leaned forward, exposing the base of his skull. "Can you see it? The scar?"

Karen ran her finger softly along the long, jagged white line. "Oh, my word. How did this happen?"

He sat up and looked at her. "Don't know. But with the hair short, this thing stands out like a sore thumb. You know they shaved my head when I first got to the hospital. Guess I was full of lice and other vermin. I didn't like seeing that scar - male vanity or something. So, I let my hair grow long to hide it."

Fully comprehending for the first time all that he had been through, Karen reached out and put her hand on his arm. "I don't know what to say. You've had to deal with so much. I'm sorry I was such a bitch to you when you first came back."

Bill laughed. "That's okay. We both had to make an adjustment."

Not knowing what to say, Karen turned again toward the sea. Bill followed suit and they sat quietly watching as the storm escalated.

Finally, Bill turned and gazed longingly at her. "Hey, remember how we used to sit on the floor with the kids playing all those old board games?"

Karen turned to him and laughed. "Yeah. You called it 'family time without electronics.'"

"God, I wish I could turn back the clock and go back to that time. I'd do things differently, Kar. Not make a mess of things like I did."

"What's done is done. We just have to go on living and doing the best we can with what we have."

Bill stared at her, then down at his hands. "There's something I never told you. Something I should have told you long ago."

Puzzled, Karen sat up and leaned forward. "Go on. What is it, Bill? Tell me."

He raised his head and stared out the window at the churning sea, trying to find the right words. "Remember way back before everything went bad, before I lost my job? There was a party that you didn't go to."

Karen nodded. "Yes, your boss, Sloane, threw that shindig for you and your team to celebrate the package you all had been working on. I stayed home because the twins were sick. What about that party, Bill?"

He looked back down at his hands, then stood up. "I think I need something a little bit stronger than wine right now. Got anything?"

"Sure. There's a bottle of Jack in the cupboard under the sink. And bring two glasses."

"Ice?"

Karen smiled. "No, I can take it neat."

He walked to the kitchen and returned with a bottle of Jack Daniels and two jelly jar glasses. He poured a shot for Karen and one for himself then sat back down. He took a sip, then faced her.

"I was angry with you for not coming. I know that was wrong. You were right to stay home with the kids, but I was mad. So, I drank too much and partied too hard."

He stopped and again stared down at his drink.

"Go on, Bill. What happened?"

"You remember Julie, Sloane's wife?"

Karen nodded.

"Well, she came on to me that night and I let her. Nothing really happened, but it might have."

Karen sat quietly, digesting what he'd said. "Go on. There's still more, isn't there? What kept her or you from stepping out of bounds, Bill?"

He sighed. "God, this is hard to say, even after all these years. I know it's no excuse but I was angry and drunk and ... well, her top was undone and I had my hand on her breast ... We probably wouldn't have stopped at that, but Marty, - you remember pasty-face Marty? He caught us. That sobered me up real quick."

Karen reached out and took his hand gently in hers. "And he told Sloane, right?"

Bill nodded.

"And Sloane got you downsized and made sure you would never get another job in the Valley. Is that what you're trying to tell me, Bill?"

He nodded again. "It was all my fault, Karen. All mine. I ruined our lives."

"But, why didn't you tell me then? We could have dealt with it."

"I was too afraid of losing you, I guess. I just couldn't man up. I'm so sorry, Karen."

Karen leaned back against the couch and took a sip of her drink. "I think I always knew something like that happened. But it's over now. Don't beat yourself up about it."

"Can you ever forgive me?"

She sighed. "Yes, I forgive you. And if we're telling secrets, I think I need to tell you something, too."

Bill lifted his head and stared at her. "What?"

Karen hesitated, thinking, then took a deep breath. "Right before we came here - actually, on the day you told me about this place and the inheritance ... I did something.

Bill frowned. "What do you mean, 'did something'?"

"You know we weren't getting along, right? I could count on my fingers the number of times we made love that last year in California. Well, I'd let my pill prescription lapse and one night, I think out of desperation, we had sex."

Tears were now welling up in her eyes and Bill reached out and took her hands in his. "You don't have to go through this. I know about the abortion. I always knew."

Karen straightened up, staring at him. "You knew? But how?"

"It was sometime before we left for here. That clinic called about the insurance. Of course, I asked about it."

"And you stayed with me? Even after what I'd done?"

"I can't say I wasn't mad at first. Yeah, I was angry and upset. But, you only did what you had to do. And the mess we were in was all my fault. How could I blame you for anything? I loved you, Karen. Always have. Always will."

He leaned toward her, keeping her hands pressed tightly within his.

"Oh, Bill," she said softly. "We made such a mess of things."

They sat quietly for a moment looking at each other. Then he reached out and gently brushed away the lone tear that was sliding down her cheek.

Surprised by his gesture, Karen gazed into his eyes. They had both revealed secrets kept hidden for so long and it seemed as if in this moment they had taken a journey back in time - back to when they had once been so good together.

Seeing the softness in her expression, Bill gently pulled her to him. When she didn't resist, he kissed her lightly, almost teasingly. She started to pull away, shaking her head. "No, Bill. No."

But he didn't listen. Instead, he pulled her tightly to him and began to kiss her with passion, probing her mouth with his tongue

As if in a daze, she found herself responding and he pushed her body down so they were laying together on the carpet, his arms around her, hands moving softly over her buttocks. She shivered at his touch and he moved one hand down farther, resting it gently on that place where her thigh joined her cheek. He kept his mounting desire under control and continued to kiss her, waiting for some signal that she was willing to go further.

Becoming aroused despite herself, Karen involuntarily pushed her pelvis slightly against his and, encouraged, he slipped his other hand up, under her sweater letting his fingers trail across her warm bare skin. She was braless and he slowly moved his hand to her front, lightly touching her breasts and teasing them with his fingertips.

Again, she tried to pull away, but he was too strong. Holding her tightly, he slipped one hand to the front of her thigh and let his fingers trail up and down, delicately caressing her. The other hand he let roam her body, lingering on those secret places he knew from experience were most sensitive.

"Oh, Karen," he moaned as he finally moved his hand up under her skirt. "Let me make love to you."

 **MAGGIE**

MAGGIE DIDN'T HAVE TO drive far. When she got to the house she was seeking, she turned off the car's lights and slowly crept up the driveway, parking close to the front. Quietly, she got out, holding her slicker tightly closed and made her way behind the bushes to the windows by the door. Cupping her hands, she peered inside. When the mist cleared away, she could see two figures on the floor in the living room, locked in an embrace, the man's hands roaming freely over the woman's body.

Tears streamed down Maggie's cheeks and joined with the raindrops that cascaded down from the overflowing gutter above. She stood helplessly, rooted in place, watching, as a profound sadness gripped her heart and she was overcome by a familiar sense of abandonment. The embrace was becoming more sexual in nature, and, as the passion inside the house grew, a cold, hard anger began to gestate inside of her, replacing the sense of loss with something much more concrete.

She stared silently at the scene inside the house until she could stand it no longer. Then, with a look of fierce determination on her face, she got back into the car and headed for home.

TERRI

TERRI SAT IN THE family room waiting for Billy to join her in front of the television. She was worried. The boy had seemed strangely agitated after dinner. He kept asking about his mother and gave Terri the impression that he thought something bad had happened to her. She checked her watch. Maggie hadn't been gone long enough to warrant the boy's fears. She thought about Charlie and his admonition to protect the boy. She looked at her watch again. Billy had gone upstairs to change and should have come back down by now.

Standing up, she decided to go talk to him and find out why he was so upset. Turning toward the stairs, she was startled when she heard the door slam.

Maggie's home, she thought as she walked to the front of the house. But when she reached the entryway, she knew something was wrong. Maggie was not there and neither was Billy.

Swiftly, she ran up the stairs, calling the boy's name. She checked all the rooms, but he was nowhere to be found.

323

He's gone out into the storm! I was supposed to take care of him. Oh, God, I've failed.

Without hesitation, she grabbed her slicker from the closet and then rummaged through the kitchen drawers until she found a flashlight.

Scribbling a quick note for Maggie, she walked out of the house, following the young boy into the storm.

BILL AND KAREN

FEELING BILL'S HAND MOVING on the bare skin of her thigh, Karen shook her head again, trying to clear the fog of desire that had somehow overwhelmed her sense of reason. A vision of Dex's face appeared before her eyes and she knew she had to stop this now before she did something she would later regret.

"NO, Bill," she cried, pushing him away from her.

He tried to pull her close again but she held her palms firmly against his chest, putting distance between them.

"I said 'NO!' This isn't going to happen."

He stared at her, his face a mask of agony. "But, I love you, Karen. And you love me, too. I know it. We can be together, like before. Don't you want that?"

He started to move toward her again but she held up her hand in a warning gesture. "Don't Bill. This is NOT going to happen. And you're wrong about me loving you. I love Dex. I think somehow I've always loved him. With you ... tonight, it's just too much wine and nostalgia. I'm sorry for all you went through, but we can't be together again. You have to accept that."

Bill stood up, turned abruptly, and gazed out the window trying to get his emotions under control. He had come so close to having her again, he felt as if he might explode.

Minutes passed and, finally, Karen reached out and put her hand softly on his shoulder.

"Are you okay?" she whispered.

Bill whirled on her, pushing her hand away. "Okay? Am I okay? No, I'm not and I probably never will be again."

Karen sighed patiently. "Bill, you have to understand ..."

He shook his head slightly, a sarcastic smile growing on his face. "That fucking fisherman. And you *always* loved him. Well, isn't that nice. And what about me? You just pity me, don't you? Well, I don't want your goddamn pity."

He moved angrily across the room, away from her, jostling her with his shoulder as he passed. He jerked open the hall closet, tore his slicker from the hanger and was about to put it on when he felt his cell buzz. Pulling the phone from his pocket, he glanced at the caller ID then turned away from Karen, answering.

"Hi, Mags. What's up? Everything okay at the house?"

He was silent for a moment, listening to her reply.

"What? I don't get it, Mags. You mean Terri? Terri took Billy out into the rain? Into the woods? Why? That doesn't make sense."

Karen looked up at the mention of her daughter's name and moved across the room to stand in front of him. "Terri? Bill, what's going on with Terri?"

Bill shook his head, indicating for her to be silent, then turned back to the phone. "I'm on my way. I should be there in about ten minutes. Stay calm. We'll get this all sorted out."

He ended the call and started to leave, but Karen stopped him.

"What is it, Bill?" she asked, a look of concern on her face. "Is Terri alright?"

Bill took a deep breath. "Maggie says she went into the woods with the boy. It makes no sense. I have to go."

A strong feeling of déjà vu passed over Karen. "You'll find her, won't you, Bill? Tell me you'll find her."

Hearing the urgency in her voice, Bill's anger quickly melted away. Gently, he reached out and touched her cheek. "Don't worry. I'll find Terri and bring her back to you. I promise."

He smiled briefly, then put his cell back in his pocket and hastily strode out into the storm.

Karen watched through the window as he backed carefully down the driveway. *It's happening again. Just like before. My child out alone in a storm and Bill leaving me to go find her.*

When the car was out of sight, she walked back to the living room, her mind in turmoil, reliving that time ten years earlier when her children had been summoned out into the night. Sickened by fear, she stumbled to the downstairs bathroom, leaned over the toilet, and vomited violently. Dizzy, she watched as the red wine and her dinner swirled vigorously round and round then disappeared like so much wasted flotsam and jetsam.

You've got to get a grip, girl, she chided herself as she rinsed out her mouth. *You know what you have to do.*

Resolved and knowing she needed to sober up quickly, she leaned in and turned on the shower, Forcing herself under the ice-cold spray, she vigorously ran a washcloth over her body, trying to prepare and purify herself for the ritual she knew she would soon have to undertake.

TERRI

ANGRY WITH HERSELF FOR dropping her guard and letting her brother sneak out of the house, Terri ran to the backyard, searching for the trail that led into the woods. The cold, hard rain pelted at her as the wind whipped about, sending shivers up and down her spine. She pointed the flashlight at the bushes, praying that the trail would reveal itself, but the growth was dense and she could see nothing but the forest beyond. She was close to panic when lightning flashed across the sky, illuminating a well-groomed pathway behind an unusual-looking bush. Pushing her way through its thorny branches, she stepped onto the trail.

It's just like the smoke dream, she thought as shadows began to close in around her, choking off the light that had led her to this place. She stood still for a moment, unsure of what to do. Did she really want to go down this path? She didn't have to do this. She could turn around now and go home ... sit out the storm, warm and safe inside. But could she live with herself if she did?

Knowing she couldn't, she began to jog down the path, calling her brother's name. The wind howled, blowing branches and debris around her, but still she ran on. Suddenly, the root of an old tree ripped from the earth and lunged toward her as if reaching out to grab her. Remembering the dream, she leapt over it, landing safely on the other side. Catching her breath, she turned in time to see the crevasse that had been opened by the root slowly close as it returned to its home in the earth.

If I hadn't seen that happen in the dream, I might have been swallowed up in there, she thought, her mind reeling in horror.

Girding herself, she shook off her fear and began again to jog down the trail. Winding and narrow, it seemed to go on forever. Gnarled branches, stripped of leaves by the wind, reached for her, slapping against her body as she pushed through the ever-encroaching vegetation. Stinging nettles tried to entwine themselves around her arms and legs, leaving painful red welts where they touched her bare skin, but she pulled them off and ran on.

Thunder rumbled in the sky and lightning flashed, finally revealing the end of the trail. Crows began to shriek in the treetops and she stopped running and stood quietly staring at the fetid swamp that lay before her. Vicious snakes and other creatures she could not name slithered in and out of its dense, rotting foliage, obscuring the stale, murky water underneath. Black flies and mosquitoes swarmed above, their buzzing ominously loud in the now-still quiet of the forest.

And on a stump, at the far side, sat her brother, his body entwined and bound by evil-looking vines, their sharp thorns piercing his tender flesh as flies and mosquitoes buzzed around his head, stopping frequently to sup on his fresh blood.

Terrified, she called to him, but the trance or coma that held him was so deep, he did not seem to hear. Then, as in her dream, another figure emerged from the forest behind him - an apparition both familiar and hideous to her. It was the Mskagwdemos!

 **BILL AND MAGGIE**

BILL PARKED THE CAR then dashed up the walkway to the house, calling to Maggie as he ran. Not finding her on the first floor, he raced up the stairs to the master bedroom. She was standing next to the dresser wearing jeans and a bulky yellow slicker, her face distraught and agitated.

"Did you find them?" he cried as he took off his coat and laid it on the bed. He moved to put his arms around her but she stopped him, pushing him away.

"You stink of sex, Bill. Stay away from me."

Surprised at her accusation, he forced a smile. "Now, Mags, you're just imagining things. You know I went over there to help and Karen invited me to stay for dinner. Nothing happened between us."

Maggie laughed unpleasantly. "Yeah, right. And there really is a Santa Claus. You think I'm pretty stupid, don't you? You just couldn't leave it alone. You had to have her, didn't you?"

Bill stood frozen, alarmed by the anger in her voice. He was about to restate his denial, but she cut him off.

"You never loved me, did you? Not once. No, you think you're too good for me. To you, I'll always be just an island girl - a hot piece of ass you can take or leave at will."

"Maggie ... I ..."

"Shut up! I'm sick of all your lies. You'll spend the rest of your life crawling around on your hands and knees trying to get whatever crumbs that bitch tosses at you and then, when she blows you off, you'll come running back here. Back to your island whore. That's the way you think, isn't it? Well, I'm not going to keep taking it. I'm not going to play backseat to that woman anymore. You hear me?"

Bill took a step toward her, hoping to reason with her. "Mags, come on now. Nothing happened between Karen and me. I'm here, aren't I?"

"Don't you come any closer," Maggie warned as she backed away from him, pulling a gun from the pocket of her slicker.

Bill's mouth fell open in surprise when he saw the weapon pointed at him. He stopped mid-stride, staring at her.

"I'm warning you, Bill. I'll shoot, and believe me, I won't miss. I know how to handle a gun."

"Maggie, be reasonable," he cajoled. "We need to find the kids. That's what important. We can settle all this stuff between us later. Then you can do what you want to me. But, please, we need to find Terri and Billy. Put the gun away."

"Oh, don't worry about them, Bill. I've got that covered. But first we're going to settle things between you and me for good."

Her words were followed by a loud clap of thunder that shook the house. Almost immediately behind it, came a brilliant flash of lightning and Maggie, facing the windows, was temporarily blinded by its bright, searing light. Bill saw her blink and in that moment seized the opportunity, stepped forward, and grabbed her hand, trying to force the gun from her grasp.

Silently, they struggled for control of the weapon, Bill surprised at the ferocity of her resistance. Finally, sure she was beginning to falter, he forced her hand down between them, hoping she would give up and drop the gun harmlessly to the floor. He thought he had finally succeeded when he was startled by a sudden flash of light, followed by a blast that left his ears ringing. He felt a sharp pain in his side and looked down, surprised to see blood beginning to spread over his shirt.

A deadly quiet fell over the room and, for Bill, everything took on an otherworldly quality as he watched the blood saturate his clothing and drip to the floor below. He looked up at Maggie with pleading eyes, but she was backing away from him, an expression of shock and revulsion on her face.

"Mags, you - you shot me!"

She stared at him for a moment then spoke, her voice surprisingly calm. "Hang on, Bill. I'll get you a towel."

She turned and walked to the bathroom and came back a minute later with one of the bath towels and tossed it at him. "Press this on the wound. It'll stop the flow."

Picking up the towel from the floor, he did as she said, then looked back up at her. She stared at him for a moment, a grim smile on her face, then nodded and reached in her pocket again. "Here's my cell. When service comes back on, you can call 911. I have to go get the kids. You'll be all right. You're nothing if not a survivor."

Then she threw the phone at him and, without a backward glance, walked out of the room.

TERRI

TERRI STARED AT THE horrific apparition in front of her, her fear escalating. Her every instinct told her to run - to get as far as she could from this place; to go back to California or to some California of the mind and forget all about Mateguas. But she couldn't. The words of the old Indian again echoed through her being. "You, young one, are strong with magic ... let the magic flow through you..."

Strengthened in some uncanny way by these words, she forced herself to stand tall and face the beast.

"You will not have him," she said strongly, her words ringing with conviction.

The hag moved closer to the boy, opening its mouth as it moved. Snakes that served as its tongues slithered in and out of swollen and rotting lips, and Terri heard its words sink deep into her soul.

"He is mine, earth child; promised to me by the great one. Flesh of my body, blood of my blood, I will have him!"

Terri reeled from the contact with the beast's unclean mind, but forced herself to put away her fear and drew strength from the faith Charlie and Harry had placed in her.

"NO! He is not yours! He's my brother and I will keep him from harm. Leave him, now!"

As she spoke, Terri instinctively stretched out her hands - palms forward, fingers splayed. Something was growing within her, something that was both a part of her and, at the same time, alien to her. Between her fingers, like some kind of ancient vestige, appeared a webbing of soft blue light. Warmth from the light radiated up her arms and through her body and as the heat inside her softly pulsed, she could feel her courage growing.

As if sensing her new confidence, the light now became brighter and elongated from her fingers, crossing the swamp toward the comatose form of her brother. The creature shrieked in horror as a thin fibrous thread of the light reached out and gently caressed its face, leaving in its stead a harsh, smoking brand. The air, now filled with the smell of burning flesh, grew heavy as the light from Terri's hands deepened in color and began to move around the boy. The noxious flies and mosquitoes that had been feasting on him sizzled when the light touched them and dropped to the earth, charred and broken.

But the boy seemed unaffected by the burning. As the light pulsed around him, color returned to his cheeks and, finally, he opened his eyes.

"Terri!" he called. "Help me!"

KAREN AND BILL

IN DISBELIEF, BILL STAGGERED over to the windows and leaned against the wall, tightly clutching the towel that was rapidly turning red to his side. He looked outside, wondering where Maggie had gone.

She's not out front. She must have gone around back to the woods. Yes, that's where she said the kids went. But why? Why would they do that? Did she threaten them, too? Oh Christ, she must be insane.

His thoughts were interrupted when he heard a car pull up the driveway. *Oh, thank God, someone's here. I'll be okay.*

The house on the hill looked quiet as Karen turned up the drive.

335

Parking the car, she grabbed the tote holding the ancient box and, unmindful of the driving rain, jogged to the center of the lawn. Once in position, with the wind whipping her hair about her head, she knelt on the ground and began to prepare for the same ritual she had performed ten years before.

First step: draw a circle with the blood powder...

When he saw the woman run up the hill, Bill began waving his arms to get her attention, but she didn't look his way. Shocked, he recognized that it was Karen and watched in disbelief as, oblivious to the wind and rain, she ran to the middle of the lawn. He saw her remove something from a small bag and then kneel down on the ground.

He yelled to her, but the wind was howling and she couldn't hear him. He tried to stand, but was becoming too weak. Any movement only made the blood flow more freely, so he let his body slip to the floor and resigned himself to just watch.

When she finished with whatever she was doing on the ground, she stood up and stretched her arms to the sky. She faced away from him, toward the sea and, her flimsy cotton skirt, drenched by the relentless rain, clung to her body making her seem almost naked in the moonlight.

Despite his weakness, Bill clung to the window ledge, his curiosity aroused. *What the hell is she doing?*

He pressed his face to the glass, straining to see better as the storm raged. The wind howled as the cold hard rain pelted against the window. His warm breath fogged the pane and, unthinking, he reached up with the towel to wipe it clean. Moving the towel back to his side, his eyes widened in shock when he saw the wide streak of warm blood smeared across the glass. He glanced down at the floor. The pool of red was larger now. He pressed the towel once again to his side trying to stem the flow. Then, unable to help himself, he returned his gaze to the window.

Her arms were still raised to the sky and in the moonlight, he could see she held something in her hand. Thunder roared, shaking the house. Black spots appeared before his eyes and he feared he would lose consciousness.

Is this how it all ends? After everything that's happened, me alone here in this house?

Suddenly, the driveway lit up with headlights as a car rapidly approached.

What now?

DEX

SOON AFTER THE STORM hit, Dex and Pete McKinney were called on by the Coast Guard to help a boater who had been caught up in the rough waters. Once they towed the boat to safety, Dex dropped Pete back at his place and decided to check on Karen and his girls.

Arriving at the house, he didn't waste time with formalities, just opened the door and walked in. Sophie was sitting alone in the living room.

"Where is everyone, Soph?" he asked, glancing around the room, looking for Karen and Terri.

"Oh, Dex, I don't know. I'm so worried."

"Hold on. What do you mean you don't know? Where's your mother?"

"Dex, I don't know! Terri went to Maggie's earlier today, just before the storm really took hold. I haven't heard from her since. Dad was here most of the day and stayed for dinner. I was feeling one of those sick headaches I get when the weather changes, so I went to bed. I took a pill and fell asleep. When I woke up, both Dad and Mom were gone. I tried to a call, but service is down."

"Think, Sophie. Where would they go? And, why would they go out in this weather?"

"I don't know. Maybe they went to Maggie's? Both cars are gone, so Mom and Dad didn't leave together. Terri used one of the bikes so Mom must have our car. Dex, I'm getting scared."

Recognizing Sophie's distress, Dex put his arm around her. "You're right. They're probably all at Maggie's. Your mom likely went to check on Terri. Storm just got too bad and she didn't feel like driving home. As you said, cell service is down so she would have no way to let you know. Now, you stay put here. I'll run over there and find out what's going on."

Sophie nodded. "Don't you get lost, too, Dex. I'll wait here. If Mom shows up, I'll tell her where you went."

Dex smiled, kissed her on the cheek, and ran outside to his truck. More worried than he had let on to Sophie, he drove as fast as he dared, listening to the sound of the wipers as they tried to slap away the rain that impeded his vision. What was Karen up to now? And why was everyone over at Maggie's place?

The answers to his questions eluded him. All he could do was hope and pray that everyone was all right.

BILL

A FLASH OF LIGHTNING streaked across the sky, blinding
Bill. He rubbed his eyes as thunder shook the house again.
Clinging to the window frame and trying to stay upright, he gazed
out at the car that had pulled into the driveway.

At last, someone's come. They'll help me. They have to.

With his strength rapidly ebbing away, he pounded on the
window, hoping to gain the driver's attention. But the storm was
too fierce and he slumped back against the wall, breathing
heavily.

Unable to stop himself, he again moved his eyes to the lawn
to where Karen had been performing some sort of ritual, but
now she was gone. He quickly scanned the front of the house,
looking for her, but she seemed to have disappeared into the rain
and wind. He turned back to the car that had come up the drive.
It was now parked and he saw a man leap out and begin to run
up the hill.

In that moment, all hope vanished. It was Dex.

340

MAGGIE

AFTER LEAVING BILL ALONE in the bedroom, Maggie walked purposefully down the stairs to the living room. She stopped briefly at the woodstove, pocketed an item, then went outside into the rain and ran over to the garage. Quickly finding what she was looking for, she jogged to the backyard and headed toward the trail that led into the woods.

Unlike Terri, she had no trouble finding this path. She knew exactly where it began. She'd found it long ago when she was just a young girl picking blueberries. The strange-looking bush that guarded the trail glistened in the wind and rain, its sharp thorns shimmering like silver daggers in the moonlight. But Maggie held no fear of them. She knew they wouldn't harm her. Her face set, she took a deep breath, and entered the woods, unscathed. Strangely, as soon as she stepped onto the path, the storm around her seemed to abate. Raindrops glistened on the grass and leaves as forest creatures began to awaken as if from a deep sleep. Bluebirds flitted by her face and wildflowers blossomed before her eyes. The crescent moon shone brightly through the canopy above, lighting her way.

It is truly magical, she thought. *How could I have forgotten? This is where I belong; here in this forest ... not back there where people are so cruel.*

She thought about Bill for a moment, feeling regret, but swiftly shook him from her mind.

Unconsciously, she slowed her pace, enjoying the smells and sounds of the forest. She stopped and picked some wildflowers and plaited them into a circle that, when done, she placed upon her head.

Now, I'm queen of the May, she laughed to herself, looking at her reflection in a puddle on the side of the trail. She sat for a moment in the grass, feeling content, but then the memory of why she was there came rushing back - her boy.

Oh Christ, why am I lollygagging? I have to get Billy out of this place. I can't let it cast a spell on me now. Once he's safe, then I can come back. He'll have my folks and he'll be better off with them than with me. And I can come back here and never have to deal with liars and cheaters again. Instead, I can have all this beauty, all this peace.

Resolved, she stood up and continued to walk down the path, quickening her pace. When she believed she was about halfway to the swamp, she stopped and put down the can she carried with her.

I have to do this now. There's no turning back from here on.

When she finished her task, she left the can on the trail and began jogging forward, eager now to reach the end.

DEX AND KAREN

AS DEX'S CAR APPROACHED the house, the earth shook with the sound of thunder and lightning streaked across the sky. He slammed on the brakes, seeing the slender form of his wife standing on the lawn, arms upraised, oblivious to the storm that was raging around her.

Jumping from the vehicle, he called out, but realized she wouldn't be able to hear him over the violent storm. Thunder shook the earth again and he zipped his windbreaker, pulling up the hood to ward off the pounding rain. With a sense of urgency, he began to run up the hill.

A fierce bolt of lightning flashed out of the clouds toward the lawn. Shocked, he stopped and stood rooted in place as the jagged spear of light ascended to the earth, striking Karen directly in the center of her being. Time seemed to stand still as he stared at her in shock - her body was impaled to the ground, surrounded by a painfully bright white light. Then, as suddenly as it had appeared, the light diminished and was gone ... and then she fell.

343

Unbelieving, Dex screamed her name as he ran up the hill. Reaching her, he knelt down and took her lifeless form in his arms. He shook her gently, calling her name as if to wake her from a deep sleep, but there was no response. With tears streaming down his cheeks, he placed his fingers on her neck, hoping beyond hope that he would find a pulse. But there was no movement.

The world began to grow silent around him. Curiously, the storm that had been raging so fiercely when he'd arrived, ceased the moment she fell. Feeling hopeless, he began CPR, but she did not stir. He tried again but still there was no response.

Looking to the heavens as if for solace, he screamed at the night sky. "WHY HER? WHY NOW?"

At a loss to know how to revive her, he reluctantly pulled out his cell. Service was back on and he began to dial 911. But, as he waited for the call to connect, he heard a soft moan come from the limp body he cradled in his arms.

Dropping the phone, he leaned down over her. "Karen? Karen?"

Her eyes fluttered open and, with one hand, she reached for him.

"No," she said weakly. "Don't call anyone."

He looked down at her, astonished. She was alive! But how could that be? It had been at least ten minutes since she the lightning struck her.

Karen," he whispered, "Are you really back? You were ..."

She gazed up at him, her eyes focusing, the color returning to her face. "Dex," she said softly. "Make love to me. I need you to make love to me now!"

As she spoke, she pulled him down to her with a strength that seemed impossible and kissed him deeply, her hands moving toward his belt.

Shocked, he pulled away. "Karen, you've been hurt. You died! We have to get you to a doctor. Now's not the time for ..."

She silenced him again with a kiss, then took his hand and placed it under her skirt, between her legs, pressing it hard against the core of her.

He was shocked to feel her nakedness and, despite himself, became aroused by the warm wetness between her thighs. He tried again to pull away but she pressed his hand deeper, letting him feel the intensity of her desire. As he struggled to understand what was happening, she moved her other hand to the front of his jeans and, feeling his erection, deftly released him.

Before he could protest further, she shifted her body to straddle him. She sunk down upon him and moved her hips sinuously to stimulate him further. Finally, giving in, he put his arms around her and pressed his lips to her neck, murmuring her name as their lovemaking intensified.

When he could stand it no longer, he rolled over on top of her, thrusting deeply inside. She moaned with pleasure, gripping him tightly with her thighs and he could feel the soft pulsing of her orgasm. She cried out his name and dug her nails into his back and he gave in to his desire and climaxed with her.

 **TERRI**

THE FOREST AROUND HER was still and quiet as the blue light continued to shoot out from between her fingertips. Billy was moving now, trying to untangle the vines that held him prisoner on the log. The foul creature that had imprisoned him had now disappeared, warded off by the power of the light.

"Hurry, Billy," Terri cried. "I don't know how much longer I can hold it off."

The boy renewed his efforts, ripping the vines from his legs despite the scratches and tears he suffered from the thorns.

We're going to make it, she thought. *We're going to get out of this.*

But as this notion passed through her mind, from out of the stillness came a mournful howl. Surprised, she turned and saw, emerging from the darkness, another creature - this one more terrifying than the last.

Terri shivered as she stared at the giant wolf that stood before her, its amber eyes boring into her very soul. As she gazed at the predator, she was consumed by an intense fear that

346

overshadowed the magic within her. Magic that was now rapidly beginning to weaken.

It's the evil thing that possessed Shawn, she thought. *Those are its eyes. I recognize them. Oh, God, what can I do?*

The memory of the night on the beach caused her panic to intensify and with it, the blue light began to flicker and retreat back into her fingers, disappearing from her hands. As it diminished, a profound chill washed over her body and she was filled with dread.

Lips curling back to reveal long, vicious teeth, the wolf seemed to smile in triumph as foul saliva dripped from its maw to the forest floor, scorching the earth with its venom. A soft growl emanated from the beast's throat as it slowly, teasingly, began to stalk her.

Wanting desperately to flee, leaving the boy behind, and never come back, it took all of Terri's strength to stand her ground. She glanced over at Billy, hoping for help, but he now seemed paralyzed again and unable to come to her aid. Her heart pounding, she whispered a soft plea for help, all the while knowing that, ultimately, she was alone - there was no one to hear.

Crows again began their horrific shrieking in the treetops as the wolf closed in on her. Almost upon her, it shifted its impressive weight back on its haunches, its body tense and ready to spring.

Terri closed her eyes, praying for a miracle, knowing death or maybe worse was only seconds away.

"Tankashila, mya kya."

Very softly at first, but seeming to come from all around her, she suddenly heard the voice of the old Indian, chanting,

"Tankashila, mya kya,
Che wo kielo,
Wakan chelo heyo,
Ah hey wa hey cheyo,
Wachio hey hey."

Slowly, the melodic cadence of the prayer that Harry Three Feathers used to bring the smoke dream began to reverberate throughout the forest behind her, becoming louder and louder with each passage. Her eyes opened wide in wonder and her fear began to dissipate. Feeling a rush of confidence, she stood tall, opened her mouth and, without hesitation, joined in the chant.

The wolf froze and cocked its massive head, listening, then began to cower on the ground. The sacred song grew louder and the beast flattened its ears to its head and tucked its tail firmly between its legs. Foul-smelling urine began to seep from its organ, as it pressed its body to the ground in fear.

The song grew louder still, now sounding like the forest's own heartbeat, until finally, the beast could take it no longer. With one sad yelp, it turned tail and ran off, disappearing into the depths of the woods.

BILL

BILL WATCHED HELPLESSLY AS Dex ran to Karen and took her lifeless form in his arms. He saw Dex perform CPR but there was no response from her. Feeling he had lost her forever, his eyes widened in wonder when she suddenly came back to life and threw her arms around Dex.

Astounded, Bill wanted to scream and beat on the windowpane with his fists, but he was too weak to do anything but watch. His face contorted in agony when he saw her lift her sodden skirt to straddle Dex, her milky white thighs wrapping tightly around his waist ... thighs that only hours ago had almost been his. He stared at the two of them, tears streaming down his cheeks, as they embraced and her hips began that erotic dance he knew so well.

He tried to turn away but was unable to, and he watched, transfixed, as their movement escalated until they reached a furiously-intense climax together. Then, exhausted, Bill sunk to the floor, looking once again at the pool of blood spreading around him.

As he stared at his life slowly ebbing away, a sound startled him. The cell phone Maggie had thrown so carelessly had suddenly come to life. With his last conscious effort, he reached out and pressed the numbers, 911.

TERRI

WITH THE DISAPPEARANCE OF the wolf, the chanting also faded and silence again reigned over the forest. Terri quickly closed the distance between herself and the boy, wanting to free him so they could leave this awful place. But as she approached, she heard a rustling in the bushes off to her right. Turning, she was startled to find that the swamp hag had returned and was staring at her with malicious intent. Backing away, she reached out for her brother and pulled him into a tight embrace.

"Be gone, foul thing!" she yelled. "He's my brother and he does not belong to you!"

In response, the creature's bloated lips curled in a gloating grin as it reached out and beckoned to the child.

Terri tightened her embrace but Billy began to struggle against her, apparently again falling under the beast's spell. In his effort to be free, he leaned down and bit her viciously on the hand, drawing blood. Unable to restrain herself, she angrily pushed him away and he ran blindly into the arms of the

Mskagwdemos, allowing that vile thing to smother him in an unclean embrace.

Determined, Terri started to move toward them, knowing the magic that had rescued them before was now spent and all she had was herself and her love to save the boy. She knew she was no match for this vile creature, but she had to try. Everything depended upon her.

She reached out to her brother in an attempt to wrest him away, but was stopped by a sound coming from the trail behind her. Someone was singing.

Unable to stop herself, Terri turned toward the sound, straining to hear. It wasn't a real song - just more of a *tra-la-la, tra-la-la* repeated over and over again in a high-pitched lilting voice. The song was getting louder and she leaned forward with anticipation, wondering who or what was coming down the trail toward them. She glanced again at the Mskagwdemos and her brother, and was surprised to see that they, too, were now transfixed by whatever, or whoever, was approaching the swamp.

Turning back toward the sound of the song, Terri was surprised when Maggie emerged from the trail, wearing crown of wildflowers on her head. Wondering if the woman had lost her mind, Terri started to speak, but Maggie shot her a warning look, as if to say, *'be still, let me handle this.'*

Terri nodded and watched as her former teacher walked directly into the swamp, leaned down, cupped her hands, and drank from the putrid water.

"It's all going to work out, Terri," she whispered. "Billy will come to you and you'll take him out of here. Okay?"

Terri nodded in response, suddenly repelled by a strong odor. It was coming from Maggie and it was familiar, but its identity remained a mystery to her.

Maggie grinned. "Take Billy to my folks' place. He'll be safe there. Oh, and when you get back to the house, your dad may need some help. He's upstairs and he's hurt."

Terri stared at her, suddenly afraid for her father. "What happened to him?"

Maggie looked at her sternly. "Just do what I say. No questions."

Satisfied that Terri would play her part, Maggie whirled around to face the Mskagwdemos who still held her boy.

"Mother," she said reverently. "I've come home. Let my boy go. Release him from your spell. He is an innocent and does not belong to you. I'll stay here with you in his stead."

The creature stared at her malevolently, wrapping one of its loathsome arms tightly around the boy's neck.

"No, Mother! You cannot do this. The wolf has fled and can no longer grant you what he promised. The boy is now forfeit. I demand you let him go!"

The hag turned back to her, leaned down, and scooped a handful of noxious mud from the edge of the swamp. Slowly, it walked toward Maggie and when it was but a foot from her, reached out and, with gnarled fingertips, smeared the foul-smelling substance on the woman's cheeks.

Maggie didn't flinch.

Seeing acceptance in her eyes, the creature then turned toward Billy and, with a nod of its head, released him. Slowly, as if awakening from a dream, the young boy's eyes focused and, seeing his mother, he tried to run to her.

"Mom!" he cried.

Terri reached out, grabbed hold of his arm, and pulled him to her.

"Billy, you can't go to her. Not now, not now."

Maggie turned her head toward the boy. "Terri's right, honey. I have to stay here. Now, you all run home. Call your granddad when you get there. Can you do that for Mom, Billy?"

Terri could see that the child was struggling with conflicting emotions. His instinct told him to run to his mother, to stay with her, while his upbringing told him he had to obey her wishes.

"Go now, Terri. Go and be swift."

Terri nodded, knowing that despite her desire to help Maggie, getting the boy to safety was more important. "Come on, Billy, we have to go. I'll come back for you, Maggie!"

353

With one last look at Maggie, Terri pushed the boy ahead of her onto the trail. He resisted at first and tried to run back to his mother, but Terri stopped him. Holding him firmly by the arm, she steered him again to the path through the woods and together they started toward home.

KAREN AND DEX

KAREN AND DEX LAY on the wet ground, arms and legs wrapped around each other in the aftermath of lovemaking. Dex recovered first, sitting up and staring at her, struggling to comprehend what had just happened.

She was dead! Dead! How can this be?

"Karen?" he said haltingly, praying she was still alive. When she opened her eyes and smiled at him, he felt a rush of relief. "We have to get you to a doctor. Make sure there are no lingering effects of that lightning strike. I don't understand what happened. You had no pulse. I tried CPR twice and there was nothing. I can't explain why you seem to be okay, but I'm glad you are. But still, you need to be checked out."

Karen shook her head. "We have to find Terri and young Bill. Maggie called and said they had gone out into the storm toward the woods. Bill was going to go look for them and now he's gone, too. I have to find my daughter, Dex!"

As she spoke, she stood up, straightening out her wet,

wrinkled skirt. She jogged over to where her tote lay and picked up some objects off the grass, then zipped the bag shut and carried it to the car.

Dex watched in amazement and shock. *What the hell is happening?* He picked his cell phone off the ground, saw it was working, and began again to dial 911. When Karen saw him with his phone, she ran over to him and knocked it out of his hand.

"Those people can't help, Dex. Believe me, they can't. It has to be me and only me. You wait here."

 **MAGGIE**

MAGGIE WATCHED TERRI AND her son until they were out of sight. Then, with tears in her eyes, turned back to the apparition that stood before her, arms outstretched, welcoming.

Smiling slightly, the once-vibrant young girl, who had been used as a pawn by so many, stepped forward and allowed herself to be embraced by the creature.

The grinning Mskagwdemos held her victim tightly against her foul body, gloating in triumph, unable to see the change that had come over Maggie's face when she knew that her son was finally safe. All the vestiges of insanity that had sparked in her eyes were now gone and in their place was only a look of grim determination.

Slowly and deliberately, she reached into her pocket for the item she had so purposefully taken from the woodstove, and, with a flick of her thumb, she lit the match.

TERRI, BILLY, KAREN AND DEX

TERRI PULLED AND DRAGGED at Billy, prodding him to move faster down the path. When they reached a bend in the trail at about the halfway point, she noticed a red can abandoned in the grass on the side, looking terribly out of place.

Suddenly, she understood. There was a warning printed boldly on the side of the container:

DANGER - CONTENTS HIGHLY FLAMMABLE.

Oh, sweet Jesus, that's what it was - the odor I smelled when Maggie appeared. It was on her clothing - KEROSENE! She doused herself with it.

Envisioning what was about to happen, panic overtook her. "RUN, BILLY. RUN NOW! RUN FOR YOUR LIFE!"

Surprised by the urgency in his sister's tone, the boy began finally to move and together they sprinted with all their might toward home and safety. Dashing swiftly down the winding trail,

358

Terri was relieved when she finally saw the strange bush that marked the entryway to the yard.

We're safe, she thought, slowing her pace as they approached it.

Suddenly, from behind came a giant WHOOSH that seemed to propel them forward. Then came the explosion, and they were thrown headlong into the yard.

Karen began to sprint behind the house toward the woods, but Dex reached out and grabbed her by the arm, trying to stop her. They struggled for a moment and then, suddenly, there was a loud WHOOSH from the woods. Startled, they stopped fighting each other and turned toward the sound. They stood motionless for a moment, as if waiting, then came a huge explosion and they were thrown, stunned, to the ground.

SATURDAY MORNING - THE ENDING

KAREN RECOVERED FIRST, RISING and running with all her might toward the woods, calling her daughter's name. She stopped short, horrified, when she saw the two bodies lying on the lawn. Fear clenched at her heart and she ran to them with Dex following close behind. She crouched down by her daughter's side, then looked up and saw black smoke billowing out from the trail - the woods were ablaze.

"We've got to get them away from here, " she exclaimed. "This whole place could go up."

As she spoke, Terri's eyes fluttered open. Recognizing her mother, she began to sit up.

"Whoa, there, Terri," said Dex, moving over to her side. "Go slowly. You may have a concussion."

Terri's eyes focused as she reached out and grabbed her mother's hand. "Maggie, she's - she's still in there. Oh, God, she set herself on fire! She ... she ... "

"Maggie's still in the woods?" Not waiting for an answer,

360

Karen glanced at Dex shaking her head, then turned back toward her daughter. "Shush. It's all over. All done. You don't have to talk about it now. Later, sweetie, later."

Terri nodded. "Okay, Mom, but there's something else. Before she did it, Maggie said Dad was hurt in the house. Said he might need help. Please. Someone has to go look for him."

Dex, checking on Billy, heard the exchange. "Bill's hurt? How? Young Bill seems okay. May have a concussion and he's full of insect bites and scratches, but otherwise, okay. You stay here with them, Karen. I'll go see if I can find Bill."

He started to rise when an ambulance with sirens blaring pulled into the drive, followed closely by a fire truck. Karen looked at Dex. "Did you call?"

"No," he said. "You get the kids up closer to the house, away from the woods. I'll go talk them."

Karen nodded then began to help Billy and Terri move a safe distance from the forest as Dex jogged over to the EMTs who were getting out of the van.

"What the hell is going on here?" asked one of the first responders. "We got a 911 from a man who said he'd been shot. Now the whole woods are on fire and what in God's name happened to those kids?"

Dex nodded. "The call must have been from or about Bill Andersen. I think he's hurt and is somewhere in the house. I don't know what happened in the woods, except that Maggie Maguire may have committed suicide by setting herself on fire. The result is the blaze you see. The boy over there, Billy, is her son. He was in the woods along with my daughter when it happened. I think he might have a concussion. He's also been badly bitten up by insects and is probably in shock."

The EMT who apparently was in charge directed one of the others to search the house, then walked over to young Billy, who appeared dazed, and began to examine and question him.

More sirens blared as a police car came screeching to a halt in the driveway. An officer hopped out and spoke briefly with the EMT then strode over to where Terri and her mother were sitting.

Karen knew they were about to be questioned and knew what she had to do.

I hope you can forgive me, Maggie, but your sacrifice has to remain hidden, she thought as she stood to greet the officer.

"Excuse me, ma'am. I understand your daughter was in the woods when this blaze started. Is it alright if I ask her a few questions?"

Karen nodded. "But make it brief. She's still in shock."

"Sure," he responded, turning toward Terri. "Just tell me what happened. Why were you all in the woods?"

"I'm not sure I remember everything. Billy, my brother, was upset and he ran away into the woods. I followed him. Maggie - his mother - must have followed me. She ... she set herself on fire."

As she spoke these words, Terri broke down and began to sob. Karen gave the officer a sharp look and a shake of her head as she put her arms around her daughter, comforting her.

"Can't this wait till later?" she asked.

The officer nodded. "Later, okay. But do either of you know anything about a man being shot?"

Karen nodded. "I'm not sure, but I'd guess it's my first husband, Bill Andersen. He was living with Maggie. They were, I believe, a couple - the boy is his. I thought they were doing okay, but he came by my house this afternoon and told me he was breaking it off. Apparently, that news may have unbalanced her. She and Bill might have argued and that may be why the boy ran away. That's my best guess. I hope someone is checking the house for him."

The officer nodded. "Thank you. I'll go see what's going on. We'll talk more later, after your girl is cleared by the docs. I'll send one of them over when they finish up with the boy."

He smiled at Karen then turned and walked over to the ambulance where the EMTs were unloading a stretcher.

Dex, who had been talking with them, returned to Karen's side. "It is Bill - Maggie must have shot him."

"How bad is he?" asked Karen, concern in her voice.

"He's lost a lot of blood, but they say it doesn't look like the bullet hit anything vital. They have a helicopter coming. It will land down on that open piece of land by the wharf. They'll take him to the hospital in town. They'll take the kids with them, too."

Karen nodded. "Good. I think Terri's okay but it won't hurt to have her checked out. The boy ... he's clearly in shock. Terrible thing, seeing his mother...."

Letting her words trail off, she stood up and helped Terri to her feet. "Let's get you over to the ambulance, honey. You're going to the hospital with Billy and your dad. Can you do this alone or do you need me to come with you?"

"I'm okay, Mom. You don't need to come. I'll stay until I'm sure Dad will be okay. You go home and tell Sophie what's happened. She must be worried sick."

Karen smiled and nodded, then turned to Dex. "Gosh, I forgot all about her. You're right. She probably is worried. Dex, can you give her a call? Let her know we're all right?"

Dex nodded as Karen and Terri walked toward the ambulance. When they were out of earshot, Karen leaned over and whispered to her daughter. "Okay. When you get there, just don't say too much. This all has to be on Maggie, honey. She shot your dad and that scared Billy and he ran away. You followed. You found him in the woods, all bitten up by bugs. Then Maggie appeared and killed herself. You could see she was not right in the head and you grabbed the boy and hightailed it out of there. No more, no less. Okay?"

Terri nodded, her face sorrowful. "I know, Mom. No one would believe the truth anyway. Gotta keep it grounded in reality, right?"

Dex spoke briefly with Sophie then walked over to the side of the house and stood quietly observing as they carried the stretcher holding Bill's unconscious form across the lawn to the waiting ambulance. Noting the IV and oxygen mask that Bill wore, he assumed that the man was still alive, but probably not by much.

The first responders lifted the stretcher into the vehicle, then turned to young Billy, who was standing now with his grandmother who had just arrived. Emma's arms were wound tightly around the boy, her face stained by tears. The EMT spoke briefly with her then helped them both into the ambulance. Terri hugged Karen and then joined her father and brother in the van.

After the doors were closed, Karen stood in the middle of the driveway as the ambulance left to meet the waiting helicopter. Dex watched her carefully, unobserved, trying to wrap his mind around all that had taken place during the night - Bill shot, possibly fatally, Maggie dead by her own hand, and Karen, killed by lightning, yet somehow still very much alive. The rain-soaked skirt she was wearing was beginning to dry in the warm morning sun and a soft breeze blew it sinuously around her long legs. Her hair, tangled and knotted by the storm's fury, was drying into a soft, curling mass around her head. To him, she was breathtakingly beautiful but unfathomable; somehow forever just out of reach. Would he ever really know her?

He saw her turn her head to look at a man who was striding purposefully toward her. Seeing her body tense, Dex focused on the man, trying to identify him. After a moment, he knew. It was Rusty Maguire, Maggie's father. Rusty's face was set in a scowl and his fists were clenched tightly by his sides.

Karen stood stiffly, apparently girding herself for whatever confrontation Rusty had in mind. Growing concerned, Dex quickly moved to intercept him before he could reach her. When he stood directly in Rusty's path, Dex put his hands up, palms forward, in an attempt to halt his friend before anything happened.

"Rusty, is there something I can help you with?" he asked calmly, shielding Karen with his body.

"My girl - my girl's gone, Dex," he said haltingly, tears welling up in his eyes. Then he pointed his finger at Karen. "That woman -

that woman and her goddamn husband - they're responsible. If that man hadn't come back from Puffin - if he'd just stayed dead like he was supposed to, then my girl, she'd still be alive."

Maggie's father began to move closer to Dex and by doing so, closer to Karen. Alarmed, Dex reached out and put his hands on Rusty's shoulders, stopping him.

"Take it easy, man. You can't fault Bill for surviving Puffin. How he did it, I don't know - it's uncanny. But, he did. And your girl, Maggie, she was always waiting for him. You know that. But now, she may have killed him. He didn't look none too good to me on that stretcher. And maybe, she just couldn't live with what she'd done to him. In any case, it's the boy you have to think about now. You need to put all these accusations and resentment aside for his sake. He's what's important and he's going to need you here - not in the hoosegow because you lashed out in grief with some sort of misplaced anger."

Dex's words seemed to penetrate. Rusty's hard stare softened and tears ran down his cheeks. Seeing the defeat and resignation in his friend's eyes, Dex pulled him awkwardly into a manly embrace as the older man began to sob openly. Patting him on the back, Dex finally pulled away.

"Get ahold of yourself. You need to go get yourself to town to be with Emma and the boy. Looked like he was in shock and you should be with him. He's going to need you strong, man. You and Em are all he has left. Okay?"

Rusty nodded, making a visible effort to get his emotions under control. "Thanks, pard," he said, shaking Dex's hand.

Dex nodded. "She was my friend. I always thought of her like she was my little sister, you know that. She's gone too soon and I will miss her."

Rusty nodded again, too choked up for words. Then, with shoulders sagging and head bowed, he turned to go. He took three or four steps forward then looked back over his shoulder, giving Karen one more hard stare. He opened his mouth to speak but thought better of it and instead, turned and walked slowly back down the driveway to his truck.

Karen stared after him, eyes cold and ungiving, but they softened when she turned to look at Dex.

"Thank you," she whispered. "That had all the earmarks of being very unpleasant."

Dex smiled, nodding. "Well, you've got to admit he does have a point."

Karen looked at him, puzzled. "What do you mean?"

"If Bill hadn't survived Puffin, then none of this would have happened. Maggie'd still be alive, living her life like she should have."

Karen's eyes narrowed and turned icy. "How can you say that? It wasn't Bill's fault someone dumped him on that island. And that girl, Maggie - she may have killed him this time. How can you even think that any of this is his fault?"

Surprised at how quickly Karen jumped to her former husband's defense, Dex began to feel a sense of loss grow around his heart.

"Okay - okay, Karen," he said softly. "I was wrong to say that. It was a miracle Bill survived before and now, well, I hope he survives this, too."

Karen's eyes again softened as she reached out and took his hand. "Let's go home. I, for one, could use a hot shower."

Dex leaned down, putting his arm around her. "You don't want to go to town - to the hospital, to be with Terri?"

Karen looked toward the wharf where the helicopter was just taking off. "No, I think she's okay. No damage. She'll stay there though to be there for her father. Let's just go home."

 **AFTERMATH**

SOPHIE, RELIEVED TO SEE her mother and stepfather, greeted them anxiously at the door.

"What happened? I heard an explosion and then sirens. A whole slew of sirens. Where's Terri? And Dad?"

Karen took her daughter by the hand and sat her down at the breakfast bar and, began to relate the events of the night before. Dex brought over a blanket and wrapped it around Karen's shoulders.

"Thanks," she said, smiling. "Why don't you get out of those wet clothes. I'll be up to shower and change in a few minutes."

Dex leaned over and kissed her lightly. "In a minute. I just want to look around first to make sure there's no damage here."

Smiling, he strode over to the living room, but stopped when he saw the disarray in the usually neat and tidy room. There were two half-full wine glasses still sitting on the coffee table, an open bottle of Jack Daniels beside them. Pillows from the couch were strewn around on the floor.

Dex's mind swirled. *Sophie said Bill was here most of the day and he stayed for dinner, too. What happened after that? Did he and Karen? Did she let him?*

He lifted his head and stared at the ceiling. *Oh, Christ, she did. And Maggie must of known. That's why she shot him and then killed herself!*

He pressed his palms to his eyes, trying to hold back the tears of sorrow and anger that threatened to spill down his cheeks.

There's something wrong with her. I've always known it. She doesn't operate like other people do. How could she go from him to me in such a short time? Doesn't she have any conscience at all?

He heard footsteps behind him and turned to see Karen walking over to the stairs that led to their bedroom.

"I can't wait to get these clothes off," she yelled over her shoulder. "You coming up?"

Without waiting for an answer, she ran up the stairs.

Dex leaned over, picked up the bottle of whiskey and walked slowly to the kitchen. Sophie was still sitting at the breakfast bar, now talking on her cell. Ignoring her, he grabbed a glass from the cupboard, walked back to the living room, and sat down.

"That was Terri, Dex," yelled Sophie, putting the cell back in her pocket. "Dad's lost a lot of blood but otherwise seems to be stable. They're taking him to surgery to remove the bullet. Terri's okay - no concussion, but young Billy has one and they're keeping him overnight at the hospital. His grandparents are there with him. Terri will be home when Dad's out of surgery. She'll text me when she knows what boat she's taking."

When he didn't respond, she got up and walked over to him. "Dex, did you hear me?"

His back was to her and he didn't turn when she spoke. She saw the glass in his hand and the bottle on the floor. "Gee, Dex, isn't it a little early for that?"

He still didn't acknowledge her, just sat quietly sipping his drink and staring out at the sea.

Not to be deterred, Sophie asked again. "Dex, I said isn't it a bit early for a cocktail?"

Turning to look at her, he finally responded, his voice tinged with barely concealed anger. "No, I don't think it's too early. And you know what, Sophie? I think I might go ahead and get stinking drunk. Yes, that's what I'm going to do and then when I'm ready to pass out, maybe, just maybe, I can swallow that load of bullshit your mother's been trying to feed me."

"What are you talking about, Dex?" asked Sophie, alarmed by his tone.

Dex laughed harshly. "Well, for starters, what was she doing all evening with your dad? You told me you went to bed so you probably don't know."

"I don't get what you're saying, Dex. You think something went on between them? I don't think so. Dad might have wanted it, but not Mom."

Dex laughed, took a healthy drink, then pointed to the coffee table. "Sure looks like something went on here last night. Wine, whiskey. And how did those pillows get on the floor? And why?"

Sophie eyes widened in shock. "What are you talking about? Are you saying they had sex? Last night? You gotta be kidding me."

Dex turned to look out at the sea again, ignoring her. "Oh, and then this morning at Maggie's house when your mother was doing her God-knows-what ritual, acting like some kind of druid priestess, did you know she was struck by lightning?"

"Holy shit! What? Lightning? Mom?"

"Went right through her. I saw it with my own eyes," he responded, turning his head and staring at Sophie's astonished face.

"And when I got to her, she had no pulse. No pulse at all. I tried CPR twice, but there was nothing. She was dead for over five minutes. You know what that means, don't you?"

Speechless, Sophie shook her head.

"It means there's no chance that if she survived she wouldn't have had some brain damage. But, suddenly, miraculously, she comes back to life. Sophie, her brain should have been fried, but

369

here she is, walking and talking like nothing happened. I tried to get her to go to the hospital to get checked out, but she refused. Says I'm wrong. Says she was just stunned. But, Soph, I studied medicine. She *was* dead and dead too long to be intact.

"So, sugar, that's why I'm drinking and I'm just going keep on drinking till I'm so stupid it really doesn't matter anymore."

Sophie stared at him, about to speak, but he again looked away from her. She reached out to tap him on the shoulder to get his attention, but then heard the sound of her mother coming down the stairs.

Karen walked directly to the kitchen, not even glancing over at her husband and daughter in the living room. She started a pot of coffee, pulled out a cast-iron skillet from under the pantry, and began to prepare some eggs. Once she had them started, she called out to Dex and Sophie. "Anyone up for breakfast? I know I'm starved."

Humming to herself, she put some bread in the toaster. When there was no reply from the living room, she walked over to the doorway.

"Dex, Sophie - what about it? Want some breakfast or am I eating alone?"

Sophie turned to gaze at her mother, her face clearly showing her bewilderment.

Karen frowned and looked from her daughter to Dex. He was again staring seaward, the bottle by his side and the half-full glass in his hand. Sophie started to speak, but Karen stopped her with a gesture.

"Soph, why don't you go to the kitchen and make sure those eggs don't burn. I need to talk to Dex - alone."

Glad to be out of the now-tension-filled room, Sophie jumped up and practically ran to do her mother's bidding as Karen walked over to Dex and stood behind him.

"What's wrong?" she asked. "Why are you drinking at nine o'clock in the morning and why aren't you speaking to me?"

Dex ignored her and took another sip of his drink.

"Dex, answer me. What's going on?"

Finally, he turned to face her. "Don't you think that maybe you should be checked out by a doctor? You were struck by lightning last night! Your heart stopped beating, for Christ's sake! Jesus, I can't believe you're asking about breakfast!"

Karen sighed. "Dex, believe me. I'm okay. I wasn't struck by lightning, though, from your angle, it may have looked that way. I told you, it hit behind me. And I didn't die, you silly. I just fainted. You're making a mountain out of a molehill."

He sat quietly for a few moments, staring at his drink, then he again turned to her, his eyes boring into hers.

"And what about you and Bill? What were you all doing last night after Sophie went to bed? Answer me that!"

Karen couldn't help but blush furiously. "I .. I don't know what you're talking about. Bill was here helping out and I asked him to stay for dinner. We had some wine and talked. That's all."

Dex laughed sarcastically. "Yeah, right. Just a little wine. Then what are those pillows doing all over the floor? You two have a pillow fight?"

Karen took a deep breath and faced him. "Okay, you have every right to be mad. I had too much to drink last night and I was lonely. But nothing really happened. I kissed him. End of story. And you made it very clear to me that you were going to look elsewhere for companionship. So, maybe I was also a little mad. But that's no excuse. All I can say is I'm sorry. But I didn't sleep with him. I wouldn't, no, I couldn't, do that. I love YOU. With Bill, there was a brief moment, but it was just nostalgia and, maybe, a little pity. But it doesn't change how I feel for you. Nothing can change that."

She waited for him to respond but he just stared at the sea, anger still apparent on his face.

Not knowing what else to do, Karen sighed. "I think I've lost my appetite. I'm going to go for a walk. You can stay here and drown your sorrows or you can come with me and we can talk. What's it going to be, Dex?"

In response, he tossed back his drink and poured another.

Shaking her head, she grabbed her windbreaker and walked out the back door.

THE BLESSED BOY

KAREN WALKED SLOWLY DOWN the beach, her mind full of Dex and the accusations he had thrown at her.

Sophie must have told him that Bill was here last night. I should have thought to straighten out the living room before I left, but there was no time. I wasn't unfaithful and I'll have to convince him of that. But about the lightning - I don't think he's ever going to believe me there.

She stopped and stared out at the waves pounding against the shore, remembering the feel of that cold, hard spear of light that had penetrated her body. There was pain, but it only lasted a moment. What followed the brief discomfort disturbed her even more. She could almost relive the sensation that had coursed through her as the lightning hit, somehow enveloping her. The memory of it was so exquisite and rapturous that she felt a blush creep up on her face as the remembered how the warmth had spread erotically throughout her body.

I was so turned on, the minute I saw Dex, I just had to have him. I don't understand why but it was something I couldn't control. As if I was compelled and driven to make love to him.

Shaking her head to clear the memory from her mind, she turned her thoughts back to present.

Dex is right - the lightning did strike me and I know I lost consciousness. But did I die? Did I actually die? Maybe, but right now I'm alive and there's nothing physically wrong with me. In fact, I feel energized ... full of life.

She kicked off her shoes and wormed her toes into the warm sand, relishing the sensation. Lost in thought, she was startled when she heard a faint rustling coming from the rocks behind her. Suddenly afraid as the memory of the ghostly wolf rose up in her mind, she whirled around. Her mouth fell open in amazement when she saw a naked toddler squeezing himself out of a small crevice between the rocks.

The child smiled at her and she watched in wonder as he sunk his tiny toes into the warm sand. He stared down at his feet for a moment, then looked up at her and laughed. Listening, she couldn't help but smile, for the sound of his laughter was the same as it had been ten years before, cascading through her mind like a thousand tiny silver bells, achingly sweet and purely melodic.

He gazed intently at her, those strange and wondrous flecks of gold in his eyes dancing in the morning sun. He smiled, and though he did not move his lips, she could hear his voice in her mind, soft and sweet like warm, melted chocolate.

"My father chose well, Great Mother," he said.

She opened her mouth to reply, but he silenced her with a gesture of his tiny hand.

"You are strong, Karen Andersen, and I am humbled before you. Because of your courage, my father says you no longer need to give him your monthly blood as sacrifice. That part of your journey has ended. You can return to your family and heal the wounds your service to him has inflicted. And that is as it should be."

Karen listened to his words and her heart leapt when he mentioned her family. *He's telling me I'm no longer under obligation and maybe, just maybe, that will help bring Dex back to me.*

The boy watched her reaction intently. When he saw and felt her acceptance, he nodded. "Take my hand, Great Mother, and walk with me a while."

He reached out his tiny hand and she clasped it in her larger one and was amazed to feel the warmth from his palm run up her arm, through the tiny crescent scar on her palm. Slowly, the heat began to move and radiate within her, suffusing her spirit with a joy so vast that it was incomprehensible. She looked down at him and smiled as, together, they turned and walked down the beach.

Inside, Dex watched as Karen stepped out onto the beach, his mind full of questions for which he could find no answers.

She's lying to me. I know what I saw ... what I felt. That lightning did strike her. And sleeping with Bill? Did she? Is she telling me the truth about that?

He sipped his drink, watching her stand motionless, gazing at the horizon.

I still love her, God help me. Somehow, I'm helpless to change that. And she does love me, too. But there's a part of her that she keeps hidden and I don't know if I can stand that any longer. I'll never have her completely like she has me. Maybe it would be better if I stayed here and let her go back to California alone. God, I feel so old. And poor Maggie - poor, beautiful Maggie. All she did was love the wrong guy. Somehow, she was the sacrificial lamb in all this madness and insanity that Karen controls. Did she know about Karen and Bill? Was that why she shot him and then committed suicide? Or was it something to do with Karen and that damned ritual of hers?

He picked up the bottle and poured himself another drink, remembering the first time he'd seen Karen at the wharf ten years before on the day her family arrived on Mateguas.

She was standing by Pete's truck. God, she looked so regal, so cold and untouchable. I knew in that moment I would do anything to have her, and from then on there was no turning back.

He continued to stare out the window at her. Suddenly, she turned and looked back toward the rocks, apparently startled by something. His curiosity aroused, Dex leaned forward to get a better view.

What's she doing? he thought as he saw her reach out toward someone or something. *Huh? She's all alone. There's no one else out there.*

Puzzled, he stood up and walked closer to the window as she turned and began to walk down the beach, her hand outstretched as if she were walking with someone.

He put down his drink, sank back into the chair, and covered his face with his hands, tears slipping through his fingers.

There's something wrong with her. There's always been something wrong with her, something not right with her mind. I knew it deep down back when we first met but never wanted to admit it. I tried to kid myself that it was something physical, something that could be fixed, but that was just wishful thinking.

He lifted his head, wiped away his tears, and sipped his drink.

Sophie walked back into the room and, seeing his distress, stood behind him, placing her hands on his shoulders. "What's Mom doing outside?"

Dex laughed, bitterly. "Why, walking with the invisible man. You know your mother - there's always something mysterious going on."

"Dex? What's happened? I hate to see you like this."

He turned his head and smiled sadly at her. "Nothing that hasn't been going on for the past ten years. Only, I think now I'm really seeing it for the first time. I think maybe your mom and I need some more time apart. Time to think things through. There's a place inside of her I can't reach - a place she won't let me touch - and I'm not so sure anymore that I want to keep on trying. Then there's your dad. Maybe she really wants to be back with him. Maybe that's what this is all about."

Alarmed by his words, Sophie looked out the window again. Her mother did look like she was holding someone's hand as she walked around the rocks and out of view. Shaking her head, Sophie sat down beside her stepfather and took his hands in hers, forcing him to look at her.

"Don't make any hasty decisions. Believe me, she needs you. I think possibly now, more than ever. And about my dad, well, there may be times when she longs for the way things once were, but that's all it is. She loves you and I think if you left her, a part of her might die. And I don't want to see that happen."

Dex looked at his stepdaughter and nodded. They stared silently out the window until Karen reappeared, her hands now at her side, walking back toward the house.

TERRI

ARRIVING AT THE HOSPITAL, Terri was briefly checked out in the Emergency Room. The doctor, finding no evidence of injury or concussion, summarily released her. Stopping by the information desk, she found out where they had taken her father and headed toward the intensive care unit. She spoke briefly with the physician in charge and found out that he was stable, but that surgery would be necessary to remove the bullet. He was unconscious and she sat by his side until they took him to the OR.

She stood quietly for a moment outside of the operating theater, whispering a silent prayer, then walked down the corridor toward the waiting room. As she passed an open door on the right, she was surprised to hear a familiar voice calling her name from inside the room.

Stopping, a smile on her face, she stood in the doorway. Charlie was sitting on the bed, a small suitcase next to him, apparently waiting to be discharged.

"Charlie!" she exclaimed. "You're all better! So much has happened, I never got a chance to check in with Harry. Last I knew, they were taking you to surgery."

The old Indian smiled and patted the bed, indicating for her to sit next to him.

"I survived the white man's medicine and all the horrible hospital food that followed. And, yes, I'm finally going home. My son is talking with the doctor now. But, what of you? Why are you here? And the boy ... what happened to the boy?"

Terri recounted briefly the events that led up to her arrival at the hospital.

"And Billy, my step-brother, he's here, too."

"Will he survive?"

Terri laughed. "Yeah, he's a tough kid. They're just worried he might have a concussion. But his mom, Maggie, she's dead. She sacrificed herself so we could live."

Charlie was silent for a moment, nodding. "That is as it should be, child."

Terri looked at him quizzically, confusion written on her face.

The old man smiled. "She was always a part of this. Without her, none of these events would have happened. Now, with her death, the circle is complete. She was a pawn of the gods to be sure, but a willing pawn nonetheless."

"I don't understand."

"In time, you will. But what brings you to the surgical wing of the hospital if the boy is okay?"

"My dad. Maggie, shot him. They say he's going to make it, but he's in surgery now. Did her shooting him have a part in all this, too?"

Charlie thought for a moment then shook his head. "No, child. I'm afraid what happened to your father is outside of all this. Simply the result of human mischief and error."

They talked a while longer but were soon interrupted when a nurse entered the room with a wheelchair.

"Okay, Mr. Red Squirrel. Your son is with the doctor now getting your discharge instructions. So, let's get you into this chair and out of here!"

Charlie nodded at her, stood up and let her help him into the chair. "I have to leave now, but I hope to be back at work at the Museum in about a week's time. Come see me, if you are still here - however, my intuition tells me you and your family will be leaving soon, home to California."

Terri sighed. "Your intuition is right. I think we'll be leaving next week."

"So, this may be good-bye."

Charlie's words hit home and she felt a tear slip from her eye, knowing how much she was going to miss this old man. She leaned over and kissed him on his cheek. "Yes, goodbye for now, but I'll be back. You'll see. I'm starting college in the fall at Scripps, studying marine biology. I'll get an internship at Woods Hole and then I'll be back. You won't get rid of me that easily."

The old man smiled and patted her hand. "Yes, I think you will be. And I hope I am still walking this earth and am able to watch as you complete your journey. In the meantime, there is always the Internet. You can email me at the museum."

Terri nodded, gave his hand one last squeeze then turned and watched as the nurse wheeled him away. Gazing at his receding figure, a feeling of profound sadness washed over her. She didn't want to leave Mateguas, but she knew it was time to go. She had completed what she'd set out to do - find her father - and, in doing so, may have somehow saved them all.

Sighing, she left the room and headed back to the surgical waiting area. Taking a seat, she picked up a magazine and began to leaf through it, but was interrupted by the chiming of her cell. Glancing at the caller ID, she smiled - it was Shawn.

"Hey, Shawn!"

"You okay? When I got to the house, they had already taken you to the hospital. You hurt?"

"No, they just wanted to check me out. I'm still here because my dad's in surgery right now. I'm waiting till he's in recovery."

"Yeah, I heard. Maggie shot him, then killed herself, right? But, that's not really how it all went down, is it?"

Terri was quiet for a minute, thinking. "You're right. There was other stuff, too. But that can't get around."

"Yeah, I know. Mum's the word. Listen, I came over when I heard they took you to town. Want some company while you wait?"

Terri smiled. "Yes, I would really like that. I think my mom's going to get us out of here and back to California as soon as my dad's out of the woods. So, we don't have a lot of time left to spend together. I'd like to make the most of what we have."

Shawn laughed. "Yeah, I figured you'd be leaving soon. Well, you'll have to get used to being texted and emailed a lot because I don't plan on letting you go easily."

Terri laughed. "Nor I you, Shawn. Not by a long shot."

KAREN AND DEX

THE BLESSED BOY AND Karen walked hand in hand until they reached the end of the beach where the rocks jutted out to the sea. The boy stepped onto the rocks, still holding her hand.

Again, she heard his voice in her head. "Thank you for sharing this morning with me, Great Mother, but now I must go. My father calls to me."

He dropped her hand and stepped away from her. When the physical connection between them was lost, she felt a sharp sense of abandonment, but that was short-lived. In its place came another emotion that, at first, seemed elusive. Confused, she watched the toddler as his form began to shimmer and fade and then, to her surprise, he changed.

Where once had stood a little boy was now perched an enormous golden eagle, its wings spread wide before her. The raptor stared at her for a moment, flecks of gold dancing in its eyes, then launched itself into the air. She gazed upward, watching as it soared higher and higher and finally disappeared from her sight. Emotion overwhelmed her and she now recognized the sensation that was coursing through her being.

"I'm FREE!" she shouted to the air. "Finally free!"

The feeling was so delicious that she lifted her head and laughed to the sky, and to her ears, her laughter now sounded like a thousand silver bells. With one more glance up to where the eagle had been, she turned and began to walk back toward the house. In the distance, she could see the silhouette of her husband sitting by the window, watching. Her daughter stood by his side as if protecting and shielding him from a world of pain. Feeling a sense of urgency, Karen began to walk faster and then began to jog, her hair streaming out behind her in the wind. As she closed in on the house, she could see Dex's features in the window and was saddened to see his face so etched with sorrow.

I'm going to lose him, she thought.

Knowing she could not survive if that happened, she ran up the stairs to the house, taking them two at time. She burst through the door and ran over to where he sat by the window. Sophie nodded to her once then left the room, leaving the two of them alone.

Kneeling on the floor in front of him, Karen reached out and tentatively took his hands in hers.

"From this day forward, I promise there will be no more secrets. No more rituals, no more bloodletting, and no more lies. I'm so sorry for what I've put you through. You didn't deserve this. Believe me, I'm yours completely. Nothing happened with Bill. I couldn't betray you that way. You must have faith in me. Don't turn from me now. Stay. You are my knight, my protector, and my only love."

Dex stared at her, his mind confused by the events of the past twenty-four hours and by the alcohol he had consumed.

"I don't know, Karen," he said softly. "Why should I believe you now? What's changed? How can I tell if you're telling me the truth?"

Karen nodded. "I know you have no reason to trust what I say. Yes, I've lied and deceived you, but I haven't betrayed you.

You have to know I would never, never hurt you on purpose. I love you. I have always loved you. And I can't live without you, can't you see that? Please, Dex, please, don't leave me now when at last we're free. Please!"

Dex gazed down at his hands, now encased in hers. Then he looked up into Karen's eyes. She seemed transparent - almost naked before him. He saw no deception, no hedging, and no hidden places now. But he also knew that if he stayed with her, he would have to accept what had happened the night before and, somehow, put the past aside and focus solely on the future.

Tentatively, he squeezed her hands.

"Okay, Karen. But no more lies. You be straight with me from now on. That's all I ask."

She nodded and was about to speak but he cut her short. "I'm not finished. Now, I don't pretend to understand everything that's happened and I probably never will. And, I'll take your word about Bill. I love you, you know that, and I'm bound to you in some strange way that no power on this earth, or beyond for that matter, can change. I don't think I could leave you, if I tried."

He stood up, helping her to her feet and put his arms around her, holding her close.

"Let's go home."

Feeling secure in his arms and in his love, she laid her head on his chest, nodding.

We're free now, she thought. *Finally, free.*

As Karen and Dex rested in each other's arms, hoping to reclaim their love, on the other side of the island an eagle soared over the charred remains of the forest. Far below, in the blackened treetops, an owl stretched its wings and peered up into the sky.

When it saw the large raptor, it nodded once and let out a soft hoot of recognition and greeting.

The eagle passed over it, but, before turning to soar away, lingered for a moment, dipping its wings in silent homage.

MARCH –
PALO ALTO, CALIFORNIA

KAREN, HER HAIR MATTED with sweat and wearing only a brief hospital gown, sat with her feet in the stirrups as the doctor examined her. "She's dilated to ten now," he said to the nurse who was standing by the bedside. "Okay, Karen, when the next contraction comes, it's time to push."

"You ready?" asked Dex, who was at her side, his arm around her, holding her hand.

"Damn straight, I am," she replied angrily. "Twelve hours of this is twelve more than I ever needed. And I'll remember that if you ever try to come near me again! Oh, oh, oh, here it comes!"

She gripped down on his hand so hard, he winced and tightened his arm around her. "You can do it, princess!"

"One more, Karen," instructed the doctor. "I can see the head, he's crowning."

The next contraction came seconds later and Karen bore down with all her might, pushing.

"Yes, yes. You got it, Karen," said the doctor, smiling. "Let's all welcome your son into the world."

He held up the baby for Karen to see, then passed the infant to the nurse, who cleaned out his nose and mouth. When she was through, the newborn let out a healthy wail. Smiling, she handed the baby to his mother. "Your son, Karen."

The baby's eyes were squeezed tightly shut and he waved his little fists angrily in the air. Karen looked from her child to Dex and was surprised to see he was crying. "You want to hold him?" she asked, softly.

Dex gingerly took the tiny baby in his strong arms, cradling him. Then the nurse gestured to him. "Here, let me have him for a minute. We need to check him out and clean him up."

Dex reluctantly handed over the child and the nurse proceeded to measure and bathe him.

"APGARS all ten, doctor. This child is pretty near perfect," she said smiling. She wrapped the baby in a clean blanket and was about to pick him up when he abruptly stopped squalling and opened his eyes. The nurse stood still staring at the child.

"Oh, my!" she said. "Doctor, come look."

Hearing this exchange, Karen sat up, a look of concern on her face. "Is there something wrong? Is he okay?"

The doctor was now peering at the infant, who was no longer fussing but was lying calmly and quietly on the blanket.

"I don't think I've ever seen anything like this before," the doctor said, clearly astonished. He turned to Karen. "Your son has the most beautiful eyes. And, he seems to be focusing already - highly unusual."

The doctor picked the baby up, wrapped the blanket around him, and placed him in Karen's waiting arms. "See for yourself."

Karen and Dex stared at the infant who looked up at them serenely. His eyes were a startling shade of blue but what made them all the more unusual were the tiny flecks of gold that seemed to sparkle in the harsh light of the operating room.

Karen gasped and turned to look at her husband.

"Is that normal?" Dex asked, marveling at the strange beauty of his child's eyes.

Karen struggled for words, her mind reeling as she remembered the feel of the hard bolt of lightning that had pierced her nine months earlier. Unbidden, old Madge Parker's words from long ago echoed in her mind.

"... Mateguas threw down a lightning bolt that struck her right between her legs, in her womanhood. And with that, the blessed boy was conceived."

EPILOGUE - MARCH - MATEGUAS ISLAND

BILL STOOD IN THE bedroom, packing his suitcase. He would be away from Mateguas for quite a while. Gerry had landed a major client in Paris and the firm had leased Bill an apartment there. He expected he wouldn't be back for at least nine to ten months. He'd hired a caretaker to make sure the house on the island, that he'd purchased from Maggie's parents, didn't go to rack and ruin while he was away. When he got back, he would renovate the old place - modernize it. Make it nice for his family.

He smiled at the thought of this - his family. He didn't mean the boy, Billy. No, Bill didn't consider him really family but that wasn't a problem any longer. The kid, suffering from amnesia, had gone to stay with his grandparents after his mother's death and, in a way, that suited Bill just fine. He was never home anyway and the kid's mother was Maggie, not Karen.

Folding a shirt, he was interrupted by the buzzing of his cell. With anticipation, he turned and walked toward the window, checking his messages as he went.

This could be it, he thought.

He knew Karen was pregnant - the girls had told him, but he found it hard to believe. *That fisherman couldn't knock her up in ten years of trying. Why did it have to happen now? She and I never had a problem. She caught with me the first time we didn't use precautions. And, then there was the other baby - the one she got rid of.*

He thought about the child she'd aborted for a moment, remembering with sadness, then he shook his head. He glanced down at the phone, holding his breath. It was a text from Terri.

Say hello to my new baby brother - Alexander Dexter Pierce!

Quickly scrolling down, he gazed at the picture of the tiny infant. Unbidden, tears sprang into his eyes.

Karen has a son!

He scrolled down to another picture, this one of Karen holding the baby. She looked tired, but still beautiful. The next picture was of Dex, beaming proudly, the child in his arms. Unconsciously, Bill's hand clenched around the phone, knuckles white with anger.

That boy should have been mine!

Staring at the picture, he couldn't help but think about how ten years before someone had callously abandoned him on Puffin Island and left him there to die. He was sure the culprit was Dex and, soon, he'd have the proof. Memories of that time were now finally beginning to surface.

The first one returned hidden within a nightmare he'd experienced shortly after Maggie's death. He was wandering aimlessly in the woods, trying desperately to find his way home to Karen when out of the darkness a shadowy figure stepped onto the path in front of him. In his dream, he'd eagerly rushed toward it, thinking he was saved, only to discover the figure was wielding some sort of blunt instrument, which it swung, hitting him viciously on the head and rendering him unconscious.

The dream ended there and he'd woken up drenched in sweat, stifling a terrified scream. But now, more snippets of that night in the woods and the months after on Puffin were coming back. Not much, for sure, and sometimes it was just a blurry picture or a feeling, but he was confident that, in time, and with help, he would remember it all. He'd spoken to Dr. Todd when the memories first surfaced and his friend had recommended a retrograde amnesia specialist in Boston. Bill planned to see the man when his sojourn in France ended.

He glanced back down at the phone, his mind returning to the present and the photos of Karen, Dex, and the baby. Again, he felt his anger start to build.

That bastard wanted her then and he did what he needed to get her. He tried to kill me and I'm going to prove it to her. Then things will be back to where they should be. Karen and me, our girls and our new son. And that fisherman will be in jail where he belongs.

He thought about the woman he was meeting in town the next evening for dinner, before his flight to Paris left at midnight.

Susan LeVeque - nice looking gal, smart, and single, too. Wants to do a follow-up piece on me. Well, a few well-chosen words, a couple of hints and a little romance, and I'll have her eating out of the palm of my hand. She'll do all the investigative legwork while I'm away and when I get back ... yes, when I get back, everything will fall into place.

He scrolled again to the picture of the baby, smiling to himself. Then he looked up and stared out the window. The sky was beginning to darken as clouds moved across the water, hiding the moon from his view. A dense fog was beginning to settle over the island, silently rolling in from the sea. Seemingly from out of nowhere appeared a large raptor - an owl - flapping its mighty wings as it flew out of the fog. It circled above the house several times, then suddenly swooped down to the lawn and picked up a small rodent.

With the tiny creature struggling in its talons, the raptor turned and began to soar directly toward the window as Bill watched. So unwavering was the owl's flight that Bill unconsciously stepped back a few paces, his mouth open in amazement.

As the bird began to rapidly close the distance to the house, an unreasonable chill coursed through Bill's body and a shiver ran down his spine. The bird's collision with the glass seemed inevitable, and he girded himself for it.

But at the very last moment, the owl stopped and hovered before his eyes as if suspended from the sky by invisible marionette strings. Bill stared at the bird, transfixed by its glowing amber eyes, as time seemed to stand still. Then, suddenly, without warning, the raptor let out a savage shriek and turned, flinging the tiny creature it held in its talons against the glass.

Startled, Bill jumped back, losing his balance, as the owl's victim spattered across the pane - blood and sinew staining the once-clear surface.

Quickly, Bill got to his feet and rushed back to the window. The moon now reappeared from behind the clouds and in the fog seemed to glow with an unnatural and eerie light. He scanned the property, looking for the bird, but it was nowhere in sight. Where had it gone? Disappointed, he was about to turn away when a movement out of the corner of his eye caught his attention.

It was the raptor, circling lazily in the sky high above, its shadow passing over the soft diffused light of the waning moon.

Bill leaned forward, his hands pressed tightly against the bloody windowpane, his gaze intent.

For what seemed an eternity, he stood that way, silent, his eyes wide open in wonder, until the owl, in all its majesty, disappeared back into the fog.

THE END

ABOUT THE AUTHOR

Born in Norwich, Connecticut, Linda Watkins moved to Michigan when she was four years old. After graduation from college (Carnegie-Mellon University '70), she relocated to the San Francisco Bay Area where she lived most of her adult life.

A Senior Clinical Financial Analyst at Stanford University School of Medicine, Linda was always writing. At work, she created 'long forms' and business plans; at home, she wrote whimsical stories, poems and songs for the delight of her friends and family. In 2006, retired, she moved to Chebeague Island, Maine where she wrote her first novel, *Mateguas Island*.

Today, she resides in Western Michigan with her three rescue dogs (Splatter, Spudley and Jasper) and is already at work on the final installment in the *Mateguas Trilogy* which she hopes to have ready for publication late in 2015.

For more information on Linda and her work,
please stop by her personal website

www.LindaWatkins.biz

Or her novel website

www.MateguasIsland.com

You can also follow her on Facebook:

www.facebook.com/pages/Linda-Watkins-Author/412758982152044

If you enjoyed reading **Mateguas Island**, please take a few minutes to post your review on Amazon.com, Goodreads, iBooks, or wherever is most convenient for you.

Mateguas Island can be purchase in print or eBook on Amazon.com or in print only at BarnesandNoble.com.

Return to Mateguas Island can be purchased in print or eBook on Amazon.com or in print only at BarnesandNoble.com

A BRIEF REQUEST FROM THE AUTHOR:

I hope that you've enjoyed this novel and, if you did, would be so kind as to leave a short review on Amazon. Thanks in advance for your help and happy reading!

Linda Watkins